A Faerie Tale Romance

CORAL SMITH SAXE

The Mirror & The Magic

ENCHANTED DESIRE

"I know I'm strange to you," Julia said. "You're strange to me. This is a strange place. Please let me have one familiar thing to keep with me." She placed her hand on Darach's arm. "I haven't yet given you reason to fear me, have I?"

At the sudden, hot spark that lit his eyes, she wished she had said something else entirely. Was he indeed afraid of her? Because he thought she was a witch? A spy? Or was there some other, more intimate reason?

She raised her eyes to his. She wanted more than anything to resist the tide that was carrying her toward him, but it was beyond her powers of will. The longing that welled up inside her, the heat of her desire, combined in such a way that she swayed toward him, as if he were the force of the moon and she the waves of the ocean.

Other *Leisure* and *Love Spell* Books by
Coral Smith Saxe:
A STOLEN ROSE
ENCHANTMENT

CORAL SMITH SAXE

The Mirror & The Magic

LOVE SPELL ◆ **NEW YORK CITY**

For the clans of
Smith, Jarvis, and Rogness—my ain folk

LOVE SPELL®

April 1996

Published by

Dorchester Publishing Co., Inc.
276 Fifth Avenue
New York, NY 10001

Copyright © 1996 by Coral Smith Saxe

Cover Art by John Ennis

Printed in the United States of America.

Chapter One

It all happened so fast.

First the sound, like the popping of champagne corks.

Then the thunk of limp forms falling to the floor. The crash of steel bowls on the tiles.

The running footsteps. And the car that sped away in the alley.

Julia Addison had seen and heard all of it. She'd seen the two killers from the tiny window in the door of the walk-in freezer at Martine's restaurant. She'd heard the sounds of their getaway when she had stepped, terrified yet desperate, out of her frigid hiding place into the kitchen where two mob lieutenants lay dead on the immaculate floor.

She hadn't been warm since.

She'd layered on sweaters and good wool

slacks and a soft hat from one of the shops in Kinloch Rannoch, but to no avail. She even had leather gloves in the pack about her waist. As she drove up into the Highlands, a constant chill still plagued her.

"No wonder, Addison," she muttered to herself. "You're the spy who ran out into the cold."

She gripped the wheel of the rented Morris Minor with gloved hands. The sky rose blue and fair above the dark treetops, but the wind outside had a raw edge. The heater in the car put out the minimum of warmth, barely warding off the chill of a Highland spring and scarcely touching the chill she seemed to carry in her bones.

Still, her relief at being out overrode any discomfort she experienced. She'd spent the past two weeks closeted in her small but cozy room at the Blackwater Inn. She'd read every book and magazine she could lay hands on, listened to all the BBC Radio gardening shows and musical quizzes she could tolerate, and written letters—letters she could never send—to every friend and acquaintance of her life, including her junior high art teacher. There was a TV in the common room downstairs, but even her passion for movies couldn't tempt her to risk going down there to sit with the other guests.

Cabin fever had gripped her last evening with a fury, when she'd found herself making paper airplanes out of magazine ads while listening to a droning interview with an expert on ancient Mongol bathing habits. She'd resolved right then to get out this morning, come heaven or hell.

And here she was, out at last. She should feel exhilarated, she told herself. "Exhilarate, Addison," she muttered. "One, two—exhilarate!—three, four—exhilarate! Oh, Lord," she moaned. "All my marbles are gone. I'm talking to myself and answering myself and giving myself orders."

She straightened up in the seat. Feeling sorry for herself made her feel angry and stupid. She was going to get out, see the beautiful Highlands she'd heard and read so much about during her stay at the Blackwater Inn. She'd enjoy the solitude of the narrow road, knowing safety at last. Mobsters from New York weren't into kilts and woolly cattle. At least she was fairly sure they weren't. All she really knew about people like Monty Gilette and his cronies she'd learned from the movies and a few news stories. Certainly James Cagney and Marlon Brando weren't from around here.

She compelled herself to relax and take in some of the sights. The road wound about as it climbed, and on all sides she saw larch, ash, and birch trees budding, punctuated by the deep greens of the younger pines and spruces. Here and there, in a sunny patch, a rhododendron flashed a bit of ruffled early color.

Julia rolled down her window—she'd never get used to using her right hand for such things—and breathed in a deep breath of the cool, moist air, ignoring the chill for the moment. Peace settled on her heart, the same feeling she'd had when she arrived so many days before, before she'd gone into seclusion. The countryside was wild and rocky, damp and often gray, but teeming with life: strong, hardy life of a sort that not only survived but thrived in the rough. She liked that.

She didn't even know why she'd picked this place to come after Martine had hustled her out of the restaurant, tossed a few of her things in a bag, and all but pushed her onto the first plane leaving for Europe. Julia had been too deep in shock to protest. After making a circuitous route through various cities on the Continent, hiding and evading, jumping at shadows, she'd simply picked the next available flight out of Dusseldorf.

She wound up in Inverness and from there had driven south until she saw signs for Kinloch Rannoch. On a whim, she decided to have a look. She'd been through a great deal in her life, and while she wouldn't exactly call herself rough and hardy, the countryside had spoken to her soul in a way no other place had before. The conical top of Schiehallion, the old and new forest lands, Loch Rannoch itself, had simply felt safe enough and foreign enough to suit her needs and her mood.

A smile began to tug at the corners of her mouth. Maybe things were going to turn out all right after all.

And then she saw it.

Her smile vanished, as did all thoughts of peace.

A single flash in the rearview mirror, the tiniest glint of metal. Still, that single flash brought Julia upright in her seat, her eyes darting back and forth between the mirror and the road before her.

Had it been a fluke? An old metal sign, a piece of forestry equipment left among the trees? A broken mirror or a reflecting strip?

She gulped. There it was again as she rounded the curve. In among the trees, the unmistakable glint of a car's front grille.

"Calm down, Addison," she told herself, gripping the wheel once more. "It's probably just another tourist."

Despite her own admonition, she sped up. She checked her mirror. Had the other car accelerated, too? She gritted her teeth. A barrier of trees blocked her view.

She slowed, still watching the mirror to see if the car gained on her. A small shock wave of fright coursed down her neck and spine. The car hung back, just beyond the curve, just out of sight, then glinted once more through a gap in the trees.

She was being followed. "Oh, God."

She cranked the window up again, knowing as she did it that it could provide no real protection against the sort of people who would be tailing her. Thugs like mob boss Monty Gilette could reach her in a locked vault, once they'd found her. Still, having the window up gave her a brief illusion of safety, and that was enough to keep her going.

She shuffled through her panicked brain, trying to think what to do. She had no idea where this road ultimately led, and she doubted that she could lose her pursuer in a race. She could double back, but that would only lead him—she assumed it was a man who was giving chase—right back to Kinloch, a dead end where she would be trapped. And if she were trapped . . .

She began searching the road ahead, looking for any sign of a turnoff, a house, or a village. They wouldn't dare try to kill her in front of a crowd of camera-laden tourists, would they? Or in the parlor of a good Scots farmer? Or would they make it all look like an unfortunate accident?

She was so unnerved that she didn't see it until the last moment. The merest opening among the trees. She swung the Morris into it, taking the turn on two wheels. Immediately the car jolted so hard she banged her head against the headliner. The so-called road consisted chiefly of rocks and ruts. And where there wasn't rock, there was mud. Sprays of it rose up and dimmed the windshield. Her wipers struggled to clear it as she glanced in the mirror to see behind her.

Alone! She gave a grim smile. But in an instant, an equally important question arose: Where was she headed?

She concentrated on navigating the Morris over the rapidly narrowing track. Low-hanging branches slapped at the windows, and several good jolts made her fear for the car's undercarriage. Still, she pushed on. She wanted to burrow into the countryside, putting as much distance between her and her pursuer as she could manage.

She took another peek in the mirror. Her heart thudded. In between the spatters of mud and leaves she could make out the oncoming vehicle. No way could this be a tourist, out for a morning's drive. This guy was after her.

"Omigod!" The shout bounced out of her as she came up against the thicket.

The road had vanished into shrubs and boulders.

She was trapped.

"No way." She slammed the car to a halt, its front end half-buried in the shrubbery. Flinging the door open, she tumbled out and leapt over the branches. She landed running, charging up the hillside, ducking and slapping at the branches that got in her way. She heard the other car halt below, heard a man's voice call out. She put on speed, glad she had worn her sturdy walking shoes. Her fanny-pack banged against her hip as she raced for safety, not knowing where—or if—she might find it.

She heard a sharp report and a sudden whine. She shrieked as a bullet shattered the slender trunk of a young ash to one side of her.

But she didn't stop. She was angry now. She'd come too far, evading these bullies. She wasn't going to make it easy for them. This was her life and she intended to live it—for as long as possible. She'd run into the next decade before she'd give up.

A small stretch of flat ground opened up before her. Some tall boulders stood about in the clearing. If she could get beyond those rocks, she thought, she might have a chance to evade him. She dug in and launched herself across the clearing.

And then she was flying.

Suddenly the very air seemed to change. Her body felt charged; she tingled and vibrated all along her limbs. The trees and the massive gray stones stood out in crisp relief, as if she had donned glasses that brought the world into crystalline sharpness. A high-pitched droning, like the sound of a moistened finger running over the edge of a goblet, filled her ears. The smell of exotic flowers hung in the air, though she saw no blossoms, and the bright tang of oranges and lemons nipped at her taste buds.

All this she experienced in the space of a heartbeat.

And then she was falling, heading toward the downhill slope on the other side of the clearing.

She hit the slope with a cry and a thump and was propelled head over heels down the path, gathering leaves and bits of moss as she went. Small rocks jabbed at her but she was rolling with such force and speed that she almost skimmed the ground. Finally she hit a mossy patch at the bottom and tumbled to a halt, feeling like one of the hedgehogs in Alice's Wonderland game of croquet.

The tingling and euphoria of her flight vanished. She looked up; the sky and treetops were spinning overhead. A face appeared in her line of vision, staring down at her with a fierce frown.

She scrambled backward, crablike, trying to get to her feet. She came up against a tree trunk. Or so she thought until she looked behind and around her and beheld a forest of strong, hairy legs. She glanced up and saw another fierce face, haloed with wild, reddish hair, and another, and another. All at once she saw she was surrounded by wild men, their faces streaked with dirt, their clothes rough and strange, and all of them wielding large, gleaming swords or knives.

Somehow she didn't think they were from New York.

"Well, Niall, is it a lass or no?" one of them said.

"Aye. Look at the bumps a' the front of her. It's a lass. That or it's the prettiest lad that's ever tried to smuggle twa of our good hens beneath his shirt."

A chorus of "ahs" emanated from the ring of men, and she saw looks of bright interest mingled with concern on their faces. Julia crossed her arms in front of her and glared at them. "Who are you guys?" she asked, trying to sound braver than she felt. The swords they carried looked as if they could cut down a fairly substantial tree in one or two strokes.

"Who are we?" asked the one called Niall.

"As if ye dinna know," said another.

"Aye, might as well ask who's yer own mother," added another.

He got an elbow in the ribs from Niall. "Don't go talkin' about anyone's mam, Ross."

Ross colored. "Sorry, Niall. I forgot me."

"Well, lass, just you stand up, slow and careful," said Niall. "Dugan, you bind her. Tommy, make sure she's no' carryin' any weapons or spellcastin' instruments."

Julia smacked at the hands that prodded and pulled at her clothing. "Back off, buckaroos," she growled. "I'm not public property."

The one called Tommy, who looked to be the youngest of the group, jumped back, his hands held up. "Buckaroos?" he asked in a quavering voice. "What kind o' devil's talk is that?"

She glared at him. "It means I won't be pawed at. Get back. I'm a third-degree black belt in ai-kido." It was a bluff, but one she hoped might give them pause.

"Niall!" Tommy gasped. "She's the one, all right. D'ye hear her?"

"Aye," Niall growled. "All the more reason to make sure she can't do her black belting work on us. Do yer job quick, man."

Tommy searched her rapidly, going through her pockets and removing her fanny-pack. Dugan, who was built along the lines of a Peterbilt truck, lashed her wrists in front of her with some leather thongs and tied a cloth about her mouth, not brutally, but securely. Julia tried to kick out at them both, but for all their size and bulk, they moved lightly on their feet, with the reflexes of cats, and they eluded her attacks with hardly a break in their tasks.

They bound her and relieved her of all her worldly possessions save the clothes she wore. The pair led her over to the man Niall, who seemed to be the leader of this party of Highland holdouts.

"Lass, ye've o'erstepped yerself. Ye shouldn't have come onto the MacStruan's lands all alone. I'll warrant even yer magic won't protect ye from the chief's wrath."

Julia stared at him. The man was clearly nuts. Cold fear coursed through her. This wasn't like dealing with Monty Gilette and his gang, however brutal their methods of doing business. These people were talking witchcraft and trespassing and swordplay. And judging from their somewhat earthy scent and their grimy appearances, their rough wool kilts and the calm conviction in their gazes, they were deeply into their woodland fantasy.

Niall took her by her elbow and began to lead her down the rocky path. The rest of the men fell into line behind them, while big Dugan went ahead.

Julia shivered again as she wondered where they were taking her. Who was this chief they had spoken of, and what were the MacStruans? What had happened to the fellow who was following her, the one with the gun? Had they killed him? Had he given up and gone away, confident that his job would be done for him by this pack of renegades from a Sir Walter Scott novel?

Panic rose within her, but she fought the feeling down. She needed to keep her wits about her. She'd find a way to escape, no matter what. Meanwhile, she needed to learn all she could about her captors.

She examined the man striding beside her. He stood tall and broad as an oak, as did most of the men, and he wore a kilt that looked more like a long blanket wrapped about him and belted at the waist. His face was clean-shaven, despite his unkempt hair, and he looked as if he had spent his life out in the wind and weather. She couldn't judge his age, though she guessed him to be in his late thirties or early forties. What would possess a man of his age to want to live out in the woods and wear blankets like wrapping paper? She'd seen few men in kilts since arriving in Scotland, and none of them dressed or behaved like the ones surrounding her now. Perhaps they belonged to some kind of club or organization that reenacted Scots history.

That must be it, she decided. They were history buffs who simply took it all a step further. She glanced at Niall's shirt, rough-woven and dirt-streaked. Okay, so maybe they took it more than a step further. But at least it was something she could understand. Maybe taking her captive was all in sport, a part of their annual games.

She took a bit of hope. They might be crazy, but they hadn't harmed her so far. Maybe as soon as she met their chief and explained their mistake, they'd release her, maybe even joke about it with her.

She didn't let herself think about the alternatives.

They climbed the rocky hills like nimble mountain goats. Julia kept in shape, but she had been confined to planes, trains, and rooms for weeks and hadn't been able to do her usual workouts. She panted as she struggled to keep up, and gasped with relief when they stopped to drink at a fast-running stream.

"I'm takin' the bond away from your mouth so ye can drink," Niall told her. "If ye scream or cry out to your fellows, wherever they may be, ye'll force me to kill ye. Do ye understand, lass?"

She gulped and nodded. His eyes told her he meant it. He would kill her. But she was desperately thirsty. She hoped he wasn't toying with her.

He removed the gag, his keen eyes never leaving hers. She licked her lips and held out her hands. "I can't drink without my hands," she said.

"Ye'll have to. I willna untie ye." He motioned to Tommy. The younger man scooped up some of the clear, running water in his cupped hands and timidly offered it to Julia. She cringed at the dark nails and callused palms, but she was too thirsty to refuse. She drank, some of the icy water dribbling down her chin. "Thank you," she murmured.

"Ye're welcome," Tommy said, pulling his hands back quickly and wiping them on his chest.

Niall tied her gag once more. Then he pulled another coarse rag out of the small pack he carried. "From here on, ye'll have to go blindfolded. Ye may know yer way to the village already, but Darach'd have ma skin if I were to show ye the way."

She shot him an outraged look and shook her head in protest. Then, seeing his determination, she gave him her most pleading stare.

He shook his head. "It's nae use, lass. Ye've called the tune and it's time to pay the piper."

The rough cloth came around her eyes. Her fear became a solid lump in her stomach, a freezing about her heart. All she had left were her ears and her nose, and the smell of the old rag didn't do wonders for her olfactory sense, at that. To top it off, they spun her about, as if preparing her for a game of blind man's bluff. Still, she willed herself to stay alert, to listen for sounds of water or birds, or to hear the silence that closed around them when they came into the sheltered eaves of the forest.

After what seemed hours, her feet landed on level ground. She didn't have to sniff very hard to make out smoke from a wood fire, animal dung, and the cool scent of grass. Chickens clucked and squawked, dogs barked somewhere nearby. Civilization, she thought, relieved. She wasn't going to be abandoned, dead, in the woods.

"Here we go. Over the threshold," Niall said, tightening his grip on her elbow.

She stepped onto a stone floor and heard the shuffling of the men's boots around her. Big, rough hands shepherded her ahead. She inhaled the scents of dust and mildew, stale cooking odors, more smoke. A house, she thought with hope. A place where people cooked and ate and slept. Something she could understand, something they had in common.

"Here she is, Darach," she heard Niall say as they came to a halt in a room that echoed with the sounds of his voice. "Just as we thought. We caught her spyin' at last."

A deep sigh came from in front of her. Julia strained to hear more. She felt someone removing the blindfold from her eyes. She blinked and stared at the man before her.

Good God, she thought to herself. I've been kidnapped by Conan the Barbarian.

Chapter Two

Darach MacStruan ran a hand over his eyes and swore under his breath. Damn, but he didn't want to deal with this.

He looked at the woman who stood before him, bound and gagged and dressed in those outlandish breeches and long tunic. He'd sent his men out to find fresh meat and they'd brought back the Moreston witch. Or so they thought.

But no one had ever seen the evil one who had caused so much harm to his people. She was little more than a rumor, though her deeds had been real enough. Was this woman she?

This one was bold enough; that was a fact. With her legs encased in those soft breeches and her torso outlined in pleasing detail by her woolen tunic, it was clear that she wasn't some modest wee milkmaid. And her eyes—above her gag, her snapping, light brown eyes had sent him a message that she was not daunted by his men or their swords. Or by him, the chief of the MacStruans. She could well be a witch.

But would a witch have been so easily caught? Would she not have used her magic in an instant to harm his kinsmen and ensure her freedom? According to Niall, she hadn't seemed to resist above a slap and a sharp word or two.

If she wasn't the witch of Clan Moreston, who the devil was she?

He shifted uneasily in his chair. Her cap had fallen to the floor and her deep ebony hair had come loose around her face. The silken sheen of those dark tresses was without compare to any he'd seen before. And her skin, unmarred by age, disease, or misfortune, was a pale ivory miracle. Her form, even beneath such odd clothing, promised soft, satin pleasures. Pleasures that he'd long denied himself.

Yet something else about her spoke to him. Something that he could not put a name to. Had he met her before? Had she been in Edinburgh, perhaps at the court, when he was a lad? She reminded him of someone, and yet she couldn't be more strange to him if she'd had green hair and three legs. That much he knew. That bothered him the most about her. Suddenly he didn't want to order the punishment he knew was expected of him.

But his men awaited his word, looking at him

with expectant eyes. He was chief. He knew his duty.

Niall cleared his throat. "Darach."

"Aye."

"Ye'll be wantin' to see what she was carryin' in the pouches of her breeches. And in her bag. Show 'im, Tommy."

Tommy came forward and laid the objects on the table in front of Darach. "Potions, Darach. And a talisman. They're sma', but I'll warrant they're as powerful as the devil."

Darach scowled at the table. He fingered the items. Odd lettering marked them all. The comfits or lozenges were wrapped in the finest glass or crystal he'd ever seen, so delicate it crinkled like stiff cloth. The tiny tube was full of red and white lozenges, soft and shiny. Tommy was right: they had to be some sort of potion. Poison, perhaps? Or did they serve some other magical purpose? A brush, a key of some sort, a silver hand mirror, and other items he couldn't name completed the inventory. Odd stuff, indeed.

He looked up at the woman, pondering. He nodded to Niall. "Take off her gag. Let her speak."

She still stood proud once her gag was removed. He saw wide, soft lips of rich rose red with pearly teeth peeking out between them. By God, the Morestons had sired one of the veriest beauties in all Christendom. Even now, his body grew warm at the sight of her tongue

24

moistening her lips, which were dry from her gag.

He shook off the sensation. He wasn't a boy to be led about by his body's whims. This woman posed a serious threat to his home and his people, whether a witch or merely a Moreston spy.

"What have you to say, woman?" he asked.

"I say where am I? And who are you? And what right do you have to kidnap an ordinary tourist and drag her off into the wilds? Is this your idea of—"

"Whisht!" Darach held up his hand. "Gods, woman, does your tongue work at both ends?"

A tint of roses came into her cheeks, and her expressive eyes flashed. "Look, mister, you're in enough trouble for bringing me here," she said, pointing straight at his chest. "Don't compound your mistake by insulting me."

The men around her gasped and took a step back. Darach only stared at the daring young woman. To speak with such boldness to a clan chief, a man twice her size and armed, into the bargain, showed either great courage or plain idiocy. He wondered which applied in her case.

"Mistress Moreston, you've—"

"That's not my name."

"Oh? And what do you call yourself?"

"My name is Addison. Julia Addison. And you're going to be in big trouble with the American consulate."

"Am I, indeed?" He pondered her words. Many of them made no sense, and her accent topped even the French for sheer oddity. She might not be an idiot, but was she mad?

He studied her again. Could eyes so clear and intelligent belong to a madwoman? She didn't look like a raver. Perhaps her peculiarity was all an act. Damn! He didn't need this right now. Not with the Morestons nipping at their sides like wolves.

"Whoever ye claim to be," he said at last, "ye must know that the penalty for trespassing on MacStruan land is death."

Her face paled. So she possessed enough sense to fear her own demise, he mused.

"Death?" she squeaked. "Wouldn't a fine and time served be sufficient? After all, I wasn't actually trespassing. I was running away from a guy who was trying to kill me—"

"Kill ye?" He scowled. "Seems ye're made for trouble, mistress. Have ye no husband to keep ye home safe?"

"I'm not a mistress. I'm a Ms.," she said impatiently. "As for trouble, you can't scare me. There's no law in England that allows the death penalty for trespassing."

"Ye aren't in England," he drawled.

"Well, in Scotland, then. Great Britain. It's all the same."

There was another gasp from the men around her. This one threatened to remove all the available oxygen from the room. She looked around her in puzzled defiance.

"Lass, you're sadly addled," Darach said. "Ye don't even ken where ye are." He rose from his chair. "I'll spare ye for now. I won't kill a witless thing that knows no better."

"Then I'll be going—"

"Nay, ye will not. I may show mercy but I'm no' a fool. Ye're to stay right here until we've learned more about ye and where ye come from. If ye've played us false, it won't go easy wi' ye."

She stared at him, outrage and fear snapping in her eyes. "And by what authority can you make me a prisoner here?"

He came to stand over her. "I am the Mac-Struan."

"So? I am the Addison," she retorted.

"Ye're chief of your clan?"

"No, I'm just a plain, ordinary American citizen. But that means I don't fall under your clan laws."

He shrugged. "Perhaps not. But ye'll be stayin', all the same. Until someone comes to ransom ye."

"Ransom me? Then this is a kidnapping." She gave a short laugh. "Well, the joke's on you, Chief MacStruan, because there's no money in my family. You won't get a penny."

"Then ye'll be stayin'." He motioned to Dugan and Niall. "Take her to the cell. See that she has food and drink. I'll not have her sayin' she was mistreated at the hands of the MacStruan."

"Aye, Darach," Niall replied. They moved to take her arms and lead her from the room.

"But you can't! Damn it! Let go of me!" She twisted about to face Darach, her face aglow with righteous anger. "You've made a career-limiting move here, mister," she snapped. "You'd best kiss your sorry tush good-bye because when my lawyers and the U.S. government get through with you, you'll be living in a refrigerator box and diving through Dumpsters for the rest of your natural born days!"

He only nodded to the two who held her. Then he turned away as Niall and Dugan hustled her, protesting, out of the hall.

Alasdair, Darach's younger brother, spoke first. "D'ye think she's as mad as she seems, Darach?"

Ross nudged him. "Ye heard her, man. Ravin'. No other word for it."

Darach nodded. "So it would seem. But I won't lay odds on it yet. She could be a crack-brained wanderer or the most cunning of spies. Time will tell." He sat down in his chair once more. "Liam, fetch paper and pen. When Niall comes back, I want to send a message to the Earl of Atholl."

"D'ye think she's the witch?" Ross asked, nodding toward the stairs. "Everybody knows the witch is the real power behind the Moreston himself."

Darach shrugged. "As I said, time will tell. Right now I have a more pressing matter to pursue. That of savin' our lands."

Julia sat down on the cot in the corner of the cell and stared at the walls. Five paces long by six paces wide, the room featured a sole, narrow window about ten feet above the floor and set deep into the smooth stone wall. A fat candle burned on a bracket near the door, adding a bit more light to the cool, darkened room. Other than these, the walls were bare, the floor was bare, and the door was barred from the outside.

How had she gotten into such a mess? she wondered. First that stupid gangland killing and her flight from the United States. Then a trek across several European countries, trying to throw her pursuers off her trail. Now she had been abducted by wild men and locked away in a cell that rivaled something out of a Monty Python movie—for the crime of trespassing, yet! As if she had had time to watch for NO TRESPASSING signs while she was ducking gunfire and fleeing for her life!

She rose and walked about the cell, chafing her wrists where the bonds had been tied. At least she was free to walk and talk and see, she thought with gratitude. And she hadn't been mistreated. Not seriously, anyway.

But she was locked up, a prisoner. God, but she hated that! She'd already spent enough time in near incarceration at the inn in Kinloch village. And here she was again, confined against her will. She'd never been a sit-still-and-calmly-wait kind of person. She needed motion and action; she needed to be on the road to something or doing something. Being locked up was tantamount to torture, to her.

Mercy, that Darach person had said. Ha! If locking her up in a dank, chilly dungeon was his idea of mercy, she didn't dare imagine what he might consider to be punishment. Who the hell did he think he was? When she got out of this place, she'd remember his name and his face, all right.

She conjured up the image of him as she circled the cell. Conan the Barbarian had been her first impression. And he was built like one: towering, massively muscled, wrapped in one of those big plaid blankets, his long, powerful legs encased in fur-trimmed boots. His hair was not red, like the rest of the men she'd seen, but deep brown and flowing to his shoulders. Heavy dark brows glowered over intensely clear blue eyes. Wide lips frowned beneath a strong, straight nose as he'd stood, feet planted, hands on hips. The epitome of lunkheaded power.

But his voice. That deep, dark voice reminded Julia of the finest dark chocolate liqueur, his Scots accent adding a soft spice to the blend. She'd been incensed by what he'd said, but utterly fascinated by the voice that had spoken those outrageous words. And he was well spoken, though his speech sounded somewhat quaint. Not a complete lunkhead, perhaps. What was he doing living up here in the Highlands like a wild animal? What must his wife be like? That is, if he had a wife . . .

She shook herself. This was not the time to speculate on her captor's marital status. She was in trouble and she alone was responsible for extricating herself from the mess. Lord knew that once she had fled New York to avoid the wrath of Monty Gilette and his goons, no one else she knew could come to her aid. Not even if they could find her in Brigadoon or MacStruanville or wherever she'd landed.

She licked her lips, her mouth still dry from the gag and from the long hike with only the bit of water she'd been given. She looked around and recalled that they'd taken her fanny-pack. She couldn't even get a breath mint or an aspirin, if she needed one. Good grief! How was she to—to—?

She looked wildly around the room, then stooped and peered under the bed. "Thank God." She sighed as she saw what she assumed was a chamber pot beneath the cot. It was primitive, but it was there. She wondered how she'd manage to wash, or even to brush her hair, since they'd confiscated her pack and all its contents. Her hand mirror was in there, the small, antique silver one her mother had left her. She wished she had it now. She could use something that was comfortingly familiar in this strange, strange place.

She drew a long breath and exhaled slowly. She was stuck here, no doubt about it. But she wouldn't give up. She wouldn't be a prisoner for long. Not as long as she still had breath.

She paced along the walls, testing the stonework and looking for anything she could use as a tool. She'd seen characters in prison movies make their escape with the help of a paper clip or a bit of a bedspring. She just had to keep looking. Unfortunately the floor of the cell yielded nothing but dust, and the cot was strung with leather straps.

She sat down on the cot once more. No matter. She wasn't about to give up. She would watch and wait and take her chance to escape when the time came.

And if Conan the MacStruan or whoever he was tried to stop her, she'd take a piece of him with her.

Edana stirred the basin with a small rock-crystal wand. The water, which had been carried to her by hand from the snows of the highest peaks, shimmered and shivered before her watchful eyes.

"And what is my love doing today?" she murmured to the waters.

Ever so gently, she sprinkled a fine powder into the basin. The tiny granules sank and dissolved, changing the water to an iridescent lavender. She stirred once more and chanted over the waters, raising her hands to implore the heavens reflected in the basin.

At last a vision began to form.

A tall man stood on a hilltop, his long hair rippling behind him in the breeze. At his side hung a mighty sword and at his feet stood an enormous, woolly hound.

"Alone again, my love?" Edana whispered, pulling her own fiery tresses back out of the way of the water. "It won't be long, sweet. Before long you'll know your true love and you'll never be alone again. Is that not so, Servant?"

The waters swirled once more, disturbing the image of the man. A reedy voice bubbled up from the depths of the basin. "It isss e'en so, mistressss," came the answer.

Edana stood back from the basin, smiling in satisfaction. She smoothed her gown down over her lush figure and shook out her abundant hair once more. The breeze lifted and caught at her wild, copper curls. She laughed and raised her arms to the welcome wind that rushed toward her, bearing spring in its arms.

The world was hers. Almost.

She cast the water from the basin out over the meadow, creating a cascading lavender arc, beautiful to behold. It fell to the grass and vanished. She tucked the bowl under her arm, took up her basket, and limped slowly back across the meadow to the castle that loomed beyond, humming a tuneful air.

"So what is this place?"

"The cell," her guard, the man named Ross, replied.

Julia sighed. She'd heard of Scots thrift, but she hadn't realized it applied to the spoken word. "A monosyllable saved is a monosyllable earned," must be the clan motto, she decided. Gary Cooper must have been their idol. Their impossible brute of a leader certainly wasn't forthcoming with any details she could use. She hadn't even seen him since he'd ordered his men to lock her up yesterday morning.

She took another bite of the porridgelike substance in the bowl she held and nearly gagged. How could anyone eat this gunk? she wondered. Ice-cold haggis with a boiled rubber-boot sauce would have been tastier. The aroma alone was an offense to her finely-tuned chef's palate. But she'd spent most of a day and all of a night in her chilly cell, and her body was beginning to protest the lack of sustenance. She tried once more to engage the man who'd brought the gunk in lieu of breakfast and who stood, ramrod straight, watching her every move.

"I know it's a cell," she said. "What I meant was, where are we? What place is this? Who is this Darach MacStruan?"

"The MacStruan. Chief of our clan."

"Is that like being the mayor or something?"

"Nay. Clan means children, kindred. For us, that's what it means as well. We're all family." She caught the note of pride in his terse speech.

"You're all brothers?"

"Nay. Cousins, uncles, brothers, most of us that are lairds. All o' that. But we all have the first MacStruan as our kin. We've all sworn allegiance to the MacStruan."

"And this place?"

He shrugged. "Our clachan. Our village. It's where we live."

"And this house?"

"Darach's house. He's a laird, ye know. A baron. O' course, so are we all lairds. But he's the chief among us, descended direct from the first MacStruan."

Julia recalled the massive MacStruan. He certainly didn't look like a baron. With his broad shoulders and dramatic warrior's garb, he looked more like some perfectly buffed actor in a swashbuckling movie. But she didn't think it likely that eight men would all be researching for a film. Besides, there wasn't a pair of sunglasses or a bottle of Evian water anywhere to be seen.

"Do you live like this all the time?"

He frowned. "I kenna what ye mean."

"I mean, like this. In this—clachan." She pointed to his woolen blanket. "Do you always dress like that?"

He looked thoughtful. "Aye. What else should we wear? I've seen trews, such as ye wear, but they're bindin' to a fella and too much draggin' in the mud."

"So you spend your days out in the woods, hunting?" As she spoke, she cast a jaundiced eye upon the grayish yellow substance piled on her spoon. She hoped no one had wasted a shot for the sake of this noisome entree. Valiantly she tried to swallow the gunk quickly to avoid any unnecessary lingering on her tongue. She was only partly successful.

"Nay, no' every day," Ross replied. "Some days we're huntin'. Some days, fightin'. Some days we're tendin' the kine. No' today, though."

She sighed. This was too weird, she thought for the hundredth time. She was getting nowhere. There had to be a reasonable explanation for these people and the way they lived. She

35

tried another tack. "Where I come from, you can't be locked up in a cell in someone's house. It's against the law."

He nodded. "None but the chief may do so here."

"This chief of yours. Is he married?"

He shot a sharp glance her way. "Why would ye wish to know?"

She shrugged. "Just curious. I haven't seen any women around here. Not that I've been allowed out and around much."

"Ye ask too many questions. It's none o' your affair."

"I suppose not. But a woman does like another woman's company sometimes."

"If there's somethin' ye're needin', we can provide."

"Oh, that's good. Then I'd like a telephone, a hot bath, clean clothes, a mushroom omelet with a glass of fresh orange juice, a cup of coffee, and a lawyer. In that order, please."

"Absolutely, lass. Soon as I finish flyin' to the moon. The MacStruan's no' so easily taken in by the likes of ye."

She decided she'd upend the bowl of gunk on his head if he mentioned "the MacStruan" one more time. Was this Darach guy a god or something? He sounded a lot more like some egomaniacal president-for-life, ruling over the world's tiniest country.

But she was too hungry to sacrifice her only source of nourishment for the sake of making a point. She had to keep up her strength in order to make her escape. Shuddering, she lifted another bite to her unwilling lips. She grimaced and swallowed.

Yes, Clan MacStruan was one bizarro little company, she thought, studying her stiff and proper guard once more. Could there really be no women around? Were there none here at all, or did this Darach character insist that they stay locked up somewhere?

Her mouth fell open. What if—

She looked at the man who stood before her. Ross, they'd called him. He wasn't as big as Darach, but he was solidly built and hardened and he carried both a sword and a knife. He looked about as macho as they make 'em, she thought. But that wasn't any real indicator. . . .

Good Lord, she thought with a start. Was this . . . had she strayed into the world's most peculiar gay resort?

She almost started to giggle at the thought. *Be cool, Addison.* It wouldn't be prudent at this juncture to be laughing to herself like a loon. Besides, she argued with herself, gay men, even on vacation, weren't likely to kidnap women— or anyone else—and drag them through the woods to their camp. At least none of the gays she'd ever known would. How many exceptions could there be? No, the historical reenactment idea was the soundest of her possibilities. She took another look at her kilted captor and decided they must be the most dedicated historians on record.

"Finished wi' yer gruel?" Ross asked.

"Gruel, eh? Yep, good name for it." She choked down a last spoonful and handed over the bowl. He headed for the door. She rose to watch him go.

He spun around in the blink of an eye, his knife appearing out of nowhere. She gasped and raised her hands.

"Get ye back on the cot," he growled. "And dinna make any more such moves. Darach says he'll no' endure any foolishness."

She sat back down, her hands still raised. "I wasn't trying—"

"It doesna matter. Sit."

She glared at him, but the glittering edge of his knife convinced her he would indeed hurt her if she moved. She watched in fear and outrage as he unlocked the door and went out. The outer bar thunked down into place and she was alone once more.

She really had to get out of here.

Chapter Three

Darach strode along the rill, his long legs eating up the distance from the clachan to the tiny loch that lay in the glen above. Liam, Alasdair, and Niall kept pace with him, each in his own fashion.

"Do ye think it was Morestons?" Liam asked. He was a good three hands shorter than Darach and of a slighter build. His owlish face looked worried.

"Who else would bother?" Alasdair replied, picking up a rock and sending it flying through the rare, clear air.

"But why kill the cattle?" Niall asked, following along with long, steady strides. "Stealin's one thing. A body can sell a stolen beast. Or eat it. But to slaughter it and leave it to rot, that's plain daft."

"Or plain malice," Darach said.

The quartet of men bore left from the loch and climbed up over a rise. Down in the narrow glen below, they could see the still, bulky forms lying in the moving grasses. Darach counted.

"Five in all. And one a calf, besides." He swore beneath his breath. "Craigen Moreston's the cravenest coward that ever was whelped. He'll no' face me, but a fat old heifer holds no fear for the likes o' him." He turned to the men. "Liam, I'll need ye to go back and get a wagon. Bring twa more o' the men. We'll need help gettin' 'em back." He sighed. "Perhaps we can salvage somethin' out of Moreston's dirty little prank."

Liam was off at once, running easily over the rocky ground, his plaid swinging about his knees. The other three started down the hill into the glen.

"D'ye think they're safe to eat?" asked Niall.

"I canna say. We'll know more when we get there. It canna be that long since they were laid low. They may be fresh enough."

There was a pause. "I dinna mean exactly that," Niall said.

Darach looked at him quizzically. His cousin colored a bit and cleared his throat before speaking. "It's the witch, Darach," he said gruffly. "How do we know she didn't poison the kine? Or cast some evil o'er them? Surely they wouldn't be safe to eat by man or beast."

Darach scowled. "It's no' happened before,"

he said slowly. "And this doesna seem like witch's work to me."

"And we have the witch," Alasdair said. "She couldn't be out here and under our guard at the same time."

"As of yestermorn only," Niall argued. "None can say if she didna put a spell upon them before we laid hands on her. Or that she couldna have done it from the cell and all."

Darach glowered at the hills. "If only the woman had stayed at Castle Moreston."

They had descended into the glen, where the cattle lay like a range of dark, woolly hills. All three fell silent as they walked around the fallen beasts.

Darach squatted down and pointed to one of the bodies. "See. That's no' witchcraft. That's the work of a mortal knife, clean and sharp." He examined the next one. "And the same for this one." He straightened. "They're stiffenin'," he said, nudging one woolly flank with his boot. "But I see no reason for us not to taste o' them. At the least, we'll get the leather from them." He put his hands on his hips and looked back up the hill. "While we're waitin', let's have a look about. The tracks of these curs may tell us somethin'."

They split off in three directions, each of them looking for any clues as to where the killers had come from and where they'd gone. Darach tramped along to the north, up the glen toward the pass.

He knew these hills and valleys as well as he

knew his own name. His childhood had been spent racing over every rocky mile of the MacStruan lands, tagging along behind his father and the other men of the clan. He knew every glen and rill, every secret grove or tiny loch, and his very heart beat to the rhythms of the land.

But today it all felt sullied to him, this clean, wild land. His old enemy, Craigen Moreston, chief of the neighboring clan, had sent his minions here to spill blood and lay waste to the lives he and his people tended with such anxious care. Cattle were the clan's best source of money, and every beast was precious. Raiding cattle was a time-honored pastime in the Highlands, and the MacStruans had done their share. Everyone knew that what roamed free, out in nature, nourished by nature's bounty, was anyone's fair game. One always had the option of stealing them back.

But wholesale slaughter of beasts just for sport—that was another matter. It was a gesture of such pure, grinning contempt that Darach wanted to unsheathe his sword and put to rout every Moreston in the whole of Scotland.

Yet he knew such an action would be utter folly. As chief, he had to be practical. The Morestons could overpower tiny Clan MacStruan in the twinkling of an eye. They possessed more land, more money, more property, more men, more arms, and more influence than the MacStruans had ever held. Yet they wanted more. And so they warred upon the MacStruans in every underhanded way, stealing away more of their land with each passing year.

Darach reached the mouth of the pass and turned to look back across the glen. What was Craigen up to? he wondered. Why this?

He thought of the young woman who'd been brought before him yesterday morning. Was she the witch who, everyone claimed, aided Craigen Moreston in all his affairs?

He shook his head. He was not a superstitious man. He knew that most things could be known or understood if only a man used his eyes and his mind. But there had been too many incidents in the past three years that could not be explained away. And if the scholars and priests he'd met in the city believed in witches, who was he to disbelieve? Besides, he knew firsthand the depths of the Morestons' evil ways. They wouldn't be above trafficking in witchcraft, he knew that much.

He strode about the area, searching for tracks. He saw nothing. He wondered what the other two men had found. Everything about this business made him uneasy. He wanted to hear that they'd found bootprints and broken grasses, drops of cattle blood upon a stone. He didn't want to think about any other explanations.

The image of mad, lovely Julia Addison came to his mind once more. Was he a fool to think that she was more insane than evil?

He shook the thought away. He had more important things to worry about. She was locked up and that was that.

He headed back down the glen to rejoin the others, trying hard not to think of odd, soft breeches, full red lips, and snapping, intelligent brown eyes.

"So, Ross, ye talked wi' her, then?"

A cheerful fire blazed away in the center of Bruce MacStruan's little house, its smoke rising up to exit through a hole in the roof. The fire's golden light reflected off the faces of the lairds who had gathered for an evening of drink and talk, and created dancing shadows on the snug stone walls. This night the men had plenty to discuss, and the witch-woman was at the forefront of all their minds.

As the eldest member of the clan, silver-haired Bruce would quite naturally command considerable respect, and did so. Over the years, however, the old laird had been nursing and honing a fuller, more majestic identity for himself. Through tortuous reasoning, a smattering of hearsay, and a dash of clan folklore, he had decided that he was not only a Mac-Struan, but also a direct descendant of Robert the Bruce. As the years passed, his self-created kinship had flowered so fully that he lived the part: assuming royal poses, offering proclamations, and answering almost exclusively to "Your Majesty." He was the Bruce. And as he was well beloved, and sound in every other way, the rest of the clan went along with the fantasy, honoring the old warrior with their respect and their good-natured tolerance.

Ross shifted on his footstool and nodded to the Bruce. "Aye, I spoke to her when I brought her gruel this mornin'. She's as curious as twa cats, that one. Asked question after question."

"Ye didna answer her, did ye?" Liam asked, aghast.

"Aye. Most of 'em were sae daft and simple, I wondered she didn't ask to be told up from down."

Niall shook his head. "Liam's right. Ye should no' be answerin' questions, let alone talkin' wi' a witch."

"We've no proof she's a witch," Ross replied, his long hands laced around his mug of ale.

"No proof!" Tommy, the youngest of the lairds, looked around the circle of men. "We all heard her wild words. We saw her strange clothes. And ye all saw the unairthly objects she kept in that pouch o' hers."

Brawny Dugan nodded. "Darach locked her awa'," he rumbled. "He thinks she's a witch."

Ross flushed. "Nay. I say he doesna think so yet. He said as much. She may be only a witless wanderer."

Alasdair, who had been perched on the deep windowsill, looking out at the rising moon, now spoke. "Ye sound a bit bewitched yerself, Ross," he said over his shoulder.

Ross's flush deepened. "Are ye sayin' ye don't even believe your ain brother, Alasdair?"

Alasdair dropped to the floor. "I make up my

45

ain mind," he said mildly. "Darach knows that. And I was only makin' an observation."

The Bruce cleared his throat. The men fell silent, awaiting his word. "Witch or no," the old man said, raising a finger, "I say she's as bonny a maid as I've ever seen. I'd no' turn a fine, wee bit like her out a' my bed on a cauld nicht."

The men laughed heartily, if a bit self-consciously. Bruce swept the group with a knowing grin. "So, ye admit the woman's been on yer minds, and no' just because ye think she's goin' to make the milk-cows gang dry."

"We're only human," said Niall.

"Aye," said Ross. "And it's been a while since—"

"Whisht," said Gordon, shaking his balding head. "Dunna ye say it!"

Ross looked apologetic. "Pardon. But the lass is fair-faced and fair-limbed. And she didna seem too awful dangerous. Except—"

Niall leaned toward him, eyes narrowed. "Except what?"

"At the last," Ross said. "She made as if she'd run out when I went to the door." He glanced around the circle defensively. "I set her back wi' my knife, o' course."

Heads nodded all around. They all gazed into the fire for a while. The room seemed a bit warmer than the fire warranted, some of them noted. Alasdair went back to his perch on the windowsill.

Gordon broke the silence. "What d'ye make of the beasts that were slain, Niall?"

Niall shrugged. "Looks like Moreston mischief."

Liam snorted. "Thievin' bastards."

Gordon looked at the ceiling. "Takes a thief to know a thief."

Liam puffed up like a bantam rooster. He nudged Dugan. "'Man's worst ill is stubbornness of the heart,' said Sophocles. Tell him some folk know what's theirs and what's not."

Dugan, long accustomed to the feud between Liam and Gordon, turned to Gordon. "He says some folk know what's theirs and what's not."

Gordon flushed to his shining scalp. "True enough! And I know my ain fowl! Tell him that."

Dugan shifted heavily toward Liam, looking bored. "Says he knows his ain fowl," he recited.

"And ye tell him—"

"Whisht!" The Bruce banged on the table with his ale cup. "Listenin' to the pair of ye is like bein' pecked to death by your damned chickens! All that happened years ago and we're every man of us gripin' sick o' the whole tale." He waved a regal hand. "Niall, ye may go on about the kine. I'd know more."

Niall described the trip to the glen and the state of the cattle. "We brought 'em back here, but I'd feel a measure more certain if we could rule out the witch's hand in this matter."

"How are we to do that?" asked Gordon.

Niall shrugged. "Darach says there's tests."

"There are tests," Alasdair said. The others turned toward their chief's younger brother. Alasdair was well educated and well traveled, in

47

addition to being a master of swordplay. When he spoke of matters outside of their tiny realm, the men generally listened.

"There are tests," he repeated, slipping off the sill once more. "But I'd not be the one to do that testin', for my soul."

"Why not?" asked Tommy.

Alasdair's eyes darkened. "Let's just say that such tests are best left to priests who have knowledge o' such practices."

Bruce studied the younger man for a moment and then nodded. "Perhaps such testin' is better left to God."

Gordon glowered around at the circle of men. "Are we to have no justice, then? Have ye forgotten what the Morestons and their evil one did to your ain family, Niall?" He swung about to Alasdair. "Do ye no' recall what happened to my sister? What happened to your da?"

Alasdair faced him blandly. "I've no' forgotten."

"Nor have I," Niall added. "I'll ne'er forget the night Darach bore your Isobel home from the Moreston's keep, lifeless as any stane." His powerful fists clenched in his lap. "My da fell wi' the auld chief. I've seen the witherin' o' the crops. I've seen the sickness on our people and the murder of our kine." He stared into the fire, anger and frustration working in his face. "Why should we no' have our justice upon the woman? When have the Morestons shown us such mercy?"

"Never in my memory," Alasdair said. "And

justice would be most sweet. But we dunna know that the lass is the one who worked the evil. I'd have a care, is all."

Gordon spat. "Let it be on my soul, then! I've naught to lose if the witch dies. You say leave testin' to God, Your Majesty? I say leave pardon to God. We canna afford to throw all we have to the Morestons and their kind. Let the priests come and test this woman. Let them decide! If she's the witch, we've dealt a blow to auld Craigen that will hit him where he lives. If she's no' a witch, either the priests will pardon her or God will do that work in heaven!"

"Amen," Dugan rumbled.

"Aye," murmured one or two of the others.

Alasdair looked about the circle and nodded briefly. "So be it for ye," he said softly.

The men fell into silence once more, sipping their drinks and gazing into the fire.

At last Tommy spoke. "Wonder what Darach's got planned?"

Heads nodded once again.

Julia scrambled off the cot as she heard the thunk of the bar outside her room. The heavy oak door swung open and Darach MacStruan entered, sword in hand.

She sighed and sat back down. Conan again, she thought. Did he really think she was any match for his bulk and that gargantuan blade? A brief scan of his height, girth, and muscled legs told her he wouldn't even need a sword to take control of her in a second.

He shut the door but didn't fasten the latch. She couldn't resist taking a speculative glance at the possibility of escape. She decided a snowball had a better chance in the Mojave desert. She had to find another way out.

He glanced around the bare, dim room. "Ye have all ye need?" he asked.

"No."

He looked at her, waiting for her to elaborate. She raised a hand.

"First," she said, ticking off on her fingers as she spoke, "I need a bathroom and a bath. Second, I need food that didn't come out of *One Hundred and One Ways to Prepare Library Paste.* Third, I need a lawyer or the U.S. ambassador or the American consul general—any of those will do. Fourth, I need some clean clothes; I've been wearing these for two days. And fifth, I want to know where in the hell I am and why you think you can hold me against my will!"

He listened impassively through her whole speech. He raised his eyebrows, checking to see if she'd finished. She waved a hand for him to speak.

"First, ye may have a bath. I'll see that ye get one brought down in the mornin'. As for clothes, I'll see what I can find. If ye dunna like our victuals, ye may go without. Ye'll eat what everyone else gets." He began ticking off on his fingers, in imitation of her. She resisted the impulse to kick him. "Fourth, I'd sooner let a wolf into my house than a lawyer. As for the others ye named, I've no idea who ye mean and no time

50

to waste findin' out. If ye want to talk to Craigen, no doubt he'll find ye as soon as he's finished skulkin' after my cattle."

Julia shook her head. "I don't know any Craigen."

His broad shoulders rose and fell, the muscles beneath his shirt rippling like shallow ocean waves. "Have it your way. As for your fifth request, I am Darach MacStruan. Chief of Clan MacStruan. This is my house, my land, my people. Ye're a stranger and ye were caught trespassin' on my land. There've been too many attacks on my lands and my folk for me to let others wander about at their leisure. Ye'll stay here, by my orders, until your folk come to ransom ye, or until ye can prove who ye are to my satisfaction."

"Couldn't you send down to Kinloch Rannoch and have one of them come up here? I was staying at an inn there and the innkeeper will know me."

He stared at her. "Ye were stayin' at Kinloch?"

"Yes!" She bounded up from the bed. "If you had given me a chance to speak, I could have told you that yesterday. All it would take is a phone call."

He scowled. "What inn?"

"The Blackwater." She watched his face and saw no change. She took a cautious step toward him. "Aren't you going to call them? Ask for Mrs. Carie, she knows me. Ask her if an American woman named Julia Addison has been staying there. Ask her if she could send someone here to pick me up. My car's stuck in the woods."

"The Blackwater, ye say?"

"Yes."

"There's no inn in Kinloch village wi' that name."

"Oh, come on!" She placed her hands on her hips. "Now you're trying to gaslight me. I know what hotel I was staying in. My stuff is still in my room there. Just call, please?" She looked up into his eyes, hoping for a hint of sympathy in their cool blue depths.

"I can't send any o' my men on a foolish chase to Kinloch. If someone knows ye're missin' they'll come for ye."

"They don't know for sure that I'm missing, and I'm fairly certain that they don't suspect I'm being held prisoner in some goofy summer camp for fans of Bonnie Prince Charlie. And you don't need to send anyone to Kinloch. Just call."

"Call?" He shrugged again. "So. Ye are addled, then, lass."

"I'm perfectly sane. Why do you keep saying that?"

"If ye think I can shout all the way to Kinloch village from here, ye must be daft."

"I didn't say—Oh, no." She felt her heart sink. "Are you trying to tell me there are no phones here?"

"Never has been any such thing."

"How about a cellular?" He shook his head. "Well, a radio, then? Fax machine?" His head moved slowly back and forth. "What do you do if there's an emergency?" she asked. "What if one of you got sick or hurt?"

"What rubbish are ye talkin'? We tend our ain."

"And you think I'm nuts?" Julia paced across the cell and back. "You must get mail. How about sending a letter?"

"Can ye write?"

She glared. "That's low. I may be an American but that doesn't mean I'm illiterate. Yes, I can write."

He thought for a moment. "All right, then. Ye may send a letter down to th' village. One o' my men may be able to go next week."

"Next week?"

"Aye. Now, if ye're satisfied—"

"I'm not satisfied!" She came to stand before him again. He towered above her, his dark features still as stone as he met her gaze. To her annoyance, she found her own gaze drifting from those dark-fringed eyes, to the striking nose, to the lines on either side of his mouth. That mouth that gave utterance to that deep, liquid voice . . .

What the heck are you thinking, Addison? This wasn't a man; this was a barbarian! Perhaps even the leader of a cult of barbarians. She needed to make every effort to get away from him, not take inventory of all his barbaric attractions. She needed to get back to a world of normal men in normal clothes. Not that she had anyone waiting for her, but she knew this Darach MacStruan just wasn't her type.

"I can't possibly wait a week," she began lamely, backing away from the solid rock wall of his frame.

"Be that as it may, that's all I can provide for ye now. I was about to say that ye may go out tomorrow. Ye'll be bound and twa of my men will be lookin' after ye, but at least ye'll be out of your cell for a bit."

Julia sighed. "Don't overextend yourself."

"I willna," he said with bland disregard of her sarcastic tone. He headed for the door. "I'll hae someone bring the tub to ye in the mornin'."

She nodded. At least he had some sense of decency, she decided. "Thank you."

He turned and looked at her, as if searching her face to see whether she was sincere. He turned back. "Ye're welcome," he said as he passed through the doorway.

Darach hefted the crossbar and let it fall into place. He listened but heard nothing from inside the cell. He left the narrow passage and made his way to the great hall.

The big room stood empty and silent. His men had left his house soon after the evening meal. They were most likely gathered around the Bruce's cozy fire, swapping lies and drinking. Somehow the idea of being alone in the house with his beautiful prisoner made him uneasy. It wasn't as if he were afraid of her. She did seem more halfwit than sorceress. And as an ordinary mortal woman, she posed no physical threat to him.

Yet he had to admit that she'd been in his house for nearly two days and he'd spent most of that time avoiding her. He'd told himself he had work to do and duties to carry out. His men could look after one small woman. The Morestons or her kin would come looking for her soon and then he'd make a decision about her. He didn't need to see her.

But tonight, after all the men had deserted his hall, he'd paced about, the sounds of his boots echoing off the high stone walls. All his attention seemed to be focused on the dim cell below the stairs. His awareness of her presence in his house had forced him to go and see her, just to rid himself of the thought of her.

He'd been only partly successful. He'd seen her, and seen that she was indeed only a woman and probably a mad one at that. He'd heard her strange accent and her nonsense words. He'd listened to her foolish babble about a Blackwater Inn and being able to call all the way to Kinloch village.

He'd also seen that fair, wee face again, with its firm but delicate chin tilted up to meet him eye to eye. She wore those outlandish trews still, and he could hardly keep his eyes and his hands from straying to the slender waist that flared so perfectly down into soft hips and trim thighs. Her lips alone, even when spouting such gibberish as "raydeo" and "gas light," were the most delicious pair he'd ever seen. He could al-

most taste the sweetness of them just by looking. As he'd thought the first time he'd seen her,
she looked like a woman made for loving.

So he'd held himself still and steeled himself
against her distracting physical appeal. He was
a man, a chief, and she was a prisoner, be she
madwoman, witch, spy, or lost traveler. To
touch her might not only prove dangerous; it
would be the basest sort of behavior in him as
her jailer. He wouldn't take advantage of her.

Still, he thought as he climbed the stairs to
his chamber, he hoped someone came and
claimed her soon. He wasn't sure his honor
could hold out for long against lively, delectable
Julia Addison.

Chapter Four

Soft mists hung over the world when Julia
stepped outside the following morning. The
clouds above the hills had dipped low, as if going for a leisurely skim over the land, close
enough for her to reach up and touch them like
solid objects. The fresh, moist air made a welcome change from the dank air of her cell.

The weather placed a far, far second in her
thoughts, however. Darach and the one called
Alasdair had come and fetched her after her
bath. She felt a bit awkward in the strange,
loose gown, undergown, and moccasin-type
shoes they gave her, but at least she was clean
from her bath in the big wooden tub that had
been rolled in and filled with bucket upon
bucket of hot water. The gown had belonged to
Darach and Alasdair's mother, Ross had told

her. So now she knew the big ogre had a mother and wasn't merely spawned from a rock.

Odd, she thought as she smoothed the soft, worn woolen of the gown. For the first time since she'd landed in Scotland, she felt warm.

But even warmth and cleanliness paled at her first glimpse of the village. If she'd found Darach's house quaint and primitive, that impression was left in the dust by the sight of the village that ringed the grassy area outside Darach's door. Chickens and ducks scuttled out of the way before them as they walked, and a couple of sheep wandered about, doing some free-form lawn mowing. A huge dog barreled out of the woods, its tongue lolling in a canine grin. The animal flung itself at Darach, who greeted it with rough affection.

"Down, Big Dog, ye daft thing," he said, scrubbing the dog's rough head. "Gang ye and hunt some rabbits. Mak' yersel' useful for a change." The animal gave Darach's face a swipe with his tongue and trotted off to stand watching the proceedings with cocked ears and interest in his eyes.

Julia wondered at the way the dog seemed to adore Darach. Everyone around seemed to revere him. What kind of power did he possess that he should inspire so much unswerving loyalty? Would they be so loyal to anyone who claimed to be descended from the so-called first MacStruan?

As they reached the center of the green, Julia looked about at what she realized constituted the whole of their village. The houses that formed a crescent about the green were all built of rough-cut natural stone and built low to the ground; black houses, they were called. She remembered the term from the tourist guide she'd read in her inn room. Thickly thatched roofs, weighted down by heavy rocks, topped most of the dwellings, and sturdy wooden shutters covered the few deep-set windows she could see. At one house she could have sworn she saw a cow looking out from one of those windows, calmly chewing its cud. Good grief, she thought, did they sleep with their cattle? Or just have them around as house pets?

As she and the two men continued their walk, figures began to materialize out of the mists. Slowly the other seven men who'd brought her here came to the edge of the grass and stared at her with unconcealed curiosity. But as she drew closer, several of them pulled back and one or two, muttering under his breath, made the sign of the cross when she met his eyes.

"What's the matter with them?" she asked.

Darach looked down at her. "Don't ye know? Ye must be used to such greetings."

"I've had my share of snubbings in my time. I've been stood up. I've even been left off the guest list at parties. But I've never had anyone treat me as if I had some kind of communicable disease." She started. "Is that what they think? That I'm sick?"

Alasdair shook his head. "Nay. They think ye're a witch."

Julia stopped dead. "They what? You mean all that silly talk when you brought me here—that was serious?" She looked back and forth between the two.

"Did ye think ye'd fooled us?" Darach asked.

"No. I'm not out to fool anybody. But I'm not a witch, a Wiccan, a Druid, or even a gypsy fortune-teller. I'm a chef!"

"Ye told me ye were an america."

"American. Yes, I am an American. And I work as a chef. Or I did until—oh, hell, that's too complicated to go into now. All I'm saying is that I'm not a witch and I don't care about getting the ruby slippers or following the Yellow Brick Road. Will you please tell that to the Lollipop Guild here?" She waved a hand at the men before them.

Darach looked over her head at Alasdair. Then he looked at the others. "She says she's a chef, no' a witch."

"A chief, d'ye say, Darach?" asked the older man, who carried a heavy walking stick.

Darach shrugged. "Ask her."

Julia shot him an exasperated glance. "Not a chief," she said to the other men. "A chef. I cook."

"Ahh." The chorus of male voices would have made her laugh if she weren't so concerned with the way they all still stared at her and fingered the knives tucked into their belts. She looked at Darach. "Don't they believe me?"

"Like as not they believe ye can cook."

"But they still think I'm a witch."

"Like as not," drawled Alasdair with a nod. "Ye've given them no proof that ye're not."

"And have I given them proof that I am?" She began to feel more nervous by the moment. Knives, strange houses, odd clothing and speech, and now witches. This had to be more than a trainee camp for the Highland games. Perhaps she had fallen into the middle of a cult after all.

They all seemed to ponder her question for a moment. Then they looked to Darach.

"Ye've done us no harm that we've seen so far," he said. "But ye're too outlandish to be an innocent."

"What does that mean? That anyone who's different from you is automatically evil? Who died and made you boss?" She could feel the heat coming to her cheeks. She lifted her chin, challenging Darach to speak in defense of prejudice.

There was another of those great intakes of breath among the group. More crossing of chests and foreheads.

Darach's eyes darkened. "My father died and made me chief."

She flushed. "I'm sorry," she said at once. "That was crass of me. But I hate bigotry of all kinds. Haven't you ever heard of a person being innocent until proven guilty?"

This time they positively goggled at her. That was the only word for it, she thought: goggling. It was a textbook example.

"Innocent until proven guilty?" The one they

called Liam still stared, wide-eyed. "What sort o' nonsense would that be? If ye didna think someone was guilty, they wouldna be in trouble in the first place! It's up to them to prove their innocence, if they can."

"That's just plain backward!" Julia couldn't help arguing. "If everyone's guilty before you've even heard their side of the story, then you might as well sentence them before they ever come to trial!"

"But if a body's innocent before ye even take 'em to trial, then ye'd be bringin' an innocent man to trial. Where's the sense in that?" Liam looked around at the group, who nodded in support. " 'Every place is safe to him who lives wi' justice.' That's frae Epictetus."

"I don't care if it's from Pee-Wee Herman; you guys are positively medieval!" she exclaimed. "I suppose you think I'm guilty of being a witch and I'll have to prove to you that I'm . . ." Her voice faded away to a squeak. "Oh, no. You can't be serious."

The faces around her were uniformly solemn. She looked to Darach. "You wouldn't—you couldn't—" she stammered. She seized his sleeve. "You can't do this. It's totally ridiculous. It's against the law."

He looked away. "I am the law."

The man named Niall cleared his throat. "We've been talkin', Darach. We canna rest easy wi' that one in our midst. We need to know if she's the witch or no."

"I'm not! I don't believe in any of that *Bell*,

Book & Candle stuff! I don't even have any crystals or incense or chimes in my apartment." Julia looked desperately at the men before her. "I'm just a plain old ordinary woman. I didn't want to come here. But I was being chased by some mobsters from New York. They were going to kill me."

"Who did she say was chasin' her?" Bruce asked Tommy, sotto voce.

"Lobsters from York," the boy replied.

"That's daft," said the older man. Tommy only shrugged.

"No, you don't understand." Julia began again. "Not lobsters—oh, this is getting too strange!"

"Are ye firm on the matter?" Darach asked the lairds, ignoring Julia's agitation.

"We are," said Gordon stoutly. "We'd have her examined."

Darach looked about the group. "And so say ye all?"

Not every head nodded, but no one dissented. Julia's heart went cold. If she could only wake up from this nightmare. But she'd already tried pinching herself and all she had to show for her troubles was bruises.

"If ye're all agreed, it will be done." Darach looked at Julia. She thought she saw pity in his eyes and fought against her fears. "Ye'll be charged and stand to the questions."

"But how can I possibly defend myself against such a ridiculous charge? I've seen *The Crucible* and I know my history." She put her

63

bound hands on his arm. "Anyone can claim someone is a witch for any reason—and nothing they do or say can prove that they are or they aren't because it's all just a lot of fear and ignorance and prejudice."

Darach looked down at her once more. "I'm no' an ignorant man," he said evenly. "Nor a fearful one. But if ye are a witch and my people suffer for my lack of testin' ye, then I'm damned for a fool and your unwitting accomplice."

She dropped her hands and looked to Alasdair. His eyes showed a brief spark of sympathy for her, then hardened as he shook his head. She looked about at the faces of the other men. Some showed fear, some curiosity, others mistrust. But none of them revealed any sign that they might champion her cause. Darach's word was indeed law.

"How . . ." Her voice stuck again. She cleared her throat, anger and indignation coming to aid her composure. "How do you propose to test me?"

"We'll send for the priest from Kinloch village," Darach said. "He'll do the questionin'."

"Just questioning?" Relief flowed into her. She'd imagined some arcane ritual involving thumbscrews and fire and . . . worse.

"If that's all that's required, aye."

"And if it's not?" A sharp quiver of fear replaced her relief.

Darach hesitated, then eyed her squarely. "Then we'll do whatever's necessary."

Julia's knees changed to water. She glanced

around the circle of men once more. "And it's what all of you want?" she asked softly.

Only one or two met her eyes. But again no one contested the decision.

"Take me back to my cell," she said, holding herself stiff against the fear that threatened to engulf her.

"Lass, ye must understand—"

"I understand perfectly, Mr. MacStruan," she said, her voice tight with shock. "Take me back."

The seven lairds trailed after Julia, Darach, and Alasdair as they crossed the green to Darach's house once more. Even the chickens seemed to clear out of her way, Julia noted ruefully. No doubt they'd been told she could turn their eggs into charcoal briquettes with a twitch of her nose.

Alasdair left them at the door, hanging back to remain with the other lairds. Darach only gave him a glance, then took Julia's arm and led her back to the little room under the stairs.

He undid the bonds on her wrists. She went in meekly and sat down on the cot. He stood by the door for a moment, as if waiting to see what she would do.

"Ye may go out tomorrow, as well," he began.

"Don't bother," she said. "I wouldn't want to terrify all you big, strong men."

"As ye wish."

He still waited by the door. She looked up to see something in his dark features that she couldn't quite place. "What?"

"It's our way, lass," he said softly. "I canna afford to take a chance wi' ye."

"So you've said."

"Ye didna have to come here."

"Didn't I?" She raised her hands. "I don't see how."

He moved into the cell, filling it with his presence, making her acutely aware of him in all his height and power. "Ye should have stayed at home, where ye belong. But if ye're goin' to trespass on your enemy's land, ye must expect to pay the consequences when ye're caught."

"If I told you that I don't know how I got here, would you believe me?"

"Are ye sayin' ye lost your wits?" He shook his head. "Anyone who can argue philosophy and law wi' our Liam, no matter how backward her notions, doesna seem too addled to me."

Her hopes sank once more. "I should have known."

"Known what?"

"That you wouldn't believe me." She rose and stood at the head of the cot. "I hardly believe it myself. All I know is that I was running away from someone who was trying to kill me. I stumbled, fell down a hill, and your men took me prisoner. That's all I know. I don't even know who you guys are—only that you're the strangest bunch I've ever met outside of a California peace-and-bean sprout cult commune." She gave a wry half-smile. "I don't suppose you're all worshipers of the Cosmic Muffin, are you?"

He scowled. "We worship God. Is that what ye worship, this muffin idol?"

She sighed. "No. I'm a plain old Protestant."

"What do ye protest?"

It was her turn to goggle. "Protest? Nothing, really. Oh, occasionally I've marched for human rights and I've written letters—oh, that's not what you mean, is it?" She chewed her lip. Given what she'd seen on the green and what little she knew of Scots history, she had to assume that they were Catholic. Or was it Presbyterian? Better not to get into denominations; she was on thin enough ice already. "I worship God, too."

He looked relieved. "That's good, then." He stepped closer. She responded to his proximity, the scent and sight and sound of him, with her whole being, causing her to shiver a bit. His effect on her startled her, confusing her thoughts for a moment.

"Ye must tell that to the priest," he said.

"Tell what?" she asked, dazed.

He shook his head. "Dunna play daft wi' me. I just said ye're no' a halfwit. And I'm no' a fool. Ye must tell the priest that ye're a believer."

"Will he believe me?"

He paused. "I willna lie to ye, lass. I canna say."

"You keep talking about these people, the Morestons. It all sounds like the Hatfields and the McCoys. Who are they?"

"Perhaps ye can tell me."

She smacked the cot with the flat of her palm.

"I've already told you! I don't know anyone by that name, and from the way you all act when you so much as mention them, I'm sure I don't want to know them." She calmed herself down with an effort. "Look, you've accused me of being a witch. I've heard you talking about the Moreston witch and I think that's who you think I am. If I'm going to defend myself against these charges, I think I have a right to know what I'm up against."

He pondered her words for a moment. "Very well. The Morestons, as ye know, are our sworn enemies. They've done naught but harm to my clan for generations. Lately they've managed to steal lands from us, plague our cattle and crops, and issue threats against my people. They seem to know where to strike to do us the greatest hurt." His mouth twisted into a bitter smile and Julia saw a spark ignite in the darkness of his eyes. "It is well known that Craigen, the Moreston, has a witch under his roof. Whether she is kin to him or a Sassenach, an outlander, no one knows. But all agree that she advises him on all matters and that she has the power to do harm and even bring death by magic."

In spite of herself, Julia felt a pang of sympathy for all that he and his people had been through. Then she caught herself. He was talking about a witch! This wasn't even real.

Still, she decided, she might as well play along. If she humored him, she might gain more information that could help her to escape. "And no one's ever seen her?"

He shook his head. "Nay. One or twa have said they'd sighted her—and lived—but their descriptions were aye so different they were useless. Besides, it's rumored that the Moreston's crone can change her shape at will, as can many of her kind. She might appear in any form." He looked pointedly at her. "Even in the form of a beautiful lass."

An odd little thrill of pleasure coursed through her at his last words. Unreasonably, her heart, and her cheeks, warmed at the thought that Darach MacStruan, who seemed so mountainous and cool, would find her beautiful, and she was astonished to know that he even had eyes for beauty.

Yet she saw his resolution to put her to this awful test. He believed she was his enemy. And so did everyone else in this village. Her pleasure slipped into chilly fear once more.

"When will the priest come?" she asked, her throat constricting against the words. She struggled against the visions of humiliation and torture that taunted her brain.

"I'll no' make ye wait overlang," he said, walking back to the door. "I'll send a man to Kinloch on the morrow to fetch him here." He put his hand to the latch, then hesitated. "If there's anything else ye need, ye may ask."

She couldn't meet his eyes. Tears welled too close to the surface and she would never, never give him the satisfaction of seeing her weep. "Nothing. There's nothing I need."

She listened as he went out, hearing again the

ominous thunking of the bar across the door. She heard his boots as he climbed the stairs. When she knew she was alone at last, she slipped down onto the cot and allowed her tears to fall.

Alasdair waited for Darach in the great hall. He'd drawn a pitcher of ale, and two cups stood on the small table at one end of the room. Darach went straight over and poured himself a full cup. He drank it off quickly, then followed it with another.

"It's a tad early to get bleezin' blind drunk, wouldn't ye say?"

Darach turned a baleful eye toward his younger brother. Alasdair shrugged. "Just askin'." He draped himself into a chair and sipped his own drink.

Darach drank off his second cup and poured a third.

"So. Ye're leavin' her to the kirk, eh?"

Darach sat, still scowling. "Do ye see I have much choice?"

"Nay, I'd say not."

Darach turned the cup about in his big hands. "If ye've aught to say to me, oganach, spill it."

Alasdair shook his head. "Not I. I value my head too much. But I canna help but wonder, do ye believe she's truly the Moreston's hag?"

Darach kept his eyes on his cup. "I don't know."

After a long silence, Alasdair spoke. "What of what she said out there on the green? About a person bein' innocent until their guilt is proved?"

"Sounds guilty as sin. Why?"

"The notion struck me as both passin' strange and yet passin' wise, as well."

"Wise?"

"Aye. Ye must admit it's easier to produce proof of guilt than of innocence. Seems that's where the law should rest its interests."

"There's never been a soul born innocent on this earth. 'Twould make no sense to assume they are."

"Ye have the right of it in the eyes o' the kirk, but I'm only talkin' about law. How easy would it be, were we to go before a court, to prove our innocence in these matters wi' the Morestons?"

"We are innocent!" Darach's eyes flashed.

"True. Ye have no quarrel wi' me on that." Alasdair lounged back in his chair. "But which would be the easier, to prove they're guilty or we're innocent?"

Darach could hardly believe his ears. Was this his own flesh and blood talking such madness? "That's as daft as askin' if it'd be easier to go up a hill or down! What's the matter wi' ye? Are ye goin' all soft over a wee lass?"

Alasdair only grinned. "I'd say it would depend upon the hill. And I'm no' takin' sides against ye, brother. I was only intrigued by what she had to say."

"Aye. She does seem to have that effect on a body."

"I wonder who this Pee-Wee Herman fella is

she was speakin' of. Some kind of judge, do ye suppose? Or maybe a prophet?"

Darach only shrugged. Alasdair quaffed the last of his drink, set the cup down with a thunk, and rose to his feet. "I'll be off then, brother."

"Where do ye ken ye're goin'? There's work to be done."

"I thought ye needed a man to go to Kinloch and fetch a priest?"

Darach groaned. "Aye. And as well ye as another of the lads. Last time Liam went, he made Fergus Dewey sae mad wi' his talk of the earth bein' round that Dewey threatened to take him before Father Martin for excommunication." He pushed out of his chair. "Leave at first light tomorrow. And be quick. No lettin' those restless feet o' yours go wanderin' about the whole of the Highlands." He gave a glance toward the stairs. "I told the lass we'd no' keep her waitin'."

Chapter Five

At the last moment, Darach chose to ride with Alasdair to Kinloch. He told his brother that he wanted to talk with some of the men there about selling their cattle, but privately he knew the real reason for the trip. He needed to leave in order to avoid seeing Julia.

Yesterday's events had shaken him—he had to admit that. If he'd known what a problem the woman would be, how she would prey upon his peace of mind and stir things up among his people, he'd have tossed her across his horse that first day and ridden off to deposit her at Craigen's door. Already he had come within a hairbreadth of exchanging blows with his brother. She had the men in such a ferment of curiosity and fear that they could scarcely concentrate on anything else. He was off now to find a priest who could try a woman as a witch. And that woman, witch or no, all too often invaded his thoughts and his senses.

He'd had a difficult time yesterday shaking off the image of her wide eyes searching his, looking for any sign of mercy or hope of pardon. The sight of her, fresh from her bath and dressed in one of his mother's old gowns, had all but made his heart stop. Moreover, because of the trews she'd been wearing before, he knew almost exactly what lay beneath the more modest attire. And that knowledge made his mind wander off, even now, onto paths that had nothing to do with priests, duty, clan struggles, or the price of beef in Kinloch.

"Are ye thinkin' o' Brother James?"

Darach looked up at Alasdair in puzzlement. No, he certainly hadn't been thinking about the grizzled old priest who'd served in Kinloch for some 30 years.

"For the test? Are ye thinkin' Brother James should be the one to do it?"

"Oh. Aye. Brother Jamie's a sound man. He'll know what to do."

"Do ye think we should set another watch over the cattle? If the Morestons try another o' their tricks, we might be able to run them off."

Darach was grateful for the change of subject. They launched into a discussion of cattle, trade, and clan business that kept his mind off Julia Addison for a blessedly long time.

The news in Kinloch was not favorable. Brother James had been recalled to Saint

Giles's kirk in Edinburgh and he had left at once. It would be several weeks, one of the monks reckoned, before his replacement would arrive.

Darach knew he could still ask Father Martin to perform the task, but the younger priest had always struck Darach as too intellectual and out of touch with real people. And to ask him to come to the clan village to examine a witch would leave the whole of Kinloch's kirk and parish without a priest, perhaps for several days.

He made his decision. The testing would have to wait until the new priest arrived. He turned his mind to cattle once again and deliberately avoided any contemplation of the motives behind his decision.

He and Alasdair completed the rest of their business in Kinloch, spent the night on the meadow outside the village walls to save the high cost of an inn room and stabling for their horses, and rode for home early the following morning. The lairds gathered about Darach as soon as he rode into the village. He told them the news.

"Ye mean to say we're to be left here at her mercy for weeks?" Gordon demanded.

"Couldn't Father Martin have come?" asked Liam.

"It's no' that lang until the new priest comes," Darach reassured them. "We'll be on our guard, and she'll be under our guard. Besides, in that time her people may come for her and we'll know if she's the Morestons' spy or no."

The men grumbled some under their breaths,

but no one contested Darach's decision out-right. Bruce posed the question that Darach least wanted to answer.

"What shall we do wi' her, then?"

"Leave her right where she is," Gordon re-torted. "Locked up, safe as houses. She's no' to be trusted out o' that cell."

Ross frowned. "That seems a bit cruel," he said slowly. "She's flesh and blood, same as we."

"But if she's let out, someone'll have to guard her every moment," Niall said. "That'll mean one less man, day and night."

"We could take her back to Craigen." Liam nodded around at them. "If we dunna want her and we canna watch over her, we should take her back where she came from."

"Deliver her straight back into his hands? So that she can work more mischief in freedom?" Tommy looked at Darach. "That doesna make sense to me."

"The lad's right," Darach said. "Even if she proves she's no' a witch, she might have learned more about us than we know. And Craigen would no' waste a moment takin' advantage."

"Chain her up!" Gordon insisted. "Give her enough to move about a bit but make sure she's secured. She's no' some princess to be expectin' courtesy from her enemies."

"Ah, hell," Alasdair said, spreading his hands. "Why not kill her now and be done wi' it? Save ourselves all that trouble."

The men gaped at him. "What the devil are ye on about?" Darach growled. His brother was not a cruel man by any reach of imagination, and he loved and was well loved by women. Why would he make such a gruesome proposal?

Alasdair shrugged. "If the wee little lass is too much trouble for all o' us, why not be rid o' her? Save us a length o' chain and some wasted man-power." He laid a slight emphasis on the word *man*. "Save us the food she'd require. Not to mention good ale."

"That's daft," Niall said, grudgingly.

"Is it?" Alasdair's eyes were wide with sur-prise.

Darach hid the grin that threatened to appear on his own face. His little brother was becom-ing quite a sage. Killing a helpless woman was beneath these men, and well he knew it.

"O' course it's daft," Gordon grumbled. "There's no call to execute the lass. She's no' committed a crime that we know of, for cer-tain."

"No?" Darach joined in the ploy.

"No," Ross said quickly. "She's done naught but trespass. She shouldna hang for that. She's no' an animal."

"But ye can chain her up?" Alasdair frowned. "Hmm. Darach, when was the last time ye chained up Big Dog?"

Darach shrugged. "I canna recall. Have I ever?"

"Verra well," Liam said, wagging his head. "We take your point. What would ye do wi' her, Alasdair?"

Alasdair turned to Darach. Darach's amusement drained away. Insolent pup, he thought. Always about mischief.

"If she's to be here for some while, it would be cruel to keep her confined to the cell," he said slowly. "She'll have a chamber, one with a sturdy lock from the outside. The east chamber has bars at the window; we'll put her there. And she may come down to meals wi' us. She may go out once a day, but only under guard, and only when we can spare a man."

The men thought this over and nodded their assent. Darach dispatched Ross to tell their prisoner the news, and sent the rest of the men off to their work. He turned to Alasdair when the two of them stood alone on the green.

"Ye take too much upon yourself, oganach," he said. "Your mischief is goin' to get ye into deep water some fine day."

Alasdair shrugged. "I only thought to save the lads from a foolish plan."

"And force my hand to a decision about Julia."

Alasdair quirked an eyebrow. "Julia, is it?"

Darach refused to rise to the bait. "Take a fresh mount and ride the north hills," he said. "Check for strays. And be on the watch for Craigen's ilk."

He turned and walked inside the house, where his inconvenient prisoner was soon to move about, free of restraint.

Julia heaved a huge sigh of relief when Ross told her of the recent changes in the clan's plans

78

for her. She wanted to hug the lanky Scotsman but restrained herself, knowing that this didn't mean she was in the clear, or that he wouldn't immediately hold up a cross and a rope of garlic to ward off her evil spirit. Nor did it mean, he made clear, that she was not going to be tested by the priest or subjected to other interrogations.

She sat down, instead of hugging him, and ate almost half a bowl of the watery, sour stew he'd brought her, feeling it was a reasonable price to pay for a chance at better conditions. This was progress, at least. Perhaps they were softening toward her, she thought. If she played her cards right, she might be permitted to leave, or get a message to Kinloch, anyway. Anything was possible.

When she emerged from below the stairs, going ahead of Ross, she breathed the smoky air as if it were fresh off the mountains. Freedom, however limited, proved sweeter than anything she could have imagined.

Darach appeared in the doorway to the great hall. She felt her joyful smile fading as she saw his glowering countenance. His suspicions showed plain in his eyes and she knew it was unlikely that he'd permit her to leave anytime soon. Still, she told herself, the orders to place her in better quarters had come from him. She owed him that much.

"I appreciate what you're doing," she said to him, gesturing up the stairs. "It's very kind, Mr. MacStruan."

He inclined his head briefly. "It's no more than a man should do," he said.

"How long will it be before your priest comes?" she asked, approaching him.

"I don't know. Days, maybe weeks. Are ye impatient to be tested?"

"No. Would you be?"

"It would depend on whether my conscience was clear or no'."

"Mine is clear. But that doesn't mean that any of you would believe me."

She looked up at him. From her height, she had to tilt her head back quite a ways to look him full in the face. She felt as if she were trying to get a glimpse of the top of a giant sequoia. He had a face as unreadable as a tree, too, she thought.

"May I have my things returned?" she asked. "I'd like to be able to brush my hair, at least."

"Ross, fetch her pouch. But leave her comfits and such. Bring only her hairbrush and mirror."

Julia opened her mouth to protest and then shut it quickly. Don't push it, Addison, she told herself. There'd be time enough to get some Tylenol or a breath mint later.

"Thank you," she said again.

He made no reply, only turned around and retreated into the hall. Ross touched her arm and she preceded him up the stairs to her new quarters.

She managed to steal a look around her as they ascended. There wasn't a great deal to see from her vantage point but what she saw interested her greatly. The view from outside, and the size of the great hall, had already told her that Darach's house, while not a mansion, was a substantial structure with two stories and a tall tower at one corner facing the hills to the west. The walls inside were of natural stone, painted white, the floors upstairs constructed of what looked like solid oak planking. Here and there a niche had been carved into the wall for a rushlight, and torches were anchored overhead, so that while there were few windows, the effect was not gloomy. A broad walkway or hallway ran from the top of the stairs across the width of the house, its sturdy stone railing overlooking the entry hall below. Several doors faced the walkway; Julia assumed they were bedrooms. Which door led to Darach's chamber? she wondered. Or did the great barbarian sleep outside in a thornbush?

"This will be your chamber," Ross said, drawing the latch of the first door at the top of the stairs.

Julia entered and stood for a moment, looking about. The room smelled musty and unused, as if it had been closed up for some time. Still, the walls were bright with whitewash, the fireplace swept clean, and the high oaken bed at the far end of the room neatly made with a fat pillow and heavy woolen blankets.

She smiled at Ross. "It's very nice. Thank you." She carried her small bundle of clothing over to the chest by the wall and laid it down before walking to the window on the opposite wall. Ross's footsteps followed close behind her own.

She stood before the modest window, its shutters open to let in the morning light. The glass was heavy, she saw, and somewhat watery in its appearance. It must be very old glass, she mused, to have settled so much. She reached out her hand to grasp one of the iron bars that covered the panes.

She turned to Ross. "Do you lock everyone into their rooms in this house?" she asked wryly.

"Truth to tell, lass, there's bars on most o' the windows in Darach's house. It's been our keep for generations. The bars keep enemies out as well as in."

"How old is this place?"

He scratched his head. "Let me think. The tower keep was first built back in the time o' the Auld Alliance, before Robert the Bruce was crowned."

Julia gaped. "That old?"

"Aye. The tower, anyways." He shot her a glance. "Castle Moreston goes back nigh that far, o' course."

"Does it?" She turned back to the window. "It's hard to believe you've kept this place up for so many centuries."

"This part o' the house is aye newer," he said. "No' more than fifty or sixty years."

"Well, it's still very nice," she said, turning to face the room again. "And all furnished with antiques, too." She ran her hand over the heavy bedpost. "Were these in Darach's family or did he buy them?"

Ross scowled. "That's a question for Darach, no' for me."

She shrugged. "It's no big deal. I was just thinking about my stepmother. She was a real antiques nut. If something wasn't at least a hundred years old with a price tag in the quadruple digits, she wouldn't allow it in the house." She gave a dry laugh. "Maybe that's why she never much wanted me around. I wasn't aged to perfection."

"Stepmother. Is that how ye came to be livin' wi' the Moreston?"

She put her hands on her hips. "The Morestons again! Did Darach put you up to this? Give you orders to grill me about my being either Broomhilda or Mata Hari for these Morestons you keep talking about?"

His shoulders slumped. "I was no' too crafty, was I?" He heaved a sigh. "Nay, Darach had no part in this. The others bade me learn all I could, lest we all come to harm at your . . . hands. . . ." His words trailed off.

She plopped down on the bed. "Look, I guess I can't blame you for trying. But if you want to know something, just ask me like a normal person. I don't have anything to hide." She felt her cheeks color as she heard these last words leave her lips. She did have something to hide—she was hiding herself. Wasn't that what had gotten her here in the first place?

Ross studied her for a moment and then crossed his arms, drawing himself to his full height. "All right. Tell me this, lass. Are ye a witch or no'?"

She faced him squarely. "I'm not a witch. It's like I told you the other day. I don't even believe in witches."

His mouth popped open. "Ye dunna believe?"

"No. Okay, I know there's the whole Wiccan thing and pagans and Druids and stuff these days, but I think it's all just a fad."

He seemed to be struggling with the notion of disbelief. She grinned. "I have to hand it to you. You guys are really great at this reenactment stuff. I have yet to see even one of you break character."

"Reenactment?"

"Yeah. You know, dressing up like that and talking about witches and living in these old houses. When does tourist season start?"

"Tourist?"

It was her turn to slump. "You guys don't give up, do you? William Wallace to the end, eh?"

He frowned. "Wallace is dead, lass."

She lifted her hands. "Yes, I know that. Okay. Let's just skip the mutual interrogations. Where's the bathroom?"

"God's truth," Ross said to the men that night before the fire at Bruce's. "She went that pale when I told her where it was."

The lairds shook their heads and pondered this new piece of evidence that the prisoner in

Darach's house was the oddest soul they'd ever come across. What would she do or say next? They eagerly anticipated the next evening, when, they were told, Julia Addison would join them for the evening meal.

The table was set for ten that evening. The lairds arrived earlier than usual, each of them glancing about the hall with an excitement that was mixed with anxiety. They drank their ale in quick sips, watching the doorway through which their "guest" would appear.

Julia donned one of the dresses she'd been given, hoping that wearing a costume might be seen as a gesture of respect for their life-style. She braided her hair down her back in a long plait and studied her reflection in the hand mirror that had been returned to her that day.

"So," she said to her image. "Here's another fine mess you've gotten us into, Addison."

She turned the mirror over and ran her fingertips over the silver tracing on its back. The initials *MJA* were etched into the center of the intricate design. Meredith Joan Addison, her mother. Julia had kept this mirror with her for years, through school and college and travels, all the places she'd been, through all the things she'd done. It was a small thing, not even very valuable in the monetary sense, but it was all Julia had left of her mother, save her memories.

She was glad Cammie, her stepmother, had never discovered it. Or if she had, she had deemed it not worthy of her attention, otherwise Julia would have been ordered to polish it weekly, and to keep it exactly in the center of the dreadful French Provincial vanity Cammie had picked out for her bedroom. According to Cammie, things of value were meant to be on display. If they weren't, how would anyone know that you were a person of worth?

Julia's sense of humor returned. She'd love to see Cammie in this place, squinting in the candlelight, trying to apply her Elizabeth Arden essentials in the reflection of an old silver mirror. If Darach and his lairds thought the items in her fanny-pack were strange, she could just imagine their reaction to Cammie's Dooney & Bourke duffel of a purse, loaded with everything from instant cooling gel to ward off the first hint of puffy eyes to her absolutely indispensable cellular phone. There'd be a mad dash for the garlic necklaces, Julia thought with a grin.

There was a knock at the door and the sound of a key in the lock. She set the mirror aside on the table and turned to see Darach's broad shoulders filling the doorway.

She caught her breath as she took in the change in him. Until tonight, she'd seen him only in his rough, work-worn plaid, his hair loose and tousled, stained boots on his feet. Tonight he wore his hair smoothed back into a leather-bound queue, a style that revealed more of his high forehead and placed greater emphasis on his remarkable eyes. His shirt was still rough-woven, but it was neat and clean and of a soft yellow that echoed a small yellow stripe in his fine green plaid. Black leggings and good black boots made his long, strong legs seem even longer and more powerful, adding the final dash to the image he presented of simple, utterly masculine grace.

Julia felt a sudden, tingling awareness throughout her own body. It was as if her very cells were responding to his presence, to his proximity. She suddenly found she couldn't speak. It wasn't as if she'd never seen a man before. Nor was it as if she hadn't known he was reasonably good-looking, in his Conan sort of way. But tonight, well, all she could think was that for a lunkhead with an attitude, he sure cleaned up awfully nice.

"It's time to sup," he said, motioning to the door.

"Oh." She started at the sound of his voice and realized she'd been rooted to one spot, gawking at him. Heat climbed into her cheeks and she moved toward the door. "Yes. Yes. Okay."

They descended the stairs in silence, Julia's senses still alive with the awareness of Darach MacStruan walking at her side. Another part of her mind wondered at her response, scolding her for her foolishness and reminding her that she needed to be looking for ways to make her escape.

They entered the great hall. Julia saw all the lairds gathered at the far end, cups in their hands. Their conversations came to a screeching halt at her arrival, she noted, and she had the ear-burning sense that they had been discussing her. She decided to seize the advantage and put them on the spot for a change.

"Good evening, gentlemen," she said, coming forward with her hand extended to Liam. "It's good to see you looking so well this evening."

Liam quickly wrapped both hands around his cup and gulped down about half its contents. She moved on to the next man.

"Good evening. It's Gordon, isn't it?"

She held out her hand. He looked at it as if it were a live squid. She turned to Niall. "Hello, Niall. It's good to see you again."

He raised his cup to her and gave a curt nod. She almost laughed aloud. These huge, hulking, sword-toting males were afraid of her! She, who stood five feet zip in her Nikes on a tall hair day, and who had heard every wisecrack about short people repeated since Aristotle, had these guys in terror for their lives. There had to be a way to use this to make them let her go.

The boy named Tommy gave her much the same reaction as the others, though his bright eyes showed as much curiosity as fear. Dugan gave her a nod and then crossed himself, as if for insurance purposes. Then she came to Alasdair.

"Good evening," she said, offering her hand.

He took it at once and pulled it through his arm, drawing her closer to him. "Good evenin'," he said, his smile growing slowly across his face. "And how is our ain wee witch-woman farin' this night? Cast any good spells lately?"

Chapter Six

Julia gasped right along with the rest of the clansmen. Then she saw the glint of mischief in Alasdair's eyes and she couldn't resist playing along.

"I'm well, sir," she said, walking with him toward the table. "But my black cat coughed up a hairball on my best broomstick this morning and it won't fly for beans."

"Terrible," he replied, his tone grave. "I'm afraid we're no' very accommodatin' to your ilk hereabouts."

"Tell me about it." She pursed her lips into a pout. "But it isn't just here. It's getting so a girl can't even sell a teensy little bottle of Love Potion Number Nine to a friend without some people trying to spoil all the fun."

"Tsk, tsk," Alasdair began.

Darach cut him off. "That'll do," he said, taking Julia's other arm. "Ye'll sit there," he said, pointing to a chair near the head of the table.

Alasdair gave her a wicked smile and sauntered off, stealing a cup of ale from Liam as he passed. She watched him go with a smile quirking her lips. Had she made a friend? Or did he just enjoy baiting his brother?

"Dugan, Gordon, ye may fetch in the pots," Darach said, taking his seat. He motioned for Julia to sit. She obeyed, her mind still sorting through the new information she'd just gleaned about Clan MacStruan.

Her heart—or rather, her stomach—sank as Dugan and Gordon came in bearing two large pots that gave out a suspiciously familiar aroma. It was more of the stewish mixture she'd eaten in her cell for the past two days. How did they all manage to look so hale and healthy on a steady diet of this stuff? she wondered.

Still, she wasn't about to offer offense by criticizing their cuisine. She watched the others digging in with gusto and joined in with a bite now and again. At least they had spoons, which looked to be handcrafted, and the wooden bowls and cups provided were beautifully carved.

"So, Julia Addison," Alasdair said from his seat across the table from her. "Where was it ye said ye were from?"

She swallowed carefully before she replied. "I'm from New York. Actually I grew up in Illinois but I moved to New York about a year ago."

"Where's Illa Noy?" Darach asked.

"The Midwest of the United States," she told him, surprised at his ignorance. "Chicago. Lake Erie. You know."

Darach shook his head. "Never heard of it."

She smiled and tried to make allowances for his provincial attitude. "It's not unusual. The U.S. is such a big place, most people think that between New York and Los Angeles all there is is cactus, sagebrush, and cowboys." She caught the men exchanging glances up and down the table. "It's a common misconception. Even some Americans think that's how the country's laid out."

"Sounds like an interestin' place," Alasdair said.

"Not as interesting as here," she said, hoping to draw them out. "I've never seen a place so well preserved or so true to the period. Ross told me that parts of this house date back centuries."

Ross sank lower in his seat as all eyes turned his way. He raised his shoulders apologetically.

"Aye," Darach said, his eyes pinning Julia where she sat. "It's a braw, sturdy house. It's survived many a siege. And no prisoner has escaped it yet."

She felt her cheeks grow hot. "You take a lot of prisoners, do you?" she retorted.

He shook his head. "Just those foolish enough to cross us."

"And if they don't escape, what happens to them?"

"It depends."

91

"That's not an answer."

"That's all ye need to know."

"I think I need to know a little bit more, see-ing as how I'm your current prisoner-in-residence."

"Ye'll have to wait upon the priest."

"Oh, come now," Alasdair put in. "This is no' a very amusin' conversation. Have ye been to Edinburgh, Julia Addison?"

She looked at him in confusion. For a mo-ment she had been utterly taken up in the exchange with Darach, so much so that she had almost forgotten they were not alone. She re-covered quickly.

"No, I haven't. I was in Inverness, just for a few hours; then I came here. But I've heard Ed-inburgh is beautiful, with the castle looking over the city and all."

"It is a fine place. Darach and I fostered there when we were younger. There's lots of amuse-ment to be found there, eh, Darach?" Alasdair's eyes sparkled.

"Aye, if a body wants amusin'."

"And you don't?" Julia asked.

"I've too much to do to go makin' merry at the slightest whim."

She rested her chin on her fist as she looked at him. "Hmm. You know what they say: all work and no play makes Jack a dull boy."

Darach merely stared at her, his eyes deep-ening in their intensity. "I'm no' a boy," he said slowly and evenly.

She felt an involuntary shiver course through

her. Once again she felt as if they had left the rest of the company behind and were conversing alone, in some intimate little place. She was such a pushover for that voice! And when he used those tones, she knew indeed that he was not a boy.

"Are all the lasses sae comely in your America?" Alasdair asked, his eyes dancing.

She gave him an embarrassed smile. "I wouldn't know," she said, flustered by his compliment.

"Ye said ye cooked," Bruce said now, leaning in from his place at the far end of the table. "Ye work at an inn, aye?"

"No. I work in a restaurant that my friend owns." Julia shifted in her seat. She wanted to get away from the topic of the restaurant. She could only deal with one mess at a time. "Do you like to cook?" she asked in return.

The older man snorted. "Nay, not I. A haunch and cup are all I require."

"Who made this?" she asked, glancing at the bowl before her.

"I did," Darach replied.

"You?" She couldn't keep the astonishment out of her voice.

"Aye. We all share duties here. Is there somethin' wrong wi' the stew?"

"No. No, not a thing." The thought crossed her mind that his plan was slowly to poison her, but she pushed the notion aside. Darach MacStruan wouldn't stoop to anything so underhanded, she sensed. If he wanted to kill someone, he'd be more likely just to snap them like a string bean.

"Good," Darach said. "I'm glad our fare is to your likin'." He pushed himself up from the table. "I've accounts to see to. Ye'll see the lass to her room, Bruce. Niall, ye're to take her out tomorrow, when ye can spare the time." He nodded curtly to Julia. "Good evenin'."

He strode from the hall, his broad back straight, his plaid swinging easily. Julia looked at the others. They quickly bent their heads, intent upon finishing their meals.

"I've an errand myself," Alasdair said apologetically. He rose and gave her a brief salute. "I hope to see ye on the morrow, Julia Addison."

"Thank you. Good night, Alasdair."

She watched him go and then turned her gaze to her own bowl. She closed her eyes and pushed it away. She couldn't look at it anymore.

They finished the meal in silence. Bruce escorted her to her room and locked her in. She sat on the bed for a while, wishing she had a book to read. A good murder story would suit her mood quite well.

She couldn't sit for long. She decided that if she was going to be confined, she'd have to work harder to stay healthy and fit. She stripped down to her undergown and did a long Yoga session, enjoying the slow stretches and deep breathing after all the tensions of the past days. She finished off and began to get ready for bed.

There was a basin of water on the table near the window, and a cloth for washing. As she bent to splash water on her face, she caught a glimpse of her hand mirror lying next to the basin. A strange, golden light emanated from its depths. She leaned over it, scowled at her reflection, then gasped as her own face vanished, only to be replaced with the face of a woman she'd never seen before.

"Who are you?" a sweet, liquid voice uttered from the depths of the glass.

Julia backed away from the table.

"Who are you?" The voice still rose from the mirror.

She took a wild look around the room, looking for signs of hidden camera, hidden video or sound equipment. Was this another test? She saw nothing but the heavy-beamed ceiling, the whitewashed stone walls.

"Oh, boy." She'd finally slipped her cable. They'd find her in the morning, huddled in a corner, playing with her toes.

Still, her curiosity was aroused. She crept toward the table again. The pale glow still gilded the tabletop.

"There you are," the voice said. "Who might you be?"

"You first." Oh, good, Addison, she told herself. That's the ticket, talk back to your hallucinations. Keep it up and you'll be at the bottom of that old wee loch before you can say "Margaret Hamilton."

Julia examined the face. Whoever the woman was, she was gorgeous, with exotic, delicate features framed by a cloud of red-gold hair. As hallucinations went, this was a doozy.

"I think not." The golden glow in the mirror seemed to shiver and the image began to break up. "How did you come there?"

"I don't know. How are you doing this?"

". . . I'll see . . . go back to where . . . find you . . ." The voice was fading, crackling like static on an old radio.

"What?" Julia leaned forward. "Where are you?"

The mirror fell silent. The glass went cloudy for a moment, then just as suddenly cleared and showed Julia the image of her own face.

Julia backed away and sat down on the bed. "Oh, boy," she said again. What the heck was happening to her? After all the talk this morning about witchcraft, had she finally succumbed to the power of suggestion and conjured up some fantasy of talking hand mirrors?

She shivered. The voice had seemed so real! And the woman had looked so completely there—not like some electronic image or projection.

Besides, she told herself, when it came to conjuring up fantasies, her natural inclination would have been to dream up the image of Ralph Fiennes or Cary Grant. Not a woman ten times more beautiful than she. And Ralph and Cary would not be demanding to know who she was and how she got there.

So what had happened?

She slipped off the bed and approached the table again. Peeking over, she saw only her plain old hand mirror sitting there, its heavy silver back the only thing that bore even a faint glow. In the glass she saw the image of her own face, looking like a deer caught in the headlights. She moved back with a shaky sigh of relief.

She really had to get away from this place.

At midday of the following day Niall came to Julia's room and escorted her out, his big hand at her elbow, his sword and knife ominously present. Julia wasn't thrilled with the circumstances, but she was again relieved to be out-of-doors and glad to be doing something other than sitting in her room, avoiding her hand mirror.

They strolled on the green in a delicate mist. The scents that floated to Julia's nostrils seemed especially clear.

"Nice day," she commented, at a loss as to how to address her guardian.

"Aye."

"Does it rain as much as they say it does here?" She was talking about the weather. Her brain truly was turning to mush.

He shrugged.

She was getting annoyed now, with herself and with these men. She decided she'd draw them out, and damn the consequences. She'd go bats if she didn't have a conversation of some sort soon.

"I always think of *Chariots of Fire* when I

think of Scotland," she said. "Have you ever seen it?"

He gave her a quizzical look, then shook his head.

"Oh, it's a great film. It won the Academy Award for Best Picture, you know."

"Best Picture?"

"Yes. It was the story of two runners who were competing in the Olympics. One of them was from Scotland—Eric Liddle? I thought he was famous."

"Never heard o' the fella."

"Well, he was from up here, I guess. And he was this terrific soccer player who could run like the wind. Only when it came time for him to run in the Olympic Games, he found out his race was on a Sunday and he wouldn't compete for a prize on the Sabbath."

He seemed to think this over. "Runnin' races is good. He's a Scot, ye say?"

"He was. He's dead now."

"Hmm. Sad, that. A good runner is a valuable man."

"Do you run?"

"Aye." His chest expanded slightly with pride. "I can still keep apace wi' our Tommy."

They walked around and around the green, talking. Niall described the various races and games the men enjoyed and pointed out hills where they'd competed in the rare air of the Highlands. Julia was fascinated. He had seemed such a stiff, solemn person, but when he talked his face came alight and he strode about with ease and even made a joke or two.

She was making progress.

Over the course of the next two weeks, she got to know each of the men by turns. At first they were all standoffish and fearful. But she kept asking them questions and commenting on their way of life, and slowly, slowly, they came around to being civil, in some cases, and downright cordial in others.

There was Niall, ever the soldier, who lived for a challenge. Tommy was a typical teenager, never totally sure of himself, but interested in everything all at once, believing he was going to live forever and taste it all. Ross was a quiet one, but Julia drew again on her love of movies and her love of food to engage him.

"And so this Babette, who cooked the fine feast, was really the finest cook in all o' Paris?" he asked, enthralled.

"Yes. And she had given all those people who had cared for her the best night of their lives."

"A fine thing," he murmured. "Fine."

Gordon was as stoic as Niall and Julia had the most difficult time drawing him out. The best she could do was chitchat. He seemed to be the one most suspicious of her. That walk was her most difficult.

Liam supplied his own conversation. In his case, she did the listening while he chatted on and on about geography, religion, law, philosophy, and anything else that he'd read about. She was astonished at the mass of medieval lore he'd accumulated.

Dugan was not into conversation at all, she decided. But he was an excellent listener. And to her delight he took her around the village, introducing her to all the animals they kept. She got to meet the cow that lived in his house, although, she soon learned, the animal actually lived in a stable built as an addition to his house, not exactly inside it. But she had her own window, so she could see out, he'd pointed out proudly.

The Bruce was perhaps the most pleasant companion of all. He took her arm with sweeping gestures and conducted her about as if they strolled in a royal procession, rather than a large patch of grass variously inhabited by sheep, fowl, and gamboling hounds. He spoke freely of the clan and the days when he was young in these hills.

"I never walked but I could run," he told her. "And the world was mine to command. Still is, o' course."

"Did you know Darach's parents?" Julia asked.

"Oh, aye. Alec MacStruan, there was a man. He could fight all day and dance all night, in his prime. All who knew him knew he was fair and firm wi' every man. And he did well by his sons. Darach was at his side for aye his whole youth, right up until he was fostered to the earl's house in Edinburgh. He might no' have shown it well or often, but he was that fond o' the lad." He chuckled. "Alec feared the boy'd come home in shame, he was sae full of the devil. But our Darach's made his da proud, God rest the man."

"And Alasdair?"

"Oh, there's a one. Wild as his brothair, and just as well loved. But more the one for pranks and jokes, is our Alasdair. And he's no' sae firm on his feet as Darach."

"What does that mean?"

The lordly old man thought for a moment. "He's aye restless, that one. He's here one moment and gone the next, like a bird that's seekin' his ain nest in the hills. Wanderin' one, I call him. And I pray it doesna lead to trouble." He gave her a shrewd look. "He's a one wi' the lassies, too, if ye hadn't noticed."

She grinned. "I have."

He patted her hand where it lay on his arm. "Guard yer heart, then, lass. He's a good man but he's still seekin' his ain way."

"I'll keep that in mind." She paused. "And what about Darach?"

"Darach? Now there's a complication, to be sure. He's the chief, lass, and his affairs are all bound up in clan. His feet are well rooted in MacStruan land. But . . ."

"But what?"

He frowned. "I'm no' sure the lad has the heart to spare."

She had wanted to ask him more but Liam interrupted them and their time was at an end. Still, she had much to ponder in her room each afternoon, after her walks with the seven lairds.

"But how can I possibly use all this to get out of here?" she asked the walls softly.

* * *

Edana paced about her chamber. The vision she'd seen in the mirror-basin the other evening had been so disturbing that she'd come close to throwing the bowl at the wall.

Who was that woman? And why, when she had cast her vision toward Darach MacStruan, had the woman's face appeared instead? Only another mirror-basin, or some very powerful magic, could intervene against her own spell and throw off her vision. There was some mischief at work. But who would dare to interfere with her magic? Who would possess such power? Moreover, there were no women in Darach's house, or even his village. Not of late, anyway. No one knew where the MacStruan women had gone, but Edana couldn't have cared less about them. She didn't want any women around her Darach. Around her love.

She pondered her options. She could steal to the MacStruan village somehow and see for herself. She could send one of Craigen's men. One or two of them could be trusted with her secrets. Or perhaps she could send the girl?

She shook her head. No, the girl was for Craigen. And she was to be Edana's masterstroke in her plan to acquire Darach, the MacStruans, and the Moreston wealth. If anything were to happen to the little chit, Craigen might refuse to marry her, in which case she would be forced to look for another girl that not only suited his fancy but who could be bent to Edana's will.

No, it was best that she work her wiles from

here, to learn more about this woman who had so intruded upon her own territory. Secrecy and solitude were always best for these matters.

Maybe the image had been a mere accident, she thought, a trick of the wind as she'd cast her spell into the mirror-basin. Perhaps the woman wasn't in Darach's house at all. A thought stopped her cold in her pacing. Could this other woman be a witch as well? Was that how she had been able to see her in the basin?

She'd have to find out. She cursed the provisional magic that only allowed her to use the mirror-basin once between sunrise and sunrise. She'd already used it once today and all she'd seen was the image of the Servant, reassuring her of her power and charm. She'd try again as soon as evening fell on the morrow.

She'd never permit anyone to steal her Darach. She'd been waiting too patiently. She'd been working too hard. She'd laid the ground for his weakening. Before long he'd be ripe for conquest. Ready for her embrace.

And anyone who got in her way would rue the day her mother first conceived her.

Humming and smiling, she sat down at her dressing table and began to brush her luxuriant, coiling hair.

Chapter Seven

After her outing with the amiable Bruce, having Darach as her escort was a major change for Julia. He arrived at her door at the appointed time, ready to lead her outside, but the set of his jaw and the darkness of his eyes told her he didn't relish this obligation.

She went with him quietly. The wind was up outdoors and she was glad of the tartan shawl and scratchy but oh, so warm leggings she'd found in the clothing chest. The clouds lowering overhead looked as sullen as Darach's countenance.

She was tempted to say it was all right and that he could take her back to her room. But something in her rebelled. She wasn't going to let him intimidate her. She needed to be outside and to experience some small measure of freedom and fresh air. The other lairds had all taken their turn and they'd survived. He could, too.

They strolled about the green in silence, the wind whipping at their clothes and tossing their hair. Julia was feeling too stubborn to try to engage him in conversation, as she had the others. Let him start it if he wanted to talk, she thought, tugging at her shawl.

"Are ye cauld? Would ye prefer to be indoors?"

She looked up at him and saw the hopeful thought in his eyes. He wanted to get rid of her, fast. Well, she wasn't having any of it.

"No," she said brightly. "It's lovely and brisk out here. I like it."

"Ah. Good."

They resumed their trek around the village. Julia felt the tension in him growing and saw his shoulders becoming more and more stiff as they went. She let him stew for a while and then stopped, her hand on his arm.

"Look," she snapped. "I know you don't want to be here with me, walking around and around. Why don't you go and do whatever you'd do normally? I'll tag along."

He scowled. "Ye'd be put out."

"How do you know?"

"Because I have to gang up the hills to see to some o' the cattle. Ye wouldna care for it and ye'd only be in my way."

That did it. "In your way?" she demanded. "In your way? Well, who put me in your way? If I'm such an inconvenience, why don't you just let me go? I'll get out of your way in a big hurry then, believe me."

"Ye know I willna let ye go."

"Then put up or shut up, MacStruan! If I can't leave and you can't stand to go for a walk with me for the short time I get to get out each day, then either take me with you or hand me over to one of the others."

"There's no one to hand ye to. They've all work o' their own to see to."

"Then take me with you."

"I could put ye back in your room!"

"Yeah, and you could put me back in your little minidungeon, too! Why don't you?"

"I'm tryin' to make this easier for ye, ye ungrateful woman!"

"Oh, pardon me. I forgot how gallant it is to push people around and lock them up and refuse to even listen to them!"

He looked angry enough to chew rivets. She wondered if she'd gone too far, but she wasn't going to back off now. She stood up to him as best she could, given the difference in their height. "If you expect gratitude from a prisoner, you're going to be sorely disappointed," she said.

"If ye expect courtesy in return for trespassin' and spyin', ye're more addled than I thought!" he shot back.

"This isn't about trespassing," she said evenly. "This is about you wanting everything your way and everyone under your thumb!"

He stepped back suddenly, his jaw working,

his posture even stiffer than before. "That's right. I'll have things my ain way. Ye want to go wi' me?" he said, his voice low and menacing. "Verra well. Let's be off."

He took her arm and propelled her toward the stables. The depth of his rage shocked her, and she didn't try to fight him as he guided her, neither violently nor gently, into the stables and sat her down on a barrelhead. She didn't move. He flung a bridle over the head of a large gray and led the horse out of the stall, pulling Julia along with him.

"Aren't you going to put a saddle on it?" she asked. His black glance checked any more words from her.

He stepped up and vaulted himself onto the horse's back. When he was astride, he reached his hand down to her. "Come then. Ye've asked to go."

Reluctantly she put her hand in his, and in an instant he had hoisted her off the ground. She had no choice but to straddle the horse behind him and hang on to his plaid with both hands.

He set off out of the village at a fast trot. Julia clamped her mouth shut, fearful that all her teeth were going to be shaken loose. Once beyond the few trees that edged the northern perimeter of the village, Darach set his heels into the horse's sides and the animal jolted ahead, streaking up the low hill before them.

Running or galloping or whatever it was the horse was doing, was a bit better than trotting, Julia thought. As they topped the rise and started down, she ventured a peek from behind Darach's broad back. She gave a soft shriek. They were headed straight into a lake! Good God, did he intend to drown her? Or was he just going to order her to jump in?

She hid her face in his plaid. At what she guessed was the last possible moment, she felt the horse swerve and shift, heading off in a different direction. She breathed a sigh of relief as she realized icy water was not about to close around her, but she kept her head down, not wishing to see any more such close calls.

Way to go, Addison. She had just had to stand up to him, hadn't she? And look where it had gotten her. On the back of a running horse, clinging for dear life to a man who was so angry with her and so strong he could probably shot-put her into the next county.

Beneath her hands she felt Darach's muscles, rock-solid and still tense with anger. Was he angry enough to harm her? Or just angry enough to take her out into the wilderness of these hills and leave her?

The wind was rising, cutting around Darach to snatch at her hair and sting her cheeks. She took a glance at the sky and saw cloud bellies dark as granite. She didn't like their look. They reminded her of Darach's face when he'd hauled her into the stables and up onto this thundering beast.

She heard Darach call out to the big animal and felt him shift in front of her as he drew in the reins. The horse slowed to a bone-jamming trot, a walk, and then quickly came to a halt.

Darach looked at her over his shoulder. "Get down," he said.

"But I—" She broke off at the flash of his eyes. She gathered herself up and slid gracelessly to the ground.

He swung off and held out his hand. "Give me the shawl."

She gave it to him, shivering less from the chill of the wind than from the ice of his gaze. He'd gone cold and quiet and she wished he'd go back to yelling at her. Yelling she knew how to deal with. Ice and snow she didn't.

He took her shawl and began to walk away, leaving both her and the horse. Her curiosity piqued, she began to follow him, keeping a safe distance.

He stopped abruptly and sank to his knees. He was examining something in the tall grass. Julia crept closer, craning her head to see. A tiny cloud of steam rose up from around his hands.

"The mother's over there," Darach said to her, not even bothering to turn around. "Gang ye and see how she is." He nodded down the slope before him.

Julia saw what was in the grass beneath his hands. It was a calf, gangly, slick, and panting for breath. She looked down the slope and saw another form among the grasses. She went ahead as he'd told her and saw the heifer, still and silent in the whistling wind.

Julia edged her way around the cow, not sure

if the animal would suddenly wake and charge her. She was a city girl, born and bred. Still, she sensed that something was deeply wrong here and she needed to help.

The cow's eyes were wide and staring. A fly lit on one glassy iris. There was no answering flinch or flick of an eyelash. Julia crouched down and laid her hand on the animal's side. It was still warm, but completely still. She'd died giving birth to the calf, Julia thought.

She stroked the brown, woolly flank, feeling sadness well up and take the place of the anger and fear she'd been carrying. "Poor lass," she crooned. "Poor little cow."

She heard steps and looked up to see Darach coming toward her, the calf wrapped in her shawl. She stood. "Is the calf all right?" she asked.

He frowned. "It's alive. But without its mam, it'll die anyway."

"But isn't there anything you can do?" She went to look at the weak little animal in his arms. "Couldn't it nurse with one of the other cows?"

He shook his head. "I dunna know. This heifer calved early. And aye alone. I canna be sure we can get this one to another cow in time."

"Well, we'll have to try!" Julia tugged at his sleeve. "How far do you think we'll have to go?"

He held back. "Julia, this wee fella's weak already. He may be sick. His mother could have been sick wi' something. It might be best to

110

leave him here. It'd be kinder."

She bit her lip. "But you don't know for sure that he's going to die. You could be wrong."

He looked down at the animal again. Anger crept into his eyes once more. He looked up and gave her a tight nod. "It'll be a tight fit. Can ye ride while holdin' fast to him?"

"I'll hang on to him, even if I have to tie him to my back."

It turned out that her suggestion was a sound one. Darach helped her fashion a sling out of the wide shawl, and then slid the shivering calf inside. He mounted up and leaned far down to help Julia up with her burden. This time he pulled her up in front of him, so that she was sitting sideways with the calf settled on her lap.

Julia watched as he took one corner of the shawl, tucked it up and around his belt, and tied it in a knot. He gave her a grim smile. "If one goes, all go."

It seemed to Julia that they rode for hours. In the graying of the afternoon light, she had lost all sense of direction. She rubbed the little calf as best she could, stroking it and talking to it encouragingly, while still maintaining a fierce grip on the horse's mane for balance. Darach's arms reached around her to hold the reins and she braced her shoulder against his chest, enjoying both the shelter from the chill of the rising wind cutting through her dress and the solid, unshakable feel of his body holding hers and the calf's in place.

But the calf was moving less and less, while

its bony little rib cage labored for breath. She bent and spoke in its ear, crooning to it. She even gave a low, experimental moo, hoping it might rally at the sound of its own kind.

"There."

Julia looked where Darach pointed. She let out a whoop of joy at the woolly brown figures huddling in the lee of a large rock, taking refuge from the wind.

She almost couldn't wait for the horse to come to a halt before she slid off. But she remembered in time that the three of them were joined and she sat as patiently as she could while Darach unfastened the knot from his belt and slid down to help her with the heavy bundle in her lap.

Her legs almost buckled under her when she reached the ground. Darach caught her arms and steadied her. "Are ye all right?"

"I'm fine. My legs went to sleep."

She looked down at the animal that hung from her shoulders. "Buy you a drink, sailor?" A faint bleat was all he could muster, but she took it as a good sign.

Darach led the way. Julia kept her arms wrapped tightly around the shawl, warding off the cold from her charge.

They came within a few feet of the small herd and Darach stopped. He carefully untied the shawl from around Julia's body and lowered the calf to the ground.

"Pull up some grass," he said to Julia as he set to work untangling the calf from the shawl.

112

She pulled up several handfuls and gave them to him. He divided them in half and handed one bundle back to her. "Rub him down wi' those."

She did as he told her, scrubbing the brown hide as he was doing. "Is this to get our scent off of him?" she asked.

"Aye. I dunna know if it matters but it couldna hurt."

When they had covered every inch of the shivering little body, Darach motioned to Julia to pick up her shawl. She clutched it to her as he walked over to the herd by the outcropping. He walked around until he found the cow he wanted, she guessed, and then began herding her over toward the calf.

Julia backed away. "Go for it, little guy," she said softly. "And don't be telling me you're lactose intolerant. That won't cut it."

The shaggy heifer plodded ahead of Darach, her head bent against the wind. She placed her nose right in range of the calf. The newborn gave another mewling bleat when it caught her scent. She answered with a questioning huff.

Julia watched, her heart thumping. "Come on, buddy, come on," she whispered.

She looked over to where Darach stood. He seemed rooted to the spot, watching the two animals discover one another. She felt a quick rush of warmth toward him. His face mirrored what she was feeling inside: fear, hope, excitement.

The heifer lowed. Julia looked back in time to see the calf struggling to its feet. On gangly

113

stilts, it made the journey to the heifer's side, and with a feeble but effective butt of its head, connected up to the first available teat. The heifer mooed again and then lowered her head to crop some grass while the newcomer drank his fill.

"We did it!" Julia exclaimed softly as Darach came around to her side.

"Aye." He put his hands on his hips. "It's no' for certain he'll make it, but at least his instincts are sound."

"At least he has a chance now." She reached out and put a hand on his arm. "Thank you for trying."

Thunder cut in before he could reply. Julia winced involuntarily and glanced up at the sky. A fork of lightning made a stab at the hills beyond.

"We'd best be gettin' back," Darach said.

They hurried to the horse, who was beginning to prance uneasily on the windy rise. Darach lifted her up before him again and she settled in just as the first drops of rain began to fall.

The drops soon became a torrent. Julia tried to get the shawl up and over her head but it was no use; the wind snatched at it and tangled it around them both as they rode. She was drenched in a matter of minutes. More thunder ripped through the air and rolled back off the hills, echoing all about them. She huddled down and tried not to think about the fact that they were riding over an open plain, with no one and nothing taller than they for miles.

"Ouch!" she cried suddenly. Hailstones began to batter them. The horse whinnied in protest as the frozen bits pelted its hide. Julia felt Darach grip the reins more tightly and urge the horse ahead.

They entered a narrow glen, then turned sharply and began to climb. The going became more rocky and treacherous, the ground slippery under the horse's hooves. What on earth was Darach thinking? Julia wondered. This was no time to climb a mountain and take in the view.

She was about to say as much when he reined in the horse. He slid off quickly and held up his arms for Julia. He helped her down and pointed into the shadows. "Go ahead!" he called over the noise of the storm.

"Where?"

A flash of lightning answered her question. There was a tiny stone hut tucked into a niche in the hillside. She ran for it while Darach found shelter for the horse.

The door to the hut was unlocked. Julia pushed it open and waited for another flash of lightning to illuminate the threshold.

Nature obliged and she stepped inside. She could smell smoke, so she knew there must be a fireplace of some sort. The other scents were dust and decay, but she didn't care. Dust was okay, for it meant that the roof over her head was a sound one, and that was all she cared about just now.

Lightning flashed again and she saw the fireplace and a narrow slit of a window on the wall to her right. She moved toward it, putting out her hands to feel her way along. She found the wall, smelled ashes, and stood, waiting, not knowing what to do next.

"Welcome to Castle MacStruan," a voice said next to her ear.

Julia levitated. "God, Darach!" she cried. "Don't sneak up on me like that. I nearly went into cardiac arrest."

"Where's that?"

"Where's what?"

"Never mind. Keep your secrets. I'm goin' to make myself comfortable."

She heard him scuffling around in the room, then caught a glimpse of him returning to the fireplace with a covered clay pot in his hands. The room went dark once more but she could hear that he was closer now.

"Have a seat, Julia Addison," he said, his voice coming from the floor. "I fear we've no chairs a'tall, but the floor's no' too hard."

Keeping one hand on the wall, she sank down to the floor. The direction of his voice indicated that they were sitting face-to-face before the hearth.

"Couldn't we start a fire?" she asked, wringing out the hem of her dress.

"We could. If we had flint and tinder."

"What about matches?"

"There's none o' those here, that I know about. I could try usin' my knife to strike a spark, but I doubt there's anything here to take the flame. Moreover, it could take me half the night to get somethin' goin' that way." He shifted and she heard the scrape of the clay pot's lid. "There's food, though."

"Food?"

"Aye. Just cakes and a bit o' hard cheese but it'll stave off the cold and all, I'd wager." She felt his hand touch the edge of her sleeve. "Here, take this," he told her.

She reached out and received a hard biscuit and a piece of dry, strong cheese. She hadn't realized she was hungry until the first bite entered her mouth. "Mmm," she sighed, chewing.

He chuckled. "It's no' sae fancy as what ye're used to, I imagine, but it's here."

"I can't imagine anything better." She wiped at the crumbs around her mouth. "Why do you say fancy?" She wished she could see. Between flashes of lightning, the place was as dark as a drainpipe. Was he making fun of her?

"Ye have a fancy way about ye. The way ye handle a spoon. How ye always look for a clean spot to sit down or touch. That silver mirror ye carry is a lady's trinket and no' a cheap one, at that."

"And that makes me fancy?"

"Aye. Or it might just be that ye put on airs."

She bristled. "What you see is what you get."

He laughed, the sound a small bit of pleasant thunder rolling through the darkened room. "As it is, I canna see much."

She softened. "That's true. I don't suppose there's any electricity in here?"

117

There was a pause. "Where would it be?"

"Are you pulling my leg?"

Another pause. "Would ye like me to?"

"No!" Heat blossomed in her cheeks. "I just want to see, is all."

"Sorry, lass. No lamps in this place either."

"You've been here before, I take it?"

"I told ye, this is Castle MacStruan."

"Yeah, right. What is it really?"

"It's a hunter's lodge, o' sorts. A traveler's rest. It belonged to a clansman years and years ago. We keep the roof in repair and a bit o' food in case the man on the hill comes by."

"The man on the hill?"

"A passerby. A wanderer or a stranger who's lost. It's the custom hereabouts." She felt a tap on her shoulder. "More?"

She took the food he offered. "Thank you. Would I qualify as a man or woman on the hill?" she asked as casually as she could.

"Of sorts, I suppose."

"But not really."

"Ye're no' a mere passerby."

"But I am a stranger."

"Ye are. But no' the sort that happens by any other day. Ye're too strange a stranger."

She sighed. "It's something about me, isn't it?" she murmured, half to herself. "I'm the exception to the rule."

"Ye're exceptional. And we dunna know if ye're dangerous."

"You can't still be hanging on to that witchcraft nonsense!" she exclaimed. "You don't really believe I'm a witch."

"I don't?"

"No, I don't think you do. For one thing, you didn't ask me to use my witchcraft on that calf today. If I'm so powerful, couldn't I have healed him or made his mother well again? Or produced a bottle of milk out of a hat?"

"Perhaps I believe that your powers are all for evil and no' for good."

"I still don't believe it. You're too sensible and straight to believe in that stuff. You may believe I'm a spy but I don't for a minute think you believe I'm a witch."

"Ah, so ye know me well?"

"I know your type."

"I see."

A flash of light showed her his face. He was leaning close to her and she caught the glint in his eyes.

She swallowed. He was too close. And when she looked into those eyes, even for that brief second, she felt that he saw into her as no one else ever had. She shifted and brushed at her wet clothes.

"How long do you think the storm will last?" she asked, at a loss to say anything else.

"It may let up soon. It may go on all night. Either way, night's fallen and we canna start for home till mornin'."

"So I guess we'd better just get some sleep." She squinted into the darkness, hoping to spy some sort of a cot or a blanket.

"Right."

She heard movement beside her and suddenly a damp strip of leather was being wrapped about her wrist. "What are you doing?" she cried, indignant.

"Makin' sure I get a good night's sleep."

Chapter Eight

She felt his big hand near hers and knew he had lashed the other end of the strap to his own wrist. He'd bound her to him.

"You can't do this!"

"I just have."

"Untie me right now or I'll scream the roof down!"

"As ye wish. No one can hear ye way out here."

"This is outrageous!"

"I can live wi' that."

"Why, you smug, sneering—"

"Ye might as well save your breath, lass. I've heard them all."

She felt a tug on her wrist as he lay down. She refused to be pulled down with him. His hand lay on her thigh, heavy and warm.

"Good night, Julia Addison," he said, yawning. "Ye may sleep sittin' up if ye prefer, but I'd no' recommend it."

"I'm fine where I am."

"Suit yerself."

She blinked into the darkness. The lightning and thunder were passing but the rain beat just as heavily on the roof overhead. It was going to be a long night.

She managed to get the shawl wrapped around her, but not without dragging Darach's hand wherever hers went. He was very obliging and didn't resist. She felt hot with anger and embarrassment as his knuckles brushed first her cheek, then her breast as she struggled with the damp wool. At last she had it wrapped around her shoulders, where it settled in soggy folds. She pushed his hand off her thigh so that both their hands rested at her side.

She sat, chilly and cross, listening to Darach's breathing in the ink-black space beside her. He was absolutely the most impossible man she'd ever met, she fumed. Suspicious. Stubborn. Arrogant. High-handed. It would serve him right if she did escape tonight. If she was fancy, if she was a witch, and a spy, then she'd show him just how tricky she could be.

She waited more than an hour, she guessed, for his breathing to quiet and slow into the rhythms of sleep. When she was sure he was well and truly out, she leaned forward an inch at a time, her own breath held. She slid her free hand down her bound arm until her fingers touched the strap. She waited to see if Darach would wake, but he made no sound or movement.

She wriggled one finger under the strap. It might be loose enough to pull her hand free, if she could contract her hand in tightly. She leaned sideways to get a better angle on the task.

All at once she was jerked over. She came down with a thump on Darach's broad chest, one of his long arms and one strong leg wrapped about her, pinning her to him.

His voice murmured against her ear. "Were ye thinkin' to answer the call o' nature, lass? If that, would ye look in on the horse before ye come back?" His arm tightened but his voice kept that same husky drawl. "Or were ye thinkin' o' makin' yer escape while I was off my guard?"

"You're never off your guard," she snarled. She pushed against him, trying to raise herself up. "Let go of me, you big troll!"

"I dunna think I will."

She stopped struggling, suddenly aware of the grip of his arm and the strength of his thigh pressed over hers. She caught her breath, taking in with it the spicy scent of him. He felt as solid as the floor beneath her but oh, so much warmer and more comfortable. Even with their damp clothes between them, she knew that his skin would be as pleasing as a fire in winter.

An odd, liquid feeling came over her as his warmth began to seep into her breasts and hips where they lay in such intimate contact with his body. She felt herself relaxing within his hold, her tensions of the long, stressful day flowing from her. She moved slightly against him, settling.

She felt his fingers toying with her hair. Good God, she thought with a jolt. What on earth was she doing? She was practically asleep on top of him. She thrashed out and broke free of his hold, rolling to the cold floor with a thump.

He tugged on the bond. "Ye have the right of it, Julia Addison; I'm always on my guard."

She opened her mouth, then snapped it shut. The man was insufferable.

She rolled up into her shawl and her gown as best she could with one hand hampered, and closed her eyes. She willed herself to concentrate on the sounds of the rain overhead. She counted the steady dripping off the eave just outside the window. At long last her body settled down, and her temper smoothed out. She drifted off, with a smile for the little calf and its new foster mother.

So he was only a semilunkhead.

He must be as mad as a March hare, Darach thought to himself. Lashing himself to her. He could just as easily have tied her to something else in the place. He could have slept outside with his horse. He could have done anything else but go out alone with Julia Addison. He'd let her goad him into taking her out here. He'd thought the venture would bore her and that she'd shrink from the very idea of getting near a cow. But they'd come upon the calf and its dead mother, and she'd goaded him again to jump in with her and take the calf to another heifer. And she'd acted not the least bit squeamish but rather seemed to have the time of her life.

The calf had done him in. Julia may not have known it, but her pleas to save it had touched off emotions he hadn't realized he possessed. Most of all, the sight of the little body in his arms, shivering and close to death, and Julia's pleading eyes, had roused him to such anger that he had had no choice but to accede to her wishes.

He'd seen too much death, lying in his arms just as the calf had lain. Those other times there could be no second chance, and as he recalled them, the anger and pain had bubbled up like a hot spring inside him, prodding him to listen to the woman before him and take the calf away.

Julia Addison had gone with him every step of the way. She'd even mooed at the creature, unafraid to make a fool of herself if it meant saving the animal's life. She'd cheered their victory and given him such a joyous smile when the calf began to nurse that his head had spun.

He shifted where he lay and felt the lash that connected the two of them. What was it about this one wee lass that so unnerved him? She was as confusing as strong spirits to his mind and body. One minute she was the sweetest maid, all dainty and fine. The next minute she was a hoyden, tramping about in those trews of hers, mixing in with his men. Then she was as tenderhearted as a dove, cooing to a sickling calf. But before he could grow accustomed to that side of her, she was off again, contrary and contentious, fighting him at every turn.

And worst of all, her slim little body, with her black waves of hair tumbling from her braid, and her glimmering pale complexion—all of her, in short—bid fair to destroy him with desire. When he had held her tonight, he had felt her soften, for a brief moment. And in that moment he had glimpsed paradise.

Och, ye sound like a lovesick pup. The woman was dangerous. And she made it clear that she wanted nothing to do with him. A troll, she'd called him.

"Bah," he whispered. So he'd made a mistake in riding out with her. So he'd made a mistake in tying her to him. No harm had been done. He would be more cautious in the future. He'd keep his peace of mind by leaving Julia Addison strictly alone.

He could do that. He could.

And for his next feat, he'd sprout wings and fly.

They rose early the next morning. Neither of them spoke much and Julia had only glared at him when he untied the strap that had held her by his side all night.

They rode home in the mists and damp of the

morning, Julia riding behind once more. Darach had handed her over to Ross, who was trying hard to look disinterested at their long absence together, but who failed miserably. Julia ignored him and went straight to her room to wash and change and dry off.

Dinner that night was Glue Stew, as Julia had begun to call the omnipresent entree. Breakfast the following morning brought a new dish, some dreadful concoction of oats and eggs. For the midday meal: more stew. She couldn't face another bite of the repellent *specialite de la maison*, and at dinner made do with the bread and ale provided. The men around her ate hungrily. She knew that they'd all been up since sunrise, working in the rare air of the Highlands, but really, she thought, their tastebuds must be dead to the world.

That evening she turned to Darach, who seemed preoccupied and hadn't touched much of his meal, either. She wondered if this would be a good time to broach the subject of her release, with the men all sitting about, listening in.

She'd thought of nothing else since their return from the hills. And while part of her was still intrigued by the images and sensations of that night in the hut, she felt more strongly than ever that she needed to get away, back to her own life.

"Darach," she began. The sound of a chair scraping back cut her off.

Gordon staggered out of his chair, his face a

bleached white, the area around his mouth a pale green. He clutched his stomach with one arm as sweat broke out on his forehead.

"I'm—" he gasped. His body twitched and he made a retching sound, but nothing came out. His eyes went wide with terror.

Julia was on her feet in an instant. She ran around the table and grabbed Gordon about the waist. With a quick motion, she applied the Heimlich maneuver to the choking man. A bit of the meat from the stew flew out of his mouth and he sucked in air like a giant vacuum. Then he leaned over and was sick all over his boots.

"Oh, boy," Julia exclaimed. "Dugan, help me, please. Ross, will you clear off a space on the table? I want him to lie down."

"Should I ride for a leech, Darach?" Ross asked. "What shall I say is wrong wi' him?"

"I know exactly what's wrong with him," Julia said crisply.

"A fit, aye, wee Julia?" Tommy wrung his hands.

"No. Good old-fashioned indigestion."

"What's that?" Dugan asked.

"At least I hope that's what it is," she went on, "and not salmonella or some other type of food poisoning."

"Poisoning?" Darach's eyes narrowed. "There's no one here who could have tampered wi' his victuals."

Julia motioned for Dugan to lift the moaning Gordon up onto the table. Tommy and Niall hurried to move more of the plates and cups

128

aside. "I didn't say anyone tampered with anything," she said, loosening Gordon's shirt collar some more. "Tommy, get me a pillow or something to lay beneath his head."

"A pillow?" He looked anxiously at Darach.

"It's all right, lad. There's a pillow in the chest in my chamber." Darach leaned over Gordon as Tommy hurried away to the stairs. "You say his food was poisoned and yet you say no person tampered with the food," he said in a low growl to Julia. "What kind of riddling nonsense is that?"

"I said he had food poisoning. Or maybe simple indigestion," Julia said, wringing out a rag in the pitcher of water. She placed the cool cloth on Gordon's brow. "It's not like someone put poison in your food. It's more like your food was poison to begin with." She patted Gordon's hand and held on as he seized up in another cramp. When his spasm had passed, she said, "Something in the stew tonight was spoiled. His body can't digest it. He's going to have cramps and diarrhea and possibly vomiting for a while until his body gets rid of everything he ate."

Darach squinted at his kinsman, pale and sweating before them. "He'll no' die of this?"

The gruffness of his voice caught Julia's attention. She looked up and saw the concern in his eyes. "No," she said softly. "I highly doubt it. But he's going to be pretty miserable— Whoops!"

Niall doubled over and staggered to the wall, one arm clasped around his waist. He looked about wildly for a basin. Ross handed him a bowl.

"Him, too?" Darach looked away as Niall lost his supper.

"That would be my guess. So that pretty much proves my theory. It's not indigestion, but tainted food. Gordon probably tried to throw up and choked on some of the meat." She put her hands on her hips. "I tasted the stew, but I didn't eat any. It smelled off to me but I thought maybe that was how you liked it around here." She faced him squarely. "I caught a glimpse of your kitchen, too, when I came down to breakfast this morning. No sink, no indoor plumbing, no air circulation except up the chimney. It's practically a Club Med for *E. coli.*"

"A what?"

"Oh, please. Don't tell me you don't even know the basics about germs and bacteria and sanitary practices?"

He scowled. "Perhaps I'm no' as learned as you, but I do know how to cook a stew. I know my way about a kitchen. I've taken care of—Ah, hell, here's another," he said as Tommy staggered in with the pillow, gray-faced and sweat-sheened.

"Thanks, Tom," Julia said, tucking the pillow under Gordon's head. "You and Niall go sit down before you fall down. Your Highness?" she called to Bruce, who sat watching the proceedings with concern and some amusement. "Could you and Ross make up some beds here in the hall? These men will need tending all

night and they might as well be all together."
She put her hands on her hips and looked
around. "We'll need chamber pots and basins.
Clean rags and several buckets of water. Also,
someone go get me a fresh, fat hen and bring
her to the kitchen."

"A chicken?" Darach asked. "What are you
planning, woman? This is no' some heathenish
sacrifice?"

She shook her head. "You're so suspicious.
Yes, I'm planning to sacrifice a chicken to the
gods of gastrointestinal peace and harmony.
Maybe they'll help me out by turning the creature into good, plain chicken broth. Would that
be too heathenish for you?"

He seemed about to retort, then shrugged.
"I'll gae and fetch her."

She turned back to Gordon and began the
process of nursing a majority of lairds through
the long, smelly, groan-punctuated night. She
left Dugan in charge of seeing the men into their
beds—the big fella indeed had an iron-clad gut,
she thought—and took Ross with her to the
kitchen. Darach stood waiting there, a fine,
rust-red hen cackling and squawking in his
hands.

"Good, you haven't killed her yet," Julia said.
"Okay." She rolled up her sleeves. "Ross, you
can start by getting out the biggest pot you have.
Start heating water in that. Then get out your
next-largest pot and heat some more. The big
one will be for cleaning up this sty and the other
for cooking this critter." She grinned at Darach.

"Do you know how this is done?"

He nodded. "But ye would hae been turned down if it were any later in the day. Killin' a fowl after evenin' prayers brings ill luck and hunger to a house."

She smacked her forehead with her palm. "Oh my gosh, I had forgotten all about the fowl-killing-after-prayers thing. Good thing Gordon upchucked early on, eh?" She smiled, softening her sarcastic tone. "I think the ill luck has already hit, don't you? I think I can help turn it around with the aid of some good old-fashioned chicken soup."

He gave her a wary look but nodded his assent.

She had to give him credit, she thought to herself hours later. He didn't flag for a moment. He killed, dressed, and plucked the fowl, and watched her every movement as she readied it for the pot. He went the rounds with her as she tended the men, and while he grimaced at some of the tasks she set him to, he did them without complaint, and added words of gruff encouragement to his stricken men. He never left her side.

It wasn't until she returned to the kitchen to tend the slowly cooking broth that she realized what he was doing. "Damn it!" she exclaimed, spinning about to face him as he went to place the dirty dishes in the washbasin. "You're tailing me!"

Chapter Nine

Darach turned slowly and gave her a long, level stare. "I'm grateful for what ye've done for my men," he said calmly. "Doubt not that ye'll be recompensed. But no, I canna let ye wander about this place wi'out anyone to watch ye. Ye're a prisoner still, make no mistake."

She hurled a wilted parsnip at his head. He ducked easily and caught it on the fly.

"You barbarian!" she yelled, hefting another root. "How can you stand there and say I'm your prisoner when I'm the only thing standing between you and the death of your men? That's right, death! You didn't even know what you put in that stew, did you? You didn't even think that you might have given everyone a case of something deadly!"

He eyed her. "Ye said it wasna fatal."

"It isn't. Not if someone knows how to treat it. Fortunately for you, I do. You were going to set leeches to poor Gordon and make him sicker than ever. If you don't know how to treat it properly, food poisoning can cause complications that can lead to death—not just a bad case of cookie tossing!"

"And what has this to do with me watchin' you?"

She launched another parsnip his way. This one caught him by surprise and she got the small satisfaction of hearing a good, solid thump square in the middle of his broad chest. "Do you think for one minute that I'd bother to help you and your men if I were your enemy? Would I be up at this god-knows-what hour of the night cooking a chicken and scrubbing your hideous old pots and pans if I was trying to kill you all?"

"Stranger things have happened."

"Aaiggh!" She turned back to the pot of broth and began stirring vigorously, muttering under her breath.

"What's that ye say, Julia?"

She slowed her stirring. He stood behind her. Close enough so that he barely had to speak above a whisper. And he had said her name. In that whisky-and-satin voice.

She swallowed against the sudden leaping of her heart. "I said 'bubble, bubble, toil and trouble, cauldron burn and fire bubble.' Got any eye of newt?"

"I'm sorry I was sae blunt wi' ye."

God, how his burr thickened and softened and melted her like butter when he spoke to her this way! She stiffened her spine against the onslaught of unreasonable pleasure that coursed through her.

"I know I'm a wee bit zealous when it comes to protectin' my ain folk."

"A wee bit?" She reached for the salt bowl, not daring to turn around and meet the brilliant blue eyes that went with that voice.

"Verra well. A great lot. And Morestons have tricked us a time too many. I need to be certain that ye willna take advantage."

"Oh, right, cooking and cleaning and nursing. That's taking advantage."

He put his hands on her shoulders and gently turned her about. "It's my duty, Julia. With the other men taken ill, there was no one else I could ask to watch over you. And because I've been watchin', I know what a kindness you're doin' for us. Because I've been watchin', I know ye're not takin' advantage." He shook his head. "But if I hadna been watchin' and anything was to happen, I could never, never forgive ma'sel'."

She gazed up at him, a bevy of conflicting emotions coursing through her. The tenderness of his voice, the sincerity of his tone warmed her—but his words angered her and hurt her pride. His nearness tantalized her and yet she knew how dangerous he could be. His total concern for his men touched her—and still she was stung by the way he treated her as an outsider, a threat to his "ain folk," as he called them. She knew she was being irrational. She *was* an outsider, and had every intention of getting back outside as soon as she could.

But it still hurt.

She turned back to the pot, rubbing a hand over her eyes. She was tired, that was all. It had been one hellaciously long day and it wasn't over yet. No wonder her emotions were twisting like kites in the wind.

"It's all right," she said, with more crispness and determination than she felt. "I know you can't help yourself."

He didn't back away. "Ye must be half dead on yer feet, lass," he said, lightly massaging her shoulders. She fought the urge to lean back into the relaxing pressure of his big hands and give in to the melting, after all. How could those huge work- and battle-hardened hands be so gentle? She gulped and slipped out from under his touch.

"Why don't ye leave off and get some rest?" he asked, seeming oblivious to her sudden fear. "Ross and I didna eat the stew. And Dugan could eat beaks and feet and no' feel the difference. We three can tend to the men. Just tell us what to do."

She heard the humble note in his voice as he asked for instructions. She turned with a small smile. "No. If you can stand it, I can. Besides, I doubt that anyone could sleep much with all the groaning going on down here."

"It does sound as if we're settin' up a guild for it, wouldn't ye say?" He grinned. "Well, then, if ye won't go to your rest, ye can tell me what it is about my kitchen that you think is sae deadly."

"Oh, my, where shall I start?" Her glance took in the entire room.

His face fell. "That bad?"

She nodded. "Worse."

"Ah."

Dawn came at last. The men had spent a miserable night, but one or two of them who had been least stricken began to rally. Julia was exhausted, dirty, and hungry. As the first glow over the hills crept in at the window, she made herself a cup of the broth and munched a late-winter apple, sure that these, at least, were safe for consumption.

Darach sat beside her, keeping his own counsel. To her surprise the silence settled comfortably between them. He had been at her heels or by her side the whole night, as he had said, but he seemed more interested in hearing her ideas on how to improve his kitchen and his food stores than in testing her for witchcraft or espionage. He had listened with keen attention to all she said and asked pertinent questions about the ways and means of sanitation and food preparation.

More than once she had turned to catch his eyes upon her, those watchful eyes, and been startled by the intensity in their blue depths. But he said nothing out of the ordinary to her and even seemed to go out of his way to show respect.

Was this progress? She wasn't sure.

She finished her breakfast and stood up from the stool where she had collapsed at long last. "I think I could sleep now," she said, yawning and stretching. "Ross knows what to do and Dugan's had a rest and can help." She looked down at Darach. "You'd better turn in, too. You haven't slept in over forty-eight hours, unless I miss my guess."

He nodded and rubbed a hand over his stubbled chin. "Aye, I will. As soon as I've secured the house."

He rose. She sighed as he followed her out of the kitchen. He accompanied her to the stairs and then watched until she shut the door of her chamber.

To her surprise, no one came to lock the door.

Darach watched Julia climb the stairs, a sudden wistfulness rising up in his heart. The sway of her hips and the flash of her ankles below her skirts delighted him, aroused him as always, but this sudden yearning caught him by surprise. He'd seen yet another side of Julia during the night. He'd known she was strong-minded and beautiful, clever and outspoken. Last night he'd seen her tender and gentle, and a true leader in a crisis. Not once had she lost her head, not even when Gordon had seemed to be choking to death before their eyes. And when she went among his men, soothing their brows

138

with cool cloths, aiding them as they heaved their suppers left and right, she remained calm and collected, murmuring words of comfort and reassurance to each man in turn.

For all her pepper-pot temper fits, her outlandish ways and words, she was a woman who'd make any man a jewel of a companion, he thought. She'd be a wife fit for a king, let alone a chief. And if she proved half as fiery in bed as she was in her defiance of him, her husband would be one lucky man indeed.

He turned from the stairs with a sharp shake of his head. He wouldn't be that lucky man. He couldn't be. He'd forsaken those dreams long ago, when Isobel had died and he'd realized that the Morestons had declared a very different kind of war.

He passed the great hall, where his men snored in chorus on their pallets. When he entered the library he found Alasdair sitting before the fire, a flask of spirits in his hand. Alasdair had been on the watch around the borders of their land when the men had taken ill. He'd taken over the task of tending to all the animals and other outside duties while the others continued nursing the sick.

Darach walked over to his brother and held out his hand. Alasdair handed over the flask and Darach took a long pull. He wiped his mouth and handed it back, then hooked a footstool with one foot and dragged it near the hearth. He sat down with a soft groan.

"Ross told me what happened," Alasdair said,

still staring into the flames. "Good thing Julia, was here, eh?"

"Aye, I suppose. 'Twas only a bit o' tainted meat in the stew. We'd have managed."

"Ah, yes. I forgot your training as a surgeon."

Darach scowled. "None o' your jibes today, lad. I'm that weary I might do something you'll regret."

Alasdair took another pull from the flask. "Ye can't make me regret anything more than I already do."

"Ye haven't lived that long."

Alasdair fell silent. Darach peered at him. "Have ye done something *I'll* regret?"

His brother shook his head. "Dunna worry, big brothair. I've no' done anything that would trouble ye more than a gnat."

"What hae ye done?"

Alasdair looked at him for a long moment, then looked at the fire. "Not a damned thing."

"Maybe that's the problem."

"Meaning?"

"Meaning that maybe ye need a bit more to occupy that clever brain o' yours. A wife and bairns, maybe?"

Alasdair choked on his drink. "Oh, aye," he said when he could speak again. "Ye're a fine one to talk of wives and bairns. Ye're the older of us. Ye're the chief. Don't ye think ye ought to take yer own advice?"

Darach reached for the flask. "It's no' the same."

"Oh, aye. I forgot. Ye're not mortal, like the rest of us."

Darach glared at him over the edge of the flask but Alasdair continued. "Do ye think we're all blind?" he asked. "Ye're as touchy as a bear with a thorn in its paw. Ye can't take your eyes off her for a moment. Ye can hardly say her name aloud. And ye must admit ye've spent the night wi' her. I'm surprised ye aren't camped beside her bed even now. Or in it."

Darach was on his feet in an instant. "Watch yer tongue, cub. What I do or don't do is no concern of yers."

Alasdair rose to face him. "And what I do or don't do is none of yers," he said evenly.

"I'm the eldest and your chief. I have a duty to see to yer welfare. I'm responsible for ye."

"Ye're no' my father!"

"Right. I'm not. Da was always too soft wi' ye."

"And ye're going to right that mistake, are ye? Ye may be my brother, but no one named ye the savior of my soul! Even ye have to admit ye're not up to playin' that part!"

Darach wanted to grab him by the shirt and toss him into the next county. He fought the urge and caught his temper before it went flying off for parts unknown.

"This is the same damned argument we've been havin' for the past three years," he said, suddenly more weary than before. He sank onto the stool.

"Too right." Alasdair remained standing, his legs apart in a fighting stance.

Darach looked at his brother. Passion lit the blue eyes they both had inherited from their mother. He recalled what his mother had told him: If there was anything as fruitless as fighting with yourself, it was fighting with your own kin. And he knew Alasdair wouldn't back down.

He rose. Alasdair eyed him warily.

"I'm goin' to my chamber," Darach said. "Tell Ross and Dugan to summon me only if they can show blood or flames." He handed the flask back to Alasdair, turned, and left the room.

His life was changing, he thought as he climbed the stairs. Changing beneath his very hands, running out of control. He hated the sensation of helplessness it brought and he raged against it. He was chief of the smallest, most eccentric clan in all the Highlands, and he loved every soul entrusted to his care with a fierce passion. It fell to him to see that things either didn't change or to control those changes and wrest them around to benefit his clan. To do any less was to dishonor the good, old name of MacStruan.

He paused before Julia's door, his anger filling him once more, despite his exhaustion. She had been the herald of these changes, he thought.

Or was she the creator of change?

Who had sent her into his life? He wasn't going to let her wreak havoc on his world. He could at least control one small woman.

Couldn't he?

"Damnation," he muttered.

He stomped past her door and went into his own room. He didn't bother with the bedcovers, simply pulled loose his plaid, wrapped himself in its warmth, and fell into a bottomless well of sleep.

The mirror woke Julia.

She shivered as she sat up in the bed. Night had fallen, filling her room with a velvety darkness. All except for one corner.

The faint glow reminded her of Tinker Bell caught in the dresser drawer. But this didn't feel quite as whimsical as pixie dust. She felt that inexorable pull once more, that calling to her.

Against her will, she slipped off the bed and padded across the cold floor to where the mirror sat on the tabletop, its lavender-gold glow reflecting on the tapestried wall.

She didn't want to look. But she had to. She leaned over the edge once more.

She gasped. The glow had become even brighter. And where she should see her own reflection, that other woman's face peered out at her.

"Who are you?" she whispered.

"Who are *you*?"

Julia saw that the face looked as puzzled as hers must be. She had the giddy thought that somehow this woman had dialed a wrong number.

"Who are you?" the face repeated.

"I'm—" Her New York basic training kicked

in. "I'm nobody. How are you contacting me?"

"You don't belong there." The voice seemed to shimmer in the air, as if coming up through water. Julia shivered even though the sound was melodious, the face lovely.

"How are you doing this? Did you wire my mirror somehow?" Anger began to mingle with Julia's fear. "Why are you speaking to me?"

"You don't belong." The voice began fading.

"Why do you keep saying that?" Julia sensed the woman slipping away, and indeed, the image was beginning to lose its sharpness, and the glow from the silver began to dim.

"Leave this place. Your life is in peril." The voice faded into a soft, silken hiss. And then it fell silent. The mirror went dark before Julia's eyes.

"What is happening to me?" she whispered into the darkness. She shook the hand mirror gently. Her image jiggled in the normal way. Nothing. No other voices, no other faces. "Damn!"

Weariness swept over her once again. She'd had her fill of this strange place and these strange happenings. She couldn't think anymore. She didn't want to think.

She felt her way carefully back to bed in the inky darkness. Then, with a last shudder, she burrowed under and went back to sleep until dawn leaked in at the window and Darach came knocking at the door, summoning her to breakfast.

Chapter Ten

A short while later, Julia spun about in the kitchen. "You mean it?" she asked, breathless. "You want me to cook for you? And you'll let me out of my room to do it?"

"Aye, if you're sure ye want the task." Darach's mouth quirked up at one corner. "It's no' the daintiest work."

"Dainty?" Julia sniffed. "I once prepared a banquet for the entire Yugoslavian diplomatic corps, their attaches, husbands, wives, children, pets, and hangers-on. And that was in one of the crummiest hotel kitchens ever to squeak past a health inspection. I'm not looking for dainty. But I don't want to end up like your men out there either." She smiled at Darach. "It'll be good to have something to do. Thank you."

He nodded. "It'll be one less thing that the

men and I have to worry about."

"Whoa," she said. "I didn't say I could do this all by myself. I can't even lift some of these pots. I'll need at least one, better two, men to help me with each meal."

"It can be done. The men are used to takin' turns in here."

"Good." She rubbed her hands together and looked about her. "First I need to make something light. The men's stomachs won't take much solid food today. Then we start cleaning up this place."

Darach's eyebrows went up. "Cleaning? But you and I—last night—how much cleaner can it get?"

She laughed. "A whole lot. So are you going to help me or just stand there like a monument?"

"I have work to do. I'll summon Ross."

"Okay."

She set to work, humming. By midday her humming had stopped. Filth and decay lay all around her. The tools she had to work with were primitive at best, the overall conditions the same. She'd need days just to dig out, she thought.

But she was in her element. Back in a kitchen, a big one, preparing meals and creating order out of the chaos. And when she served the men the tasty vegetable broth and soft egg custard she'd concocted, they were visibly grateful.

To her amazement, Darach left her alone most of the day. Of course, she had Ross or Dugan with her all the time, but he didn't seem to need to watch over her personally. She mused on this as she cleaned up after the evening meal, trying to decide whether to be grateful or sorry for his absence.

She went to bed that night tired but satisfied. Whatever Darach's motives for enlisting her in his household, she at least had something over which she could exercise some control. The kitchen would be her domain and she would belong there, if nowhere else in this strange world. If she could prove herself to Darach and the others, perhaps they would let her go.

Several days passed, full of hard work and pleasant hours getting to know each of the lairds. The men had rallied quickly and all had returned to their work within a week's time. Each of them came to Julia, one by one, and expressed his thanks for her care, as well as extravagant praise for her cooking. She warmed herself in their regard, though she noticed Darach kept silent and distant from her. Was he waiting to see if she was going to slip something into the soup and wipe them all out? She suspected as much, a thought which gave her only grim amusement. As if she would know what to do all alone in this weird place, with all of them dead! As if they hadn't come near to doing themselves in with all the spoiled food and dirty utensils she'd found.

The subject of spoiled food brought to mind her current dilemma. If she was going to cook, she needed fresh food each day. She could figure out how to preserve some foods for later, but she needed fresh produce, herbs, and seasonings to prepare anything decent on an everyday basis.

"Ross," she asked one morning as they prepared eggs for breakfast, "is there a market near here? We're going to need supplies soon."

He frowned. "Ye'd have to go to Kinloch Rannoch if ye want to go to market."

She grimaced. "I don't suppose Darach would allow that, would he?"

Ross shook his head. "I doubt it. And even if ye did gang there, we've few coins to spend. What is it we're needin'?"

"Oh, fresh vegetables and fruits. Cheese. Butter. Spices. Fish. Flour, rice, potatoes, sugar, salt, pepper—" She looked at his crestfallen face. "Too much?"

"I dunna know. I don't know what some of those things are. But I can tell ye we canna afford more than a bit o' flour and salt at market when we do go." He brightened. "But vegetables we have. In the gardens."

"Gardens?" She clasped her hands. "That's wonderful! Oh, please take me to them, Ross!"

"Well . . ."

"Please?" She turned on her most wheedlesome smile. "If you want to get sick again," she said, shameless in her arguments, "if you want Darach and the others cooking for you again—"

"This way." He led the way to the back hall and out into the sunshine.

Ross escorted her all over the area that had been set behind a rustic fence of interwoven branches. A wealth of familiar plants grew there, including broccoli, onions, cauliflower, lettuce, peas, and leeks, along with several that Ross named for her. "And I've laid in herbs as well," he said. "Rosemary and fennel, thyme, parsley and pennyroyal, see? Are they aught ye can use?"

"Absolutely. This is going to be a great garden in a few weeks," Julia said. Ross puffed up with pride.

"Aye, I make sure there's good dung laid in and around and worked into the soil. There's sun here most days. My house is there." He pointed to one of the neat little stone cottages. "I can look out my window and watch for beasts and such that might want to taste my crop."

"Right. We'll have to think of some way to chase off the rabbits, especially when those lettuces ripen. Those little varmints couldn't care less about fences."

"Varmints?" Ross's face brightened. "Ah! Vermin, ye mean."

"Yeah. You could call them that." Julia smiled. "Let's get to work," she said, rolling up her sleeves. "There's weeding to be done."

She and Ross worked in the garden for hours, oblivious to the sun's journey across the sky. Julia had many questions about the clan to ask as they labored.

"Ross, why don't Liam and Gordon speak to one another?"

Ross heaved a sigh. "It was chickens. Was it eight years ago, now? Or ten? I canna recall, it's been that lang. Gordon found twa or three chickens roostin' at his back door. He claimed 'em and took the eggs for his ain. Liam came visitin' of a mornin' and saw the hens. He squawked worse than the fowl, sayin' they were his biddies and he'd have them back and the eggs as well."

"Didn't Gordon eat the eggs?"

"Aye, but bein' reasonable has nothin' to do wi' this matter." Ross grinned and shook his head. "For all his learnin', Liam's a man like any other."

"Did Gordon give back the hens?"

"Nay. He refused. Alec, our chief then, Darach's da, went out one nicht and took twa hens frae each man's brood. He had 'em dressed and roasted, then called the men before him and asked for each fellow to identify his ain birds. Well, o' course they couldn't, and they knew they could nae langer fash the chief o'er this matter o' the fowl. But they've no' spoken directly to one another in all this time."

Julia gaped at him in amazement. "But they seem to get along."

"Oh, aye. There's naught that one wouldna do for the other. But it's the principle o' the matter, don't ye see?"

"No, I don't."

He shrugged. "Neither do I. But that's who they are and how they are."

"You guys are amazing—"

Darach came roaring out of the kitchen door. Too late, Julia recalled she had broken yet another rule.

"Julia Addison!" he bellowed from the far side of the garden.

She stood up from the patch of kale she was thinning out. She brushed her hands off and walked toward the fence, taking her time.

"What are ye doin' out here?" he demanded when she drew nearer.

She swept an arm out over the greening plants. "Gardening."

"I didna give ye permission to go—"

She held up a hand. "Stop right there. No, you never gave me specific permission to come outside. But you did entrust to me all the cooking and food preparation, right?"

He glared, but held his silence.

"Right," she answered for him. "Ross was kind enough to show me his gardens. They're wonderful. They'll be a terrific source of fresh foods all summer." She placed her hands on her hips. "Now, if you want me to prepare foods that'll keep you all strong and healthy, then you need this garden to thrive. Are you going to come and weed and fertilize and water it every day?"

"O' course not. I canna spare the time."

"I didn't think so. But I can. Once the kitchen is in better shape, I'll have more time to work out here. Ross is a wonderful gardener. He can help me and see that I don't fly off on a pea-pod airplane."

She could tell that he wanted to argue, to put his foot down. But he couldn't. He looked at Ross and looked at the plants that they'd tended already. He scowled and pointed his finger at her. "So be it. But dunna let me catch ye slippin' any rose petals into the food. I had them once in Edinburgh. They taste like a man's eatin' a whore's perfume."

He stomped off.

Julia turned to Ross, wide-eyed with wonder. The two of them burst out laughing. A flock of birds rose from the trees nearby, startled by the sudden commotion. Julia fell silent and looked around her, listening.

"It's amazing how many kinds of birds I can hear up here," she said. "And insects. And even voices, echoing in the hills and glens. Back in the city, it's too noisy to hear anything that isn't right in your ear."

She stopped in the path, a chill suddenly coursing over her skin. She held up a hand as Ross started to reply.

She trained her ears all around. Then, shading her eyes, she searched the blue, blue sky above.

"It mustn't be," she murmured. "It can't be." She shook her head. "It isn't."

Ross was watching her, concern on his long, thin face. She raised her hands and shrugged. "You don't have any noise pollution up here," she said. "And almost no air pollution."

"No," he said cautiously.

"It's astounding what you can hear in this

152

place. And see." She sniffed. "And smell. I never noticed it before. You don't even have any planes going over. You must be way out of the flight path for everybody."

"Aye."

But that was impossible. Sooner or later a plane or a forestry helicopter had to fly over. Something. There had to be some sounds of civilization. Hadn't there?

She sank down on the broad tree stump that sat in one corner of the garden. Though she hadn't admitted it until now, she had been wondering if perhaps, just perhaps, she might have somehow fallen through some loophole in the laws of physics, and she was, indeed, 500 years in the past. Everything was too convincing here, too wild, too young, if that was the word she sought. There was an innocence in the air itself, as if the scents and substances of her own twentieth century had never touched this place.

And the men never slipped. Never once did any of them use a phrase that betrayed modern times, unless it was one she herself had introduced. Never once had they faltered in their day-to-day manners and life-style—it was all convincingly medieval. Her reenactment theory was shot to pieces.

She began to quake. Ross placed his hand on her shoulder. "Julia? Are ye ill?"

She clenched her hands in her lap to keep them from shaking. "No. No. I'm not ill." She looked up at his long, kindly face. Tears rose in her throat. "But I think I'm lost."

He squatted down beside her. "Lost?"

"I don't belong here. I belong in another place. Another time." She gave a short laugh. "Only I don't really belong there, either."

"I canna follow ye, lass."

She bit her lip and forced back tears. "It doesn't matter," she said quickly. She must sound like a madwoman to him. Or perhaps a witch. That, she didn't need.

She smiled. "It's nothing. I was just—remembering something, that's all. I'm all right now. Shall we take these goodies inside?"

Ross led the way out of the garden. She followed behind, her mind and spirit curiously still, as if she had stumbled upon some truth that had settled into her for good. She went about preparing the evening meal, thankful for Ross's quiet nature and respectful distance.

Time travel. The idea had been simmering on one of the back burners of her mind for some time. She had pushed it aside, hardly allowing it to form into words. It was too preposterous.

And yet the preposterous explanation was the only one that fit. She had somehow crossed into *The Twilight Zone* and was now ensconced in the Highlands of the late fifteenth century. In the middle of a lost time, in the middle of nowhere, in the middle of an ancient clan. She was a pawn in a feud that was fought centuries before her birth. She was among men who were dust long before the Pilgrims set out for the New World, before there was baseball, dental floss, or penicillin. She was baking apple crisp for a house full of ghosts.

She began to shake again. She grabbed a cup of ale and sat down on the little three-legged stool that stood near the hearth. She took a sip of the strong drink, wrapping both her hands around it to keep from spilling it into her lap. Questions were forming in her brain like kernels of popcorn exploding over a hot flame. How had it happened? Could she go back—or was it forward?—into her own time? Would she end up in some time other than her own, wandering back and forth through the ages?

And how was she going to tell Darach?

She gave a little whimper as she huddled on the stool. This was too much. Darach and his men were still fearful that she might be a witch. They were more than half convinced she was a spy. And she was certain that they had some sincere doubts about her sanity.

She clamped down on a hysterical laugh that bubbled up within her. If she were to tell them what she now thought had happened to her, she would remove all their doubts in one sweeping pronouncement. They'd probably hustle her off to an exorcist, and she wasn't at all sure that she could blame them.

She looked up and saw Ross glance quickly away. *Get a grip, girlfriend.* She might feel this truth in her very bones, but this was neither the time nor the place to go public with her conclusions. She'd have to bide her time. And when she went to make her escape, she'd better have a damned good plan.

She took another bracing draft of the ale and went back to the oven.

The lairds were especially jovial at the evening meal two nights later. Julia had prepared roast venison, a salad of tender new greens, and steamed dumplings. She felt proud of how well everything turned out, despite the limitations of the old kitchen.

After the food had been cleared away and a roaring fire built in the hall, the men treated Julia to a round of utterly hair-raising tales of battles their forefathers had fought and their own escapades in peace and war. As the hour grew late and the fire died, Alasdair told a ghost story about a weeping lass and her dead lover that literally raised the hairs on the back of Julia's neck. She shivered in delicious fear, feeling Darach's solid presence next to her and the safety of having all the other men round about.

But when Darach escorted her to her room and bade her a brief good-night before locking her inside, sadness welled up within her. She wasn't one of them. And she was no closer to freedom than she'd been the first day she'd stood before him in the great hall.

She tried to shrug it off as she undressed for bed. But what had worked for her all these years since her mother's death didn't seem to work in this odd place. She couldn't pretend that she hadn't missed the kind of closeness she'd witnessed among the clan members these past weeks.

Cammie, her stepmother, had told her often enough that she was such a gem because she was so grown up and self-reliant, even at age nine. That was when the parties for important people had begun, with Cammie and her father, as newlyweds, the laughing, beautifully dressed hosts. Julia had been trotted out for her one appearance of the night, after a full inspection by a *tsking* Cammie, who would send her off, murmuring that it was "a blessing the girl was so intelligent, at least."

Julia shook off these memories as she climbed into bed and blew out the candle. She was self-reliant. And she was intelligent. She'd done more things in her life than Cammie and her country-club set had ever dreamed. And she most certainly wasn't one of those whining, nurture-your-inner-child types who blamed all their problems on their upbringing. She knew she alone must resolve whatever conflicts came her way.

Still, she'd never been confronted with a conflict quite like Darach MacStruan and his clan. And she didn't think she could be blamed if a small twinge of longing crept into her heart when she thought of belonging to such a close-knit group. Or belonging with anyone, for that matter.

She'd had relationships with men, it was true. One had even been serious for a time. Until Julia had grown restless and dissatisfied and moved on to a new place, a new interest. It was a pattern that had started and ended most of her relationships.

A recollection of Darach's voice came to her, along with the warmth of his nearness, the tang of his earthy, wool-and-leather scent, the look of his tall, powerful body as he strode about in his kilt. Her mind had told her to get a grip, but her body had cheerfully disobeyed, rousing heat within her and prompting tendrils of desire to curl around her midsection.

Was it belonging she wanted? Or just to climb that big, glorious body and get lost in the velvet of that deep, rich voice, murmuring outrageous love words in her ear?

She rolled over and pounded the pillow, groaning into its depths. Such thoughts and dreams were more dangerous than the swords of all the lairds combined. She knew now that she was in the wrong place, the wrong time. She couldn't, wouldn't let him get to her. Especially not that way. Not in a way that would trap her in those steel-banded arms, or imprison her beneath . . .

"Aaiggh!"

She bit the pillow.

The mirror was "awake" again. Julia knew it as soon as she woke in the chill of midnight. In the darkness it lit the table by her bed with its ethereal glow.

She tried to ignore it. She went so far as to put the bed pillow over her face to hide the light.

The Mirror And The Magic

Her efforts were all in vain. She could no more ignore the mirror than she could fly. She needed to know why, after all these years, her mother's looking glass had suddenly begun to speak to her.

She slipped out of bed, went to the door, and listened. All was quiet as far as she could hear. Reluctantly she went to the table and got the mirror.

She climbed into bed again and, with a sigh, took up the mirror. Its lovely, opalescent light grew and her own image gave way quickly to the face of the woman she'd seen before.

"You're still there?" The quavering, liquid voice floated to Julia's ears.

"Y-yes. I'm here. Where are you?"

"It doesn't matter. You must leave at once."

"Why?"

"You are in terrible danger. Don't you sense it?"

"How do you know this?"

"Beware of the chief. His heart is dark. You must go and not return."

"But how can I?" Julia whispered. She groaned. "Oy vey, I can't believe I'm having a conversation with a mirror!"

"Do not fear. I am as real as you. The glass holds the power."

"Fine. But how can I leave? I'm not even sure where I am!"

"You don't have much time," the woman said. Her voice was growing clearer. "Things must go back to the way they were."

"You mean—go home? You don't unders—"

The door burst open. Julia shrieked as Darach crossed the room in two strides and grabbed the mirror from her hand. He raised his arm and aimed for the wall.

Chapter Eleven

"Darach, no!"

Julia was out of bed in a flash. She grabbed Darach's arm before he could let the mirror fly. "Please don't!" she begged.

He glowered down at her, his face lit by the rushlight in the hall outside the door. "I'll not have ye practicing yer witchery in my ain house!"

"I'm not a witch, I swear! How many times do I have to say it?"

"Words come too easy to ye, Julia," he said. "It's deeds that count. What kind of deviltry were ye tryin' to work wi' this thing?" He brandished the mirror before her.

"Nothing! Nothing." She cast about for an explanation. How could she explain what she didn't understand herself? "I'm lonely, Darach,"

161

she said, knowing as she said the words that it was the truth. "I was talking to the mirror because I was lonely." She reached up and touched its heavy silver backing. "It's the only thing I have left of my mother's," she said softly. "Ever since I was a girl, I've kept this mirror and felt . . . closer to her."

Darach lowered his hand, but he didn't release the mirror. "Your mother's dead?"

Julia nodded. "And yours?"

He shook his head. "Gone."

"I'm sorry."

He looked at her. What was going on behind those eyes? she wondered. He seemed on the verge of telling her something, then seemed to think better of it. He looked at the mirror, turning it over and over, studying it.

"I know I'm strange to you," she said. "You're strange to me. This is a strange place. A strange time. Please let me have one familiar thing to keep with me." She placed her hand on his arm. "I haven't yet given you reason to fear me, have I?"

At the sudden, hot spark that lit his eyes, she wished she had said something else entirely. Was he indeed afraid of her? Because he thought she was a witch? A spy? Or was there some other, more intimate reason?

She glanced down and realized that all she wore was a thin linen undergown. A surge of warmth began to creep up into her cheeks despite the chill around her. Her hand was still resting on Darach's arm and she felt the powerful, corded muscles of that arm shift beneath her touch.

She raised her eyes to his. She recalled her wayward thoughts as she had gotten into bed that night. She wanted more than anything to resist the tide that was carrying her toward him, but it was beyond her powers of will. The longing that welled up inside her, the heat of her desire, combined in such a way that she swayed toward him as if he were the force of the moon and she the waves of the ocean.

She stood up on her toes and kissed his stern, beautiful mouth. His arms came around her, pulling her up and into him, melding their bodies perfectly. She slipped her arms about his neck, letting the heat of his big frame soak into her through the fragile cloth of her gown. Nothing had ever felt so entirely right to her before. His lips teased and coaxed at hers, urging more from her, promising more in return. She sighed, feeling herself turning to liquid in his embrace.

Suddenly he reached up and pulled her arms away, setting her back from him. His breathing was ragged.

"What is it?" She put her hand to her mouth, feeling suddenly bereft.

He shook his head. "Ye play the game nicely, lass. But I willna fall into your trap. If ye think ye may lull me wi' kissing, you're wrong. I'm no' the sort of man who makes decisions wi' what's beneath my plaid." He handed her the mirror. "Keep it. For now. But if I see any signs of mischief, it will go hard on you, lass. Know that. The priest is still to come."

Julia watched him go, her heart aching, her feelings stung to the quick. And the sweet warmth of his lips still clinging to hers. When the door was shut, she heard once more the click of the heavy iron key in the lock.

She ran to the bed and wept.

Darach prowled about his room. His shadow loomed up the walls in the firelight, which was the only light he wanted. He wasn't sure that he wanted light shed upon the thoughts he was having. Or the feelings.

What had he done? Against all his better judgment, he'd put what for all he knew was an instrument of evil back into the hands of a witch. A witch who wove webs of lies with the face and demeanor of an angel. A witch who spoke with such sincerity and emotion that he was spellbound. A witch whose kiss was so sweetly passionate that even now his body and spirit raged against him for denying the torrent of need that she had aroused in him.

He looked above the mantel, where his great-grandfather's sword hung in its place of honor. Darach's father had told him many times of the bravery of his forefathers and how the Mac-Struans had fought with Wallace and other patriots to free Scotland for the Scots. He'd been entrusted with that legacy. So many of his people had been slain, so many had given their lives for the name and freedom of the MacStruans.

His duty was to see that his sires had not shed their blood in vain.

And yet he couldn't bring himself to cast this woman out. Nor could he bring himself to destroy her and end her threat to his clan forever.

"Why, damn it?" he growled.

Big Dog whined, raising his head from the bone he was gnawing near the hearth. Darach pointed at the ragged mutton leg. "I'd better not find rats in here come mornin'," he said sternly, finding a target for his anger. "Finish it or bury it!"

Big Dog padded to the door, bone clenched in his jaws. He looked balefully at Darach from over his shoulder.

"Ah, hell." Darach went and opened the door. "Right then, go on. I'll sleep better wi'out yer snorin' anyway."

Big Dog gave a sniff and trotted off toward the stairs. "Daft animal," Darach muttered, shutting the door. "He's as taken wi' her as the rest of them. Probably goin' to sleep in her room right now. Sleep on her pillow while she . . . ."

He groaned. Saints, he was jealous of a dog!

He had to be bewitched. Nothing else could have him in such a sweel over a bit of skirt. Somehow she managed to addle his senses every time he got near her. Kissing her and holding her slim little body against his had only made it worse. In that moment, the half-formed thought that he had met her somewhere before had returned.

Suddenly he stood still. It had come to him

at last. He had met her before, but not in any human realm. She was a being straight out of his dreams. Though he'd never confessed it to another living soul, in those rare moments when he would permit himself to have such longings or fancies, he felt the touch of a woman, the scent and feel of her form. He knew what she would be like: fiery, sweet, and wise without guile. A woman made to complement his deepest needs. Julia.

The very idea shook him to the marrow.

He needed to get away from her, he thought once more, resuming his pacing. Do some work. What was that quote that Liam had spouted to Tommy not long ago? "Love yields to business. If you seek a way out of love, be busy; you'll be safe then." Even if he wasn't in love, he was perilously close to its dangers. A long, hard day's work, every day would keep him out of harm's way. He'd make sure he stayed away from the house from dawn to dark. That way he wouldn't have to see her or hear her. He'd be able to clear his head and figure out just what to do with her.

The only trouble was, his dreams were filled with ideas of what to do with Julia Addison. And not one of them involved leaving his own bed.

That was the hell of it. He wanted her with every sinew and fiber of his body. But was it a desire he might feel for any normal woman? Or had she bewitched him, cast a love spell to ensnare him and render him vulnerable to his enemies?

His thoughts circled around themselves like a serpent swallowing its own tail. Everything led back to that one question: Who was she?

He thrust his fingers into his hair, raking it into wild disarray. How could he possibly find out, short of testing her before an inquisitor or going to the Moreston himself? He snorted. As if Craigen Moreston had ever told the truth in his life. And he'd already vowed that she'd not be persecuted for witchcraft while she remained in his custody.

He wasn't about to hand her over to his enemies, either. If she was one of them, let them come and claim her. He would keep her here, in his own house. With him.

He went to the table and poured himself a cup of ale. He downed the contents quickly and followed with another. And another.

He shunned his bed, hoping that the hard floorboards beneath him would prevent those vivid, yearning dreams from disturbing his rest for one night. The ale would aid in his search for oblivion.

When dawn came, he woke with a smile and an aching in more than his back. He groaned and fell back before the cold hearth. She'd done it again. She'd invaded his dreams. And the images his fevered mind had conjured throughout the night would have awakened passion in a statue.

He flung himself up and out. He handed the

keys to Bruce, who was on the watch. "Tell Julia she has the run o' the house, but no more." Then he was gone, off on a tour of his lands that would take him all day to complete.

Edana wanted to fling the basin across the meadow. When she had tried the mirror-basin before, she had seen nothing and had known relief. But now she had looked into the basin twice and seen that woman! This was no accident, nor some trick. The woman was there, in Darach's house, and she possessed a mirror of some power. And while Edana had done her best to frighten the woman away, she couldn't be sure the woman would accept her warnings.

She bent over the waters once more. "Servant. Is my true love's heart still mine to be claimed?"

The waters muddied and swirled, as if agitated by an unseen hand. "It iss not ssso," the watery spirit replied.

Edana's heart contracted. Darach loved another? Her Darach? "It cannot be," she said. She spoke over the waters once more. "My love has taken no other to wife?"

The water smoothed and rippled. "It iss e'en ssso, mistress."

"Ah." Edana sighed her relief.

Still, the woman was there. She was not wedded to Darach. She might merely be some whore. Or perhaps she belonged to one of the other clan members. She shook her head. Possible, but not likely. All this time she'd been watching the MacStruan, her basin had never shown her anyone but Darach or one of his men who was in close proximity to him. Whoever she was, this woman was near to him.

Was she also dear to him?

Edana looked into the waters. The visions had disappeared; the water was returning to its original state. She smiled at the reflection of her own face floating there. At least the woman wasn't more beautiful than she. She didn't have to worry on that account!

But she did have to find out who was coming between her and her love.

And then she'd have to get rid of her.

Whistling cheerfully, Edana carried the basin over to the window and dumped the water into the shrubbery below. A cat yowled out in outrage from the darkness below. Edana laughed. "Silly old Malkin," she called out. "Serves you right for lying in wait for some hapless tom!"

Julia spent the next day in the kitchen again, reorganizing the pantries and scouring the place from top to bottom. The work was a good outlet for all the confusion and frustration that had haunted her through the night just past. But it was only a partial success. She wondered if there was enough work in the whole of Scotland to keep her mind off of Darach MacStruan and the fire that had been ignited between them last night.

She frowned. The fire that had been ignited within her, she thought, correcting herself. He'd set her aside and left without so much as a backward glance. No, that kiss hadn't been nearly so stirring for Darach as it had been for her.

It was impossible, she told herself for the hundredth time. She couldn't make a relationship with Darach MacStruan. Not only because he was such a difficult man, but because he was a man who belonged in a separate time altogether. How could she possibly have a life with a man who existed hundreds of years before she was even born? She had no idea if she was stuck in this time or if she'd go sailing back to the 1990s or some other time at any moment.

Ross came in near midday, a young, skinny cat snuggled in his plaid. Julia exclaimed in delight and hurried to find a saucer for some cream.

"Nay, lass, dinna feed it," Ross said, holding up a hand.

"But she's so thin!" Julia cried. "Look. You can see her little ribs poking out."

"Aye. All the better for her to prove her worth."

"Her worth?"

He nodded. "This lassie's sae hungry she'll eat a mouse right down to the squeak. Put her in th' pantry, close the door, and in no time the whole place'll be free of the varmints." He grinned with pride at his use of the new word. His grin faded in a moment, however, as he looked about. "Dinna ye tell Darach, though. He's a dog's man and won't hold wi' a cat in his house." He grinned once more. "For all his ferocity, the Big Dog's no' a fine mouser. Won't waste his time on such a tidbit."

"Well, Little Cat," Julia said, scooping the wary animal up into her arms. "Judging from the evidence I've seen, you're in for a feast." She gave the cat a gentle toss into the pantry and quickly shut the door. "Let's hope she doesn't get into any of the other foods," she said to Ross. "I think I've sealed up as much as I can." She sighed. "What I wouldn't give for a Tupperware party in the neighborhood."

"Tupperware?"

"Yeah. Special containers for keeping food fresh."

"Ah. I could see if Gordon can make some for ye. He's a fair tinker."

Julia tapped her chin with a fingertip. "A tinker, eh? You know, maybe he can help me. Can you get him to come here? I can show him what I need if I can find a pen and some paper."

She spent the rest of the day conferring with Gordon and when he left, she was satisfied that she'd soon have made some major improvements in the kitchen supplies. If she stuck around long enough, she thought with grim humor, she might bring this place kicking and screaming into the Renaissance.

After Gordon had gone, she heard a meowing and scratching at the pantry door.

"Little Cat," she said, hurrying to open the door. "I'm sorry, girlfriend. I forgot you were in there. How goes the hunting?"

Little Cat strolled through the passage with

an air of complete belonging and self-satisfaction. She went straight to the hearth, found a corner that suited her, and settled down to have a leisurely wash. Julia laughed. "That good, eh? Well, I doubt that even one of your great prowess could have cleaned them all out in one afternoon, kiddo. Tomorrow you can show your stuff again."

Little Cat gave her a solemn, green-eyed stare and then, deciding a bath was more important than anything a human had to say, returned to her task. Julia pondered for a moment. How was she going to hide this little fuzzball from Darach? And, for that matter, Big Dog? BD was a sweetie, but would he tolerate another animal cutting in on his territory? Would a small cat fall into the proper size range for a canine appetizer?

"Looks like you and I have the same problem, kiddo," she told her as she started on the evening meal. "We don't belong here, we aren't wanted here, but here we are. And we're both going to have to walk on eggs to avoid ticking off the powers that be."

She heard her stepmother's voice once again, whispering to her before some party or family gathering. "Try to fit in, dear," she would say. "No one expects you to be a part of my family right away. But make an effort, all right?"

Julia sighed. Now that she thought about it, her whole life had been about finding someplace where she belonged, where she fit in. From high school, to college, to Yoga and meditation, chef's school, the I Ching, fire walking, archery, hypnosis, modern dance, disc jockeying, rolfing, organic gardening—the list was embarrassingly long—she had been searching for a clue as to who she was and what she wanted to do with her life. She thought she had found her niche when her old friend Martine Coburn gave her the job as assistant chef in her new restaurant. She was happy with cooking, liked the city, enjoyed the other people working at Martine's.

But she hadn't felt as if she belonged there. If she was honest with herself, all she'd done was put in her time there, and gone home alone.

Cammie had been right. She didn't fit in, no matter how hard she tried.

And now here she was. In the last place—the last time—on earth where she could fit in.

She looked about. She'd had Ross and Tommy put up new shelves and pegs to store pots, pans, and utensils. The floor had been scrubbed many times over and she had sprinkled sawdust mixed with dry herbs and grasses to absorb any lingering smells. She'd put in a request for some of the whitewash she'd seen on the walls of the house and the outsides of the lairds' cottages and was planning to add extra lamps to brighten the room. With Little Cat curled on the hearth, bread baking, and a roast of beef turning on the spit, her new workplace was cozy and welcoming.

But this room wasn't hers. It was Darach's. And Darach had made it plain that she didn't belong. Not in his house, not in his clan, not in his homeland.

She clapped her hands together. Self-pity was not her style. She needed action. It was time to start thinking about leaving. There had to be some way to retrace her steps and find a way back to her own world and time.

She jumped as someone cleared his throat behind her. She whirled about to see Alasdair standing in the kitchen doorway, hands on his hips, looking about the room in wonder.

"Well, well," he drawled. "This place shows a loving hand."

She felt herself color with pride. "Do you like it?"

"Mmm." He came toward the ovens, sniffing appreciatively. "If it's ever been cleaner, I canna recall the occasion."

"Oh, surely when your mother was here . . ." She halted. "Oh. Perhaps you'd rather not speak of her."

"Why not?" Alasdair stuck his finger in the pot of sauce she was stirring.

She slapped his hand. "Stay out of that. You want to get us—them—all sick again?" She stirred more vigorously. "I only meant that with your mother gone and all, you might not want to talk about her."

"Oh. Aye, I suppose. Still, she was never much of a hearth dweller. You're the one's made this old dungeon sparkle."

"Thank you." She took a fresh spoon and dipped it into the sauce. She lifted the brown liquid up for him to taste. "Here. Taste this and tell me what you think."

He opened his mouth and let her spoon it into him, both of them laughing as some dripped down his chin. She wiped it off with a fingertip.

"Takin' up cookin', oganach?"

They both whirled to see Darach standing in the doorway. His expression was carefully bland, but Julia saw a spark of anger dance briefly in his eyes. Alasdair backed away from her, but she held her ground. She put a hand on her hip. "Do all you MacStruans have to come and go like ghosts?" she demanded. "I had a spoonful of hot sauce in my hand. We both could have been burned."

Darach stepped into the room, his eyes moving quickly from her to Alasdair and back again. "Oh, aye. We'd not want to have anyone over-heatin'."

She ignored his sarcasm. "Dinner will be ready in about half an hour," she told him. "If the gods of the peat-burning fires are with me. You have time to go clean up." She looked pointedly at his muddy boots, which had already dripped clumps of wet earth on her immaculate floor.

Darach sniffed the air. "It smells fair. No eye of newt?"

She tried to glare at him, but she caught the tiny lift of his mouth and couldn't help smiling. "No. No toe of frog, either, I'm afraid. And the only thing I've used the broom for today has been sweeping the floor." She gestured to his feet.

He looked down at last. "Oh. Ah." He bent down and began to pull one off.

"No!" Julia cried. "Not in here! Out! Out the back door and leave them out there until they're dry."

"Ye're a bossy wee thing a' of a sudden," he grumbled. But he went to the door and deposited his boots outside.

He padded back in his bare feet. He sank down onto a footstool and sighed. "Spring's comin' on fast," he said to Alasdair. "The cattle hae been makin' merry up there to the north. Like as not some are breedin' even now."

Alasdair nodded. "They'll need to be brought down soon. Leastways, the heifers."

"The sooner the better. I thought we'd go out day after tomorrow with some of the lads and bring them down to the glen by the oak woods."

"I'll spread the word."

"Do it. And see to our Bruce while you're about it. His bones are troublin' him again."

Alasdair left quickly, as if glad to be away. Julia watched him go and then turned back to the vegetables she was slicing for the pot. "Why are you so hard on him?" she asked.

"Am I hard on him?"

"You're always treating him like a serving boy. I don't know what an oganach is, but Alasdair didn't like you calling him one, I could tell."

"It means young man, that's all." There was a

pause. "Are ye takin' up my brothair's cause, Julia?"

She turned with a frown. "Alasdair is a grown man. He doesn't need me to defend him."

"True enough. But the lad has a lot to learn."

"Who doesn't?"

Darach blew out a breath. "It's no' somethin' ye'd understand."

"No? Maybe you're the one who doesn't understand. From what I've heard around here, you were your father's fair-haired boy. He guided you every step of the way. But who was there for Alasdair? If you ask me, he's done pretty well on his own."

It was his turn to frown. "Ye don't know our ways. I'm the MacStruan. My father had to make sure I was ready to be chief."

"And what if something happened to you? Wouldn't Alasdair become the MacStruan?"

"Aye."

"Well?"

He rose from the stool. "That's what I've been tryin' to tell ye. He needs to learn. Bein' the MacStruan doesna mean goin' about at all hours or readin' books or ridin' horses as ye wish."

"No, it just means telling everyone to jump and expecting them to ask how high on their way up."

He came to stand before her. His eyes searched hers. "Ye don't know me as well as ye think," he said, his voice low and tense.

She wanted to back away from him but the

oven was behind her. She raised her chin. "If I don't, it's no fault of mine," she said.

"Would ye have me as a teacher?"

She was suddenly warmer than even the heat of the oven warranted. His voice had changed somehow. His tone was still challenging, dangerous. But she wasn't sure where the danger lay, or what he was challenging her to do. The man was maddening.

"I don't need a teacher," she said, for want of anything sufficiently withering.

"No?"

"No!"

He raised his hand. For an instant she thought he was about to strike her. Instead he caught one of the curls that had escaped from her braid and tucked it back behind her ear. She almost jerked away from him with the shock of such a tender, intimate gesture, the sensation of his fingers touching the sensitive flesh of her ear. He lowered his mouth to hers and kissed her slowly. Deliberately. Completely.

"Leave Alasdair to me," he said, lifting his head and setting her away from him. "I know what's best for my ain brothair."

He turned and left the kitchen. Julia turned back to her vegetables, her insides still trembling from their brief encounter.

How did he manage to affect her so deeply? All he'd had to do was stand near her, touch her ear. She'd been feeding Alasdair, touching him and laughing with him, but she hadn't experienced anything akin to the total arousal she felt whenever Darach came within a yard of her.

Then he'd gone and kissed her. God, she hated that. All it took was one sweet, warm kiss from that outrageously sensuous mouth of his and she was a bowl of crème brûlée. And when he'd finished reducing her to mush, he'd strolled off in his smug, arrogant, "I'm the MacStruan" way, leaving her to go along with whatever he said. And she'd stood there like a carp, gaping after him.

"Cuthach," she muttered to herself. She stiffened and gasped.

Little Cat gave a sniff from the hearth. Julia looked at her in wonder. "Now where did that word come from?" she asked, her chopping knife in midstroke. She shook her head to clear away her confusion. "The word means madness," she said softly. "But how could I possibly know that?"

Little Cat licked her chops, yawned, and curled back up into a comfortable ball behind the wood stack. Julia went back to work, trying hard to forget the eerie sensation of that unbidden word.

Chapter Twelve

Auld Bruce's house needed fixing, Darach reported to Julia the following morning. He and some of the others were going to help the older man with the repairs.

"If ye like, ye may come out to the green," he said, never looking up from his oatmeal.

Julia nearly choked on the last bite of her breakfast. "I can what?"

He looked up. "Come ye out on the green. It bids fair to be a clear day. Stay on the green where we can see ye, and ye can stay out as long as we're workin' on the Bruce's house."

She decided it was best not to question his change of heart. She smiled and nodded. "I'll be ready right away."

* * *

The day was indeed clear, with the sky a blue of such intensity and clarity that the sight took Julia's breath away. She strolled about the green, looking at all the houses and reveling in the chance to be somewhere other than the house or the gardens.

The lairds devoted most of their time to working on Bruce's repairs, but she never lacked for companionship. One by one the lairds paid her a visit, each one putting his characteristic spin on the tour of the village. Niall, ever the soldier, told her about his father's house, where he lived, and how his father had fought for clan and king in the old days. Ross fetched his pipes and skirled a lively melody for her, scaring the chickens into the underbrush and chasing the birds out of the trees. The Bruce came and rested himself on a tree stump, managing to transform the old wood into a throne from which he issued royal commands to the men at work on his roof. Liam bent her ear with a detailed account of all the geologic and botanical wonders of the place, confiding, out of hearing of the others, that he personally was working on a radical new theory that the earth was, in fact, spinning around and around even as they spoke.

Dugan tramped up after a long session of hoisting rocks to the roof by ladder. He carried a well-worn leather bag with him and, to Julia's complete astonishment, pulled out two wooden knitting needles and a ball of rough yarn. He sat and conversed, in as few syllables as possible, about the weather and the animals, all the while knitting a meticulous, even piece of woolen that looked capable of resisting even the chilliest winds.

Tommy came last of all, gamboling over the green like Big Dog, his energy, as usual, as boundless as only a teenager's can be, Julia thought. He dragged her to her feet and ushered her about the house that he was building, pointing with pride to every beam and post and stone laid there by his own hands.

"It's beautiful, Tommy," Julia said. "I can't believe you're building a house all by yourself at your age."

The lad puffed up with pride. "I'm no' so young. I'm eighteen. Or will be, this summer. And when I marry—" He broke off suddenly.

Ah, thought Julia. Aloud she said, "And when you marry . . . ?"

"When I do marry. I don't know who," the boy stammered. "I don't know any maids here and the next village is the Moreston's and beyond that it's a long walk, as far as Loch Rannoch, nearly, before ye come to any . . . girls. . . ." He grinned. "But when I do marry, I'll have a bonny, snug house, wi' a real fireplace like Darach's, for a wife and bairns."

"You will indeed."

"Will ye be marryin' our Darach?"

Julia's jaw dropped. "Will I be what?"

"Will ye be—"

"Never mind, I heard you." She raised her hands to the sky that peeped in through the roof

182

beams. "Darach! Darach! What is it with you guys that all you can talk about is Darach? I don't go around talking about the mayor of New York City!"

"Ye're goin' to be marryin' him, this mayor?"

Julia looked at the young man and sighed. He was absolutely in earnest. And he was clueless. For that matter, she thought, he wasn't the only one.

"No, Tom. I don't think I'll be marrying the mayor of New York. Or your Darach."

"Why not? I think you'd make our chief a fine, fine wife, wee Julia. If I was Darach, I'd—"

"Thomas!"

Alasdair vaulted in from the window hole. "That'll do, youngling."

"But don't ye think, Alasdair, that Julia and our Darach—"

"No' another word."

Tommy's face fell and then he shrugged. "I guess ye auld folk don't think much about love and all that. Hope I'm not like that when I'm your age."

Alasdair made a playful jab at the boy. "Your time is comin'—dinna ye hasten the inevitable. Get along and start laying fires and heating water in the kitchen. Get yer mind off love and . . . other matters. Julia will be wantin' to get a meal goin' before midnight."

Tommy left the way Alasdair came in and Julia couldn't help laughing. "He's exactly the way I was when I was seventeen," she said. "I couldn't wait to get out into the world and try everything on for size." She gestured around the house. "Though he's way ahead of me, I'd say. I certainly didn't have the skill or the wherewithal to build my own house when I was his age."

"Tom's a good lad. He'll make a fine man, if he doesn't lose his head in some mischief first." Alasdair cocked his head to one side. "Don't take his prattlin' about love and Darach too seriously, Julia. They're all sae rolaisteach at that age. It's the curse of the MacStruans."

Her eyebrows shot up. "Are you serious? You and Darach were once hopeless romantics?" A shiver shot down her spine. She knew the word. She knew the word! How could that be? It was as if there was some magic about this place that was slowly, inexorably making her one of them.

"Oh, aye," he said, oblivious to her reaction. "Ye should've seen Darach at court when he was fostered in Edinburgh. Da nearly had to go fetch him home in disgrace for his ways with the ladies."

Julia was amazed and elated at this bit of news, though a twinge of jealousy tempered those feelings. So Darach MacStruan was human after all. Or at least he used to be. "What happened after that?"

Alasdair thought for a moment. "He settled down, I suppose. Da was always good at puttin' the fear o' God into us, one way or another."

"And did he give up the ladies?"

He gave her a shrewd glance. "Nay."

She had to grin. "You're a loyal brother, Alasdair."

"I should hope so. Darach's a right pain in the arse often enough, but we share blood."

"It must be nice to be so sure of your family."

"Sometimes it's all there is between ye and the wolves."

She gazed at the floor, suddenly feeling more foreign than ever in this foreign place. "Would you consider me a wolf?" she asked.

She felt his hand beneath her chin. He lifted her face until she met his eyes. They were filled with friendly concern. "Don't tell me. He's been holdin' ye off by claimin' that ye're a witch still."

"I don't know about holding me off. But he thinks I'm the enemy, I know that. Even if I'm not a witch, he's made it clear I'm an outsider and not to be trusted."

Alasdair took her arm and drew it through his. He led her toward the doorway. "Dinna ye worry, lass. Darach's cautious, is all. Wi' everything."

"Cautious? He's downright paranoid where I'm concerned."

"Paranoid?"

They stepped out into the sunlight. "Yes. He treats me like I'm going to plant a bomb in the middle of the green and blow all of you to kingdom come."

Alasdair laughed. "I can see him thinkin' that. He's like an auld hen, my brothair. When it comes to his ain folk, he fair clucks with protectiveness."

Julia grinned up at him. "Now that's an image I would never have come up with in regard to Darach."

"Watch. He's comin' now, thunder ridin' his back and lightnin' in his eyes. But mark ye, he's watchin' the nest."

She looked and there, indeed, was Darach, bearing down on them, his face dark as a storm. He was issuing orders before he came to a stop. Julia had to work hard to conceal the smile as she thought of Alasdair's description.

"Niall needs help wi' the last o' the stanes," he said to Alasdair. "That is, if ye can spare a moment."

"At your service, my liege," Alasdair drawled, and sauntered off.

"Tommy's in the kitchen. No doubt the water's heated by this time. The men are hungry."

She gave him a radiant smile. "All right," she said, mimicking Alasdair's saunter. "My lord."

He caught her arm. "If I were indeed your lord, ye'd know it."

She gazed up at him, still smiling. "Is that the fatal charm that won the ladies' hearts in Edinburgh?"

"What's my brothair been tellin' ye?"

"Enough to know that you aren't as rough and tough as you pretend to be."

He pulled her closer. "Ye think not?" His tone was low and distinctly threatening.

She swallowed but kept her smile. "I think you're a fake, that's what I think. You talk tough but inside you're a bowl of mush. You act like you don't care about anyone or anything but you're as susceptible to love as the next man."

"And ye think I was in love wi' the ladies at court?"

She nodded. His eyes had grown so dark and wild. She could almost feel the intensity of his feelings rolling off of him.

He jerked her quickly into his arms, pinning her against the rough wool of his plaid. Without another word, he bent his head and kissed her.

Julia felt as if she were being dipped into flames. The rough magic of his lips heated and tormented her, rousing a sudden fever that seemed to originate in the marrow of her bones. His hands slid down her back, pressing her against him, allowing her to feel his strength and power, his own heat. The kiss went on and on, teasing, tempting, drawing a soft moan from deep in her throat. She felt as if her legs would no longer hold her.

As suddenly as his embrace had begun, he ended it. He set her away from him and looked at her with a cool smile.

"And was that love, Julia?" he asked, his voice rumbling from deep in his chest. "Twa bodies bangin' against one another? Is that what passes for love where ye come from?"

He turned abruptly and was gone.

"Damn it," she muttered. "He did it again."

When her knees at last agreed to work properly, she hastened to the kitchen and began cooking with a fury that was only matched by the storm that was raging inside of her. Tommy watched her, but wisely kept quiet, especially after they heard Darach slam through the front door and stomp upstairs to his chamber.

It was a very quiet meal.

The next morning, Darach and the men went off to bring more of the cattle down from the hills, leaving Julia at home with the Bruce. She was grateful for the older man's easygoing presence and the fun of playing along with his pretensions to royalty. It had been another uneasy night for her, what with wondering if the mirror was going to talk to her again, the whys and wherefores of time travel, and trying not to think about Darach's hot, angry kiss.

Bruce accompanied her to the garden, where a light mist was falling, interrupted now and then by bursts of golden sunlight. He sat on a rock and related many stories of the lands around the MacStruan clachan, and the people who had struggled and worked and played and died for the love of the land.

As she listened and worked, Julia could imagine men and women coming and going, driving cattle past the spot where this garden now stood, young people meeting at the legendary dancing places, children racing after the wild birds and rabbits. Despite the bloodshed and suffering she knew were substantial parts of their lives, she couldn't help thinking of how they'd banded together in clans, combining their fortunes as one family.

"Your Majesty," she asked after Bruce had

fallen silent for a few moments, "are the clans today the same as in the old days, when they first began?"

Bruce pondered her question. "I'd have to say the clans are no' as they were even when I was a chiel. But clans are still important, especially here in th' Highlands. It's how most of us still live, though I know some in the cities keep to their ain selves."

There was another question that had been on her mind for some time. "I thought clans were large groups of people who'd pledged allegiance to one chief," she said. "But Clan MacStruan is small, more like one family. Why aren't there more of you?"

He regarded her cannily. "What might ye mean?"

"I mean why are there so few MacStruans? Darach has told me that the Morestons have far more people in their clan."

"Weel, it's no' a cheerful story, lass."

"I don't mind."

"There was once nigh as many MacStruans as Morestons. But where the Morestons gathered forces by conquerin' or forcin' allegiances wi' other clans, the MacStruans have always gone their ain way. Then, o' course, time and bad times take their toll. War. Famine. Sickness. The MacStruan chiefs have held their line, but the clan's diminished these last twa or three generations."

"Darach says the Morestons have killed a lot of your clan."

"Aye. And taken land from us, in one way and another. There's only so many people a piece o' land can support. Some of our kin left for other parts o' Scotland and even England, sad to say." He gave her a rueful smile. "I never thought the day would come when there'd be this few clansmen on this land. I've hopes for our Darach, though. And Alasdair, as well. The twa o' them could give us a brace o' bairns, if they'd just decide upon it." He shot her a sharp look. "Which o' them do ye ken will choose a wife first?"

She shook her head, avoiding his keen old eyes. "I wouldn't know. I think it all depends on whether or not they kill one another first."

He chuckled. "Ye have the right o' it, lass. They're like two cats in a sack, some days. But ye can depend upon it, no outsider had better come between 'em. They'll close ranks sae quick the man—or woman—willna have time to draw the next breath."

"I know. Darach's made it pretty clear what he thinks of outlanders like me."

"Has he?"

"Yes. Clan comes first, last, and in between with him."

"Ye mustn't take it too hard, wee Julia. It's just our way."

"I know. Never mind." She got up, brushing off her skirt. "I'm beginning to know what Harrison Ford must have felt like."

"Who's that?" His face was a cheerful blank.

"Of course, you wouldn't know. How can I explain? You see, Harrison Ford was in this

190

movie, *Witness*, where he gets wounded in a murder investigation and he runs away to this farm with this beautiful Amish woman." She knelt down and began to weed the shallots. "He lived with them, worked with them, ate with them, slept in their beds, even wore their clothes, but anytime he tried to get close to one of them or questioned their way of life, they'd tell him he couldn't understand because he was an outsider. That's how I feel here."

"And ye believe we're Amish?"

She grinned. "No."

"Hmm." He gave her a puzzled smile. "Are ye runnin' frae a murder, wee Julia?"

Chapter Thirteen

Her head snapped up at his words. "What makes you say that?"

"This Harrison Ford fella. He was wounded in a murder, ye said. And ye say ye feel as he did. Are ye runnin' frae a murder as well?"

"Oh, boy." Julia buried her face amid the foliage. She'd accidentally given herself away. Just as she was beginning to win some of the clan's trust, here came a new suspicion for them to hold against her.

She decided that when life hands you lemons, make a sorbet. She moved closer to where the Bruce was seated. "That was just a movie, Your Highness. But it was a great story. You'd like it, I think."

"Aye? Well, tell it, lass. Ye know I love a good tale."

So as she worked, she related the plot of the movie in as much detail as she could recall. Bruce listened, a look of rapt fascination on his weathered face. When she came to the climax of the movie, with the shoot-out in the dairy barn, he thumped his staff with approval. "That Ford is as canny as any Highland reiver!" he exclaimed.

She grinned and stood up. Wiping her hands on her apron, she nodded toward the house. "Glad you liked it. I'd best get some food started. Would you deign to aid me in the kitchen, Your Highness?"

He pushed to his feet. "I shall, m'lady Julia."

Later that night, with the men seated around the cozy ingle in his cottage, the Bruce retold the story of *Witness*, in its entirety, to the other lairds. When he'd finished, they sat back in wonder and satisfaction.

"Who'd have known wee Julia would have such a tale in her head?" Ross said.

"I would," said Gordon. "She's no' exactly the most ordinary maid ever to wear skirts. When she does wear 'em, o' course."

"She said they called these tales movees, did she, Your Highness?" asked Liam. "I've ne'er come across such a word. Must be an outland term."

"Wonder if she has more to tell." Tommy's eyes were bright. "Though I think the lass in the tale should hae gone wi' Harrison. But then, he was an outlander."

After that, Julia was engaged every night. The

lairds took to staying in the great hall after the evening meal and while they contributed their own stories, the highlight of the evening was the time when Julia would tell them another "movee."

She was glad of all those nights she'd spent at home while she was in school, watching video after video, as well as all the movies she'd seen in theaters. She didn't know what she'd do when her store of films was exhausted—would she be forced to resort to reruns? Or trot out old plots from TV dramas?

Darach seemed as entertained by her tales as the rest of the men. He still stayed aloof from her, taking a seat in the shadows of the hall as he listened and sipped his ale. She seldom saw him in the day, except at meals. He was always hunting or herding, she was told. She wondered if he was so reluctant to be near her, why wouldn't he let her go?

But there it was. She was still a captive. And she'd have to make the best of it until she could make her escape or Himself the MacStruan decided what he wanted to do with her. She could guess which would come first.

The days spent with the lairds were delightful. When she found Tommy practicing the Heimlich maneuver on Big Dog, she took the boy under her wing and began to tutor him in safety and sanitary practices. He came eagerly to the kitchen when it was his turn to help, and his ability and the deftness of his hands made Julia proud.

"You should think about medical school," she told him one afternoon, after he'd snapped into action and successfully treated a minor burn to Liam's hand.

He colored. "Nay. I'm no' the one to be in school. I couldna leave the *clachan.*"

"Oh, I'm sure they'd let you out if you wanted to go. I know they're kind of tough on the whole clan business, but if you wanted to go, I think they'd let you."

He smiled. "It's no' that. It's me. I wouldna want to leave home and travel to Edinburgh or some big place like that. I have my house here, and my people. Market days in Kinloch once a year are enough for me."

She didn't argue with him. The summer was coming on and the Highlands put on their best show. Flowers of all kinds cropped up here and there, even in the rockiest places. The sheep had lambed and the wobbly legged babies leapt and tumbled about on the meadows. Julia spent more and more time outside with the lairds, in all weather, savoring all the new scents and sights and sounds.

Darach threw the paper on the table. "What the devil do they take me for?" he growled at Niall. "Do they think they can spit on my father's name?"

Niall crossed his powerful arms over his chest. "The Moreston's been a busy wee man."

Darach paced about the library. "He's been that and more. He can't shake us off our land, so he's gone to the earl and asked for the boundaries to be drawn again, just to be certain there's been no mistake made." He returned to the table and pounded his fist upon the offending letter, bearing the seal of the Earl of Atholl. "And if they canna find a mistake in his favor straightaway, I'll eat my saddle."

"Ye'll have to go to the earl," Ross said. "It's been said his ears are not open only to the chink of coins."

"Aye, but he's a man and an earl. If there's more money to be made with the Moreston, he'll side wi' Craigen. It's only practical," said Gordon.

"Still and all, he may lend Darach an ear. He knew your father, lad. The earl will no' forget Alec MacStruan's aid when he was in a bind." Bruce stood by the fire, his staff held straight before him.

Darach stopped his pacing by the Bruce's side. "Think ye he will? Even after Craigen's been sending him cattle and all?"

Niall snorted. "Our cattle, he sends."

Darach acknowledged this with a nod, but he waited for Bruce to reply.

"'Tis worthy of the attempt," Bruce said. "I dunna how it can hurt. And if ye succeed in pleadin' our case to the earl, ye'll have saved us a fight."

"Are ye sayin' we shouldna fight for what's ours?" Gordon rose from his seat, eyes flashing.

"Whisht, o'course I'm no' sayin' that." Bruce drew himself up. "Ye forget who ye're addressin', *oganach*. Ye'll no' take that tone with yer sovereign."

Gordon looked at Darach. Darach flicked an eyelid at him. He made his obeisance and apology at once.

"Right." Darach looked around at his men. "Ye know what to do in my absence. I'll be back as soon as I may."

"What of Julia?" Bruce asked.

Darach frowned. "What of her?"

"Ye're no' goin' to take her wi' ye?"

Darach wanted to demand if the old man had lost his wits. But something in the Bruce's voice told him that their local sovereign was quite serious.

"Nay," Darach replied. "I'll take Alasdair wi' me. He's spoilin' to be off. Julia will stay here, under the care and guard of all of ye. She's to be treated as well as ever, but she's no' to be allowed to leave the clachan or wander about unattended."

Bruce gave him a look that told him he disapproved but would hold his tongue out of respect for his chief. What was the fellow on about? Darach wondered.

He understood some of Bruce's motives when he went to tell Julia of his plans. She was in the hall, supervising Tommy in the setting of places for the midday meal.

"You're going away? For how long?" she asked, her dark eyes searching his.

"I canna say. I have to speak to the Earl o' Atholl. It's three days ridin' there and back, and no tellin' how lang he may keep us waitin'." She looked worried as she turned away from him. "Ye'll be cared for here, same as always," he added.

She turned back to him. Tommy had gone to the kitchen. She lowered her voice. "Do you have to go?"

"Aye, I do. I'm sorry, lass. What would the lairds do of an evenin' if ye were no' there to tell them a movee tale?"

"Will Alasdair be here?"

He felt his heart contract with anger and jealousy. "Alasdair rides wi' me," he said tersely. "Ye'll be fine here on your ain."

"But—"

"I must go and pack. It's a lang ride." He swung about and strode from the room.

Alasdair again! He slammed open the clothes chest in his chamber and began tossing things onto the bed. He might have known. Alasdair was all the things he, Darach, was not. Tall and slim, yet strong, his brother moved with such easy grace that all female eyes were upon him wherever he went. Alasdair's manners were far more courtly and pleasing to a maid. No saucy maid would ever call him an ogre. And men were drawn to Alasdair's quick wit and unparalleled skill with a sword. It was no wonder Julia preferred he stayed here with her while his beast of an older brother rode away for days at a time.

But she had kissed the ogre. He sat on the

bed, his best shirt in his hands. She had kissed him, not Alasdair.

The memory of that kiss in her room had sustained and tormented him for days. In an instant, he could conjure up the feel and taste of Julia, the sound of her, the sight of her, her special scent of minted water. It had been so fine to him that he'd been unable to resist kissing her again, despite her anger and mistrust of him.

How could he be so besotted with a woman he hardly knew, a woman who was most likely his enemy? And how could he be so base as to be jealous of his own brother? He and Alasdair had their differences, but it wasn't right for a man to permit a woman to come between him and his own flesh and blood.

"Bah," he said and returned to his packing.

Rain fell in torrents the next morning. How appropriate, Julia thought. Saying good-bye to Darach fit in perfectly with the cold rain dripping from her nose and running in rivulets down her back.

· "If you happen to see any pepper or sugar in one of the markets where you're headed, you might pick it up." She felt like an idiot. She was making stupid small talk when she really wanted to beg him to stay or, at the very least, take her with him. She felt ashamed and annoyed at her weakness for the man, but she simply couldn't help herself.

"I'll see what I can manage," he said, tightening the strap on his saddle pack. "Ye might look in upon the Bruce," he said. "He's hale but I know the rains bother him more than he'll ever confess."

"I will. I'll bake him some scones. They're his favorite."

"Well." He turned from his horse. Alasdair stood nearby, making his last preparations.

"Yes. Well, you'd better get started." She smiled, feeling as if her mouth were being worked by thick, resistant rubber bands.

"Aye. Ye should—"

"Well, wee Julia! We're off!" Alasdair swept around from behind her and grabbed her up in his embrace. "And what would it cost a man to get a wee kiss for the road?" he asked, his smile flashing.

"Put me down, you idiot!" She punched him on the shoulder playfully. She couldn't help smiling back at him. At least someone was glad about this journey.

Alasdair put her down but not before he'd planted a loud, smacking kiss on her cheek. "There!" he said cheerily. He swung her around to face Darach. "She's a' yours, big brothair."

Darach's face was darker than the rain clouds over their heads. Julia cringed inwardly. She would have kissed him willingly, if he'd asked. But this way—

Darach snatched her to him. His mouth was upon hers at once, cool and wet with the rain running down his face. She wanted to beg him to stop and she wanted him to go on and on, kissing her for days on end.

She pulled away, the impulse to stop winning out. She didn't want to be kissed because of some unspoken dare between Darach and his brother. She wanted Darach to want her for herself alone. He let her go and she stepped back, her hand clutching at the collar of her gown.

Alasdair gave a long, low whistle and mounted up. He raised his hand to her and smiled. She could only stare at him, surprise and hurt rendering her silent. His smile faded, replaced by a look of sincere contrition. He waved again and moved off, heading toward the northern mists.

Darach swung up onto his horse. "Keep well, Julia," he said softly.

"I will." She could scarcely squeeze the words out around the lump in her throat.

He gave her a nod and then he, too, rode away, the mists swallowing him up in a matter of moments. Julia stood gazing at the spot where his big form had disappeared, the rain sliding over her cheeks and into the corners of her mouth. It was odd, she thought. Somehow the rain tasted salty.

Darach's absence had its compensations. Ross and the other lairds relaxed their watch of her and she was able to scout around the edges of the village and identify paths that might lead her back to the world outside of Clan Mac-Struan.

But she had also begun to worry about her plans to leave. If she had indeed managed to land in the middle ages, it definitely put a kink in her escape plans, she thought to herself as she rambled about the gardens one morning, choosing the freshest produce of the day. Where would she even begin to rediscover the wormhole or time wrinkle that had carried her here? And was it even possible to repeat the process?

Another problem she faced was the clan itself. She'd grown so fond of them so quickly. She'd made a place for herself in their midst and, however tenuous their acceptance of her might be, she enjoyed it. She wanted to know the whole story of their lives, how it all turned out. And she didn't want to read it in a history book, if such a thing could be found.

She bent to select a few tender young onions. She didn't want to think about the other, large, blue-eyed, well-muscled reason for her concern about leaving the clachan. But she had to face it, she told herself, shaking the dirt from the bulbs. She was falling in deeper every day. Leaving Darach would only get harder the longer she remained. Besides, she had absolutely no shred of evidence that he wanted her to stay, even if it were possible. He'd made it clear that she was a prisoner, not a guest.

She tossed the onions into her basket. Whether she was in the fifteenth century or the twentieth, she still had no idea if she could make a relationship with Darach even if he freed her: He was undeniably attractive to her, so much so that his very presence some days made her feel slightly weak-kneed. She'd dreamed of him many nights, especially since the night they'd spent in the old hut on the mountain, dreams that would have received an emphatic X-rating, had they been films. The tension of holding back her desires was increasing with each passing day.

But she was attracted by more than his physical form. She admired his easy command of his men, which, despite her jibes, was respectful and never petty. She appreciated his plainspoken honesty, his passionate care for his people, his acceptance of his odd little clan with all their foibles. She even enjoyed his thundering temper and was beginning to understand some of the difficulties he had with Alasdair. Her mind held a thousand questions she wanted to ask him. Her body longed for a thousand ways to explore his. Her heart knew a yearning that could only be fulfilled by him and the outpourings of his heart. For the first time since her mother had died, she felt truly connected with another human being.

Yet she knew he considered her too strange, too foreign. He was bound up in his clan and his love of this land and with his struggle to be a good leader of his people. He had no room in his life for her.

She added some fresh lettuce to the basket and moved toward the garden gate, a heavy sigh trailing behind her on the breeze. It was a bitter knot she'd tied for herself. She lived in an impossible time. She loved an impossible man.

She shook her head. Her mind was starting to spin from trying to examine all the permutations of time travel, dreams, and love.

Not a good recipe, Addison, she told herself as she exited the garden and headed for the kitchen. It was a mix that was certain to produce nothing but mud. She needed clearer vision if she was going to cope with all of this.

Vision. The word brought a sudden shiver. The visions she'd been seeing in her mother's old mirror were not the sort she wanted. They were yet another ingredient tossed into the mix. Were they real? As real as traveling back in time, she supposed. What did they mean? Who was the woman who spoke to her through the glass, and why was she warning her against Darach?

She went inside and put her basket down on the table. Things were getting more and more weird, she thought. And when the going gets weird, the old saying went, the weird turn pro.

"Hell, girlfriend," she murmured to herself as she began to wash the greens. "That makes no sense."

Yet somehow it did. The face, the voice in the mirror—that was a pro. She knew it as surely as she knew a paring knife from a pot roast. Everything was tied together somehow. And she would feel a whole lot better when that mystery was unraveled. Somehow she needed to know the truth. Without it she was lost.

The Mirror And The Magic

* * *

Darach dove into the icy loch and came up sputtering. The ride had been muddy and wet, and though it was still misty, he needed to rid himself of the grime of travel before they arrived at the earl's home.

Alasdair, always restless, had gone ahead to secure lodging for them in the nearby town. He and Darach had had little to say to one another for most of the ride. Darach knew he was bearing a grudge for Alasdair's behavior on saying good-bye to Julia, but he couldn't bring himself to discuss it. His feelings were still too volatile, too new to bring out in the open, and the confusion they brought was difficult to credit, let alone express.

Julia. The name was everywhere in his mind, his blood, his body. She was his worst torment. She was his sweetest dream.

How had it happened? he asked himself once again. He'd known enough women in his time, but none of them had crawled into his soul and set up a home there. Yet here was this wee bit of a lass, with a tongue like a needle at times, and like the softness of a feather's touch at others, and he was captivated.

He dove again and surfaced, gasping. She infuriated him regularly. She drove him mad with desire and foolish with jealousy. He was perilously close to losing his head over the lass. For one thing, he was fairly certain that she was neither witch nor Moreston, but he clung to both those notions to defend his need to keep her near him and also to hold her at bay. She had him coming and going. He held her prisoner, and yet she was quickly turning into his jailer.

Dammit! He scrubbed at his hair. He was supposed to be in control! He was the one who was supposed to keep his head, lead his people, and not be led astray by a pair of luscious lips and a quick wit. He needed to make a decision about Julia Addison. He must either let her go and remove her confusing presence from his life forever, or he had to find a way to minimize the power of his feelings for her.

He waded to shore and dried himself off. A traitorous voice within him offered up yet another solution: he could also choose to make her his. So she was mad, maddening, and utterly foreign—she was still a woman and he was a man. Why shouldn't he have a chance to taste all those pleasures he'd been dreaming about for so long? Why shouldn't he enjoy her company, share her thoughts?

"Och, ye're sae lathered up about her, ye're talkin' nonsense," he scolded himself.

He pulled his best shirt and a fresh plaid from his pack. As he dressed, he recalled the task before him. He had come here to petition the earl not to grant any more boundary changes to the Morestons. He needed his wits about him. He couldn't afford any more mistakes like the one that had cost his people lives and land two years ago. He couldn't allow anyone else to be lost as Isobel was lost.

He belted on his sword and raked his fingers

through his hair. He stared out over the loch, where mist was rising in tendrils from its surface. The glen beyond stretched green and lush between the hills. He heard birds calling in the woods behind him.

This was what was important, he told himself. The land. The land and his clan.

In that moment he made his decision.

As soon as he returned he would let Julia Addison go free.

Chapter Fourteen

Despite her confusion and longing for Darach, Julia made use of the time while he was away. Tommy was progressing at a great rate in his lessons, and her twentieth-century know-how was challenged to find new and more advanced skills for him to learn. She was taking knitting lessons from Dugan, as well as learning a great deal about chicken husbandry. Liam supplied her with Gaelic and Latin terms for the plants around the clachan, as well as an endless supply of quotes for all occasions. Ross was becoming a fair cook under her tutelage, and all the lairds joined in her morning Yoga sessions.

One evening, after stories around the Bruce's cozy "ingle," as they called the circle of fire in the center of his floor, the men all rose as one and began a strange and wonderful ritual.

"Smàladh an teine," Liam explained to her as the men smoothed the ashes and laid large squares of peat and ashes over the embers. "We call it 'smoorin' the fire.'"

Dugan began to chant in his rumbling bass voice.

> "The Sacred Three
> To save,
> To shield,
> To surround
> The hearth. The household,
> This eve,
> This nicht. This nicht,
> And every nicht,
> Each single nicht."

Julia was delighted. "What a wonderful way to say good night," she said.

"Not only good night, but a blessing on the house," said Liam.

"And best o' all," offered the Bruce, taking her arm as they walked to the door, "in the mornin' the fire kindles as quick as a thought."

He bade them all a good rest, and Ross and Tommy escorted her back to Darach's house, where they were staying in their chief's absence. She climbed the stairs to her room with a smile.

It was like having seven older brothers, she thought. Eight, counting Alasdair. She knew she couldn't make the number nine, for her feelings for Darach were far from brotherly. Yet it seemed as if the other lairds were coming to accept her for who she was now, and included her in most of their activities and even some of their plans.

On the fifth day after Darach and Alasdair had ridden away, the lairds took Julia fishing. Delighted to be out and eager to try her hand at some fish dishes for the men, she dressed in her slacks and sweater and joined them on the hike to the burn, where they said the best fish were to be caught.

Tommy raced ahead and back as they went, and Bruce decorously took up the rear with Julia, whose Highland stamina was not up to par yet. The burn proved to be a fast-running stream, rocky and cold, and the men set out onto the rocks with long-handled nets to catch the plentiful trout.

Julia watched and helped, then, spying some herbs on the bank, hopped over the rocks to examine them. She was happily cropping some wild mint when she saw a figure standing a ways off, among the bracken that ringed the edge of the woods.

She stood and shaded her eyes with her hand. She couldn't make out a face, but the figure was dressed in a plaid and holding his arm as if he'd been injured. She started toward him.

He was of medium height and strongly built, but all Julia saw was the blood that dripped from his left arm. "Hello," she called out as she approached. "Do you need some help?"

"Aye," the man called. His voice sounded

tight, as if it was an effort to speak.

She hurried over to him, wiping her hands on her slacks. "You've hurt your arm. Did you cut it?"

He nodded. She stood a few feet away from him. "I know a little bit about first aid. Would you like me to look at it?"

He nodded, a weak smile lighting his wind-worn features. She returned the smile as she stepped up and peered at the blood-soaked shirt. "I may have to cut that away," she told him. "Do you have a knife or a—"

Her words were cut off. The man sprang behind her and quickly wrapped a leather strap about her throat.

Julia clawed at the choker, her panic a live thing within her. She stretched her mouth wide to scream, but a harsh whisper was all she could summon up. Her breath was close to running out, her chest burned, and her face felt as large as a balloon. She was going to die, she thought, her heart pounding out a frenzied beat. She was going to die out here in the woods, alone.

All at once, her basic self-defense training came back to her. She raised one foot and smashed it down on his instep. Using his surprise to her advantage, she elbowed him, hard, in the solar plexus. He dropped the choker with a yell. She dealt one last blow, slamming her foot against his shin. She heard the bone crack and down he went, gasping in pain. She fled toward the burn.

Ross caught her as she tore over the rocks and

into their midst. "Halt, Julia, what's the matter?" He held her away from him and looked her over. His face went white and hard. "Who's been at ye, lass?"

The others began gathering around her, nets in their hands. Julia could only gasp for breath, glad that it was coming and going as it should, but shuddering with pain at the raw, ragged feeling inside her throat. At last she could speak. "Over there," she said, pointing to the woods. "He—tried—choked me. . . ."

Ross, Tommy, Niall, and Gordon were off before she finished speaking. Liam and Bruce helped her to a seat on the rocks and brought her cool water to drink and a wet cloth to bathe her neck.

"Wee Julia," Bruce said, his voice as stern as any king's, "are ye hurt in any other way save your neck?"

She shook her head. "No. He just—" She held up her hands. It was too painful to speak through her swollen throat.

"Good, good." Liam patted her hand. "Ye're hurt, but still alive. Did ye get a look at this fellow?"

She shook her head once again. "Too fast," she whispered.

Bruce thumped his staff. "Insolent blackguards!" he cried. "There'll be hell to pay for this mischief!"

"Aye," said Liam. "We'll no' let ye go unavenged. We'll hunt him down and see that he's made to pay for his crime, dinna ye worry."

She couldn't do much more than sit there, shaking. The others came back at a run.

"We couldna find him, Julia," Gordon said. "Did ye see which way he ran?"

She stared at him in amazement. "Ran? I can't imagine how he could have run anywhere. I—I broke his leg. I'm sure of it."

"Ye did?" Niall's expression was skeptical.

"Yes," she croaked. "Self-defense classes. I smashed my foot into his shin. I heard the bone snap."

Ross looked upset. "Julia, lass, there's hardly a sign o' anyone havin' been there. Save for this." He lifted a thick leather strap.

"That's what he used—" She pointed to her throat to illustrate. Ross held the strap against her neck and nodded. "It fits the mark," he said to the others. "But it is no' possible ye crippled him, lass. He's run like a rabbit, out o' our hands."

She rubbed her hands over her face. "I don't understand—" she began.

"Whisht," said Bruce. "Ye must rest now, lass. We'll search again." He motioned to Niall and Ross. "Ye gang there, at the south. Tom, ye gang wi' Gordon and take the east. I'll take the west. Liam, ye stay here wi' Julia. Stop her talkin'."

The men dispersed as Bruce directed and it seemed to Julia that they searched for more than an hour. When they returned at last, whistling to one another in the woods, she could tell from their faces that they hadn't found anything more.

"I don't understand it," she said to Ross. "Why was he pretending to be hurt? If he wanted to kill someone, why didn't he just grab me while I wasn't looking and get it over with?"

Tall Ross gazed back at the woods. "There's no grasping the works of some men's minds," he said. "I've known a few in my time that could only go by the name of evil, they were that cold in the heart." He gave her a wan smile. "But we're here now. And ye must stay close. Darach would make mincemeat of us if aught was to happen to ye. And I wouldna blame him."

Julia spent the next day or two being cosseted by the lairds. She was given the place of honor at meals, scarcely allowed in the kitchen, even when she heard the sound of fisticuffs break out from behind its doors. Bruce brought her strong spirits, liberally laced with wild honey to soothe her injured throat. Liam did his inimitable best to talk so steadily that she wouldn't have a chance to use her voice, even if she wanted to.

While she was napping, the lairds held a clan council meeting in the great hall of Darach's house. The idea that Julia had been attacked, nearly killed on their land, was not only troubling, it was an affront to their pride.

"If we canna protect one wee lass wi'in our ain borders," Niall said, "what are we to do if the whole clachan is attacked?"

"Darach wouldna be fit to live wi', should aught happen to our Julia." Tommy nodded his head wisely at the others.

"We canna permit murderers to plague anyone in the clan," Gordon said stoutly. "No' wee Julia, no' Darach, no' even one of our chickens."

Liam's brow was furrowed. "But dinna this event seem odd to the lot o' ye?" he asked. "None but Julia saw this fellow, before or after she was hurt. And she swears by all she holds dear that she broke the villain's leg ere she came away. Yet, when ye went searchin' for him, but moments afterward, he was nowhere to be found."

"What are ye gettin' at?" Niall crossed his arms over his chest.

"I'm only sayin' that it's a most peculiar man who could sneak up wi'out any o' us seein' him, make to choke a lass, and then run away wi' a broken leg."

"Are ye sayin' Julia dinna break his leg?" Tommy looked indignant. "If ye dunna believe she can, I'll set ye straight on that. Julia knows tricks we all could use in a fight."

"Nay." Liam glanced down to where his hands were twisting in his lap. Then he faced the men. "I'm sayin' it looks like witchcraft."

There was a general cry of outrage from the others. Bruce thumped his staff for order. "Calm yerselves!" he cried. "Let the man finish."

"I'm no' sayin' Julia's a witch," Liam said. "I'm sayin' that this fellow that appears and disappears sae blithely may be a witch himself. That, or under the protection of a witch."

There was a profound silence. Gordon was the first to speak.

"Dugan," he said slowly, "tell him it's no' sae

daft an idea. Especially when ye add in the truth o' what Tommy said. If Julia says she broke the man's leg, break it she did. And still the fellow escaped."

"I fear ye're right," Bruce said, before Dugan could load up and repeat this speech. "And therein lies the rub. How may we protect our Julia—and ourselves—from such hale and fearsome forces?"

"We've no guarantees," Niall said. "Magic doesna come out and fight in the open, like an honest soul should. But we canna abide another such attack. We must double our vigilance."

"Aye," said Ross. "We've been lax in our guardin' o' Julia. We thought Darach was bein' too harsh wi' the lass and let her gang freely. And look where it landed her."

"I'll take first watch." Dugan thumped his chest. "If any stranger comes nigh our Julia, I'll quarrel wi' him."

"That's the way," Bruce said, nodding approvingly. "We'll set up a watch on her. She's no' to be alone for a moment. Understood?"

The men nodded. Liam looked worried. "What'll we tell Darach?"

Silence fell once more. Every man looked at the others, pondering the implications. Not only had they permitted Julia to roam free, but through their carelessness she'd come to harm. The source of that harm might even now be roaming their lands, like a wolf circling its prey.

Bruce gave voice to their options. "We may tell him," he said. "And take the consequences like men. But the chief will be that much more worried about Julia and the Morestons. Or we may keep this back from him, double our guard, and will that nothing happens again."

Niall sat back on his stool. "There's no question. We must tell him."

"But if this was merely a chance encounter?" Ross asked. "What then? We'll have worried Darach over a simple attack from a vagabond in the woods."

"Is that what ye truly believe?" Niall's eyes were narrowed.

"Nay." Ross sighed. "I was only thinkin' o' some way to spare Darach, especially if his visit to the earl goes badly for us."

Bruce nodded. "Ye have the right sentiment, Ross," he said kindly. "But Darach's chief o' the MacStruans. He wouldna wish for any o' the clan to keep such an important matter from him, just to save him the worry. 'Twould be disloyal for any o' us to do as much."

"Besides," Tommy piped up, "Darach's in love wi' Julia. He'll want to know if she's in danger, and no' just because he's chief."

"Whisht, lad," Liam said, nudging the boy. "Ye dunna need to speak o' Darach's personal affairs."

"Well, he is," Tommy persisted. "And I dunna know about the rest of ye, but if she were my love, I'd be that angry wi' any man who knew she was in danger and didna tell me."

"That's well," Gordon said, holding up a hand. "But the matter is no' love here. It's survival. I say let's get to work. We'll know what to say to Darach when he comes."

So it was agreed. Julia found herself attended day and night by at least one, and sometimes two, lairds. She wondered at first if they feared that she was planning to leave. But their behavior was so attentive and obliging, she began to think that they were, indeed, concerned for her well-being after the attack in the woods. And as they doubled the watches on the borders, she knew that they feared another and possibly more serious assault. She decided not to mention it, even though a flock of hovering Mac-Struans was annoying at times, and surreal at others. It was enough to know they were acting out of duty and respect, for her and for their clan. She was going to miss them so much.

Chapter Fifteen

"Servant, is my love safe from the clutches of that woman?"

"He iss far from her reach," sighed the water.

Edana stepped back, her smile radiant. Willem had accomplished his mission. The spell of invisibility she'd given to him had worked like a charm. He'd taken the wench out and put her to death, as she had instructed. Today, when she looked into the basin, the woman did not appear or speak to her. All she saw was the rippling, wavering face of her Servant. She had made yet another obstacle disappear from her path.

She frowned. Leaning back over the bowl, she spoke again to the Servant of the mirror-basin. "Servant, is what you have told me the truth?"

"Misstress, I may not lie to theeee."

"No, no. Of course you can't. It isn't possible for you to lie." Edana's smile returned. "Very well. That little matter is out of the way. Now, if Craigen and the Earl of Atholl have done their part, it is almost time for me to reveal myself to my love."

She disposed of the water and laid the basin down on the grass. She moved about the meadow with her odd, limping grace, selecting herbs and flowers for her store of charms and potions.

"Ahh," she cooed. "A lovely bit of henbane, nestled like little jewels here among the rocks."

She gathered the poisonous greens into the pouch she wore at her waist. You never knew when plain old poison was called for, she thought. It had certainly come in handy when Craigen had come to her asking her to rid him of his inconvenient sire.

They'd made quite a pair, she and Craigen. He'd been more than generous with her. But then he'd hardly dare to be anything else, knowing her as he did.

Yet it was time to move on. She was a woman in love, and while her love was patient and enduring, she couldn't wait forever. Craigen and she had a bargain: He would bring about Darach's financial ruin and she would work her will on his people and his lands. That way they would both have their revenge on the MacStruan. And she would have him for her own.

"My, things are a wee bit twisted about, aren't they?" she said to herself as she hunted for mushrooms. But then, what in life wasn't complicated? Love and revenge, death and lust, power and danger. Was there any other way?

She sat on a fallen log and recalled the wild mix of feelings she'd experienced the first time she'd met Darach MacStruan. It had been in Edinburgh, where her family had sent her in embarrassment for her odd ways and her hideous leg. Banished from London to the wild north, she had managed to thrive at the court of James IV. There was no denying her beauty despite her physical deformity, and she could be charming and even witty when she so desired.

There was an added benefit to landing in Scotland, too. In the back streets and out-of-the-way inns of Edinburgh, she'd met folk who practiced the craft that she had discovered when she was still a child in London. Witchcraft.

She was already a skilled practitioner of the black arts when Darach MacStruan strode into the court, his dark hair as glossy as a raven's wing and his eyes exactly the shade of blue that appears in the center of a flame, the place where fire burns the hottest. She desired him on sight, and her desire kindled quickly into a glorious obsession.

But she made a fatal error. In her youth and inexperience, she tried to attract Darach in the way any other woman might: with charm and allure. She had plenty of both. Yet the dark-haired young chieftain was utterly immune to her. It was astounding. She, who had never known failure, tasted a defeat made doubly bitter by the fact that Darach MacStruan hardly even seemed to see her. On the two occasions they met, he wasn't even able to recall her name! And after excusing himself from her side, he went directly to the milky-pale Caroline Farquharson and began a liaison with the pastyfaced chit. It was hardly to be credited.

As fortune would have it, however, Craigen Moreston was waiting in easy reach. Sick with jealousy over Darach's easy conquest of his beloved Caroline, he'd first taken up with Edana in hopes of making Caroline jealous in return. His ploy went completely unnoticed by the Farquharson heiress and his loss was made even more ignominious by Caroline's refusal to take him back, even after Darach had set her aside and moved on to another lady.

When their own sham romance cooled, Edana and Craigen remained friends, of a sort. Craigen learned of her special gifts and was eager to employ her. He begged for a love philter that would melt Caroline's heart, but Edana convinced him it was useless. Love spells were among the most difficult to execute, and human hearts were so wayward that the charms often went awry. Else why would she not have used one on Darach?

They entered into a pact. Craigen would keep Edana in his household, providing for her every need. In return she would aid him in becoming the richest, most powerful laird in the central

Highlands. She had also sought out a young woman whom he could take to wife, a girl so lovely that Craigen kept her locked in the tower, under Edana's watchful eye, until Edana determined that the time was right for the marriage and its consummation. She had seen to it that the girl was already legally named as Craigen's heir, promising that the wench would give him many strong sons, and quickly, too. And if, perchance, something should happen to Craigen, well, Edana would be close at hand to aid the grieving young widow in managing her affairs. Close at hand, with Darach on her arm.

"And now that I've rid myself of that silly little drab of Darach's," Edana purred, "I am ready to complete my plans."

She rose and stretched her arms to the sky. How good it was to be on firm footing again. How good to know that soon she would have her love. And revenge.

"What the devil is a' this?" Darach repeated.

Dugan collapsed heavily out of his headstand. Niall untangled his legs from the Lotus position. Liam toppled out of his Sun-Salute, landing in a heap on the grass. Julia scrambled to her feet, brushing off her slacks. She searched Darach's face. He looked good, healthy and whole. Just angry. What else was new?

"It's Yoga," she told him, smiling. "I was teaching the men how to be more flexible and peaceful. It's good for meditation."

"You think my men are common mummers and acrobats?"

"No. Yoga isn't a game. It's a way of keeping fit—"

"They'd be more fit if they spent their time at their work, not flappin' about like chickens wi' the ague! Niall, come to the hall. Gordon, I saw twa of our kine on the hillside, headed for the woods. Take Tommy and get them back." Darach swung down off his horse and handed the reins to Alasdair. "Tak' care of him, then come to the house."

Julia saw Alasdair flush. He seemed about to say something but changed his mind after a second glance at Darach's thunderous expression. He led the tired horse away to the stable.

Darach strode across the green, barking orders left and right. Julia hurried to catch up to him.

"How did your meeting go?" she asked. "You came back awfully quick. What did the earl say?"

Darach halted and swung about to face her. "I'll thank ye no' to lead my men astray," he said between clenched teeth. "We canna afford such foolishness."

Julia bit her lip and nodded. His face softened somewhat. "I ken ye mean well, Julia, at least wi' most o' what ye do. And we're that grateful to ye for the food and the cleanin' and all that ye do. But times are hard, lass. We canna sit about tradin' songs and stories and dance steps. We have to fight for our livelihood every day."

He shouldered his pack once more. "I want a wash. Then I must speak with Niall and my brother."

She reached out and placed her hand on his arm. "I do understand. I'm sorry if I distracted the men. But they do seem to enjoy it. They need a break sometimes. And things have gone well here while you were away." She searched his face, trying to see what was written in his eyes. "Things didn't go so well with you, did they?" she asked softly.

He shook his head. "They did not."

"I'm so sorry."

He moved away from her, his jaw working. "I won't give it up, though. That land is Mac-Struan land and I'll be havin' it back or die."

A shudder ran through her at the bleak rage in his eyes. She knew he was as good as his word.

He stopped in his tracks. "What the devil is that?" he demanded.

Julia looked and saw Big Dog trotting across the green toward them, a spitting, wriggling puff of gray fur held in his muzzle. "BD!" she cried, running over to the cheerful hound. "No, no! Put her down!"

BD looked at his master. Julia saw thunder and lightning in Darach's expression. BD swung his huge head back to Julia and then carefully deposited the hissing Little Cat at her feet. She scooped up the outraged creature and faced Darach. "She's been mousing for us," she said, smoothing LC's dog-dampened fur. "She stays in the kitchen most of the time."

"Keep it out o' my sight or I'll feed it to the wolves." Darach strode on to the house.

BD snuffled up to Julia and gave LC a friendly lick. The cat swiped at his nose. BD shied back with a yelp. Satisfied that her dignity and position had been avenged, LC settled in the crook of Julia's arm, purring.

Julia groaned. "Perfect timing, you two," she said to the animals. "But then, with Himself the MacStruan, you could be in your dotage before you caught him at a good time."

She heard a soft cough behind her. She turned to see Bruce looking at her with his head cocked to one side. "What's on your mind, Your Grace?" she asked.

"When I was king, I oft had the same trouble as he." He nodded toward Darach's back. "'Tis hard for a king to laugh and sport. It's a sore heavy crown we wear."

She sighed and took his arm. "So I'm learning, sire. I just wish I knew some way to ease his pain." She felt Bruce stiffen and hurried to amend her words. "I don't mean ease it that way, Your Highness. I only wish I could see him smile a bit more."

Bruce patted her hand and they walked on toward the house. "What the man needs is a fool," he said. "Someone to shew him that the world is no' so dark and *greich* a place as he believes." He shook his graying head. "But then, he's young. And his blood's as hot as his sire's. It'll tak' time."

226

The Mirror And The Magic

They both set to work on the evening meal. Once the main course was under way, Julia excused herself and went to change into a dress. Tommy fell into step behind her and accompanied her to her chamber, but she was used to that by now.

She ran a comb through her tangled curls and was about to fasten them back into her usual clasp when her eye fell on her mirror. She didn't want to see it right now, no matter what image floated on its silvery surface. It had been quiet for days and she wanted to keep it that way. All she wanted to know was how Darach was feeling and what the earl had said.

She tossed her hair back over her shoulders, slipped on her shoes, and went softly downstairs to the great hall. For once there was no escort. She heard Darach's deep, rumbling voice as she stood outside the doorway.

There was a pause. "Ye might as well come in, Julia. There's no need to be peepin' at the keyholes."

Her cheeks went hot at his words, but as he didn't seem angry, only resigned, she went in, wondering again at the sixth sense he seemed to have about even the slightest change in the air. She looked around the table at Niall, Alasdair, Ross, and finally Darach. They looked, to a man, tired, grim, and resolute. Her eyes met Darach's and he held her gaze for a long moment. He motioned for her to sit down.

"You know what needs to be done," he said

to the others. "We'll speak again after the meal tonight."

The other men left with tight nods to Julia. As they filed out, she turned to Darach, watching him as he stared at the far wall, his fingers drumming the table.

"How bad was it?" she asked.

There was a long pause. "The Earl of Atholl said I was spoilin' the peace wi' my petty claims. He said there was naught he could do, the deed had been done." He paused again. "He said there was no' enough of us MacStruans to look after so much land, so why should we want such a burden."

"What a jerk," Julia murmured.

He looked at her, startled for an instant, then gave a mirthless grin. "Aye, that about describes the worthless—Well, never mind."

"What will you do next?"

He sighed and slouched in his chair, stretching his long body as best he could. She was so glad he was back. Just looking at him was a feast. She felt again the thrill of pleasure of looking at the relaxed power of him, the leashed strength. But she knew his strength could be unleashed at any moment. She needed to know the cost to him and to his people.

"If the Morestons want our land, we intend to make them pay the price." He toyed with his knife, letting it roll over and over his fingers.

"Meaning?"

"Meaning we tak' their kine. We tax any of their clan that crosses our path. We rout them out and burn whatever houses or crops they plant in our fields. We'll quarrel wi' them, in other words."

"But—isn't that terribly dangerous?"

"Aye. So's starvation. And shame."

"But you're not starving. Couldn't you take him to a higher court?"

"Courts can do naught for us. Morestons hae the money to buy anyone they wish to have it all go their way." He put down his knife and finished off his drink, tipping the cup to drain out the last drops. "Our way is the only way we can win. The only way we can hold our heads up."

"For God's sake, Darach, there are fewer than a dozen of you and hundreds of them! You'll be like lambs to the slaughter. Your pride's not worth that, surely?"

He eyed her sourly. "Takin' the side of yer ain folk, again, Julia?"

She bristled. "My ain folk, as you call them, live in Illinois, as I've told you a hundred times already. I don't know any Morestons. I only know what you've told me. You do remember telling me about them, don't you?"

"Aye. I hope that wasn't a mistake my people will pay for."

She hopped up from her chair and came to stand across from him, her fists on her hips. "You're talking about going out and risking your necks! Pardon me for caring!"

"Ye're not o' the clan. 'Tis no' your concern."

"Oh, right. Well, that may be true to a point,

but what happens to me if you all go out and get yourselves killed?"

He leaned farther back and eyed her up and down. Heat rose in her cheeks once more, and she felt his gaze tingle along her skin like a touch. She held herself still and continued to glare at him.

"Ye'd manage," he drawled. "Ye've managed well enough here."

"What?"

"Well, haven't ye? Ye come to us out o' nowhere, ye won't say where your loyalties lie, and yet here ye are, wearin' our cloth and eatin' our food and sleepin' under our roofs. Kissin' my brothair. Aye, ye'd manage well, no matter where ye landed."

"Are you saying what I think you're saying?"

"You tell me."

"You think I tricked you into taking me in? You think I'm using my sex as a tool to get you to help me? Is that what you think?" She grabbed at the laces of her gown. "Who captured whom?" she demanded as she hauled the dress off over her head. "Who locked me up in that little hole of a room down there under the stairs?" She tossed the dress on the table. Big Dog gave a whine from his spot at Darach's feet.

"Who found you all having a salmonella bakeoff and took over all the cooking and cleaning around here?" She ripped off the undergown next and stood before him, stark naked except for her shoes. "As for kissing your brother, he kissed me exactly once, on the cheek. Whereas you, you big, cement-headed troll, have gone far beyond a peck on the cheek. And furthermore, I'd like to see any one of you big lunkheads try to fit into that!" she yelled, flinging the undergown at his head.

She stomped out of the room and up the stairs, taking little pleasure in Darach's amazed and appreciative stare. She heard a groan and the crash of pottery on stone as she hurled herself into her room and slammed the door.

Muttering to herself, she snatched her still-damp underthings off the clothesline she'd rigged up and pulled them on. She'd manage! She'd manage, he'd said. All right, she'd show him who could manage.

"Excuse me for living, MacStruan!" she yelled.

Darach held the chemise against his chest, staring at the spot on the wall where he'd flung his cup. What had the Lord in heaven been thinking to send him such a problem as Julia Addison? Didn't he have enough to worry about without this worrisome, beautiful, baffling, independent *bean ceadalach*—madwoman— messing about in his life? Didn't he have enough trouble keeping track of his own lairds and their odd ways? And did she have to go about practicing her wild ways on him and his men? Yoga! What the devil was that? Cement-headed, what did that mean? Sam and Ella! Who were they? Why couldn't she be a nice, meek wee maid and go drooping about, immersed in self-pity for the prisoner that she was?

And why in the names of all the saints did she have to strip down to her sweet, bare skin before him, blind him with desire, and storm out, just to prove a point?

He looked around for something else to throw at the wall. He lifted Ross's abandoned cup, but a whine from under the table distracted him momentarity. There was no point in destroying his own property simply because he was vexed.

Vexed? Hell, he wasn't vexed. He'd been poleaxed.

Big Dog came out to stand at his side, his huge head placed carefully in petting range. Darach ruffled the dog's ears. "Did ye see her, fella?" he asked softly. "Paradise walking about on twa legs."

Big Dog snuffled and shoved his head harder against his master's hand. "Oh, aye, I suppose she's no' your sort. But damn me if she isna' mine." And damn me if I'll ever get another glimpse of that sweetness again, let alone be permitted to touch it, he added silently.

But she was so contrary! Was there ever a lass for arguing and fighting like Julia? She stood up to him at every turn, insisted on butting into his affairs, took charge of his own men at the blink of an eye. Who the devil did she think she was?

And still he didn't have the answer to the most important questions of all: Who the devil did he think she was? Was she mad, or was she a Moreston?

And did he care?

This last thought brought him out of his chair, angry at the traitorous turn of his mind. Of course he cared! The safety of his clan depended upon his caring, as well as his ability to think straight and clearly. He recalled the decision he'd made the other morning at the loch. He'd made too many mistakes already. He must let her go, send her away. And he had to do it soon.

He strode to the door, Big Dog dancing along, toenails clicking on the flagstones. Dammit, he didn't want to let her go. But he had to do it.

Out on the green, he took a deep breath of the clear, cold air, its freshness helping him become more alert and focused. He had a raid to lead. It was time to send out a scout. He'd deal with Julia soon enough.

He was soon absorbed in the details of planning the cattle raid. But his men noticed the faraway look on his face from time to time, and the way his gaze would sometimes stray to the walls of his own house.

Julia sat back in the chair and scrubbed a hand over her eyes. She had been poring over Darach's books for more than an hour and her frustration made the task doubly hard. She recalled enough of her high school Latin to permit her to read about half of what was written. From those clues, she could puzzle out maybe an eighth more, but beyond that she was lost. To top it off, there didn't seem to be anything in the books that addressed the subject of travel through time.

She wanted to give up. She'd begun right after breakfast, as soon as Darach had gone out to make the rounds of the cattle with his men. She knew they'd laid their raiding plans, but Darach would tell her nothing. Out of pride, she refused to ask the lairds, either. She wouldn't give Darach the satisfaction of knowing how much she cared about all of them. But she knew they were most likely sneaking about on Moreston land right now, herding their enemy's cattle away to their own hills.

She had made up her mind last night, as she lay in her bed, listening to the lowing of the cattle and the wind among the budding branches. She had to find out exactly what had happened to her. That was where she had to start, in order to get away and get back to her own time.

Her departure would mean one less mouth to feed, she'd told herself when her heart protested leaving the clan, leaving Darach. One less soul for the chief to watch and worry over. All she had to do was figure out how to accomplish it.

She leaned back over the book that was opened wide before her. She couldn't help imagining what a book such as this one would bring from the book dealers in New York. Librarians would be peeing their pants for a peek at such a volume, she thought, with its heavy leather binding, its gilt-touched illuminations.

The Mirror And The Magic

"A good tale, is it?" a voice drawled.

She started and looked up to see Alasdair leaning in the doorway. He was tossing an apple up and down in one long, elegant hand.

She shook her head. "No. I'm afraid it isn't. Or if it is, I can't tell."

He stepped into the room. "Can ye no' read?"

"I can. English. But my Latin is rusty."

He came to her side and leaned over the book. "Ah. The *Rosa Anglica*. A most learned text. Planning some surgery on my brothair, lass?"

She laughed. "No. I don't think anything would cut through that thick hide of his."

Alasdair chuckled. "Ye've a point. But what do ye wish to know from auld friend John of Gaddesden? Englishman though he be."

"I . . ." She shook her head. "I can't tell you. You'll lock me up again and this time you'll throw away the key."

"Why no' let me be the judge o' that?" He pulled a stool up beside her. "I'm no' Darach, ye know."

She looked at him thoughtfully. "It must be a real pain sometimes to be his brother."

"Aye, it has its trials. And its rewards."

"You love him, don't you?"

"I do. The great woolly beastie." He cleared his throat. "But back to the book. Ye say ye canno' read the Latin. I can read it. Where shall I start?"

She bit her lip. "Are you sure? I want to know about spells and charms."

Alasdair pushed up from his seat. "I'm off."

"I was afraid you'd say that. Please, Alasdair." She caught at his plaid. "Don't tell Darach about this. You can forget I ever mentioned anything about it. I don't want you involved."

He scowled. "Why do ye want to know such things? They're no' for healin', are they?"

"No."

He went to the door and shut it, then crossed back to stand on the far side of the table from her. "All right. I'll no' be sae quick to judge ye, lass. Tell me what's got ye huntin' for such unairthly knowledge."

Julia told him. As she described her experiences, he kept a studious, stern expression on his face, but she could see from his eyes, so like Darach's in their blue brilliance, that he was intrigued. When she had finished, he stroked his chin and gazed at her with keen interest.

"So ye think ye've come here under magical means no' of your ain makin'? And that there's some magic way by which ye could gae back again?" He considered for a moment. "It sounds as mad as auld mad MacPhee."

She slumped. "I was afraid you'd say that, too. You're probably right."

"Just because it sounds mad doesna mean ye're wrong." His smile flashed at her. "Mad MacPhee was the finest cattle breeder in the Highlands. No one cared much that he talked to his furniture, once they'd had one o' his bulls mate up wi' their heifers."

"You mean it? You'll help me then?"

He turned the book around his way. "Let's

see. Auld John begins wi' the head and works his way down to the feet. Choose a body part, lass, and we shall see if there's a charm that pertains to your problem."

Julia jumped up and ran around the table to give him a hug. "Thank you! Thank you!" she cried. "I can't tell you how good it feels to have someone not write me off as a nut-case foreigner!"

He colored as red as a berry and patted her shoulder. "Let's get to work, then," he said huskily. "It would be best to keep this from Darach," he added. "He's no' likely to tolerate any talk o' magic."

"Tell me about it."

"There's no time for that. Let's be about it before Himself gets back."

Chapter Sixteen

They worked all day in the library, discarding one idea after the other, until at last, as the shadows in the room grew long and Julia began to feel cramped and chilled, she rose and stretched.

"Well," she announced as Alasdair sat back and looked at her questioningly. "We gave it a shot. But I don't think any of this is what I'm looking for. I know the moment everything changed. It was just before I fell down the hill and the lairds found me. I wish I could recall what it was that was so different about that moment. It was all so weird." She yawned widely, covering her mouth. "I'm sorry," she said.

"'Tis no matter." He tipped back on the chair, his long legs balancing him perfectly. "But what ye just said pricks my mind. That about the moment when ye say ye went from one time to another."

"Yes?"

"Aye. What if ye went back there? To that place? Might it no' tell ye something, give ye some recollection?"

She gaped at him. "I am an idiot. You are a genius. Of course! That's it! I have to go back to the spot, I'll bet. It was near a bunch of big stones, all in a circle. I'll go back there and then—" She slumped into her chair once more. "It's no good."

"Why not?"

"First of all, Darach won't let me out of the village. Second of all, even if I could get out of here, I was blindfolded for most of the trip, remember? And I was in a panic to begin with. I couldn't find that place again with a map."

"Ye won't need one."

She looked at him.

"Ye'll have me to guide ye. Besides, those were the standin' stones ye saw. They've been the marker between the eastern limits o' our land and the Morestons' for aye generations."

"But—"

The door blew open with hurricane force. Darach stood in the doorway, his great shoulders filling the space in silhouette. Even with his face half in shadow, Julia could read the distrust and anger in his eyes.

"This is a charmin' scene," he growled.

"Darach—" Julia began.

"Save it." He jerked his head at his brother.

"Get along and help Dugan and Niall. Ye've been sportin' lang enough."

Alasdair got up slowly, unfolding his long, lean frame and taking a challenging stance that matched Darach's to perfection. "Who says I've been sportin'?"

"I do. Hangin' about indoors wi' a woman. Behind closed doors. What else would ye call it?"

"I don't know, Darach. Ye seem to've made up your mind awful young."

"That's rich comin' from ye, youngster. Now do as I say. Niall and the others need yer help."

Alasdair seemed about to refuse. Julia held her breath. Then Alasdair relaxed and sauntered toward the door.

"Thank you, Alasdair," she called after him. "I'm much obliged for your help."

He turned and gave her one of his brilliant smiles. "Think nothin' of it, lass. 'Twas pure pleasure."

He strolled out. Darach made way for him, but kept his hands clenched at his sides. When Alasdair had gone, he turned to Julia.

"So, another of the lairds has fallen under yer spell?"

"Alasdair is a friend. He was helping me read some of these books. My Latin isn't too good."

"A lass like you doesna need the Latin."

She hung on to her temper. "Perhaps not. But I'd think you'd have the good sense to know that even a man like you needs his only brother!"

She brushed past him. He caught her wrist. "Don't go yet."

She glared up at him. "Why shouldn't I?"

"If ye're lookin' for trouble, ye don't have to go lookin' in my family's books."

She sighed. "I'm not looking for trouble. I'm looking for a way home."

"What does that mean?"

She shook her head. "I didn't expect you to understand. Let me go, please. I've got to go see about dinner."

He pulled her closer. She was held close to his side, looking up into those angry eyes that also seemed to speak of something else, something she didn't want to name.

"I'm no' a man to be trifled wi'."

"I'm not trifling with you or anyone else. I'm trying to find a way home."

"What does that mean?"

"You figure it out."

"Ye take chances, lass."

"I have to."

He tightened his hold on her, slipping his arm around her waist. "I won't have ye messin' wi' my baby brother."

"He's not a baby."

"Nay. He's not. He's as headstrong and stubborn as you are."

"Is that why you try to bully both of us?"

His mouth was mere inches from hers, his eyes boring into hers. "Is that what I am, Julia?" he asked, his voice suddenly soft and much, much more dangerous. "A bully?"

She swallowed against the rising speed of her heart and breathing, her mouth suddenly dry. She could feel the heat of his body against hers, the steady rise and fall of his own quick breaths. The steely arm that encircled her waist held her fast but not brutally so, and she damned herself for the thought that she wanted to stay right here in his arms.

"N-no," she murmured. "You're not a bully. But you're close to it." She raised her eyes to his, braving the intensity of their blue fire. "You try too hard to control everything and everyone around you. Don't you ever get tired of trying to make the world go around every day?"

He flushed a dull, sullen red. "I'm the chief," he said tersely.

"I know," she said sadly. "I know."

He let her go abruptly. "Go see to yer meal. Tommy's in there, likely cuttin' his toes off wi' the carvin' knife."

She took her chance and scurried away, relieved that she was out of the too exciting, too pleasurable circle of his embrace. She ate her supper in the kitchen that night, with only Big Dog for company.

But when she went to bed that night, the dreams returned, those half-waking, half-sleeping images of Darach: Darach walking toward her, Darach holding her, Darach rising above her like a great, loving force—

She shook herself awake, then got up and padded to the window. She opened the shutters and looked out over the moonlit green. Two fat sheep grazed contentedly on its lush grass. No light shone from any of the cottages that circled the green, though the moon cast a bright reflection off their white-limed walls. Such a beautiful place, she thought. A place of laughter and song, sorrow and tears, hard work and simple rewards.

And she must leave it. Now. Lest her heart lead her into disaster.

She turned away and began to dress. She slipped past a snoring Dugan without stirring a hair on his head. Shortly before dawn, the fat old sheep gazed at her with mild interest as she crossed the green and headed up the trail into the woods.

"It's gettin' nigh onto time, Darach."

Ross stood before him, his eyes alight and hopeful. Darach gave him a nod and a smile. "So it is," he said, putting the finishing touches on the bridle he was mending. "What say the others?"

Ross grinned. "They're fair ready to fly up the hills. We can be ready to leave first thing in the mornin'."

"We'll do some hunting on the way," Darach said. "It'll be time for that, as well. But tomorrow morning should be fine."

"Are ye—" Ross left off, uncertain.

"Am I what?"

"Will ye bring Julia?"

Darach muttered an oath. "Damn. I'd no' thought o' that. She'll have to come. There's no one to stay here to watch over her." He set his tools aside and got to his feet. "I'll tell her to make ready for the trip. Mayhap she can prepare some food to take along."

"Ye're goin' to tell her . . . the secret?"

"In time, aye. There won't be a secret once she's been wi' us, will there?"

"No, I guess not."

"Call her down, Ross. She's sleepin' late this morn, it appears."

"Aye, Darach."

Ross was back soon, his face creased with worry. "She's no' in her room, Darach."

"Well, then, she's either in the kitchen or the pantry. She's no' allowed to go anywhere else."

"I looked there."

Darach frowned. "She has to be somewhere in the house. Ye search again in the kitchen. I'll try the library. Maybe she's taken to the books."

Darach met up with Alasdair in the great hall. "So, do ye ken it's time once again?" the younger man asked affably. "The men have that look in their eyes."

"Aye. Have ye seen Julia this morn?"

"No. I got my own breakfast early, before she'd risen."

Darach hurried to the library. A quick search told him she was nowhere about. He strode back into the hall.

"What is it?" Alasdair asked.

Ross appeared once more, with Niall at his side. "Darach, there's something ye should know."

Darach scowled. "I dunna have time—"

Niall raised his hand. "It's about Julia."

Darach searched their faces. He didn't like what he saw there. "Tell me."

"While ye and Alasdair were away to the earl's, Julia came out wi' us for some fishin' in the burn."

"What? Ye took her out—where are your wits, man?"

Niall raised his hands again to placate him. "We ken now we did wrong, Darach. But while we were out, Julia slipped away to the meadow, lookin' for herbs, she said."

Ross took up the tale. "She saw a man, bleedin' at the shoulder and beckonin' to her frae the woods. Ye know Julia, she'd no' hesitate to aid a creature in need. She went to him and. . . ."

"And?" Darach felt his heart contract with fear.

"She was attacked. He slipped a strap about her neck and choked her."

"Dammit! Why did ye no' tell me this before?"

Niall took over again. "We planned to, Darach. We knew it was our duty. But ye brought home such bad tidings and we got sae caught up in plannin' the raid, it got set by."

Darach looked about the room, searching for aid in grasping this news. "But I saw no marks on her," he said at last. "And she's in proper spirits."

"Aye," said Ross. "But we all saw the marks. She could scarce speak a word for three days."

"The man," Darach said, his hand on the hilt of his sword.

Niall shook his head. "We couldna find him. Nor no trace o' him. Only the strap." He glanced at Ross and licked his lips.

"And?" Darach prompted, knowing his men all too well.

"Julia says she broke the man's leg and that's how she escaped. Tommy showed us how she'd taught him to do it and it could have happened so. But we ne'er could find the fellow, for all the blood she saw and his leg broken into the bargain." Ross shifted on his feet.

"There's more?"

"Aye," said Niall. "Because he vanished so and we couldna find him, we were . . . well, as it was . . . we thought it might be that. . . ."

"Spill it!"

"We think he might have been a witch," Ross blurted.

Darach sagged. "Ye don't."

"We do," Niall said, beginning to rally behind his fellow lairds. "And we think it's somethin' ye should know if Julia's turned up missin'."

Darach didn't answer. He took the stairs two at a time and burst into Julia's chamber. There was no sign of her there either. The ashes in the fireplace were cold, the bed was cold, and there was no sign of her breeches outfit or her pouch.

"Damn it!"

"She's gone, then?" Alasdair stood in the doorway. Ross and Niall crowded up behind him.

"Aye." Darach pushed past them and headed for his own room. Alasdair followed. He watched as Darach flung things into his saddle bag and belted on his sword.

"Think ye she's gone to the Moreston?" Alasdair asked.

Darach grunted. "I'd never claim to ken what Julia's goin' to do next. Maybe she has. Maybe she's simply gone roamin', lookin' for her america or dumpsters or whatever. But I'll bring her back or know the reason why."

He looked around the room, making a mental check of anything he might have left. His eye fell on his knife and he picked it up and slipped it into the top of his boot. He turned to his brother. "Ye and Niall lead the men up the hills, as planned," he told him. "I'll join ye up there, as soon as I catch our wild bird that's flown."

"Ye'll no' hurt her?" Alasdair's eyes were suspicious.

"Ye take too much upon yourself, lad. Never ye mind what I'll do wi' Julia. Ye get the men safely up into the hills."

Alasdair caught his arm as he went past, out the door. "I'm just tellin' ye, Darach. Hurt her and ye'll answer to me."

"Ye alone?"

Alasdair flushed. "Aye, if need be. But I'll wager the rest of the lads will stand wi' me on this. Julia's grown dear to us."

Darach gave him a long, steely stare. "Do your job, oganach," he said. And he was gone.

* * *

Julia traveled along the edge of the burn, staying alert for any familiar sights or the sounds of pursuing MacStruans. She'd been walking for hours, going along as best she could by instinct, memory, and the small amount of information that Alasdair had given her about the standing stones.

Another lovely day, she noted with a sigh. She'd always thought of the Highlands as being wet and cold year-round, but once the morning ground mists had vanished, she was walking through sunny glens and warm, shady woodlands. Flowers and blossoming shrubs sprang up in patches here and there, and she had the feeling that she was part of one of the first mornings of the world.

She wished she knew where she was going, though. She knew she was looking for one of the ancient circles of stones put up long before even the Romans had marched over the British Isles. Now that she thought of it, one of those self-same stones had probably made her trip and fall, sending her tumbling down the hill and into the hands of Clan Looney Tunes. If she could get back there, perhaps some of this Alice in Wonderland stuff would fade and she'd be back in her own world, with her own car. *With lobsters from York chasing me.*

That thought brought her to a sudden standstill. She was still on the run from those thugs who'd been chasing her ever since that chilly day in Martine's kitchen. She was a witness to a gangland murder, and that hadn't changed.

She was going to be in danger from them even if she was free of the hold of Darach MacStruan.

She had another awful thought. What if that man in the woods, the one who had choked her, had been one of the mobsters? Were they trying to make her believe she was crazy somehow, and not capable of identifying the men who'd committed those murders back in New York?

Oh, damnation, Addison. It was all too confusing. *Just get on the road and get out.*

She trudged on, her watch expanding to include gunmen with termination on their minds and woodland assassins with injured legs. Even as she walked, though, she considered her options. If she managed to get back to where she'd started on that strange day that seemed ages ago, what was she going to do? Clearly Gilette's men had tracked her all the way from New York, across the Continent, around some of the Greek islands, and finally, to a village in the Scottish Highlands. They'd find her, no matter what.

She stopped at a fast-running bend in the stream and took a drink. She sat down on a rock and rested, bathing her forehead with the chilly water.

What would Darach do? she wondered idly. If he'd been a witness to a killing, would he have gone to the police right away? Or would he have hit the road, as she had, shoving his things into a suitcase at the urging of his friend and taking the first flight out of the country?

Somehow she didn't think he'd have run. He

was not above stealing cattle from his enemies; he was not above fighting and killing, or above ordering everyone about as if he were Caesar himself. But to witness a cold-blooded murder and tell no one what he'd seen? Uh-uh. He'd have taken his Conan the Morally Upright self on down to the local precinct and reported in. It would be his duty, as he'd so often said. And, she thought with a sigh as she rose to continue her hike, he wouldn't have tolerated hiding away, as she had.

She grinned at the idea of Darach MacStruan in hiding. For one thing, Darach would be hard-pressed to conceal his striking face and his warrior's body, let alone his regal airs and arrogant ways. For another, he'd probably just pick up those goons of Gilette's, bang their heads together, and toss them into the freezer, lest they threaten his clan.

She kicked at a tree root. He was the most irritating man! So damned gorgeous and so damned bossy. She never knew if she wanted to bop him upside the head with a Louisville Slugger or jump his bones. As often as not, she wanted to do both.

Sadness captured her heart as she thought that she'd never have the chance to do either one. She was going out of his life forever. There would never be a time to learn if his kisses made her world tremble, time after time, as they had done so far. She'd never know the pleasure of being enclosed in his powerful arms and held against that rock-solid chest. She'd never have the chance to learn the answers to all the questions she had about him.

Would he care? she wondered. Beyond being totally ticked that his prisoner had escaped, perhaps to run to the dreaded Morestons, would he give a flying flip if she disappeared?

There was a rustling in the brush on the ridge above her head. She glanced up but saw nothing. Still, something made her freeze and listen. She heard panting, like a dog who'd been running awhile.

"All right, Big Dog," she called out. "You've found me. Come on out and bring Darach with you." She should have known she couldn't escape him, after all. She looked up with a grin of resignation.

Her grin faded as she looked into the pale eyes and rough gray coat of a wolf.

Darach was in a fine temper by the time he reached the burn on the far side of the woods below the village. Guiding his horse carefully along its track, he could make out a footprint here, a broken branch there, all signs that told him that someone had passed this way recently, someone who wasn't at all careful about concealing her path. He also noted that, as far as he could tell, she was alone.

The madness of the lass! What was she about? These lands held a multitude of dangers for the strongest of men. What chance did she think she had out here alone?

Unless she knew her way. Unless she had

made arrangements for someone to meet her.

He hated the thoughts he was thinking. He'd thought he knew Julia. She was a trifle outlandish, a mite eccentric, but he'd lived with eccentricity almost all his life. She'd been kind to his men, thorough in her job, faithful in most every way.

But she had fled. She'd taken advantage of his willingness to show his trust in her and she'd stolen away like a thief in the night.

He wanted to shake her. He wanted to turn her over his knee. He wanted to bind her to him and never let her go. That was what put him in an even fouler temper. His innate honesty refused to deny that he wanted Julia in his arms, in his bed, in his life. And that was a large part of why he was so hot to find her.

Fool! He railed at himself in English and Gaelic, called himself every kind of idiot, but he couldn't let go of the longing and the fierce desire that swamped his senses whenever he so much as thought of her. Did she have any notion of the havoc she wreaked upon him just by walking past him? Did she have the slightest inkling that she invaded his dreams every night and tormented him so sweetly therein that his hands clenched down on the reins even now?

She couldn't have. Barbarian, she'd called him. Ogre. Bully. Hadn't he seen her often enough with Alasdair? Alasdair, who championed her cause at every turn and whose refined features and learned ways would appeal to a lass of Julia's tastes far more than his own rough style.

"Damnation," he grumbled, steering his mount around a fallen log. The merest thought of Alasdair and Julia sharing even the most chaste of kisses caused his blood to heat like an ironsmith's forge. Brother or no, he wouldn't tolerate that!

A scream ripped through the silence of the woods. He gathered the reins and spurred his horse across the meadow, heading toward the sound. He heard it again, even over the pounding of hooves.

Sweet Jesu! It was Julia!

Chapter Seventeen

Julia faced the wolf, too terrified to move. She'd always heard wolves were shy creatures who'd run away rather than challenge a human being. But this beast looked utterly fearless and most definitely hungry.

She saw him gather himself to spring and her body came to life. She leapt away, out of his path, a scream erupting from her throat with gratifying power. Her back came up against sheer rock; her feet tangled in a root that snaked along the ground. She twisted about to see her pursuer, frantically working at the vine that held her captive only a few feet from those terrible jaws.

The wolf faced her again, his feet braced. She smelled the heat of him, the wildness. He hunkered down again, growling, ready to pounce.

She screamed as another furry body hurled itself from the rock above and engaged the wolf in battle. Savage growls and grunts emanated from the whirling tangle of fur, teeth, tails, and ears.

"Oh, God! Big Dog, look out! Get away!" she screamed. She managed to free her feet and lunged toward the pair.

"Back off!" came a shout.

She looked up to see Darach leap from his running horse and streak across the meadow, his knife in hand. To her horror, he waded into the fray, slashing at the wolf with a power that seemed as savage as any beast. There came a loud yelp, and Big Dog was tossed clear of his opponent. Now it was Darach and the wolf, wrestling and grunting together among the rocks and vines.

Julia hung back, fearful that any interference might cost Darach his life. Big Dog lay on the other side of them from her. She tried edging toward him.

There was a sudden, gurgling cry, and Darach leapt back from the wolf, his knife upraised and bloody. The animal flopped to the ground, gave one last violent lunge, as if to continue the fight, then fell once more, stilled by death.

"Darach!" She flung herself into his arms, shaking and sobbing. "Are you all right?"

His arms closed about her for a moment, holding her tight against his chest, which still heaved with the effort of the battle. She raised her head to look at him and he kissed her, roughly, thoroughly.

When he lifted his head, she said, "Oh, Darach, I thought—"

He thrust her out at arm's length. "What the devil were ye tryin' to do?" he cried. "Have ye porridge where your wits should be?"

"What—?" She was shocked at his sudden turn from tenderness to rage.

"Ye could hae been killed! I could hae been killed. Big Dog could hae been killed!"

"Big Dog!" she gasped. She twisted out of his grasp and ran to the big animal's side. "Oh, BD, you've got to be all right. You saved my life, you big sweetie!"

She moved her hands all over him. He had several bites, but none of them looked too deep or serious. She lifted his head onto her lap and lifted his eyelids. His eyes were clear and not rolled back in his head. She shook him gently.

"He's been knocked out," she said to Darach, who hovered nearby, his own face mirroring her concern. "Do you have any of that liquor you guys carry around?"

He loped off without a word and was soon back with a flask. She took it and said, "Hold his head up and help me pry open his muzzle. I'm going to try to get some of this into him."

Together they managed to pour some of the liquor down Big Dog's throat. The animal came to life with a loud snort and shook himself free of their hold. He coughed a couple of times and then gave them both a stare of such obvious annoyance that they both laughed.

"Atta boy," Julia said, rising to go and stroke the huge head. "You're as hardheaded as your master. No wolf is going to get the best of you."

"Many thanks," Darach said dryly.

She straightened up. "Thank you, Darach," she said solemnly. "I know I wouldn't have survived without you. I don't know if BD here would have, either."

"Ye're welcome. Now, why the devil were ye out here in the first place?"

"I need to go, Darach. I have to get back to my old world. You've told me often enough that I don't belong here, and you're absolutely right. I thought if I went off on my own, I'd save you the trouble of feeling responsible for me. If I went on my own, it wouldn't be the same as if you had let me go."

He swore under his breath. "Ye thought to save me the responsibility of being the one who let ye escape? Ye'd save me the trouble of wonderin' if ye had gone to the Morestons? Save me the trouble of thinkin' of ye lyin' dead here in the wilds?"

"No, I didn't think that. I meant well, I swear." She could feel her own anger rising. "You can't blame me for wanting to get out of someplace where I don't belong, where I can never fit in. And how do you know that I don't have responsibilities of my own, in my own . . . world? You don't have the market cornered on duties, you know."

"I do not. But I do what's my duty and leave

the rest alone. I don't go tryin' to take on the tasks of others!"

"The hell you don't! You're the champion of I'd Better Do It Myself Or It Won't Get Done Right. I've watched you snatch responsibility right out of your own brother's hands because you can't let go of your control over him and everything else to do with Clan MacStruan."

"Ye would take his part."

"Aye, that I would!" She was startled by the burr in her accent, but she was too angry to stop and contemplate the ramifications. "Alasdair is a good friend to me and he doesna think I'm a porridge-brained ninny."

"I never said ye were a ninny."

"You said I had porridge for brains not fifteen minutes ago."

"Oh. Aye, so I did. But ye scared me that bad, lass! I thought ye were goin' to be killed."

"Oh, right! So you rode in to the rescue and now you think you own me!"

"If ye aren't the damnedest, most confounding little—" He lunged forward and grabbed her by the arms. "Listen to me, Julia, I'm no' goin' to apologize for wantin' to have ye alive and here, wi' me!"

With that he crushed her to him once more and kissed her. It was as if her whole world were melting away and being remade. Her feelings for Darach ran so deep and strong that they frightened her. She wanted him with such complete passion that she longed for a way to burrow inside him and take root there.

She wound her arms about his neck, anger and love and longing mingling in the kisses they shared. Darach lifted her completely off the ground, holding her in an embrace that was as right as her own name. She clung to him, willing this moment to go on forever.

"Julia," he murmured against her neck. "Ah, Julia, if I'd lost ye!"

She hushed his mouth with hers.

BD gave a whine beside them, then a warning bark. Darach let Julia down gently, his hand moving to his sword. Julia looked at Darach.

"Another wolf?" she whispered.

He shook his head. "This one goes on twa legs, if it is. Come." He held out his hand. "We ride."

He gave a low whistle to Big Dog and hurried Julia to the waiting horse. He climbed up and pulled her up behind him. "Hold on."

They took off up the meadow and over the hills. Julia glanced back. For a moment she thought she saw someone standing in the spot where the wolf had perched, waiting to spring at her. She blinked and the figure was gone. But she would swear she'd seen it. And that it was a woman clad all in green.

It wasn't long before Darach and Julia met up with the lairds on the trail. All of them had bows and arrows, knives, and swords with them. Julia tugged at Darach's plaid. "Are they going to war?"

He grinned. "Nay. Not unless the deer in these

woods have taken to wielding cannon and sword."

"Oh, hunting."

The men crowded around them. "Where'd ye go, Julia?" Tommy asked. "We were that scared when we found ye gone."

His innocent concern touched her heart. Not everyone thought she'd run off with evil intent, she thought. "I went off to find the spot where you and the others found me that first day," she said, knowing that she was telling only half the truth. "But I was foolish to leave. I shouldn't have gone off on my own."

"Amen to that," said Alasdair. "I'm glad you're safe, Julia."

She gave him a brief smile but kept silent about the trouble she'd gotten into, or how Darach had come to her aid. Darach had all but said he suspected her of loving Alasdair, and that Alasdair returned those feelings. She wanted no such mistaken beliefs.

"So what have you got?" Darach said.

The men showed a brace of wild fowl, several fat rabbits, and an adult deer. Darach clapped Niall and Gordon on the backs for the deer and praised the others for such a good catch in such a short time.

"Shall we ride, then?" he asked.

"Aye."

The men had several horses among them. Two of them had been pressed into service as pack animals. Julia never failed to wonder at the strength and lung power of all the men, even auld Bruce. They could walk and even run up and down these wild, rocky hills and glens for miles uncounted and never seem to tire. Even Big Dog trotted along as if this were a short stroll in the park. She slid down from behind Darach when they stopped to let the horses water and tried keeping up with the group. She managed for a while but, slowly and surely, she began to flag and had to accept Darach's boost back up onto his mount.

"I don't know how you do it," she said, gathering up the reins he handed to her.

He smiled. "We're born to it, I suppose. Ye'll come to have the wind to run up and down the Highlands, too, someday." He strode on at her side, guiding the horse here and there over a dangerous patch.

She heard his words again, ringing in her heart. *Ye'll come to have the wind to run up and down the Highlands, too, someday.* He'd spoken as if he not only expected her to stay, but he wanted her to stay. For the first time, he was treating her as if she weren't a mere outlander, but someone who was, at least in part, a member of his people.

They began to climb higher as they emerged from the woods. Rocks and crevices sported low, scrubby plants, and the wind whipped around the steep trails with a crisp, stinging freshness. She leaned toward Darach. "This can't be the way back to the village," she said. "I didn't come this far when I was on my own.

And I don't remember these mountains."

"We're no' goin' back to the village tonight."

"It's impossible!"

Edana was beside herself. She wanted to fling herself after the departing couple and scratch their faces into pulp. Another woman still occupied a place in Darach's life—in his arms—the same woman she'd seen in her mirror-basin. The same woman her loyal Willem had sworn he'd killed.

She gritted her teeth. It was well that Willem had disappeared from Castle Moreston recently. If he dared show his face there again, she'd make certain he writhed in such torment he'd beg for the relief of hell's fires.

She marched to and fro on the ridge, fists clenched, nails biting into her palms. How could it have happened? The mirror had told her the deed was done—

"Fool! Imbecile!" she railed at herself. Her mind replayed her mistake.

Servant, is my love safe from the clutches of that woman?

He iss far from her reach.

The idiotic basin had taken her question literally! Darach had been with the Earl of Atholl; of course he was out of her reach. For the basin to answer her as she wished, she needed to ask it precisely what she wanted to know, else the Servant would only respond to the words she spoke. And she had not thought to require the Servant to show her the woman's whereabouts—alive or dead.

She put her hands on her hips. The gypsy woman who had been her teacher had forgotten to tell her of such complications. Honestly, she thought, it was getting more and more difficult to depend on anyone.

She looked down at the body of the wolf below and gave an exasperated sigh. If only she'd known the woman was out here alone. She could have sent Grif after her on purpose. As it was, he'd found her on his own, but Darach had done away with her pet.

Her Darach was so strong! She smiled at the memory of his fierce struggle with the ravening Grif. She could make use of that strength, too.

But he'd been trapped once again by that she-wolf in breeches, Edana thought as she turned away from the ledge and headed back toward the castle. Men were such fools. She sighed again. She was going to have to rescue him from the clutches of this annoying intruder. And she'd make sure the job was done right this time.

She pondered her choices on her solitary walk home. Sometimes she wished she hadn't struck that bargain with Craigen. He was taking an abominably long time to bring Darach's clan to their knees, and he only listened to her counsel half the time. Another foolish male. With this woman in Darach's life, she might have to step in and make things happen a bit faster.

She frowned. No. No, she wasn't going to hurry this. She'd worked too long and hard to rush things now. She'd find a way to be rid of the woman. After all, she was merely a woman and Edana had already gotten rid of one woman who'd dared to come too close to Darach. What was another in the name of true love?

"Where are we going?" Julia asked again.

"Ye'll know when we get there."

"Darach!" She gave him an exasperated glare.

He grinned. "Dinna fash yoursel', impatience. Ye'll learn all in good time."

"I'll fash myself if I want to!" she retorted. "And what does that mean, anyway?"

"It means don't go rushin' about, pesterin' to be told everythin' all at once."

"Beast!"

He grinned that maddening grin and turned away to talk with Niall.

They climbed up one hill and down another, then entered another wood. The days were long up here in the north, Julia knew, but it was growing late. She wondered if they would camp for the night. She didn't like the idea of sleeping out in wolf country, even surrounded as she was with men capable of killing a wolf in hand-to-hand combat.

They climbed up out of the woods as the sun was beginning to lower itself toward the western peaks. The men stopped at a stream and to her surprise, went off behind the shelter of some trees and waded in for a bath. She looked at Darach in wonder.

"They like to be clean when we come up

264

here." He gave her another of his wicked grins. "Do ye mind if I do the same? Perhaps ye'd like to join us?"

"No, thank you," she said quickly. "I've never been one for group bathing."

He shrugged and began to undo his belt and plaid. He was down to his long shirt alone when he looked up to see her gazing at him, wide-eyed. He chuckled and shook his finger at her. "A more modest maid would look away," he scolded.

"I'm not a maid," she said tartly, coming to her senses. "Go off and have your bath, ogre. I won't assault your virtue."

"Damn the luck," he said sorrowfully. He walked off, whistling to himself, swaggering a bit in a way that told her clearly he was putting on the show for her benefit. Big Dog trotted off with him, tongue lolling cheerily.

She dismounted and tied the horse to a tree near the others. She wandered down to the water's edge and dabbled her fingers in the chilly rush. She glanced downstream to see the men at their baths, just visible in and among the lacy branches of the overhanging trees.

She sat on a rock and drew her knees up to her chest. She heaved a sigh of peace and satisfaction. Such beautiful men, she thought with admiration and pride. Though she couldn't see every bit of them, she could make out their powerful muscles, the glow of health and strength about them, the many shades of auburn hair, save for the silver-topped Bruce. And in the midst of them, splashing and playing like a schoolboy, was dark-haired Darach, his shoulders far and away the broadest, his height the greatest.

She gazed across the stream to the wild hills around her. The barren splendor of the landscape was growing pale lavender and blue in the waning light. Clouds scudded here and there overhead, casting shadows and then lifting to permit the last golden bars of the sunset. No wonder the clan felt so possessive about this place, she thought. *If I'd learned to survive and thrive in such a unique and challenging world, I'd want to defend my right to be here.*

She glanced again at the men splashing and shouting in the water, BD joining them in thrashing, yipping glee. She wondered how they must feel, living so completely as a part of this land. What would it take for her to live that way? Or to be accepted by the people who lived in such close harmony with its wild ways? Would she be forever an outlander to them?

"What the heck are you on about, Addison?" she murmured. There was no way she was going to stay in the Highlands with these people. She had to get back. She needed to set right the business she had left in New York when she had run away. She belonged in the city, in a world of delis and bookshops and cabs.

She smiled at the idea of taking the lairds out for Sunday brunch at Goldfarb's deli, not far from her tiny apartment in the city. And getting the whole bunch of them onto the subway would be a stitch, she thought, along with watching their faces as the cars and trucks and Rollerblading messengers crammed the streets during business hours.

What a contrast to this place! She looked around again, trying to imagine leaving it for the city. To her shock tears rose, unbidden, to her eyes and filled her throat.

What was this? she wondered, brushing at her eyes. She'd wandered around the United States most of her adult life. She'd never shed a tear upon leaving anyplace. But the mere idea of parting from the harsh, wild Highlands threatened to break her heart.

"Ready to go on?"

She started as Darach came up behind her, dressed again in his shirt and plaid, slicking his hair back with both hands. She caught her breath at the sight of him, the drops of water glistening off his high cheekbones, the easy, animal grace of his stride over the rocks. He was the embodiment of masculinity, she thought, with all his fierce love of the land and his people, the heat of his temper, the strength of his body, the tenderness of his soul. Her heart rose up as she admitted, once again, that she was falling in love with him, falling faster and farther with each passing day in his company.

"What is it?" he asked, coming to her with a hand outstretched. She took his hand and let him help her up from the rock. "Have I got a salmon stuck in my ear?"

She laughed. "No, not that I can see. I was just woolgathering."

"Woolgathering, eh? I'd best warn the sheep."

"Silly," she said, smiling up at him. "Are you going to tell me where we're heading?"

"It truly is a secret," he said, his face growing more solemn. "I canna tell ye. And I must blindfold ye for the last of the way."

"Blindfold me?" She stopped. "Why?"

"It's better that way."

"You still don't trust me, do you?"

He hesitated. "Nay, I canna say that I dare," he said. There was a note of apology in his voice. "But there are others that I know I can never trust. Because of them, I canna let ye see how we get where we're goin'. It would be a danger to the clan. And it would be a danger to ye, Julia."

"A danger to me? Are you saying that someone might try to hurt me to learn how to get wherever it is we're going?"

"Aye." He frowned. "The lairds told me what happened while I was away. It seems someone's already tried to harm ye."

"Well, hell." She thought about this for a moment, her mind whirling with possibilities. "Why did you bring me here, then? Why not leave me down in the village?"

"Ye would no' be safe down there, either. I canna spare a man to watch ye. Besides, ye ran off, remember?"

"So, wherever we're going, all the men want to go and no one wants to be left behind?" Julia tapped her chin with her fingertip. "Hmm."

He shook his head and laughed. "Ye're more curious than ten cats, Julia Addison. When will *ye* trust *me*?"

She looked at him in wonder. His tone was laughing, but she could see from his eyes that he was serious. She was about to respond when he turned and gave a piercing whistle. She heard the men come splashing out of the water.

Darach untied his horse and boosted her up as the first of his men answered his summons. "It's about time," he said to Niall and Liam with a grin. "Were ye waitin' for some lily-scented soap to come floatin' down the burn?"

"Naw," said Niall, tucking his shirt securely into his plaid. "I was waitin' to see if the midges would carry off our Liam, here."

Liam slapped at one of the monstrous insects. "I've studied and studied and I canna find a single reason why they should prefer me to the likes o' him," he said, jerking his head toward Niall. "As the Emperor Hadrian retorted to Florus:

I've no mind to be a Florus,
Strolling round among the drink-shops,
Skulking round among the cook-shops,
Victim of fat-gorged mosquitoes.'"

He smacked at another buzzing invader. "They nip at me like I was one o' wee Julia's daintiest cakes." Big Dog added to the indignity by trotting up and giving himself a thorough shaking, all over Liam's front.

"See they don't feast on anythin' vital," Niall said with a wicked smile. "Ye may have a use for it soon."

Darach interrupted before Liam could reply. "Let's get started. We've no torches wi' us to carry on after dark."

The other men returned, damp and smiling, and soon the party was on its way. Julia was grateful for the ride on Darach's horse, despite the rocky path that jostled her right, left, and center. She'd been traveling since sunrise, and her feet were starting to complain.

She looked about at the men. Why had they wanted a bath all of a sudden? While they were by no means filthy, she knew that baths were not daily occurrences back in the village. And the looks on their faces; they all looked like Elvis pilgrims at the gates of Graceland, waiting for their turn to go inside.

She looked at Niall. Stern, soldierly Niall kept breaking into a grin as he went along. Liam, of all people, was humming a tune. Tommy kept racing ahead and dashing back, his energy more boundless than ever, if that were possible. Everyone seemed filled with a secret joy. Heavens, even Liam and Gordon smiled at one another—had a truce been called in the notorious chicken feud?

Darach called a halt after a short while and, looking genuinely apologetic, tied a kerchief over Julia's eyes. "I'm trustin' ye no' to peek," he told her. "For your sake as well as ours."

The rest of the trip was more jostling, as far as Julia was concerned. All she could make out was that they were climbing, winding back and forth as they ascended. To her relief the last leg was relatively short. She felt Darach's horse come to a stop. She heard whispers from the men around her. A short bark of laughter rang out now and then, followed by several voices hissing for silence.

"All's well, Darach." She heard Ross's voice nearby. BD gave an affirming woof.

"Right then," Darach said. "Get the horses unpacked."

She felt his hands lifting the kerchief away. She blinked in the half-light and gazed around her. They seemed to be on a ridge. She looked off to one side and gasped. A drop of nearly 500 feet plunged to the rocky streambed below. To her right rose a sheer rock wall.

"Where are we?" she asked, sliding off on the horse's right side rather than brave the tiny space of rock between her and the rocks far below.

"On MacStruan land, believe it or no'." Darach motioned her ahead of him and began to lead the horse around a high boulder topped with scrubby, low-growing plants.

"Way up here—" She fell silent as she rounded the rock wall. "Oh, my gosh," she breathed. "So that's what all the secrecy is about."

Chapter Eighteen

Julia was filled with wonder. Standing before the gaping entrance to a cave stood a group of smiling, cheering women and children. There was a rush all around her. The lairds and their ladies came together in a noisy, joyous embrace, children dancing about in excitement and screeching happily. BD raced in circles, barking thunderously, pausing here and there to jump up and lick someone in greeting. Julia's mouth snapped shut lest she get a mosquito appetizer, but she turned wide eyes on Darach.

"They stay up here," he offered. "Once a month, we come up to visit."

Julia found her voice. "Is this—is it some kind of religious rule or something?"

"Aye, ye could say that. We're bound to care

272

for our families by all the laws of God and nature."

She couldn't help smiling at the expressions of joy before her. "So this is where all the women and children of your clan have been hiding out. I was beginning to wonder if . . ." She caught Darach's sharp gaze. "Yes, well, never mind." She clasped her hands together. "This is marvelous!"

A tall woman came forward out of the press of reunited families. She leaned on a staff and while she wasn't exactly old, her dark hair was shot with silver.

Darach went forward and embraced her. "Mother. Ye're keepin' well."

Darach's mother! Julia noticed that Alasdair hadn't joined the throng. He came to greet their mother, too. Julia drank in the sight of the regal-looking woman flanked by her two tall, handsome sons, one dark, the other fair. But the resemblance was clear. It was also eminently clear that this woman held a power over these two warriors that no one else could claim.

The woman thumped her staff. "And who is this?" she asked, pointing to Julia with an imperious finger. "What hae ye brought me? Another nun for our wee convent?"

Darach and Alasdair both colored at their mother's words. Darach motioned for Julia to come forward. She wanted to stick her tongue out at him for treating her like a servant, but somehow the woman standing next to him had her almost as cowed as the brothers.

"I'm Julia," she said, offering her hand. "Julia Addison."

"An outlander?" Darach's mother turned to her son with a frown. Julia dropped her hand in embarrassment.

"Aye."

"Where did she come from? No' from Kinloch, surely."

"We're—I'm no' sure, Mother."

Julia fidgeted. They were talking about her as if she were invisible.

"And ye brought her up here?"

"I couldna leave her in the village alone."

"Julia's been stayin' wi' Darach," Alasdair put in.

Darach shot him a wrathful glance. His brother looked all innocence, but Julia spotted the glint of mischief in his eyes.

"Has she indeed?" The older woman motioned to Julia. "Come closer, lass. I'd see what ye look like." Julia came forward as bidden—or commanded, she wasn't sure—and stood for inspection. She'd heard stories of meeting people's parents for the first time. Boy, would she have one to share if she ever got back to her own world.

"Hmm. Ye're a fair enough lass, that's certain. And ye have a generous mouth." She scanned Julia's figure. "I'd say ye could carry a bairn or twa. But why the devil are ye wearin' trews, lass? Are they no' powerful binding?"

Julia couldn't help grinning. "No, just the opposite. They're quite comfortable. Men and women both wear them where I come from."

"And where would that be?"

"New York, most recently."

"New York? What was wrong wi' the auld York?"

Julia smiled. Queenly though this woman was, she could learn to like her. "Nothing at all."

"Nothing save it's *English*." She made the word sound roughly equivalent to *road kill*. "Forgive my sons and their boorish ways, Julia Addison. It seems I must introduce my ain self to my son's guest. I'm Mairi Urquhart Mac-Struan."

Julia kept a straight face as the woman offered her hand. Darach and Alasdair looked like hooked fish, she thought. As she shook hands with Mairi MacStruan, she felt a wondering admiration at this woman who could overpower two such fearsome males. For all their swords and bluster, in their mother's presence they would always become small boys.

"Well, Julia Addison. Shall we go in? My sons seem to think it meet to leave an auld woman standin' out in the dark and cold."

She led the way, leaning on her staff. Julia and the two brothers trailed in her wake. The clan parted to allow Mairi passage into the cave, and Julia heard many murmured greetings from the lairds. Mairi MacStruan nodded and accepted their recognition with royal aplomb. Darach might be the MacStruan, but his mother was a power to be reckoned with, she thought.

"She outdoes even the Bruce," she muttered to Darach. "What an incredible woman!"

"Whisht," he said. "Don't let her hear ye. There's no livin' wi' her as it is."

She looked up at him and saw fondness in his eyes. He might be in awe of her, but he loves her, she thought. She liked the tender light in his eyes, a light that softened his hardened features and added grace to his rough demeanor.

So he's good to his mother, she told herself. That's no reason to get all mushy. She was still an outsider to them all, and she would soon be leaving for her own world. She'd be a fool to get in any deeper than she already was.

Right, a small voice said within her. *And I'm Mick Jagger.*

The rest of Clan MacStruan swarmed in behind them. The cave was enormous and high-ceilinged, Julia saw, with smaller chambers leading off in several directions. In the center of the main chamber there was a large fire ring with a sturdy iron spit hanging across its width. A fire was already kindled, and the smell of roasting meats and cooking onions reminded her that she hadn't eaten since early that morning. The women parted from their men with many fond pats and kisses and went to the fire to prepare the meal. A rough-hewn table served for chopping and mixing; a barrel of water was kept filled by boys and girls trooping back and forth with buckets. They all seemed more than capable of cooking up a feast in such an unusual kitchen.

Julia took a seat on a tree stump that had been dragged into the chamber. "I can't believe this," she murmured. "You live here? All the time?"

Mairi MacStruan nodded. "Aye, we do."

"Whatever for?" She clapped her hand over her mouth. "I'm sorry. That was rude."

"Nay, it wasna rude. 'Twas honest. Did Darach no' tell ye about us?"

She shook her head. They both glanced at Darach, who was helping the men carry in the supplies and fresh meat they'd borne up the mountain. Mairi sighed. "That's like him. My son carries the weight o' the world wi' him, even though it's no' his place to do so." She looked at Julia. "No doubt he thought to protect ye from the Morestons, should they come lookin' for us."

Julia looked down at her hands. "No, I don't think that's it. At least, that's not the main reason." She paused, then lifted her eyes to Mairi's. "Darach thinks I'm a spy for the Morestons. It's either that or I'm a witch. He can't seem to make up his mind."

"And are ye a witch?"

"No."

"Cam' ye from Castle Moreston?"

"I don't even know where that is."

"I won't abide a liar," Mairi said severely. "Are ye prepared to stake your life on those words?"

"Yes, but it won't make any difference to Darach. He won't listen to me."

"Ah. It's like that, is it? Himself willna let you

go? Which is he more afraid of, I wonder? Losin' his pride or losin' his lass?"

"I'm sure it's his pride."

"Dunna be too sure. Losin' Isobel was a blow that came nigh to knockin' the pins out from beneath my son."

"Isobel? I thought she was Gordon's sister."

"Aye, she was. And she was pledged to Darach. Did he no' tell ye that either? Och, the lad holds his tongue tighter than a miser's purse strings."

"Pledged to him? Do you mean pledged to be married?"

"Aye. And the wedding but twa days away, besides."

"The Morestons murdered her," Julia said, her voice shaking.

"They did. They came in the night, killed the watchman, and stole her out from our house whilst all slept. We hunted night and day for her but we knew where she'd been taken. Craigen, the craven-hearted swine, had stolen her. When Darach and the others came to Castle Moreston to demand her release, a serving man came bearing the puir lassie's body out from the keep. There were marks o' witchcraft on her body. Darach was half mad wi' the grief of it for aye a long time."

"That's horrible," Julia said, tears filling her throat. "No wonder he hates them so."

"There's reason enough for the hatred between our clans. Our strife wi' that lot goes far back among our sires, but the flame seems to have grown hotter and more personal between Craigen and Darach. They were both in Edinburgh fostering wi' the earl as young lads. I had hopes that a friendship might grow, but something happened there that set the pair of them at each other's throats every time they crossed paths. And when Craigen became chief, almost his first act, before his da was in the ground, was to set fire to the woods at the western edge of our lands. My husband and his brothair had been hunting in those woods. They had no place to go except onto Moreston land. They were killed on sight. Then came Isobel. And all the strivin' after the lands. I doubt there'll ever be an end to it all."

"It's like a gang war." Julia started at the words that popped out of her mouth. She had seen firsthand what such a war could bring about. She'd been on the run because of people who lived for such trouble. And by running she'd left Monty Gilette and his kind to kill and terrorize people again and again. It was a thought that didn't sit well on her conscience.

She recalled her companion. She reached out and touched Mairi's arm. "That must have been a terrible time for you. I can only imagine what it must have been like to lose your husband."

"It was. Although I always had the fear that such would be his fate, I never spoke it aloud until I saw his body, so strong and hale and as still as any stane."

"And Niall's father was killed with your husband? And Gordon's sister. Darach's fiancee. No

wonder he wants to hide you away up here."
Julia's heart went out to the clan members who
were working around her and Mairi. So many
senseless deaths! So much pain. So much more
that Darach was carrying around that she
hadn't understood before.

The call for supper interrupted her reverie.
Eager to be of help and needing to move lest
she be awash with tears, Julia excused herself
and jumped up to go to where the women were
dishing out bowls of leek soup.

"That smells heavenly," she said, leaning over
the pot. "Let me help serve?"

A small but sturdy sparrow of a young
woman, all dressed in brown with thick brown
hair, smiled shyly at her. "Are ye sure ye want
to help? After all, ye're the chief's lady, aren't
ye?"

"I?" Julia blinked. "No. I'm just Julia."

"I'm Rose. That's my Niall, over there."

"Ah! Oh, I'm pleased to meet you. Niall is a
fine man."

"That he is, though I'd no' have him hear it all
the time, if ye take my meanin'." Rose grinned
and patted her belly, which was rounding out
prettily from under her gown. "He's so sure I'm
carryin' a lad beneath my apron he's already
found the bairn his first horse. Won't he be
flummoxed if a wee lassie pops forth?"

"It'll be the making of him," Julia said
warmly. "And you and that bairn could use a
rest. You sit and I'll dish out this wonderful
soup."

"If ye're sure—"

"I'm sure." Julia took the big wooden spoon out of Rose's hand and set to work ladling soup into the various wooden bowls stacked by the fire. She glanced at Rose, who was staring at her slacks. Rose blushed and looked away.

"I know," Julia said with a chuckle. "My *trews*, as you call them. I must look pretty strange to you, especially when not even your men wear pants."

"They look . . . they're—" Rose stopped, coloring even more.

"Shocking?" Julia asked, arching her brows wickedly.

"Well, aye!" Rose dropped her voice. "Julia, ye can see every line of your limbs!"

"I know. And you know what else?" Julia leaned toward her conspiratorially. "They're comfortable as sin, too!"

"Julia!" Rose covered her mouth, shock and delight in her eyes. She glanced around. "What does your Darach make o' them?"

An odd thrill of pleasure went through her at the words *your Darach*. But she shook her head. "He's not my Darach," she said, handing bowls of stew to another woman, who carried them off to the men gathering about the fire.

"He's not?"

"Nay." She smiled at Rose. "It's a long story."

"Ah."

She glanced at the woman who sat looking at her with calm interest. "What was Isobel like?"

she asked, hating herself for the question but unable to resist asking.

"Isobel. Ah, there was a one. The sweetest lass ye'd ever want to meet. So mild a body sometimes didna know she was there." She sighed and rubbed her belly comfortingly. "Och, that was a terrible day when Darach brought her home to the village. He locked himself away and we could scarce coax him out to go to her funeral."

"It must have been awful. To lose his bride-to-be." Hurt and jealousy mingled in her own heart, despite her efforts to override them with sympathy.

"Aye. Everyone loved Isobel."

Julia turned to the pot, hoping to hide the confusing mix of emotions she was experiencing. So Darach had not only been engaged to be married, but he'd been engaged to the sweetest woman on the planet. There wasn't a chance in the world that anyone would ever say as much about her, she thought. No wonder Darach always kept her at arm's length. No wonder he always seemed angry whenever they got close.

"Alasdair looks fit enough," Rose commented.

Julia looked to where the tall, auburn-haired man stood conferring with Tommy, who had his arm about the waist of a sweet-faced young girl. "Yes, but he always does," she said, smiling. "His lady is a lucky one to have caught him."

"His lady? Alasdair has a lady?"

"Well, yes. Darach told me he's bespoken."

Rose looked perplexed. "I wonder when that happened? It's always been Darach naggin' at Alasdair to get himself a lass, but ye know Alasdair and his wanderin' ways. He always says he can't pick just one; it'd be sae borin'.'"

"You mean he isn't engaged to anyone?"

"Not that I know of. Ye'd be the one to know, bein' down to the clachan wi' the lot of them."

"Hmm." Julia tapped the side of the kettle with the spoon. Here was another secret in the MacStruan clan. Why had Darach told her that Alasdair was engaged when he wasn't and had no intention of becoming so?

"I see Herself beckoning for ye," Rose said, nodding toward Mairi. "Ye'd best look lively."

"She's amazing, isn't she?" Julia handed the spoon over to Rose.

"That's no' the half of it! Get along. She'll be thumpin' that staff and shoutin' at us if ye don't."

Julia hurried over to Mairi's side. "Julia Addison, I want ye to sit beside me and tell me more about yerself." She eyed her up and down. "But first, I want ye to get out o' those ridiculous clothes. Go wi' Jeannie, here, and she'll find ye a proper gown."

"But I—"

"Are ye refusin'?" Mairi's voice had an edge of steel.

"No, but I—"

"Verra weel. Jeannie, take her to my things. I've somethin' that'll fit her in the bottom o' my chest."

Mairi waved them off. Julia trailed after the scurrying girl, wondering what Mairi would demand of her next. She decided she didn't want to think about it.

A short time later she returned to Mairi's side, clad in a gown of soft, olive-green wool with a delicate linen undergown. The hem trailed, but Jeannie insisted that was acceptable; Julia turned up the cuffs of the sleeves. "Do I pass inspection?" she asked Mairi, smiling.

"Don't be pert, lass. Ye look proper, that's all I ask. Now, then. Sit down, eat and drink, and tell me about this new York of yours."

Julia obeyed. The food was delicious, the wine cool and sweet, the company formidable but fascinating. Over a second cup of wine, she tried to tell Mairi MacStruan about the Big Apple.

"Ye say all the buildings are sae tall ye have to crane your head to see up?" Mairi looked at Julia reprovingly. "I've been to Edinburgh, lass, and Aberdeen as well. And I've heard many a traveler's tales of London. There's nae such a thing as buildings tall as mountains, save for a castle here and there. Would ye no' say ye're stretchin' things a mite?"

Julia shrugged. "I wouldn't lie to you."

"Ye wouldna?"

"Nay."

"Then why do ye pretend no' to care for my Darach?"

Julia choked on her wine. "What?"

"Oh, ye heard me, lass. Why do ye avoid

talkin' about him? Ye're workin' sae hard no' to glance his way, your neck must be takin' wi' the cramp."

"But I—"

"Oh, aye. Ye say ye're but a prisoner of his. But I think ye're tellin' me another tall tale."

Julia shook her head. "I do care for him. In a way. But he doesn't care for me. He thinks I'm his enemy. And when he doesn't think I'm a Moreston, he thinks I'm a witch. And when he doesn't think I'm a witch . . ."

"Aye?"

"When he doesn't think I'm a witch, he thinks about Isobel, I imagine, and how I can't measure up to her memory."

"Did my son say as much to ye?"

"No, not in so many words. But—"

"Then why do ye believe my son is no' in love wi' ye?"

Julia could only stare at the older woman, openmouthed. There was a hint of amusement in Mairi's eyes, but Julia could tell she was serious.

"I'll leave ye to think on it." Mairi thumped her staff loudly. The hubbub in the chamber quieted a bit. "Some music, I think. Ross MacStruan, to your pipes."

"Aye, Mairi." Ross darted off to find his pack. Tommy's companion, whose name, Julia had learned, was Lara, brought out a beautiful skin drum. Liam brought out a battered stringed instrument that looked to Julia like a cross between a lute and a guitar. Before long Dugan

285

joined in, playing a recorder. Dance tunes and marches, ballads sung in turn, sad airs and stirring rants—they played them all. Even Niall sang; a suggestive ditty about a maiden gone fishing, and received a playful cuff on the ears from Rose.

Julia sat in the circle before the fire, gazing about her at the faces that ringed the light. Niall and his Rose, Tommy holding hands with shy Lara, the Bruce beaming on them all, Mairi MacStruan looking even more regal at his side, her tall staff in hand. Big Dog had plopped himself down by the cave entrance with a satisfied woof and was now dozing, one ear cocked to listen for any approaching danger. Soon the children were tucked into bed in the chambers beyond the big cave, and the adults chatted and sang as they finished off the last of the feast.

Such beautiful, funny, loving people, she thought. What a special bond they enjoyed, part of them through blood kinship, like Tommy and Alasdair and Ross, and some of them, like Niall, through loving allegiance to the name and honor of the MacStruans. Clan meant children, Ross had told her, and it did seem as if they were all children and all parents together, taking care of one another. Membership in the clan connected them, much as they were connected in the circle around the fire. Was there anything like it in her own time? It had never seemed so to her.

She sighed and smiled. Yes, the mystery of the MacStruan women was solved at last. She looked across the fire and saw Rose smiling her way. She returned the smile, but couldn't help wondering how these women stood it, being hidden away here in the hills, never going below to the beautiful glens or to their own homes. She'd go nonlinear in less than a day, she thought, if she had to spend her life here.

"More wine?" Darach seated himself cross-legged at her side. It was the first time she'd seen him since they'd arrived.

She held out her cup. "Yes, please. It's delicious stuff."

"Honey and apple mead," he said, refilling her cup. "My mother has casks of it laid in every year. This'll be the last of it until autumn, when the apples ripen." He looked around the fire ring, a satisfied smile on his face. "What think ye of the rest o' my folk?"

"I think they're wonderful," she said sincerely. "You're very lucky."

"Aye, that I am." He gave her a wry grin. "What did my mother have to say to ye? I saw ye over there wi' yer heads together."

"Hmm. I don't know if I should tell you." She felt suddenly mischievous. "You might get angry."

"I wouldna doubt it," he drawled. "The pair of ye have given me more grief in my life than all my men combined."

She gave him a playful push. "Oh, poor Darach!" she mocked. "How he suffers!"

He edged closer to her, his voice lowering to that warm, deep rumble that always seemed to melt her bones. "I do suffer, Julia."

"You do?" She peered at him over the rim of her cup, hardly daring to think what his intimate tone implied.

"I suffer from want . . . of peace!" He laughed at her surprise, then went on in that teasing, velvety tone. "Ye could help me find it, wee Julia."

Chapter Nineteen

Darach reached out one long, strong finger and traced a circle around her kneecap. The soft fabric of the gown slid over her skin, caressing her.

"Ye could help me find peace," he repeated, his eyes bright with mischief and more.

A shiver of excitement rode down her spine. "Could I?" she asked, matching his teasing tone. "But why should I?"

"I'd make it worth your trouble." His finger slid down her calf, half tickling, half caressing.

"But if it's trouble, why would I want to do it in the first place?" Her voice was growing husky, and she quickly took a sip of the cool wine.

"Oh, the trouble I'd cause ye would be no trouble at all." His big hand slipped beneath the hem of her skirt and circled her bare ankle like a bracelet.

"I—" She looked up. Several of the couples around the fire had left, and more were making their way to the shadows by the walls. With their arms about one another's waists or holding hands, they made it plain that the time had come for them to celebrate their reunion in a more private way.

"Darach." Mairi came to stand beside him. He rose at once and Julia stood with him. "I'm goin' to my bed. I expect to see ye in the mornin'. We've much to discuss."

"Mother, we've both said our piece. My answer is still the same." Darach's tone was respectful but firm. He leaned down and kissed Mairi's cheek. "Sleep well."

Mairi gave him a cool stare. "I've not said all I'm goin' to say, laddie. And don't say ye've heard me till yer ears have attended my words. I'll see ye in the mornin'."

"Aye. In the mornin'."

Julia hid the grin she felt coming at the sight of big, powerful Darach MacStruan bending to the commands of his mother. Mairi kissed her son, then turned to Julia.

"And ye, lass. Ye come after. I would speak wi' ye, especially."

"I will, Lady MacStruan."

"Lady! Hmph! I'm no' a lady. Call me Mairi. It's the proper way."

"I will. Mairi."

"Good night, then. Get a bit o' rest, the pair

of ye. Ye both look like somethin' that fool dog of Darach's has been worryin' at."

She moved away, with Jeannie, her hand-maiden, scurrying ahead with a candle to light the way. Julia turned to Darach. "She's one heck of a lady," she said.

"'Lady! Hmph!'" he said, mimicking his parent. "'I'm no' a lady!' She's no' a lady but she's a woman and a half, that one."

Julia turned back to the fire. Tommy and Lara sat there still, but from the looks they gave one another, she knew they weren't looking for any other companions. The highly charged atmosphere of the cave made her feel like a wallflower at a high school dance.

Darach cleared his throat. "Come outside wi' me. Ye'll not see stars like these where ye come from, I wager."

Grateful to get away, she followed him out into the cool night. Big Dog raised his great head and gave a snuffle as they passed, but he went back to his rest at once.

Darach led her away from the entrance to the cave, up a short path to a narrow ridge above. As they rounded the lone tree that stood there, bent and gnarled from the wind through the hills, Julia looked up and gasped.

Darach was right. She had never seen anything like this anywhere, at any time in her life. The stars hung so thick and close overhead she was tempted to reach out and touch one of them. The only thing she could think of was diamonds, thousands upon thousands of diamonds, spilled across a huge expanse of deepest black velvet.

"I'm the richest man in all Scotland," Darach said softly.

"You are. And no one can take these from you."

"Aye. And they'll ne'er grow auld. Nor will they wither and die."

"Not like people."

He looked at her. "Ye know what it is to lose someone ye love."

"I do. When my mother died, I thought I'd go on hurting into eternity." She smiled up at him. "But other people can help, even if they can't take her place."

"Have ye found those people?"

She leaned her back against the tree, avoiding his eyes. "I don't know. Maybe. But you certainly have."

"Have I?"

"Yes. All those people down there in that cave. How wonderful it must be to have all those people around you, all of you working together and caring for one another."

He stood silent, looking up at the sky.

"Don't you agree?" she asked.

"Aye, they're good folk."

She laughed. "Good? They're the best, the salt of the earth. You're not only rich in stars, Darach, you're rich in family."

"A family lives together, under one roof."

"Not always. Sometimes it's not possible. I don't think your house is big enough to hold your whole clan, small though it is."

He gave a brief laugh. "Nay, true enough."

They stood silently together for a few moments, gazing at the stars. Then Julia summoned the courage to say what she'd been thinking that evening by the fire. "Darach. You're right. This is no way to live."

"What do ye mean?"

"I mean like this. Husbands and wives separated. Children seeing their fathers and uncles and older brothers only once or twice a month. People living in caves, no matter how clean and dry and well stocked."

"It's not safe for them to come down."

"Because of the Moreston's threats?"

"Aye. He's sworn to kill off everything I hold dear."

"But he hasn't done anything more than fight you in court and kill some of your cows, that I can see. At least not recently. Don't you think he might be bluffing?"

"Nay."

She looked at him. He looked like a part of the mountain, so stiff and rigid was his stance. She knew he must be thinking of Isobel. But she couldn't let the matter drop. She'd seen the longing in the eyes of the MacStruan women, the boredom and loneliness they shared.

"Darach, the women can help. They're clan, too. Let them come down. Let them help you protect your lands and support their men."

"Julia, I've made my decision. There'll be no questionin' it."

She straightened. "I beg your pardon? I'm not one of your lackeys! I will question anything I damn well please!"

"And it will avail ye not! The women and children stay here until I can bring about peace."

"And how long will that be?"

"Dammit, Julia, stop now! Ye don't want to anger me!"

"Yes, I do!" she exclaimed. "I want you to wake up and smell the coffee, MacStruan! Peace could be a long, long way off. Do you want those kids in there to grow up in a cave, hardly knowing their own fathers?"

"I have a duty to protect my people. If I was to let them come down, those bairns might no' grow up at all! Is that what ye want, Julia?"

"Of course not!" She crossed her arms. "All right then, if it's so treacherous down below, I'm staying up here with the women."

"Ye will not!"

"Why not?"

"Ye're comin' back down wi' me and the men!"

"Why should I? You've made it clear you don't want me around! You insult me at least half the time. You lock me in my room whenever you feel like it. Why don't you leave me up here so I won't aggravate you anymore?"

"Dammit, Julia—I don't want ye to go away!"

Before she could reply, he yanked her to him and enfolded her in his embrace. He smothered her words with a kiss that seemed as much anguished as angry. Even as she responded in kind, she braced herself for his rejection, for him to set her away from him as he had done the other times he'd kissed her.

But his kiss went on. And when at last he raised his lips from hers, it was only to repeat her name, over and over, as he showered still more kisses over her cheeks, her forehead, her eyes.

The hunger within her heart rose up and urged her to respond. She had been storing up her feelings inside her for weeks. And she knew that it was too late now to halt their expression. She lifted her arms and twined them about his neck, murmuring "yes" into his ear. "Yes."

He swept her up then, and with her arms still tight around him he carried her down the rocky little path and across the brook to a darkened grove beneath the stars. He set her down in the center of a ring of fragrant pines, his hands on her waist. "Julia, I—"

She put her hand to his lips, shaking her head. She wanted no explanations, no questions tonight. All she wanted was him.

Slowly she reached down and pulled her gown off over her head. She kicked away her shoes, rolled her stockings off, and stood before him, clad only in her thin undergown.

He raised his hands and pulled the clasp from her hair. The heavy waves tumbled to her shoulders and she shook them out, glorying in the sheer pleasure of physical sensation. Then, ever so gently and slowly, he raised the hem of her undergown and lifted it off and away.

She stood before him, clad in starlight and trembling with delicious anticipation. She could feel her heart beating faster as his eyes seemed to drink her into their depths.

To her astonishment, he sank to his knees before her, his head bowed.

"Darach?" What could this mean, this tall, proud warrior chief on his knees before her?

He lifted his head. "Ye're more beautiful than anything I've ever beheld," he said, his voice tight. "I want to honor ye, Julia."

Her heart contracted for an instant, then expanded with still more love than she ever thought possible. She knelt before him on the thick carpet of sweet-smelling pine needles. "Let's honor one another," she whispered.

Smiling into his eyes, she unfastened the heavy clasp that held his *breacan*. She smoothed it off his shoulder, then set about undoing his belt and sword. After a few awkward fumblings, she set them aside and pulled the rest of his plaid away.

Her eyes had grown accustomed to the dim light in the grove. She could see the pulse that beat at the base of his throat, and the quick rise and fall of his chest. As she removed his boots she smoothed a hand along his hard-muscled legs, ruffling the dark hair and enjoying the feel of their latent power.

He had untied the opening to his shirt. She gathered the garment into her hands and pulled it up and over his head. She set it aside and sat back on her heels, gazing with fascination and delight at the magnificent body that, so far, she had only been allowed to imagine.

He was as muscular and lean as she had thought, with a thick mat of dark hair that covered his chest and made a tapering trail down to his navel. His skin glowed with health and warmth. Here and there, though, she saw whitened, formidable scars, marks that reminded her that she was not with just any man, but with a warrior, a man who had wielded a sword in many battles and who had been cut by the swords of others. The sight of all that power and ferocity, quiet and laid bare to her vision, touched her deeply. She knew that appearing in any way weak, vulnerable, or unguarded was anathema to Darach. His trust, as well as his passion, brought tears to her eyes.

"Whisht," he murmured, reaching up to touch her cheek. "What cause d'ye have for tears, love?"

"You're so beautiful."

"Och, ye are an addled one." He grinned. "I'm as crisscrossed with sword bites as a kitchen table, and I'm no slender youth like our Tommy." He rubbed his hands over the mat of hair on his chest. "And I'm as woolly as one of our kine in winter."

"You're beautiful," she repeated.

"Have it your way," he said, smiling. "So long as ye're pleased."

He reached for his plaid and spread it out on the ground beside them. He stood and reached for her hand, pulling her to her feet. He put a hand to her cheek and caressed her, sliding it along her shoulder and down to the curve of her waist. "Is this what ye want, Julia?" he whispered.

His hand stroked over her belly, causing her to shiver. She closed her eyes as he trailed his fingers up and around her breast, circling and circling around. "Is this what ye want?" he asked again.

She was swaying on her feet, hypnotized by the slow, slow progress of his loving. She nodded, unable to speak.

"Ah, that's good," he murmured. "We agree at last, my Julia."

He placed his hard, callused palms flat against the taut little peaks that he'd aroused. She gave a soft sigh of pleasure and arched up toward him.

"Not yet, sweet. Let me give ye all."

She wasn't sure she could stand all, let alone stand to wait. But she stood, quivering like the faint breeze among the pines overhead, accepting his slow, sweet gifts.

In the dim recesses of her conscious mind, she wondered at the change in Darach Mac-Struan. She'd imagined him touching her so many times, but she'd never dreamed that this big, hardened, obstinate man would be such a tender, thorough, passionate lover. He seemed utterly indefatigable, utterly impervious to the quite obvious needs of his own body. He showered her with kisses, bathed her in caresses, tasted and touched and soothed and aroused every inch of her body. He lavished her breasts with heated attentions, suckling and smoothing and cherishing. His hands and lips found pleasure places she hadn't even known existed on her own body, and he kissed and stroked her from head to toe, taking infinite care to leave no spot untouched. And when at last her knees threatened to give way, and her moans of pleasure turned to urgent pleas, he laid her gently down upon his plaid and covered her completely with his warm, hard form.

"Darach," she murmured against his neck, burying her face in the hot, spicy refuge of his skin. "I don't think I can stand any more."

"Nay, sweet?" He parted her legs with his knee and settled himself between her thighs.

"Nay."

He moved up ever so slightly. She arched up, trying to pull him to her. He held still. "Ken ye feel what I'm feelin', Julia?"

"I—Yes. Darach!"

He raised himself up on his hands so that he could gaze straight into her eyes. She saw such tenderness there and such intense passion it almost took her breath away.

"Are ye ready to be wi' me? Truly, love?"

She nodded. "I want to be wi' ye, love. Completely." She closed her eyes as he eased forward again.

"Look at me, sweet."

She opened her eyes and saw his handsome face, starlit and shadowed and intent with his loving of her.

"I want to see ye when I come to ye."

She couldn't have looked away if she'd wanted to. He raised his hips and, his eyes never leaving hers, joined them together in one smooth, firm thrust. She cried out with the sweetness of their union and clung to him, shaking.

"Whisht, love," he murmured, gathering her to him. "Whisht. The best is yet to be."

And he was as good as his word.

Alasdair turned from the sight of the couple standing in the center of the grove. His stomach roiled with anger and frustration.

So Julia had made her choice and Darach had staked his claim, he thought. And once again he was second best, the younger brother, the second in command.

He'd had enough. He couldn't stay around here and see Darach and Julia in the morning, both of them wrapped in afterglow, exchanging glances and touches and intimate words. He'd had enough of that already, watching the rest of the clan reunited.

He headed back to the cave, grabbed up his pack, and was off while the rest of his world enjoyed the pleasures of their beds.

Chapter Twenty

The following day was one that would remain honey-drenched and magical in Julia's memory. All thoughts of time and partings were forgotten. She and Darach rose late from their bower, languid and lazy, sorting their clothes from the tangle among the leaves and branches. They washed in the icy brook, Julia spluttering and gasping in shock while Darach pretended the water was as warm as a tub by the fire. When they were dry and dressed, Darach took her hand and led her through the woods and across the streams, to the crags and down into the glens, showing her the wild beauty of his land.

They spoke little, yet she sensed that volumes passed between them. A glance, a touch, the simple act of sharing the day together with no intrusions or duties to distract them was bond enough. They came together often to share a kiss or an embrace, and by midday sought out the coolness of another dry small cave Darach knew, there to expand upon the delights they'd known the previous night.

They lunched on berries and wild carrots they found, neither of them particularly hungry for sustenance beyond their loving. While they ate, Julia watched as Darach's face, so often creased and set with tension of late, relaxed and softened into an almost boyish peace. She couldn't remember ever seeing him smile so often. She felt healed and replenished herself, finding peace in his tender regard and in the utter solitude they shared.

"We needed a vacation," she said aloud, leaning against his solid side as they sat on a sun-warmed rock overlooking a narrow glen.

"Vacation?"

"Yes. You know, a time to get away from it all."

He pondered this and nodded. She peered up at him. "Oops, maybe I shouldn't have reminded you."

"Nay, it's all right. I was surprised, is all. I didna think I could leave my cares behind. But I have. Wi' ye, sweet Julia."

"You ought to do this more often. I'm afraid the stress is going to do you in."

"Stress?"

"Yes. The pressures of being the chief, having all the lairds looking to you for leadership. The

Morestons. Alasdair. Me." She grinned as she said this last.

He quirked a smile her way. "Aye. But I don't think I want to get away from ye, lass. If I'm gettin' away, you're goin' to be right by my side."

"I'm glad," she whispered, laying her head upon his shoulder. "Just remember, all work and no play makes Jack a dull boy."

"I told ye before I'm no' a boy," he said in a soft growl.

She looked up at him with a smile. "Yes, I know that. I knew it then, and I most definitely know it now."

He put his arm around her and they continued to watch the shadows of the clouds pass across the green glen.

Alasdair tramped along the path, heading aimlessly up the hillside on the other side of the village. He'd hardly slept last night, letting his restlessness carry him along as far as he could go without getting utterly locked in the darkness of the forest. Now, at midday, the sun cast fat, golden shafts of its light through the forest canopy. He scarcely noticed the beauty of the day about him or heard the bird songs that threaded the skies overhead.

He had been furious at first when he'd seen Darach and Julia locked in each other's arms beneath the stars. But as he'd walked, he'd come to the realization that envy, not jealousy, was what had ignited his temper. Somehow, if he had been in love with Julia, he knew that he would have spoken by now. And he would have cheerfully waded in and taken Darach's head off with his own hands at the sight of them together.

What he wanted was what he sensed they shared, a passion that seemed to make them both come more alive in each other's presence, that prompted them to such heat that they must find expression in temper, or creation, or in an embrace. It wasn't mere lust; he knew what that was and how easily it could be satisfied and dismissed. This was something different, he told himself. Something that couldn't be ignored, something that grew, somehow, rather than diminished, when it found expression.

"Och, the wanderin' philosopher," he muttered as he climbed the narrow ravine near the Moreston border. "In love wi' the idea o' love."

"And what would be wrong with that?"

He had his knife out in the blink of an eye. He glanced around the clearing where he stood, looking for the owner of the voice.

"Come out and show yourself," he called. He was but a pace or two from Moreston land, he thought ruefully. The old standing stones nearby lay just inside the MacStruan border. Had he walked into a trap?

There was a rustle of leaves to his left. He whirled.

"I'm here." Someone tapped his right shoulder and he almost rose up into the air. He didn't think, he reacted. He seized the intruder by the hair and made ready to divide his enemy's body from his soul.

His mouth fell open and he nearly dropped his knife in surprise at the sight that greeted him. This was no hardened Moreston henchman or hunter.

It was a lass.

Fathomless fawn-colored eyes returned his stare with an astonishment that he knew must mirror his own. He set her back a ways from him, still holding her pale, red-gold braid in his grasp. He looked her carefully up and down, not even cognizant that his boldness might give offense.

She was someone—or something—that could have stepped out of a tale of yore. Her almond-shaped golden eyes held no fear of him, only wonder, and while he could see the pulse beating fast in her slender throat, she didn't seemed overly frightened. Her green cloak and rust-red gown, with her pale, ginger-gold hair, made her look as if she were a part of the forest itself: wild, eternally young and ancient of days, full of mysterious life and nature's secrets. Verdant. Beautiful. Magical.

"Are ye real?" he whispered at last.

The young woman nodded, her eyes never leaving his.

"Who are ye?"

"I am Celandine. Celandine Talcott."

Sunset was drawing near when Darach and Julia returned to the caves. The clan had spent the day much as they had, Julia noted, judging from the satisfied smiles and intimate touches that passed between the couples. The children had been fed and toted off to their beds. The lairds gathered at the fireside, awaiting Darach's word.

"So," said Niall, rocking back on his heels with an ill-concealed grin.

"So?" asked Darach.

"Ye passed a pleasant nicht, I trust?"

Darach gave him a bland stare. "Concerned for ma health, are ye?"

Bruce clapped him on the shoulder. "O' course we're concerned, lad. It's no' every day that our chief takes a woman for his ain." He lowered his silver brows. "Ye treated our wee Julia right, did ye not?"

Heat spread from the base of her neck to the roots of her hair at Bruce's words. She waited for what Darach would say in reply.

"I think we have some plannin' to do," was all he said. He looked about. "Where's Alasdair?"

"We havena seen him today. He didna sleep here, that any of us knows." Niall grinned again. "Not that we were payin' all that much attention."

Darach gave a brief smile, but his eyes looked worried. "Damn the lad and his wanderin' ways. His restless feet'll land him in hell if he doesna learn some sense."

"I saw him last night," Tommy ventured.

"When?"

"When I went out to relieve myself. He was

comin' back from the grove. He looked as hot as a bear wi' a thorn in its bum."

"The grove?"

Julia met Darach's eyes over the heads of his men. They both knew what Alasdair must have seen if he had been in the grove last night. Her heart ached for the man she was coming to view as a real brother. Had Darach's suspicions been correct, at least as far as Alasdair was concerned? Did Alasdair feel more than mere brotherly love for her?

Her spirits, so buoyant from the past hours spent in Darach's company, now sank as she took in the darkness of his glare. Here was a new trouble he could lay at her door, she thought. If she caused him to lose his only brother, what might happen to the tentative love they'd so recently discovered?

Darach swung his attention back to his men. "He must have gone off last night. But he would have come back by now. Niall, you lead the others back to the village. He may have gone back there, but there's something about this that bodes ill, to me. Ross, Tommy, Dugan, come ye wi' me."

The men set off at once to make ready. Julia crossed quickly to Darach and took his arm.

"You think he saw us?" she asked softly.

"Aye." He pulled his arm away slowly. "I've got to find him."

She tugged at his plaid, holding him. "You know, don't you, that I—"

"That ye what?" His eyes searched hers.

"That I don't feel . . . that way . . . for him?"

He looked disappointed somehow. "Aye. I believe ye, Julia." He gave her a quick kiss. "Mind what Niall tells ye, ye headstrong lass. I'll see ye safe at home." He started away.

"I'm not going with Niall."

He turned and came back, his eyes snapping. "What did ye say?"

"I said I'm not going with Niall and the others. I'm staying here."

His eyes narrowed. "Not this again."

"Yes, again. I'm a woman. I don't belong down in the village with you men."

He bowed his head and groaned. "Saints, Julia, ye're goin' to be the death o'me." He looked up and placed his hands on her shoulders. "We need ye down there. Who'll look after the lads if they're ill? Who'll do the cookin' so we don't kill ourselves wi' your eecoleye?"

She stiffened. "Is that all I am? Nurse and cook? Well, any of these women here can cook and clean and nurse you big louts better than I can, I'm willing to bet. Why don't you take one of them?"

"I don't want one o' them!"

Heads turned all around the cave. Darach looked about with embarrassment. He lowered his voice. "I don't want one o' them," he repeated. "Besides, I can't keep watch over ye if ye're up here."

"You—I—you—!" Julia could only splutter in her outrage at his words. "What the hell do you mean, keep watch over me?"

He put a finger to her lips. "Whisht, woman. Listen. I only meant to say that—"

"You only meant to say that after all this, after last night, after today, after all of it, you still don't trust me! You still think I'm one of your damned Morestons, don't you?"

"Julia, it's not that—"

"Damn you to hell, Darach MacStruan," she hissed. "Danm your ever-watchful chief of Clan MacStruan eyes!"

She whirled away from him, heading back into the rear passages.

"Darach!" someone called behind her as she fled. "We'd best leave while there's light."

She kept running until she found an empty, silent niche in one of the far chambers. There, she sank to the ground and wept in frustration.

Mairi went out to bid her son good-bye. She leaned on her staff and peered up into his glowering face with wry amusement.

"So, ye've toppled at last," she said, chuckling. Darach's frown deepened. "She's a meet match for my thornbush," Mairi went on. "See if ye can hold a place open for her in that crowded heart o' yours."

Darach looked down at his mother, his eyes suddenly touched with anguish and confusion. "I don't know if I dare," he said, his voice gruff.

"Ye mean for the sake o' your heart?" asked Mairi, her bright eyes growing tender at the sight of her son's pain. "Or for her sake?"

"For her sake, o' course." He shook his head.

"Nay, I tell a lie. I'm that afraid of her, Mother. I'm afraid she'll see I'm not much of a catch. I'm afraid she'll vanish into the air wi'out me." He looked away to the hills. "But I'm afraid *for* her, too. If anything were to happen—"

Mairi nodded. "I know. I know it's hard not to think o' Isobel. But that's past, son. Take heart for the future! Get ye wed, before she decides for auld Bruce, ye daft thing. Get some bairns! Or get some bairns and then get wed, it makes no matter t'me—as lang as ye do it soon."

"Ye're a wicked auld woman," Darach said tenderly, gathering her up into his embrace.

"Aye. And your wee Julia's a young one. Make her wicked happy, son. Ye've put the light in her eyes already—now put one in her heart and in her belly."

"Och, what would I do wi'out so many o' my kin to advise me at every turn?" Darach asked the skies. "Just once I'd like to try."

Mairi pushed him away and gave him a swat on the shoulder. "Get out of here. Find that foolish brothair of yours. Then see ye stay home long enough to kindle the common fire."

"So says the witch of the MacStruans," Darach said with a grin, swinging up on his horse.

"And well ye know it," Mairi said, grinning back.

Niall soon came to stand before her, his mouth twisted in a wry smile of apology. "We need to ride out, Julia," he said. "The light willna hold."

"I told Darach that I intend to stay here with

the women and children."

He nodded. "I heard. But he gave orders. I'm to take ye home, on my horse or across it."

"Just try it, buster."

"Julia." He squatted down until he was eye to eye with her. "He's the chief. If I didna obey, he'd have every right to send me packin' from the clan. Or worse. Ye wouldna wish that to happen, would ye?"

"Niall, don't try to guilt-trip me. It won't work. I was raised by the queen of guilt. You're his closest friend. He loves you and he needs you. He'd never toss you out of the clan."

He made a harumphing noise in his throat and stroked his chin, considering. She stared at him squarely, waiting to see what he'd try next. She knew that if he wanted, he could indeed haul her up out of here and toss her, bound and gagged, over his horse's back. But she was willing to bet that Niall would only do that as his last resort. In the meantime, perhaps there would be a chance to sway him. She didn't think she could stand to go back to the village while she was still angry at Darach.

"Julia, lass," he began in a wheedling tone.

"What's this?" Mairi came shuffling along the corridor, Jeannie going along before her with a torch. "Julia? Why aren't ye makin' ready to gang wi' the others to the village?"

Julia clambered to her feet. "Mairi, I want to stay here."

"Don't be daft, lass," Mairi said, giving her staff an emphatic thump. "Why ever would ye want to stay here wi' a bunch of auld women and squalling bairns? Your place is down below."

"My place?" Julia bristled. Who did the woman think she was? The Queen of Everything?

"Aye. Ye came to Darach. Ye came to his village. Ye didn't come to us up here in the hills. My son needs ye."

"He needs me! What about me?"

Mairi stared at her incredulously. "Did ye no' hear me? Ye came to Darach. What ye need is there wi' him."

"That's the most sexist, ridiculous, high-handed—"

"Whisht!" Mairi thumped her staff once more. Julia had the brief thought that the woman had no real need of its assistance, she only used the big oaken branch to scare people into doing her bidding. She tried staring back in defiance.

"Ye needn't take up yer chin so wi' me, lass. I learned such tricks at my mother's knee. I'm no' sayin' ye're to gang down and be his slave. Ye're a woman and in these hills that counts for more than all that tender English lady pap ye probably learnt as a bairn." Her imperial manner softened. "Are ye willin' to concede ye love my son?"

Julia wanted to deny it. She hadn't said as much to Darach, but if not love, what had the past day and night been all about? She gave a nod.

"Good. I didna ken ye were a fool. And will ye

also concede that ye would turn to ravin' if ye were to be shut up in these caves for weeks on end?"

"Yes." Grudgingly.

"And will ye also concede that ye have more that ye need to learn? Things that canna be learnt hidin' in the hills?"

Julia stared at her. "How do you—"

"I'm no' sae foolish as ye might think, clumpin' about here among the rocks as I do. But I know the look of a seeker when I see her. Ye've become part of a mystery and it fair drives ye wild that ye canna solve it. So I say stop tryin' to summon up pity for yourself. It doesna suit ye. Gang ye down wi' the lads. Find the secret yer heart longs to learn."

Julia's shoulders slumped in resignation. "You are too much," she said, smiling. "I wish you were coming with me."

"A wicked auld woman, my son called me." Mairi chuckled and motioned for them all to move back up the passage. "And ye'd best take it to heart, lass."

On impulse, Julia reached up and gave her a kiss on the cheek. "I'll see you soon," she said. "Just try and stop me."

Mairi's laughter rang around the stone walls. "Ye may see me sooner than ye think," she said, shaking her finger. "So see that ye have your house in order."

Niall took Julia's arm and hurried her out to where the rest of the men waited, packed and ready to travel. Julia swung into the saddle as

Rose rushed up with a small cloth bundle.

"Some of ma cakes," she said breathlessly. "Ye said ye liked 'em so."

"Thank you, Rose." She leaned down and gave her a hug. "Take care of yourself. And the wee one. I'll see you soon."

"May it be so."

Rose and the others waved until they passed beyond the trees. Julia rode home in silence, Big Dog at her side, thinking about all the events of the past two days. She dismounted and went into the house. She was too weary to do anything more than collapse into bed, with BD snoring on the hearth, LC curled up by his wooly flank.

Edana was humming again.

Craigen Moreston left off listening at her chamber door and moved down the hall, frowning. He went to his own chamber and shut the door.

The witch was getting to be more trouble than she was worth, he thought as he poured himself some wine. She'd been useful to him in the beginning, when they'd both come back from Edinburgh and he'd taken on the position of clan chief. Her spells had sickened or driven off all his opponents within the clan. She'd managed to scare the MacStruans into silence, for the most part, by foretelling—and forestalling—their chief's wedding.

He made a sour face at the memory of that time. Edana had been working an enchantment on the girl, Isobel, when one of his own men had stumbled, drunk, into the girl's room and killed her when she began to scream. Edana had been beside herself. She had wanted to turn the girl to the dark before they sent her back to Darach. The drunken man had died a hideous death by one of her charms.

And he, the Moreston, had to give up hope of getting more of the MacStruan lands in ransom for the lass. The outcome had not been all bad, he mused, going to the window, which looked out toward the woods between his land and the MacStruan's. That overproud pup Darach had been taught a lesson and been hurt where Craigen himself had been hurt years ago in his foster father's home in Edinburgh. Darach had stolen the only woman Craigen had ever loved. She'd taken one look at that tall, glowering oaf and left Craigen before he could blink. And the hell of it was, Darach couldn't have cared less about his lovely Caroline. He'd dallied with her for a short time, then sent her off while he pursued another lass at the court.

Caroline had left and gone home to Glasgow, shattered and unwilling to accept Craigen, even as second-best. Craigen took the blow full in his heart. He had vowed then that the whole of Clan MacStruan would pay for his loss.

His cause hadn't been hurt when he found out, through Edana, that there was rich ore in the hills owned by the MacStruans. It was only meet that he get Darach's treasure, since the MacStruan had stolen Craigen's. And Darach

315

and his ragtag little clan would be poorer by more than half.

He looked about the chamber that he'd furnished with everything he could find that filled his fancies and catered to his love of luxury. Recalling Caroline always made the opulent room seem more empty than a cell.

He picked up a crystal bowl and smashed it on the hearth, putting all his frustrations into the action. Damn Darach MacStruan! He could have had all he wanted, if not for that wretched bastard. If only Edana would tell him the time had come.

He needed a wife, he thought, pacing to the window and back. He needed a woman of his own. And if he couldn't have the one he loved, he'd have the most beautiful young treasure he could lay hands on. She was here, in his own house, and as yet he hadn't been permitted more than a chaste kiss. Edana had forbidden it, and he feared the witch too much to cross her. And as it was Edana who had brought Celandine to him, he couldn't be so ungrateful—or foolhardy—as to offend her.

But the time was drawing near, he hoped.

Was that what Edana was humming about? Was she consulting her mirror-basin to see if all the signs were right for his marriage to beautiful Celandine?

He hoped so. He didn't like to think what else the witch might be planning.

Chapter Twenty-one

Edana flicked at the old clothes she'd donned. Rusty with old dirt and damp, tattered and patched, they looked as if they'd been dragged through three wars and a flood. Perfect for her needs.

She lifted the pouch of trinkets to her shoulder and smiled. She didn't need a mirror to tell her she looked the image of an old peddler woman. Celandine's wondering eyes told her all.

"Well," Edana said briskly, her own lovely voice betraying her true age. "I'm off."

"Where?" Celandine rose from the cushions where she was seated, cross-legged, watching her companion change from a beautiful young woman to a stooped old hag.

Edana merely laughed. "Never you mind. You

317

don't need to worry about a thing, my little one. Leave all to me. You concentrate on being as lovely and as innocent as you are."

"So I can't go along." Celandine sat back down, her slender shoulders sagging. "I'm so tired of being a prisoner in this house!"

"A prisoner? Tut, lass. You're the Moreston's betrothed. You're not a prisoner. You're the most honored person here, save Craigen himself. And when the time comes and he takes you to wife, you'll have the world at your feet."

"And then can I go outside when I please?" The younger woman flounced impatiently on the cushions.

"You'll not want to," Edana said brightly. "You'll be so happy in your husband's bed and getting his children that you'll never long for anything else in the world. I'll make sure of it."

Celandine's delicate nose wrinkled. "His breath is of onions," she whispered. "And he's always looking at me like I'm a piece of honey cake." She shuddered.

Edana went and put a finger under the girl's chin. "So you are made of honey," she said, smiling. "And together you and I shall catch ourselves a kingdom with that honey." She straightened up and shifted her pouch once more. "I shan't be too long. Watch for me at sunset. And mind you go and play your harp for Craigen. He loves your music so and he's feeling as restless as you today. Mayhap the pair of you can find solace in your music."

Edana exited the room by the special door

that led down the east side of the castle. It was less watched, and most of the guards were susceptible to the simplest charms, so she used this route when she needed secrecy.

She hummed on her way to the woods. With each step she took inside the sheltering trees, her body bent even more. Her red hair first looked like fire, then slowly faded to the color of old, white ashes. She could feel her skin sagging, her lips pulling dryly over her teeth. By the time she crested the last rise above the MacStruan's village, she was completely transformed. No one would recognize her in this guise. As for that, of all the MacStruans, only Darach had ever laid eyes on her. And he hadn't cared who she was at the time.

She smiled, feeling with her tongue her crooked and chipped teeth. He'd know her soon, though, she thought. And he would be so happy.

Julia was baking bread. She had the dough spread out on a slab of smooth rock and was kneading the springy ball with extra energy. Good therapy, she told herself. Better to take out all those aggressions and anxieties on the dough than to act them out on the people around her.

In reality, her fingers itched to wrap themselves around Darach's neck and shake him till his teeth played like castanets. She knew she'd be more likely to shake herself silly before she so much as moved Darach, but she didn't care.

He was such a royal pain in the *ton*.

She grinned as she thought of the word. Alasdair had taught her that word, so she knew how that Gaelic word, at least, got into her head. And he'd had every right to use the phrase in reference to Darach last night.

Darach and the others had given up looking for Alasdair and returned to the village, grim-faced but not hopeless. Everyone in the clan knew that Alasdair was a wanderer, possessed of restless feet. He'd most likely show up sooner than later, they all said.

And so he had. He rolled into the house shortly after nightfall, looking especially pleased and cheery, if not a little dazed.

But Darach had risen from his place at the table, where they'd been finishing off a late meal, and read his brother the riot act. Julia had never seen Darach so fierce in his criticism of Alasdair. Yet as she watched him, the idea came to her that some of what he was feeling was guilt. Darach believed that Alasdair was in love with her. But it was Darach who had won her heart. Now he was fearful that he had hurt his brother and he'd been fearful that Alasdair had gone off in anger. If anything had happened to Alasdair, he would never have forgiven himself.

She could understand his feelings, but she couldn't for the life of her figure out why he'd chosen such a ferocious means of expressing them. He and Alasdair had come to the point of drawing their swords, when the Bruce had intervened by what was an obviously fake attack of coughing and choking. Later, when she and Darach were alone in the kitchen, she had challenged his treatment of his brother.

"Why did you light into him like that?" she demanded. "You were that far from getting into a sword fight with your only brother!"

"It's none o' your affair," he began.

"The hell it isn't!" she snapped. "I'm not putting up with any of that outlander crap anymore! I live with this clan, I feed this clan. I cook for you, play with you, nurse you, sing with you, eat and drink with you, and, in case you've forgotten, I've slept with the chief of Clan MacStruan!"

"He's got to learn sometime!" Darach retorted. "He canna go off and scare the whole of the clan like that."

"Why didn't you tell him that?"

"I did."

"No, you didn't, you big beastie! You ragged on him about his wandering and about his responsibilities. You got up in his face and told him he was a disgrace and a slacker. You told him you'd toss him out on his rear if he disappeared again without telling you where he was going."

He glowered at her. She nodded. "You know I'm right. I was there. You didn't say you'd missed him or that you were worried about him or any of that. Just a swift right hook to the jaw."

"Hook?"

"Never mind the linguistics! You treated him

shabbily and you know it."

"Alasdair knows what I meant."

"Does he? Is that why he was ready to pull out his claymore and hack right back at you?" She put her hands on her hips. "You're not the easiest man in the world to get to know or to understand. Yes, everyone knows you're a good man and a good leader. All of us are loyal to you—including Alasdair and me, the outlander. But sometimes you have to find ways of telling people what you mean and what you want without worrying about your image as the rough, tough, shoot-'em-up sheriff of Dodge City!"

"Ye're meddlin' again, Julia."

"You bet I am."

"Ye're tryin' to change me into somethin' else but what I am."

"Not true. I'm trying to make you see that you have a couple more choices when you deal with other people."

"I am how I am."

"Really? Then what you are is a major lunkhead, which is what I thought the first time I laid eyes on you."

"Fine. I'm a lunkhead. And I dunna need a lass tellin' me how to manage my ain folk."

"That's right, you don't. You need a good swift kick in the kilt!"

"Fine!"

"Fine!"

And out he'd stormed, leaving her to kick at the stove in frustration and then dance about the room, holding on to the injured foot.

Alasdair had come into the kitchen. That was when she had learned her new word.

"He does love you, you know," she'd said, handing him a plate of steamed vegetables.

"Aye. And I love him. But I'm startin' to wonder if we can live in the same house any longer. Or in the same village, for that matter."

"Don't you dare run off. Don't let him get away with treating you like that."

Alasdair cocked a brow. "Interestin' talk from Darach's ain true love."

She felt herself color. "No, it's not. It's because I love him that I want him to see that he can't treat everyone as if they're children or cows or something that he has to keep in line or they'll go off and do something daft." She dished up some of the venison she'd grilled. "I do love Darach. And I love you, too. I never had a brother but I couldn't imagine a better one than you."

He accepted the plate with a wry smile. "I'm glad Darach's taken ye into his heart," he said. "I could no' imagine anyone better for the big lunkhead."

"Oh-ho! So you were listening at the keyhole, eh, Mr. MacStruan?"

"Well . . . it wasna so difficult to hear the pair of ye."

"In other words, we were yelling like a couple of . . ."

"Lovers?"

She'd shaken her head and started to clean

up. "I don't know, Alasdair. We love each other, but is that enough?"

Those words had echoed through her thoughts and dreams all night. When she'd climbed the stairs, she waited for a moment in the hall, hoping that Darach would emerge from his chamber and invite her to join him. She'd hoped in vain. Sighing, she'd gone to her own room alone.

Morning had come and she still hadn't seen him. Ross had said that Darach's horse was already gone from the stable by the time he'd risen, shortly after sunrise. She was alone in the house, with her thoughts and her bread. Thoughts about staying, about leaving, about a circle of old, gray stones.

A knock came at the outer door. Wiping her hands on a piece of toweling she went to answer it, assuming it was Ross or Tommy wanting her to come see the newest produce in the garden. She opened the door with a smile, then stepped back quickly, startled.

"Oh, dinna be frighted, lassie," the old woman said cheerily. "Ye've no' met me before, have ye?"

Julia took another step back. "Uh, no . . . I don't think we've met. . . ."

"I'm Lizzie Lindsay. I come up frae Kinloch frae time to time to sell my goods to the MacStruans. And who would ye be, ye pretty wee thing?"

"I'm Julia. What can I do for you, Ms. Lindsay?"

"Oh, no, dearie. Call me Lizzie. Everybody does." She patted the large leather pouch she had slung over her shoulder. "Is the chief about? He likes a trinket now and then for his ladies, he does."

"Does he now?" Jealousy pricked at her. Which ladies were these? she wondered.

"I kin come again, lass. It's only 20 or 30 miles down to Kinloch." She turned and started to shuffle away.

"Wait!" Julia beckoned the woman back. "Darach's not here. But at least come in and have something to eat and drink. I had no idea you'd come such a long way."

"Oh, I couldna take your victuals," Lizzie said.

"You must. I know about the code of hospitality here in the Highlands. Darach would be outraged if he knew I'd turned someone away from his door."

"Well, if ye think it well." The woman shuffled over the threshold and peered about with her milky old eyes. "What a fine kitchen. Your husband is a right lucky fella."

"I'm not married." Julia went to the pantry and fetched fruits, cheeses, bread, and ale. She hurried back to find the old woman seated next to the hearth, petting LC. Oddly, LC, usually the most amiable of creatures, took one sniff of the woman, arched her back, spat, and then swiped at the gnarled hand that touched her.

"Little Cat!" Julia cried. LC streaked off to parts unknown. "I'm sorry," she said, hurrying over to the woman's side. "I hope she didn't hurt you. She's usually very friendly. She probably smells another animal on you. Do you have a cat?"

Lizzie shook her head as she sucked at her finger. "Dinna fret yourself, lass. Cats are sae fickle sometimes, is all."

"Here, let me get you a plate and a cup."

Julia bustled around and put together an attractive plate for her guest. She came and sat by the hearth while the woman ate and drank.

"Do you make the things that you sell?" she asked, making conversation.

"Some, aye. Open my pack and have a peek, lass."

Julia lifted the heavy pouch and laid it on the hearth. She opened the flap and reached inside. "Why, these are lovely," she said, fingering some embroidered linens.

"Gae ahead. Look all ye like. Mayhap ye'll find somethin' that ye're dyin' to have."

Julia lifted out several bundles done up in clean old cloths. She opened them one by one, exclaiming and remarking on their contents. She held up a quaint thimble in the shape of a sitting hen. "I ought to get this for Dugan," she said with a laugh.

"Aye. Dugan does love his fowl. He's traded eggs and hatchlings for my goods many a time."

"So you come up here often?" Julia held a silver comb up to the light.

"Oh, aye. Years and years." Lizzie set her plate aside. "Now that's a piece I got from a fella who'd brought it all the way from London town." She pointed a crooked finger at the design on the comb's side. "Is that no' a cunning image of a rose?"

"It's lovely."

"Try it, lass. It'll look sae fair on ye, wi' yer dark tresses."

"Oh, no. I couldn't. I can't afford it."

"Whisht. Try it. We'll talk about price after." Lizzie rose from the stool. "Here, let me catch up yer side hairs, like so. . . ."

"Ouch!" Julia grabbed at her head as the woman pushed hard on the comb. Her eyes swam with tears at the pain.

"Just a wee bit farther," the woman said.

"No, don't—it's—"

Julia's stomach rolled and her breath came in short, harsh gasps. She caught a glimpse of the old woman's face as she crumpled to the floor. How strange, she thought dreamily. The woman had two faces. A young one and an old one . . .

And then she thought no more.

Edana straightened and wiped her hands on her skirt. "There. That's done." She scooped all her goods back into her pouch and shouldered it easily. "Good-bye, Julia," she said, gazing down at the young woman who lay so still on the floor. "And you needn't worry. There'll be no charge."

Chapter Twenty-two

"So, lad. Are ye plannin' to ignore the lass forever?"

Darach glared at the Bruce. The old man took
liberties no one else would dare. Except, of
course, Julia.

"Nay."

"Well?"

"Well, what?"

"Are ye no' going to go to her?" Bruce
smacked him on the arm with his cap. "She's
been waitin' all night and a mornin'. Long
enough, do ye no' think?"

"It's no' the right time. I need to know more
about her—"

"Ye're no' thinkin' o' havin' the priest up here
to question her? After all that's been said and
done? Wee Julia's nigh a part o' the clan, lad."

The Mirror And The Magic

Darach pulled a sour face as he groomed his horse. "Your Highness, I dunna think she'll be wantin' to speak to me."

"Boidsear! Are ye truly sae ignorant o' women? After all the mischief ye got into when ye were fostered—"

"Saints! Leave off!" Darach punched the air with his fist. "The whole lot o' ye think ye can arrange my life for me! Who's chief o' the MacStruans?"

Bruce pulled himself up stiffly. "Ye're the MacStruan, lad. But ye'd do well to recall I'm king!"

The older man turned sharply and marched out of the stables, his staff beating a military tattoo as he exited. Darach leaned his forehead against his horse's withers. He'd offended the Bruce. He'd offended Julia. He'd offended Alasdair. Who'd be next? Big Dog?

God, but he'd missed Julia last night. He'd been tempted to go to her room and wake her up. But he feared she'd send him away and he couldn't have borne that from her. Not now.

He needed her. The shock of the thought made him jerk upright. He needed her. He knew it. But what the devil did it mean? Was he to give in to her every time she stood up to him? Did it mean abandoning things he'd been taught since he was a bairn and adopting her ways?

Or did it mean that for the first time in his life he had a partner, someone with whom he could share all his ideas, all his cares? To his astonishment, the idea suited him to the ground.

He tossed down his grooming rag and bolted out of the stable. Even if he had to go on one knee and beg her forgiveness, he wasn't going to let Julia spend another night away from him.

He burst into the house. "Julia!"

He got no answer. He raced for the kitchen. "Julia, love, I—"

He got no further. For a long, horrible moment, he stood in the doorway of the kitchen, staring at Julia's crumpled body lying on the floor. He fell to his knees beside her and gathered her up into his arms. He looked around wildly. There was no one around except the wee gray cat, who was mewing at him and padding in anxious circles around her mistress. But the outside door was open wide.

He patted Julia's cheeks. No response. She was so white, he thought, his heart contracting in his chest. He began to shout for help.

He hauled her lifeless body up off the floor. It was then that he saw the glint of silver in her hair. He'd never seen that before.

Ross and Alasdair came pounding in the back door.

"Darach! What's—" Alasdair bounded forward.

"It was this." Darach's voice was actually shaking. He held up the delicate silver comb. "Saints, her blood's on the tines!"

Alasdair felt Julia's wrists and throat. "She's

still warm, Darach. And I feel a pulse at her throat. She's alive."

"But she's sae pale."

"Let's get her to a bed."

Darach seemed to come to his senses. "Aye. Ross, gather the others. Ask them if they've seen anyone comin' or goin' this mornin'."

"Aye, Darach."

Ross raced out the back door as Darach pushed through the kitchen door with Julia in his arms. He mounted the stairs, hesitated before her chamber door, then marched past to kick open the door to his own room. He laid her on the bed and began chafing at her wrists. Alasdair pulled out a flask and offered it to Darach. Darach took it and lifted Julia's head so that he could tip the liquid into the corner of her mouth.

"Come on, Julia. Wake up, love!"

Tommy raced into the room. "Where is she?" he cried.

"She's here. But we canna get her to waken to us." Alasdair motioned the boy to stay back.

"Julia's taught me some o' her medicine," Tommy said, breathless from running. "Let me help!"

"What's she taught ye?" Darach's eyes never left Julia's still face.

Tommy ran around to the other side of the bed. He looked at her. "Is it something she's eaten, do ye know?"

Darach shook his head. He held up the comb.

Drops of red glistened on each of the sharp tines.

Tommy frowned. "What's that?"

"This is the trinket that drew her blood."

Tommy took the comb and held it up to the light. "There's more here than a cut to the head," he said. "There's some kind o' powder all along the teeth." He sniffed it. "It smells rank."

"Poison," Darach said flatly.

Tommy nodded. "I'm no' sure how to treat this, Darach. Julia told me mostly about poisonings in the stomach." He reached for the flask. "But she's taught me a bit about cuts. We can use strong spirits, she says, to purge the wound of infections. It may help to remove some of the poison in the cuts."

Darach yanked out the hem of his shirt and tore a strip off the hem. "Here. Use this."

Tommy soaked the cloth in the liquor and began dabbing at the spot where the comb had been driven into Julia's scalp. "The tines went in deep," he said. "Why would she push a comb sae far in?"

"She wouldn't," Darach said, his eyes never leaving Julia's still, white face.

"Then who—" Tommy's eyes went wide as he looked at Alasdair. "Sweet Jesu, do ye think it was the witch?"

"If it wasna the witch herself, then it was one o' her Moreston lackeys," Darach said.

"How would they hae come into the house?" Tommy asked. "No one here would hae permitted a stranger to walk onto our lands, let alone come into yer house, Darach."

Alasdair answered. "Ye forget, Julia doesna know any o' the Morestons. And no one knows what the witch herself may look like."

Darach nodded. "Whoever did this, they looked trustworthy to Julia. She let them come in. She even fed them."

Tommy swore an oath, then looked up at Darach and flushed. "Sorry," he said. "But Julia's been kind to me."

"Dunna fret yourself," Darach told him. "It's what we all want to say." He looked down at Julia. "God help me! She's no' breathin'!"

Tommy went into action at once. Grabbing Julia from Darach's grasp, he pushed her down on the bed.

"Lad, get your finger out o' her mouth! She'll—"

"Whisht!" Tommy cried. "I know what I'm doin'."

Darach had never felt so completely helpless in all his life. Julia, his beautiful and odd wee Julia was in peril and there was not a thing he could think of to do for her, save watch and pray as a 17-year-old lad ministered to her in the strangest ways.

He felt Alasdair's hand on his shoulder. He looked up and nodded his thanks briefly. Then back to the bed, where Tommy seemed to be kissing Julia with great energy, if a decided lack of skill.

"What's he doin'?" he whispered to Alasdair.

"I canna say. But he's been a faithful pupil.

And Julia helped us when all the men were sick wi' the stew. If there's aught to be done, Tommy'll do it."

"Please, God, let it be so."

Now Tommy was pumping his hands on Julia's chest, causing her body to jerk rhythmically. He kept glancing at her face, as if watching for signs of life. Then he went back to kissing her.

"He's tryin' to blow the life back into her!" Darach whispered, awestruck.

"He's done it!" Alasdair cried. "Look! She's breathin'!"

Tommy sat back, sweat dotting his forehead. Darach scooped Julia up and held her against him. To his utter joy, she moaned and shoved her elbow into his ribs.

"You're crowding me—Oh, God, I'm going to be sick!"

Alasdair raced for a basin and got it to her in the nick of time. Darach looked around and saw Tommy and Alasdair grinning like idiots. Then he realized his face most likely carried the same foolish expression.

Julia straightened up at last. Tommy pressed a damp cloth into her hand and she wiped her mouth.

"What happened?" she asked, her voice scarcely more than a croak. "I feel like I was run down by a garbage truck."

"We think ye were poisoned, lass," Darach said gently.

• She scowled at him. "Poisoned? Oh, hell,

have you been trying to cook again?"

Darach was too overjoyed to take umbrage. "Nay. I was nowhere near the kitchen. Do ye recall anyone comin' in?"

She shook her head, then clapped her hands to her temples. "Ow, damn, that hurts!" She probed at her scalp. "What the . . ."

Darach prodded her gently. "Was there anyone else in the kitchen wi' ye?"

She sat there for a long moment, staring into space. "A young woman," she said slowly. "No, an old one. Yes, a very old woman. Dressed in rags. She came to the kitchen door. She said she came here often to sell trinkets to the clan." She looked at Darach. "She said her name was Lizzie Lindsay."

All three men started. "What?" she asked. "You do know her, don't you?"

"In a way, yes," said Alasdair.

"She used to come here to sell her odds and ends," Darach said. "But lass, auld Lizzie Lindsay's been dead and in her grave near four years now."

"Uh-huh." She slid down on the bed and Darach helped her stretch out with her head on the pillows. "So we're back to square one. You figure either I'm crazy or I'm lying, right?"

Her words entered his heart like an arrow. He shook his head. "Nay, love. I think ye have the right of it. Ye were taken in by a witch."

She closed her eyes. "Oh, please. Not that again."

Tommy patted her hand. "It's true, Julia. She

put a poisoned comb into yer head."

She looked up and took the silver bauble he held. "This?" she asked wonderingly. She touched her temple again and winced. "Poisoned?"

"I think so. There's a white powder on the teeth o' the comb and it doesna smell a bit like your hair." He blushed and shot a glance at Darach.

Darach was too preoccupied to care about Tommy's youthful, and possibly lustful, observations. He caressed Julia's arm. "Julia, lass. How are ye feelin'?"

"Like hell with anchovies."

He grinned. "Ye're better then."

"If this is better, I don't want to know what dead is like." She closed her eyes. "I ache all over. And my mouth is so dry. Who punched me in the chest?"

"I did."

She peered at Tommy out of one eye. "I thought you liked me."

"Ye stopped breathin'," Darach told her. "Tommy here blew the air back into ye."

Both her eyes opened in wonder. She groped for Tommy's hand. "You did CPR on me?" she asked.

"Aye, Julia. I did just what ye told me."

Her face crumpled. "You did CPR on me," she repeated tearfully. "You guys do care."

"Whisht," Tommy said, embarrassed but still proud. "I only did as I was taught. I can't wait to teach Lara."

"I can imagine," Alasdair drawled. He laughed as Tommy colored even redder.

"Pay him no mind," Darach said. "Ye saved Julia's life, lad. I owe ye."

"Ditto," Julia said dreamily, her eyes closing once more.

"Nay, don't go to sleep," Tommy said, shaking her. "Darach, set her up again. Alasdair, fetch some water. I don't dare give her anything stronger."

The two brothers did as they were told, their eyes meeting in an amused glance over the end of the bed. *Tommy's come into his own,* Darach thought. *And well he wears it.*

There was a scuffling at the door. Ross came bursting through, with the rest of the lairds almost on top of him. "Darach, I tried to keep them out but they wouldna listen to me!"

Gordon pushed forward. "How's wee Julia?" he demanded, glowering about the room as if one of them might have done the deed.

"Not wounded, sir, but dead," Julia intoned, raising a limp hand in salute. "That's from *Philadelphia Story,* for all you film fanatics."

Gordon grinned and ran a hand over his bald pate. "That's our ain Julia, all right." He turned to the other men, who stood clogging the doorway. "She's alive."

"Tell him we heard, Dugan," Liam said.

"We heard, Dugan," the big fellow muttered, staring into the room. Liam scowled but was ignored.

"All right," Tommy said, herding them all out

into the hall again. "Ye've seen her. Now let her rest."

"Since when are ye chief here, laddie?" Niall bristled.

"Do as the man says," Darach said, rising to stand by Tommy.

The men left, mouths gaping. Tommy returned to his patient, swaggering a bit as he went.

LC trotted into the room and leapt up on the bed. Darach headed toward her, ready to toss her as far as Inverness. Then the wee thing nuzzled up against Julia's side and settled in, purring. Its slanting green eyes studied him with mild curiosity and complete confidence. Julia smiled and scratched behind the cat's ears.

He groaned. "Hell, what was the point in all those initiations and bein' named chief o' the MacStruans?" he asked of the walls. "The bleezin' cats have more say in my ain house than I!"

"Puir auld ogre," Julia murmured.

He grinned. "Welcome back, wee Julia."

Edana could hardly wait to get back to her tower room and consult her mirror-basin. On the way home from the MacStruan's village, she had changed back into her usual lovely form. She cast off the tattered clothes as soon as she could and sent for a servant to bring water from her special supply.

In the privacy of her chamber, she poured the water, scattered the precious powder. "Show me my love," she cooed and waited for Darach's image to appear. She smiled with delight as his face took shape in the settling water. How handsome he was, she thought. How utterly—

She stiffened. What was that? Another image was superimposing itself on Darach's.

"It's her." Edana ground out the words through gritted teeth. That wretched woman was still in the house. There she was, sitting on a bed, brushing out her black hair and looking only a bit wan for her brush with death. How could her poison have failed?

"Tell me, Servant. Is this an image of a living person?"

"It iss e'en so, mistresss."

Edana trembled in her rage. "I ask you, Servant. Is my love's heart mine still?"

"Hisss heart belongss to another, mistresss."

She stifled the scream that rose in her throat. She would stay in control, she told herself. She would rid herself of this obstacle. It would require more drastic measures, she knew. And she would have to be more subtle. But this Julia woman would die.

Julia was sick for several days. The effects of the poison had been mitigated by Tommy's quick action, but she had still gotten a small dose of the deadly stuff in her system. Tommy stayed with her through that first day and night, along with Darach, then surrendered his post to Darach and went home to sleep the sleep of a champion.

The lairds had not been idle. Every path and

deer track was searched for clues. Alasdair questioned Julia closely about the old woman, and she'd done her best to recall everything, but much of the morning was lost in a haze.

While she slept, Darach gathered the lairds in the great hall. He set up a rotation for all of them to act as guards over Julia, day and night.

"She willna like it," Niall said.

"Don't I know it," Darach replied. "That's why I'm chargin' each of ye wi' the task. And it's up to ye to think of an explanation if—hell, this is Julia we're talkin' about—*when* she asks ye why ye're hangin' about." He nodded to Tommy. "Ye have the excuse of being her physician." He looked to Alasdair. "Ye live in this house, so ye can say ye're only bein' companionable. As for the rest of ye, do your best."

"Aye, Darach."

Darach crossed the burn at a narrow spot, his long legs straddling the distance with ease. He judged that this was the area where the men had been fishing the day Julia was attacked. He shaded his eyes against the sun as it emerged with sudden brilliance from behind a cloud. A short stretch of meadow led to the eaves of the forest.

Though he couldn't see them from here, he knew there were charred stumps and bare patches in that wood, bitter reminders of the fire set deliberately by the Morestons. While he was away in Edinburgh, living in luxury, his people had been at the mercy of their old enemies. The Morestons encircled the site where his father and his uncle were sleeping and had set the trees and bracken alight. The deadly circle of flames had wakened the pair, but it was the smoke that sealed their fate. In a matter of moments, they were lost in the thick, foul darkness.

A more evil trap could not have been laid. When the MacStruan chief and his brother stumbled out of the woods, choking and hacking at the burning brush around their legs, the Morestons had ambushed them. When Mairi MacStruan brought her complaint to the earl, the Morestons had stoutly claimed that the two men had come over their borders in the night, wielding swords. They'd only done what any citizen might, by law: They had defended their own lands and people against men who were known to be their sworn enemies.

Mairi had come home, broken with grief and frustrated rage. She'd sent for Darach right away, and then taken to her bed, ill and silent. It was months before she returned to normal life, and even then she was much diminished in health and vigor. She had rallied for Darach and Isobel's marriage and had stayed firm in her support of her son in his time of grief and of learning the ways of a clan chief. But she had gone willingly enough to the hills with the women when one of the maids of the village had been assaulted and savagely beaten one evening a year ago.

Darach began to cross the meadow, searching the grasses for any signs that might remain of the day Julia had been attacked. His heart roared in outrage at the mere thought of anyone threatening her. The fact that the villain had chosen the eaves of this haunted forest to commit his crime made it doubly heinous. If this, and the more recent attack on Julia, didn't show the fine, black hand of the Moreston, he'd climb to the top of Schiehallion and crow like a rooster. What was more, this time, he wouldn't let the villains get away with their crimes.

He squatted as he came under the shadow of the pine wood. He peered into the dim recesses, seeing gold bars of sunlight piercing through the branches here and there. Cocking his head, he listened. It was uncannily silent.

He glanced about, the hairs on the back of his neck prickling. There should be bird song, he thought to himself, or the bleating of the deer to their young. Even the insects had halted their midday hum.

Slowly he put a hand to his knife. He rose and turned in a circle, half-crouched and ready for attack. Still he saw no one, heard no footsteps.

He kept up his guard, but continued his search. Slowly the sounds of the forest resumed and his feeling of apprehension passed. There had been no rain to speak of since the attack and there might still be prints to follow. He paused at a thick clump of bracken. He squatted once again, examining the lush ferns with a light hand. Dark drops marked the green fronds, small spatters that Darach recognized as dried blood. He broke off a leaf and sniffed it, then rubbed it between his fingers.

Someone or something had bled on this spot, and recently, too. Whether it was man or beast, there was no way to tell. But it corresponded with Julia's story of the bleeding stranger who'd stood in the eaves and beckoned to her for help.

He rose with a muffled growl. His Julia had too soft a heart. She'd minister to the devil himself if he but showed her a bruised thumb. And look where her tender heart had gotten her: choked and then poisoned.

He prowled about the spot where the blood had fallen, his heart and his conscience nagging at him to admit that it was not only Julia's kindness that had put her in danger. He was responsible himself. He had brought her into danger by loving her.

He smiled to himself in wonder. One moment he'd been determined to let her go and remove her disturbing presence from his life. The next moment he was hunting her down, bringing her back into the fold of his clan, bringing her into the realm of his heart. He had done what he'd told himself was unthinkable: He'd staked a claim on beautiful, mad, outlandish Julia. And he was prepared to defend that claim to the death.

Death. He stalked farther into the woods. He couldn't allow the Morestons to take her as they had taken Isobel. He knew with every sense and instinct in his nature that the Morestons were behind these attacks on Julia. They were trying to strike at him through her, all because he wouldn't sell his clan to the greedy bastards. He couldn't let her become a victim of his failure as a chief. This time he'd not make the same mistake as before.

He would bind sweet Julia to him, protect her, defend her, hide her away if need be. But she would be his and his alone, forever.

Chapter Twenty-three

Darach came home from his search looking sober yet calm. Julia caught him watching her throughout the evening meal. When they gathered at the fireplace for stories, he asked to hear the story of Bogart and Bacall in *Casablanca*.

She told it willingly, since it was one of her favorites, but her concentration wasn't all it might have been, for those deep blue eyes were trained on her every moment, looking ready to devour her. She found herself warming, felt her heart beating a little faster as she spoke. There was no mistaking the message in his eyes, she thought, but what had brought about such a change?

When she was finished, Liam stood and cleared his throat for attention. He folded his hands on his stomach and blinked solemnly at the group that ringed the fire.

"The other lairds and I have a proposal to put forth to ye, Darach," he said. "Will ye hear it?"

Darach looked a trifle annoyed, but he gave his assent. Liam nodded his thanks and cleared his throat once more.

"As ye know, the traditions o' our fathers and mothers go back generations, before the time of St. Columba, before the northern men in their longships, before the Stane of Scone was set in place for the crowning of—"

"Will I live lang enough to hear the end o' this proposal?" Darach drawled. The men laughed and Liam smiled sheepishly.

"I shall get to the heart of the matter, and that is that our hearts have been won by the movee tales of our ain Julia. The adventures o' the Indiana Jones, the gruesome tale o' the Alien, the tragic love o' that laddie Romeo for his lady Juliet—these are tales that shine wi' the best o' our auld tales." He turned to Julia. "Having said this, wee Julia, I would tell ye that we have a name for the likes of ye in the Highlands: seanachaidh, a teller of tales. From ancient times, the seanachaidh have sat before the hearths—"

"The proposal," Niall prompted.

Liam shot him an irritated glance, then turned to Darach. "In brief—"

"God, make it so," muttered Gordon.

"In brief," Liam continued, ignoring him, "I have been commissioned by my fellows to ask that Julia Addison of the New York be named as seanachaidh of Clan MacStruan."

Darach looked at Julia, his eyes dancing. "What say ye, Julia Addison? Will ye agree to be chronicler of Clan MacStruan, relating its mighty deeds and its joys, its battles and its sorrows?"

"And will ye tell us that *High Noon* story again, Julia?" Tommy put in.

"I—I don't know what to say." She looked around at the group of men who were smiling and nodding their approval. In their weird and wonderful MacStruan way, she knew they were paying her a high compliment. "I'm honored," she said, looking at Darach. "I'll do my best to live up to the title, if you really want me."

"We do," Bruce said, beaming.

"Aye," added Dugan.

"Then stand, Julia Addison," Liam said. He lifted a basket from the floor and removed a short staff, the head a knob carved with a stylized design of interwoven knots and thistles.

Julia stood, mist edging her vision. She glanced at Darach. He nodded solemnly.

"Accept the slat-sgeulachd, the staff of tales," Liam said, holding it out to her. "And let all know that ye are the bard o' the MacStruans."

Julia took the staff and held it out in front of her. She looked around at the men who had chosen her to be the chronicler of their lives. "I accept the slat-sgeulachd with pride," she said solemnly. "And I will watch and listen and tell your stories and mine as best I can."

"Hear! Hear!" cried Bruce. The others took up the cry, stamping their feet and whistling.

Julia beamed at them all. Tommy leaned out from his seat on the floor near the hearth. "Now, wee Julia? *High Noon?*"

Darach stood. "Let our new seanachaidh have her rest," he said before Julia could reply. He took her hand, lacing her fingers with his. He nodded to the men, who, for once, elected to be discreet and exit promptly, making their farewells as they passed through the door.

In the silence that followed their departure, Julia turned to Darach, feeling suddenly shy. He lifted her chin with one finger and placed a feather-light kiss on her lips.

"I'm sorry I quarreled wi' ye, lass," he murmured, his voice soft as the rabbit-fur slippers she wore.

"I'm sorry, too," she said, putting her hands on his shoulders. "I was being a nag. I know you'd never do anything that wasn't for the good of the clan. I—I think I get jealous of them sometimes."

He cocked a brow. "Jealous o' that gaggle o' lunkheads?"

She smiled. "Uh-huh. I get jealous when I see how much you love them and how they always come first with you, even if it's not the best for you. Even if you get a wee bit pigheaded about it."

He placed his hands on her waist and pulled her close. "Clan comes first, it's true, sweet. But my ain Julia is the bard of the MacStruans. She's the MacStruan's lady. She's clan."

She stared at him, her mouth slightly open

with wonder. "You—you mean that?" she whispered.

He took advantage of her, shamelessly, and kissed her breathless. "Aye, love, I mean it," he said, pressing his lips to her temple. "If ye'll have me."

She threw her arms about his neck and held on for dear life as he carried her off to the stairs.

Edana lifted the apple to the light. "Perfect," she murmured. "So rosy and plump. Who could resist you?"

She put the lid on the small black pot and fastened the cord that bound it. "Wouldn't do to have anyone getting into that, would it?" she asked the white cat who sat on the tabletop, watching her mistress. The cat gave a throaty yowl and jumped down, heading for the window.

Laughing softly, Edana uttered her last words of incantation over the poisoned fruit, swirled her cloak about her, and vanished into the shadows. The cat howled to the moon from the window ledge. As if in answer, the sound of laughter rippled through the night, twining with the mists above the trees.

"Tell me about Isobel."

They'd been lying on Darach's bed, fully clothed, necking like teenagers. Julia had the delicious sense that they were playing hooky. Darach had slipped up behind her in the garden that afternoon and swept her off to the bedroom, his eyes saying all she needed to know. For the first time in a long while, she felt as if they had all the time in the world.

In this sweet, almost innocent intimacy, she dared to ask the question that she'd been keeping in her heart ever since Rose had told her the story in the caves.

Darach closed his eyes. "That's all done, Julia. Let it rest."

"No. I can't." She inched closer to him. "I need to hear about her. What she was like. How you got engaged. How you felt about her."

"Isobel's dead," he said, his voice hollow.

"I know that. But—"

He opened his eyes. "But what? What has Isobel to do wi' you and me?"

"You loved her, didn't you?"

He sat up. His silence grew long.

She gazed at him in wonder. "You didn't love her?" she asked softly. "But everyone said, you and she—I don't understand."

He put his head into his hands. "I know what everyone thought. They said it often enough, how Isobel and I were sae perfectly matched, how we were sae in love. But it was a sham. At least, it was for my part."

Julia sat up and put her hand on his shoulder. "If you didn't love her, why did you agree to marry her?"

He raised his head and stared at the wall. "It had been planned since we were bairns. And it was fine when we were young." He shrugged.

"Then I went to Edinburgh. I met one or twa women there—"

"One or twa?"

He shot her a sour glance. "All right. So there was more than one or twa. But I learned more about the world there, and that women are as different from one another as men."

"Very enlightened of you."

He ignored her sarcasm. "When Da was killed, and I was summoned home, Isobel was grown up. She was the same sweet, shy lass I'd left. More so. And as fresh as a violet frae the glen." He rose and began to pace. "There was nothin' about her that any man couldna love. Or learn to love."

"But you weren't any man."

He shook his head. "I couldna. I liked Isobel. I loved her as my kinswoman. But I never felt the love I knew she craved o' me. The love that should be between a man and a woman when they pledge their lives to one another."

"You were going to marry her anyway?"

"Aye. I gave my word, and to break faith wi' Isobel would have been to break faith wi' all. I'd be no chief to lead the MacStruans. So, aye, we made the marriage plans."

"And then she was . . . taken."

He stood looking into the fire. "She was stayin' in my ain house, carin' for my mother, who'd been ill. She was that good, always carin' for others."

Julia rose and went to him. She put her hand on his arm. "You can't keep beating yourself up for what happened to Isobel. It was out of your control."

He shook off her hand. "But it was in my control! Can ye no' see? I had the chance to bargain for her life but I wouldna. I let my pride lead me and I refused to strike a bargain wi' Craigen. Isobel perished while I was playin' the great chief who would never give in."

A lump formed in Julia's throat. He was in such pain, she thought. He'd been carrying it around for years.

"Darach," she said, touching his arm once more. "You couldn't have known that Craigen would kill Isobel. You don't have a crystal ball that can foretell the future. You did what you thought was best for the clan, as you always do. You couldn't give Craigen your lands and let him walk all over you." She peered up into his tortured face. "Too often," she said, the sadness trembling in her voice, "people like Craigen kill their hostages anyway. Even if you had given him everything he asked for, Isobel would still be dead."

"Ye might be right. But the fact remains, I didna love her enough and I didna do all I could to save her. Her death will be on my soul for eternity."

"And what about me?"

He looked at her, his eyes stormy with pain. "I'm sorry, lass. I thought I was past Isobel's death, but it isna true. I'm no' a fit match for ye. I'll only bring ye sorrow. It's the curse of the MacStruan chiefs." He walked to the table and poured himself a cup of wine.

Julia went after him, her heart a chilly rock inside her chest. "That's it?" she asked. "You failed once and so it's all over?" She frowned, fighting against the tears that threatened to flood forth. "Do you feel about me the same way you felt about Isobel? Do you not love me either?"

He stared at her, astonished. "Nay. Do ye no' ken what ye are to me, Julia? Ye're my sun and moon, my soul and body. God, sayin' I love ye doesna tell it by half."

"Then why are you pushing me away?"

He gripped her shoulders, anguish in his eyes. "I fear too much for ye, love! I'm in trouble deep wi' the Morestons. I dunna know if I can protect ye or my clan. I'm no great champion at romancin', as ye know now. I bear the scars of too many bitter mistakes I've made. I have sae many memories of lives lost and I ken there will be more. I canna bear to see ye hurt, Julia!"

She was weeping openly now. "And I canna bear never to see you again!"

He crushed her to him, his anguish a palpable entity in his embrace. She sobbed into his chest, freeing all the fears and doubts she'd been holding in for so long. She also wept for the sorrows Darach had borne and the doubts and fears he carried on his broad, but terribly human shoulders.

He carried her to the bed and sat on the edge, cradling her in his lap. He rocked her in his arms and let her cry until her sobbing halted and her tears slowed. She sat up and wiped her eyes.

He shook his head. "What am I to do wi' ye, Julia Addison? Ye come into my life like a clap o' thunder and ye commence to turn every corner o' it upside down. Hae ye no shame or pity in ye?"

"No." She gave him a teary smile. "I majored in Shameless in college with a minor in Pitiless. Graduated with honors and distinction in tormenting big, bad Scotsmen."

His face grew more serious. "But lass, ye know ye canna stay. I dunna know what the Moreston might do to ye, but I'm no' about to wait around and find out. Craigen is out to get the mountain—the mountain where our women and bairns are hidin'. His witch has already threatened your life twice. The pair o' them will try again."

"I'm not going and you can't make me."

"Julia, do ye no' ken—"

"I ken plenty! Now do you love me or no'?"

"I love ye to distraction! But—"

"No buts." She took his face in her hands. "I love you to distraction, too, Darach MacStruan. And I willna be parted frae ye." She set one fist on her hip. "So are ye man enough to stand by me, ogre?"

He pushed her over onto the bed and pinned her shoulders. "Ogre, am I? Ogre for lovin' ye, lass? Or for carin' about ye?"

She grinned up at him. "Aye."

"I ought to—"

She got her fingers up under his plaid and tickled his ribs. He twisted, laughing, trying to escape her torment. She scrambled off the bed and bolted for the door.

He was across the room in a flash, his big hand slapping the door shut just as she reached for it. She ducked under his arm and fled, giggling, toward the far side of the bed.

He stalked her, his heavy boots clumping ominously. She grinned at him. "Now, Darach, remember your blood pressure. And that old football injureee—"

He lunged for her.

Chapter Twenty-four

Alasdair waited at the standing stone. He paced around the old rock with its worn carvings and kicked at the smaller, fallen stones that ringed its base.

Days, he thought to himself. It had been days since he'd first seen Celandine in the woods. They'd scarcely talked that first time, only stared at one another in wonder, exchanging names and promises to return, until a distant sound had frightened her into fleeing.

He'd come to this spot every day, hoping just to see her again. By now he was desperate, fearing she might never return. Or that it had all been a dream.

He heard a rustle in the woods. He looked up expectantly, but drew his knife all the same.

Once again she seemed to materialize beside

him. The golden strands in her hair shimmered in the late-afternoon light, and her eyes sparkled with unconcealed joy. On impulse he grabbed her and kissed her.

He pulled back, looking down into her lovely, gamine face. Her eyes remained closed, lips parted like a new-opened rose.

"Again," she whispered. "Oh, please, again."

He placed his hands on her shoulders. Desire and honor warred within him. Saints, she was so lovely, so tempting, he thought. And she was utterly guileless in her passion and in her demeanor.

"Come," he said, taking her by the hand. "We must talk."

"All right." She went with him and together they sat on one of the broad, flat stones of the circle. "What would you know?"

"First, who are ye?"

She laughed, a silvery, rippling sound that enchanted him. "I am Celandine, remember? Celandine Talcott. Does my name mean nothing to you?"

He thought hard and then shrugged. "I'm sorry."

She frowned. "I thought surely you knew who I was when last we met. You—Well, it's no matter." She lifted his hands and pressed them beneath her chin, smiling at him once more with her moonbeam of a smile. "I'm the betrothed of Craigen Moreston."

Alasdair thought he was going to be sick. He yanked his hands loose from hers and jumped to his feet. She stared up at him in alarm and confusion. "Alasdair? What is it?"

"Ye! Ye're a Moreston?"

"Aye. At least, I shall be."

"Are ye—are ye a witch?"

"No, of course not." He regarded her warily. She nodded reassuringly. "I am not a witch."

He drooped with relief.

"I'm one of the Fair Folk."

"God in heaven."

She trotted after him as he began pacing once again. He turned back to her at last. "Listen to me, lass. Is this some game ye're playin'? A prank?"

Her look was all innocent wonder. "A game? You want to play a game?"

"No. No, I dunna want to play any games." He clenched his fists. "Are ye serious? Ye're Faerie? And ye're to marry wi' the Moreston?"

"Aye. Edana, she's my guardian since my parents died, she says that I must wait to be wed until next month when the signs say I'll be most ready to receive his seed."

He closed his eyes. This was getting wilder and wilder by the moment. And Darach thought he had problems with a mere mortal Sassenach like Julia.

"Do you believe me?" Celandine asked, touching his arm.

"Do ye want to wed wi' Craigen?" The words came hoarsely from his throat.

She hung her head. "No."

He gripped her shoulders. "Then ye must

358

come away wi' me. Even if ye're as mad as auld Mad MacPhee, I can't leave ye to that mongrel Craigen. Saints, Celandine! He's been keepin' ye like a prize fowl, fattening ye up for the kill."

"But Edana—"

"Ye owe no allegiance to the Morestons, lass." Alasdair stroked her hair, his hand trembling with fear for her. In a matter of hours, she had entered his heart. He had to be with her, keep her safe.

"It's not the oath I made to him. It's a promise I made to her."

"To this Edana? Is she no' a Moreston?"

She shook her head. "I may not tell anyone. But I have promised. Edana has been good to me. Like a sister."

He growled deep in his chest. "'Twould be a cruel sister who'd hold ye to such a promise. I'll kill Craigen before he touches ye," he said fiercely.

An owl called in the woods. Celandine raised her head like a startled deer.

"I must go," she whispered, pulling away from him.

He pulled her back and kissed her, hoping to both silence her and persuade her. She kissed him back with equal fervor, but when the kiss ended, she had slipped out of his grasp somehow and was running for the trees.

"Celandine!"

"Wait for me, my love!" came the soft reply.

Chapter Twenty-five

Julia went up and over the bed and dropped to the other side, racing for the tapestry that hung from the wall. She ducked behind it, her laughter muffled against the heavy weave. Darach's booted footsteps followed right behind her.

"Ye're trapped, lass. Ye'd best give in."

"Never!"

She felt his hands moving along the hanging, coming closer and closer. She inched toward the far end.

"Julia," he called softly. "Are ye no' forgettin' somethin'?"

She held still, listening. What sort of trick was he planning to play?

"Aren't ye forgettin' that ye said ye couldna bear to be parted frae me?"

"Why, you rat, you!" she exclaimed. She leapt for the edge of the tapestry. He caught her in an instant, scooping her up and hauling her to the bed. She shrieked and kicked at him playfully. "That was a dirty trick," she huffed. "Taking advantage of a poor, helpless woman."

"Poor, helpless woman?" He guffawed. "The day ye're any of those will be the day that Dugan gives up his victuals."

"Are you saying I'm not a woman?" She pretended offense. "Then you're not a man, Ogre MacStruan."

He pulled her across his lap and kissed her hard. She succumbed immediately to his heated demands, returning his kiss in kind. After a long, long moment, he lifted his head and cocked an eyebrow at her.

"So, lass, you think I'm no' a man a'tall, eh?"

"I didn't say that. But I think you're awfully touchy for a man who goes about dressed in a skirt."

His face darkened but then he caught the sparkle of mischief in her eyes. "Is that so?" he asked, his voice dropping low. "And what of a lass who goes about in breeches?"

She smiled. "I haven't had any complaints."

"No, that ye haven't. Do ye no' like my plaid?"

She reached up and toyed with the heavy brooch that fastened the long piece of wool at his shoulder. "I do like it," she said softly.

His hand trailed over the plush knit of her sweater. "And this tunic of yours. It has its merits, I vow."

361

She shivered at the sensation of his big, hard hand caressing her back with such gentleness. "You like it?"

"I like it." His hand stopped in the middle of her back. "But I'm no' too sure about this."

She felt herself warming as his finger hooked into the back of her bra. "It's considered the proper thing to wear where I come from. And men often find them quite . . . exciting . . . to look at."

"Do they now?" His eyes sparkled. "Is that when they're on or when they're off?"

She chuckled. "On."

"Hmm. 'Tis an interesting notion." His fingers slipped around to the front of her sweater. The soft fabric slid upward. "I wouldna want to go against your customs too much," he said.

"No?"

"No."

She closed her eyes as the sweater continued to slide upward. She raised her arms and Darach slipped the garment off over her head. She opened her eyes to see him gazing at her in fascination and appreciation.

His fingertips traced the lacy edge of the brassiere, sending sparks flying through her. She straightened with pride at his warming regard.

"I see why yer menfolk want to see their women dressed in these," he said. "At least, why they'd want to see the likes of ye in one." His hand cupped her. "'Tis a fair silken package for sae sweet a gift."

He bent his head and kissed the place where

her breasts began to swell above the pastel peach lace. Julia wondered if there was a Victoria's Secret to be found in this place. The things she could show him . . .

"Is there more to see?" he murmured, tasting her neck.

"What do you mean?"

"Is there aught else beneath?"

"Why don't you find out?"

He lifted his head and smiled the most delightfully wicked smile. "I thought ye'd never ask."

He lifted his hands to her bra. He paused, frowning. He toyed with one of the straps, lifting and pulling it.

She twisted around so her back was to him. "See the clasp there?" she asked, lifting up her hair. "Just unhook it."

"Unhook it," he murmured. "Just unhook it."

Mastering the clasp took a while. Thorough as he was, he insisted on hooking and unhooking it until he was sure he could snap it free with one hand. At last, satisfied with his new skill, he freed her and sat back.

She lifted her hands to her shoulders and smoothed the straps down her arms. He took them the rest of the way, setting the bit of lace and satin aside on the bed.

"Ah, Julia Addison," he said. "Ye're the finest thing I've ever seen in my life." He bent to kiss the swells of her breasts, his lips grazing over her skin, causing her to shiver with delight.

He sat back again. "So. What else do the

women wear in your world?"

She tilted her head and raised her brows. "Why don't you find out for yourself?" she asked again.

He accepted her challenge. Lifting her easily about the waist, he placed her on the floor, standing between his knees. He studied her slacks for a long moment.

"You undo the button at the waist first."

"Buttons. These I know of." He made short work of it. He squinted at the zipper. "Ye're sure ye're no' a witch?"

She laughed. "Aye, I'm no' a witch," she said, imitating his lovely soft burr. "I'm a woman."

"Amen to that."

She took his hand and guided his fingers to the little tab at the top of the zipper. Slowly, slowly, they eased the zipper down.

"Ahh," he said wonderingly. "Such a device. But thank God no man has to wear such a thing near his privates."

She laughed again. "I've got news for you. In my world, they do."

His mouth fell open. "Ye can't mean it!" He shook his head. "Damn me, but the men in your land must be made of iron, to go about with their family jewels in peril all the day long!"

"Well, I think they'd say the same about you in your plaid."

"I'll ne'er understand it. But it does beat laces. Ye're not bound into your kirtle so as to keep a man out of where he wants to go."

He placed his hands on her hips and began

to ease the slacks downward. They slipped past her hips, fell to the floor, and she stepped out of them. She took a step back, allowing him to see what she wore beneath.

He gave a low whistle. "Lass, that wouldna keep ye warm on the hottest summer day." He made a circular motion with his hand and she revolved for him. "And what do ye call that?"

"Panties," she said. "Or briefs."

"Brief's the word, I'll grant ye that."

"You don't approve?" She turned back around to face him.

"Approve? Lass, if I get any more enthusiastic I'll shame m'self." He reached out for her and drew her back between his knees. He stroked the scrap of lace-trimmed satin, causing Julia to jump with the shock of pleasure.

"Easy," he crooned. "I was just testin' the dry goods."

She couldn't help laughing. "You say the damnedest things."

"I? I say? List' who's talkin'! Mistress Laser Beam Coffee Maker Dumpster Radio herself." He ran his hands around her hips. "Does this have one of those confounded clasps?"

She shook her head. He looked relieved.

She slipped her thumbs under the elastic and slid the panties away. He sat back on the bed and began to study her, inch by inch, from her toes to her hair. She thought she'd feel embarrassed. No one had ever looked at her in such a tangibly lustful way before. But she felt utterly at ease with Darach. And proud. And more aroused with each passing moment.

"Saints, Julia. Ye're somethin' out of a dream."

He pulled her to him and kissed her. She pulled back and eyed him squarely. "Now you."

She climbed up onto the bed and knelt before him. His deep blue eyes held hers as she placed her hands on his shoulders.

"How does this work?" she asked.

He tapped the brooch. "Try this."

She worked the slender, carved pin out of the circle of his brooch and freed the length of plaid at his shoulder. He shrugged and it fell to his waist. She pulled his arm free of the loop it made. "No buttons, eh?" she asked, fingering the laces at the cuffs of his shirt.

"No buttons. No clasps. No teeth fasteners to slide up and down and catch at a fellow's . . . skin."

She undid the laces at his close-bound cuffs. Then, on impulse, she leaned in toward his chest and undid the lacings at his neck with her teeth. He caught his breath. She sat back, smiling smugly.

"Ye're a tease."

"Am I?"

"What if I'd done that wi' those silky wee briefs of yours?"

A quick flush of excitement raised her temperature even more as she thought of his mouth touching such a sensitive area. He gave a soft growl and held out his arms. "Well?" he demanded. "Are ye goin' to leave me thus?"

She sat back on her heels and put a finger to her chin. "Hmm. I don't know. It's a bit like Christmas. I want to unwrap the package but then it won't be a surprise anymore."

"Leave the surprises t'me."

"All right." She gathered his shirt up and pulled it off over his head. She let it fall to the floor as she gazed once more with fascination and delight at the sight of him. "I love to look at you," she said softly, touching her fingertips to the thick mat of dark hair that covered his chest.

"I'm glad ye like what ye've seen thus far."

"And what else do the men of your country wear?" she asked.

"What d'ye mean?"

"You know," she said, smiling impishly. "Underneath."

"Why don't ye find out for yourself?"

She reached for his belt buckle. The good, heavy leather slid away from his waist. All that remained was his plaid, wrapped loosely about his lower body. She reached for the fabric. "You'll need to stand up."

He slid to the edge of the bed. Gently she tugged at the long length of wool and off it came, slipping to the floor to join the tangle of clothing already cast there.

And there he was before her, his warrior's body revealed to her in the bright light of the fire. She smiled up at him. "I could gaze upon you for hours."

He came and sat beside her on the bed. "Forgive me, sweet, but I'll have to indulge that wish another time. I need to touch ye. Now."

His urgency ignited hers. She slid toward him and wrapped her arms about his neck. "Touch me, then," she whispered. "Touch me everywhere, anywhere. I'm yours."

He pressed her tenderly into the feather bed and pillows, loving her. He lifted her over him and watched her find her pleasure, his eyes sparkling. He carried her in his arms to the tapestry that hung on the wall and, bracing her back against it, he loved her as he stood, holding her easily as they rocked together in slow, wild rhythms. He lay down beside her and cradled her into his body, playing languidly with her until she was beside herself, then turned her and loved her once more, staring down into her face with complete delight and passion.

Julia cuddled against him, tired and utterly sated. She stroked his cheek and wound his leg with hers.

"I love you," she whispered. "Do you know that?"

He took her hand and kissed her fingertips. "As I know my name, sweet. As I know I love ye, my ain Julia."

She turned in his arms and snuggled up against him, so happy in the knowledge that she was precious to this most amazing, complicated, masterful, vulnerable, overwhelming man. They'd marry soon. That is, if she had anything to say about it. She wasn't about to give him a chance to send her away. She hugged him in delight, her plans dancing in her head.

He tugged the covers over them both and soon was breathing the soft, even breaths of sleep. Julia smiled to herself as she gazed at the fading fire. Monty Gilette and his goons had done her a great big favor when they chased her into the Highlands. Into the Highlands and straight into love. Love and another feeling she had never fully known in her life—belonging. She was the MacStruan's lady.

She no longer cared that she was living in the strangest community she could ever have found. She no longer cared that water came from wells and streams, and cooking was done over peat fires, and sanitation was a daily battle. She didn't care any longer if she was from the twentieth century, stuck somehow in time. She wasn't going anywhere. She'd found a love and a family to fill her heart.

A family! The idea brought another delightful shiver to her. What if a bairn was already growing inside of her? A wee MacStruan planted there by the MacStruan, her love?

She couldn't sleep. Despite all their exertions so far, she was too excited by these new feelings, her new future, to sleep.

Gingerly she lifted Darach's arm from where it was draped over her waist. She slipped out of bed and donned her slippers and Darach's big shirt. She breathed deeply of the scent of him that lingered on the garment. He was hers. She wanted everyone to know it, to stake a claim on him like a lioness defending her territory. She wanted to be at his side forever.

But first she was hungry.

She let herself out of the chamber and padded downstairs to the kitchen. Little Cat came to greet her, making it plain that nocturnal visitations were absolutely correct in her rules of etiquette, especially if there was a possibility that salmon would be forthcoming.

Julia scooped her up. LC's furry belly felt very round and firm. She held the cat up to look her in the eye. "Is that my cooking I feel? Or have you been kindling the common fire with some local tom?" LC remained silent. "Oh, so you're taking the Fifth on this one, huh?" Julia giggled. "Well, I'm not ashamed to admit that that's exactly what Darach and I have been doing. And I hope the fire catches quick." She put the cat down and rubbed her own flat stomach. "Quick, do ye hear?" she whispered.

I'm turning absolutely primitive, she thought with a chuckle as she lifted a covered plate of cheese and bread down from one of the shelves. She found a gorgeous red apple sitting on the tabletop, its bright skin beckoning.

She smiled. One of the lairds had probably brought it in for her. Ross, most likely. It was far too early for ripe apples, but he'd found one rogue apple and saved it for her. She did belong. She was beginning to believe it.

She lifted the round fruit and took a bite. It was the sweetest, juiciest—

She didn't get to finish the thought. She felt a fire in her stomach and weakness in all her limbs. She collapsed and something hard connected with her skull. She had the brief, ridiculous thought that she really ought to clean the kitchen ceiling. Then her world caved into darkness.

Chapter Twenty-six

"Darach? Darach!"

Darach muttered a curse under his breath and burrowed deeper into the bed. He reached out to pull Julia in closer to him. He found only a cold spot where she should have been sleeping.

He sat upright, shaking his head. "Julia?" he called, squinting around the room.

"It's Alasdair!" came a voice from outside the door.

Darach rolled from the bed and went to yank open the door. In the back of his mind, he noted something wrong about the door, but he was too groggy to bring it to consciousness.

"What?" he growled, giving his brother a baleful stare.

"Is Julia wi' ye?"

Darach twisted around to search the room once more. He turned back and shook his head. "Is she no' downstairs in the kitchen? It's near mornin'."

"It is mornin', full. And aye, she's been in the kitchen, but she's no' there now."

"Why the hell are ye askin' me all this?" Darach padded over to retrieve his shirt from the floor. He noted that Julia's clothes still lay where they'd fallen the previous night, along with his plaid and boots. But he couldn't lay hands on his shirt. An odd feeling began to form in his belly.

"It struck me strange when I went into the kitchen a wee bit ago," said Alasdair. "There was a plate on the floor, broken, and a bit of food left out. Ye know Julia with her safety and sanitation creed," he said with a short laugh. "She could no more leave a broken plate on the floor and food out for the vermin than she could grow a beard."

Darach yanked on his boots and went to grab a shirt out of the chest. "Nay, she wouldna. And she wouldna go out dressed in my shirt alone. I latched the door from the inside when we retired last eve. It isna latched, so I know she left on her own."

Alasdair's face paled. "Jesu, Darach, ye don't think—?"

Darach faced him as he tossed his kilt over his shoulder. "What is it ye're thinkin'?"

"Ye dunna think she's run off, do ye?"

Darach thought of last night and the way Ju-

373

lia had cherished him, welcomed him, and how she had insisted on being allowed to remain with him. There was nothing about her that showed she was false in any way. "Nay," he answered.

Alasdair looked somewhat relieved. "Good. I was afraid ye might be thinkin' she went off to the Morestons or flew out wi' the kitchen broom."

"Not in my shirt," Darach said, lifting his belt and sword. "And not wi'out first usin' the broom to sweep up that broken plate." He fastened his belt and tucked his knife into the toe of his boot. "But I'm thinkin' she is wi' the Morestons."

He was past Alasdair and headed for the stairs before Alasdair could say the name Darach didn't want to hear: Isobel. Images of the night Isobel was taken and the night he had borne her home had long since been seared onto his brain. This was too like that awful time. And he'd been fool enough to think it couldn't possibly happen twice!

Julia came to with a groan. Her mouth was horribly dry and bittertasting, and she felt as if a flock of vicious woodpeckers were slam-dancing inside her skull. She tried opening her eyes.

She closed them against the glare of sunlight through mist.

"Darach," she murmured, putting out her arm to his side of the bed. She came up with a handful of leaves, moss, and dirt. "What—where?"

She sat up, her ears ringing madly. "Darach, how did we get out . . . here . . ." Her words faded away as she opened her eyes to see that she was in the woods by the standing stones. "Oh . . . no. No!"

Things weren't right. The trees were all wrong. There weren't enough of them.

She had an acrid taste of citrus in her mouth, the scent of dying flowers in her nostrils. Both sensations were fading fast.

She'd gone traveling. Every sense she possessed told her she was back in her own time. Far, far away from Darach and the clan. "No," she whispered. "No, it's not time. I didn't mean for this to happen now. I just—" She couldn't go on. A cry of grief came welling up within her like the rush of floodwaters.

She heard a footstep.

She scrambled to her feet, instantly wary. A man stood a few feet away from her. He was wearing a brown leather bomber jacket, blue jeans, and Nikes. If she had any doubt that she had traveled in time, he pretty much removed it.

He held out his hands. "Don't be afraid. I'm not going to hurt you."

She gasped. "You! You're the one who chased me! You shot at me! What are you doing here?"

"I've been following you. Are you all right?" He took a step toward her.

"Get back!" She glanced around, looking for

a branch, a rock, anything to defend herself.

"Ma'am, I fired a warning shot to get you to stop running," he said, pausing. "You wouldn't stop when I shouted at you."

"Of course I wouldn't. I'm not stupid." She backed away, wondering if she could outrun him. She was getting her Highland wind, but would that be enough? This guy looked awfully fit. Perhaps if she could lull him for a moment or two she could get a head start.

"So you're an American?" she asked conversationally. "You must be one of Monty's boys. I have to say you've been pretty smart in following me."

"Actually, Ms. Addison, I'm not here on behalf of Mr. Gilette. I'm with the FBI."

"Oh, sure," she said. "Right."

He reached into his coat pocket. She shrieked and ducked, hands over her head.

"Whoa! Lady, I'm not going for my gun. See?" He held up his hands. She saw a shiny card and a badge in one of them. He held it out to her. "My ID," he said. "Special Agent Williams. I've been tracking you for weeks."

Julia took the proffered identification between her thumb and forefinger, as if the little leather folder might explode at any moment. She examined it closely. She squinted back and forth between him and the photo on the card.

All her bones suddenly ached. She drooped as she handed back his ID. "Yeah, well, it looks good, but anyone can make up a phony ID."

He sighed. "Yeah. Ms. Coburn said you'd be

hard to convince. She gave us a tape to play in case you weren't sure I was the real thing."

He took a minicassette player out of his pocket and handed it to her. She took it and sat down on one of the stones, her head aching. She was so tired, and she wasn't sure she cared much what happened to her right now. She wanted Darach. She wanted to go home.

Still, she was here. And she knew that she had unfinished business in this time. She looked at the object in her hand. The tiny machine seemed strange, somehow, though she knew what it was. She turned it over a couple of times, then managed to find the PLAY button and pressed it.

"Hey, Julia. This is Martine. Girlfriend, if you're listening to this, then I know Mr. Williams has finally found you. I know I sort of pushed you into running away after Gilette's men offed those guys in my kitchen. But the guys here at the FBI and the NYPD have convinced me it's best if you come home and tell all about what you saw. They'll see that you're protected every step of the way. They promised me that 'cause I said I'd test my new cutlery on them if anything happened to you. I think they took me seriously."

Julia stared at the tape. It was Martine's lovely, husky voice. But had they coerced her into making this? If they had, she'd take them apart, one piece at a time. The tape continued.

"Anyway. I know what you're thinking. You're thinking this is a bogus tape and I made it at gunpoint or they used a computer to put my voice on here. But listen to me, Jules. This is the real thing and I'll prove it. It's real 'cause only I would know what happened the night we snuck into Lido's. Remember? We used his PC to re-write all Tony's menus so dinner the next night read like a roadhouse nightmare. I'll never forget your specialty of the day: Pork Rinds a la Maison Denny's. Nobody knows about that except us.

"So, go ahead and take a chance, Jules. For my sake as well as yours. And so we can put scum like Gilette away for good. Go with the nice man. He's harmless if you don't tick him off. Tell him all you know. And I'll have your chef's hat all clean and starched when you get back."

The tape clicked off. Julia stared at the cassette player, then stared at Agent Williams again. "All right. I'll tell you everything I know. Then I'm out of here. Capisce?" She gathered Darach's shirt around her and settled herself on the stone.

"You want to talk out here?"

She looked around. "Sure. Why not? We'll be okay unless the Morestons come along. But I'm pretty sure they're not going to. Not today."

"The Morestons?" He rubbed his cheek. "Ms. Addison, you're not involved in gang activities here, too, are you?"

She drew herself up in her best imitation of Mairi MacStruan. "I'll have ye know I've never been involved, as you call it, wi' any gang activity anywhere. I was an innocent bystander when that killing happened in New York."

"So you did see someone get killed?"

"I did. I was in the freezer, taking out Cornish game hens for that night's special. I looked out the window of the freezer—it's a walk-in—to make sure that nobody was standing by the door, because I had an armful of cold birds and didn't want to clonk anybody coming out." She shivered at the memory.

"Would you like my jacket? I think it's going to rain and that . . . dress . . . doesn't look too warm."

She waved him off. "No, no. Now that I've been up here for a few months, I'm getting pretty used to it. But I'm always cold when I recall that last night in New York."

He looked puzzled. "A few months?"

"Aye. I've been here since early May. It's almost September now."

He sat down at last. "Ms. Addison. When I shot at you, did you fall?"

"Well, kind of. It was more like I went flying down the path over there."

"And did you hit your head or anything?"

"No. I had a couple of bruises here and there, but nothing on my head." She peered at him. "Why would you think I'd hit my head?"

He coughed. He looked around at the standing stones. He glanced up at the sky. He looked everywhere but at her.

"Mr. Williams?"

"Ah, Ms. Addison, do you know what day it is?"

"Yes. It's August the twenty-seventh."

"No, it's May fourteenth. The same day that you drove your rental car off the road and ran into the woods. That happened only a little more than an hour ago."

She stared at him. Then she looked around herself. He was right: Everything was the same as when she'd left; he was the same; only she had changed. She struggled to make sense of it all. "But when I fell down the hill over there, I was taken prisoner by the MacStruans. I've been in their clan's village for weeks, months!"

He got up and paced about the circle. "I'm real confused here. I didn't see anyone named MacStruan or Moreston up here. Just you, Ms. Addison. I've been beating the bushes up here for over an hour, looking for you." He turned to face her, frowning. "But when I saw you running, you were wearing a sweater and a hat and pants. You disappeared from sight and when I circled back here, I saw you lying on the ground. Now you're wearing that shirt thing. And you say that you've been in some clan encampment?"

"Aye." She waved her arm to the left. "All this, from the stones to the wee loch on the other side of the village and then some, is MacStruan land. Or it was."

"Ma'am, this is a reserve. All this land is protected by the Scottish Natural Heritage Society."

She rubbed her head. There was a hot, sore knot on the back of her head. She had been hit. Or she'd fallen. And she was deeply confused. She knew she had come back to the twentieth century, but no time had passed, as it had in the fifteenth.

She leaned forward. "Tell me something. Is there an inn in Kinloch village called the Black-water Inn?"

"Sure. That's where you've been staying."

She rubbed her head. "Agent Williams, could we go there now? I think I need some time to figure out what's going on."

"Good idea." He offered her his hand to help her up. "Your car is pretty well enmeshed in that thicket you drove into. I think one of your tires is blown. But my car is only a short distance from there." He looked down at her slippered feet. "Are you okay in those?"

"Oh, aye. I wear them all the time." She looked up at him. "Or at least I think I wear them all the time."

They returned to Agent Williams's car in silence. She took her place in the passenger seat and buckled herself in. He climbed in, started the heater going, and reached under his seat to hand her a Thermos. "Here. It's tea. Good and strong. You could probably use something to brace you."

She filled the cup as the car warmed. As the heat from the tea seeped into her chilled hands, she thought of how this same tea had been made months ago and it was still warm. Or was it only a couple of hours ago that it had been brewed?

She screwed the lid back on the Thermos and set it down on the floor at her feet. She took a good long draft and swallowed. She looked at Agent Williams.

"Will you at least think about going back to New York to testify?" he asked.

Julia thought hard for a moment. When she nodded, he put the car into gear and began to back down the dirt road. She hung on to her teacup, sipping quickly to avoid having her drink end up in her lap. A sharp pain entered her heart as they left the MacStruan borderlands. She knew she was leaving a part of herself in this place, with Clan MacStruan.

Calm down, Addison, she told herself. She wasn't going to give up. She'd take this opportunity to find out more about the MacStruans. She'd testify against Monty Gilette, just as she knew she'd testify against Craigen Moreston if she could. She'd see justice done. And then she'd hurry back to the Highlands, to the stones. They must be the portal between her time and Darach's, just as she had guessed that day with Alasdair in the library. She'd hurry back to Darach, with a satisfied mind and a clear conscience at last.

Darach rode as if speed were the only thing that could save his sanity. And maybe it was so, he thought. He had to get to Castle Moreston before anything could happen to Julia.

When Isobel had been taken he'd waited, refusing to bargain with Craigen. He'd waited until he'd known her life was in peril. And he'd been too late. Isobel's blood was on his hands. Please God, he wouldn't add Julia's to that stain.

He chafed at every rocky patch or stream that hindered him, forcing him to slow down lest the horse be injured. He wished for wings, like the fantastic machines that Julia had described to him. He'd soar over the trees, over the hills, and land—like an avenging eagle—on the topmost tower of the Moreston stronghold.

But that was not to be. He pushed on, Alasdair and Niall at his heels, Big Dog racing to keep up. Only a few more miles, as the crow flew. He wouldn't allow himself even to think about what he might find when they arrived at that evil house.

Craigen Moreston stared at the woman lying on the bed. He lifted her limp hand and let it fall to the bed once more.

"Angus, ye idiot, ye've killed her," he said quietly. "Do ye think she's of use to me dead?"

Angus cringed at the white heat in his chief's eyes. "I didna hit her, Craigen," he said. "I swear! She was lying on the floor in the kitchen, just where ye said she'd be. There was no trouble takin her. She seemed asleep."

"Then why is she lying here with no breath left in her body?"

"I dunna know! She just went all cold like that when we passed the standing stones near the border. She was alive when I took her, Craigen.

I'd stake my life on it!"

"So you have." Craigen gave a nod to another man who stood silent in the shadows.

Angus began to scream. Craigen waited until he was carried off down the stairs and out of the tower before he said, "Ye can come out, Edana."

Edana slipped from the alcove behind the tapestry. She limped over to the bed and looked down at the woman who lay there. "Tsk," she said softly. "Another of Darach's dead brides. When will he learn?"

"She is dead, then?" Craigen took a hand mirror from off the nightstand. He held it under Julia's nose, knowing even as he performed the task that no breath would cloud its surface.

"Aye, she's gone."

"Damn the luck!" Craigen tossed the mirror onto the bed, marched to the table, and poured himself some wine. "I wanted her alive, to use for ransoming the last of the MacStruan lands."

Edana shrugged and toyed with one of Julia's curls. "You still can."

"What do ye mean? I can't trade on a corpse!"

"Darach doesn't know she's a corpse."

Craigen scowled. "The man's no' an idiot. He'll want to see her before he makes any bargain wi' me."

"Will he?" Edana hummed a little tune.

"Dammit, witch, stop! I hate that and well ye know it!"

She laughed but the sound held no mirth. "All right, Craigen. Listen to me. Listen well. Darach loves this one."

"So? He loved the other one as well."

"No. He did not. He was marrying her to please his father—his dead father, as you well know. No, he didn't love that scrawny, whey-faced Isobel, his cousin. But this one—he'd give his last drop of blood for this one."

"But not if she's dead!"

Edana faced him with a wide-eyed stare. Craigen shrank a bit, but held his ground. "Verra well. Tell me how to make a dead woman live again."

"Use Celandine. She's of a size with this one and of similar build."

"Oh, aye. And her hair's as red as the sunrise. That'll fool MacStruan, for certain." Craigen sneered and took another sip of his wine.

Edana smiled at him. "Craigen, you know I care not whether you get Darach's land. All I want is Darach brought to his knees. Now I can aid you, or you can mock me and I'll be off." She made as if to leave.

"No, damn it. Ye know I need ye. Ye say we can pass Celandine off as this one? Do it, witch, and I'll give ye the MacStruan on a silver plate."

"Call her. If I know my Darach, he'll be pounding at the gate within the hour."

Craigen gazed at her. "Your Darach? It never fails to amaze me how a woman can make a grand love affair out of a wave o' the hand. I doubt the man recalls yer name, witch."

"Time's wasting," Edana sang out, bending over the MacStruan's woman.

Chapter Twenty-seven

"Come out, Moreston!"

Darach cupped his hands around his mouth. "I know ye're in there, hiding like the coward ye are! Show yourself!"

A robed figure appeared on the parapet of the tower. "What is it ye're wantin', MacStruan?" came the hoarse cry that Darach knew to be Craigen's.

"Ye know what it is I want!" Darach shouted up. "Let her go and I'll no' burn ye down."

"And who might this lass be?" Craigen called out. "Someone dear to ye?"

"Let her go."

"Perhaps we can reach an understanding, MacStruan."

Darach paused. What was the toad up to now? "No bargains, Moreston. I'm the one call-in' the tune. Let her go or I set my men to torchin' everythin' in sight."

Craigen's voice was sneering. "All your men? How many would that be, MacStruan? Surely ye could count them all—ye've a full set o' fingers to use!"

Darach only stared at the figure on the parapet. "I'm waitin'. But I'll no' wait overlong."

Craigen seemed to be conferring with someone out of view. Darach motioned to Alasdair and Niall to move forward, their torches held high.

"Moreston. Ye've no more time!"

"Wait, MacStruan."

Darach nodded to his men. They halted. "What now?" he asked. "Ye were ever the one for chattin'."

"I'd treat wi' ye, Darach."

"Ah," Darach murmured. "So it's Darach now, eh?" He shouted up to the parapet, "Keep your treaties."

"Are ye sure? I think ye'll want to hear me out this time."

Darach crossed his arms. He was chafing to be inside that tower, to be with Julia. But he knew Moreston's tricks. He would have to wait and see what was in store.

"I'll give ye the lass, MacStruan. In exchange for the hills."

"He wants the mines," Alasdair said in disgust. "He took Julia for the mines."

Darach said nothing.

Craigen called out again. "Did ye hear me?

I'm offerin' ye the lass for the hills. It's more than fair, Darach. Ye haven't enough people to watch your cows, let alone work your mines. And the lass will be yours."

"Don't do it," Niall whispered hotly. "Ye know ye can't trust him."

Darach still kept his own counsel. He raised a hand to signal the tower. "Bring her out, Moreston! I'll no' treat wi' ye if ye've harmed so much as a hair on her head."

Moreston bowed and backed away from the edge of the parapet.

"Darach! It's your birthright! Ye can't gamble it away," Niall urged.

Alasdair shot him a glance and shook his head. Niall flushed but fell silent.

"Do ye think she's in there, Darach?" Alasdair asked.

"Aye. I know she is."

"What of the—"

Alasdair didn't finish. Another figure was approaching the parapet.

"It's wee Julia!" Niall said excitedly. "She's all right!"

Darach continued to stare at the figure above him. His Julia, he thought. He should feel joy at seeing her well and standing before him. But he felt nothing.

Alasdair edged his horse closer to Darach's. "It's no' her, Darach."

Darach whipped around to face his brother. "How can ye tell?"

"I'm no' certain, but I think it's another lass.

This one doesna resemble Julia about the mouth, if ye can see from here."

Darach looked. The same lovely black hair. The same height. The same long neck. But her mouth?

He squinted. "God help me," he whispered. It wasn't Julia.

Alasdair made a sudden choking sound. Darach looked at him again. His brother's face had gone ashen, his eyes standing out wide. "What?" he growled, feeling his uneasiness increasing by the moment.

"It's her," Alasdair murmured.

"Her?" Niall asked. "Julia?"

"Nay," Darach snapped. "It's another, not Julia." He put his fingers to his lips and gave a piercing whistle.

From out of the sheltering woods came the rest of the lairds, riding forward, unlit torches in their hands. Darach faced them. "Craigen's played us false once too often. Stand watch." He swung off of his horse and handed the reins to Niall. "I'm goin' in."

New York hadn't changed, that was for sure, Julia thought. Not that she'd been allowed to see that much of the city since she'd returned. Williams had virtually smuggled her into the U.S., then hustled her into this apartment high over the city. She hadn't been outside of a building or a car since she'd left Scotland.

A prisoner again, she thought. But this was her choice. When she'd come back in time to the exact day she left it, she knew that she had business to finish in this time. Loose ends. And while her heart ached for Darach, the lairds, and the Highlands, she had a feeling deep within her that she was doing what was right. It was her duty, and a MacStruan was nothing if not honorable.

She grinned. She thought of herself as a MacStruan these days. A member of the clan. It was a thought that had warmed and sustained her since she had left the standing stones with Agent Williams. She also kept herself going through the sometimes grueling, often boring hours of the Gilette hearings by planning her return to the clachan. She was going back. No matter what it took, she'd find a way back to Darach. As soon as she finished her obligations here. Then there would be no more ties to this time that could compete with her ties to the Highlands and the whole of Clan MacStruan. Ever since she had left, perhaps even before, she had felt as if a part of her soul were missing.

She turned to look at Agent Williams and his partner, Agent Diana Kennedy. "How much longer am I going to have to stay here, do you think?" she asked.

Williams shrugged. "We'll have the word from the grand jury soon, I hope. But you've got to stay here until it's over."

Kennedy rose from the couch and went to stand beside Julia. She looked out at the view.

"If you crane your neck until it's really painful," Julia said dryly, "you can see Central Park.

Or some trees, anyway."

"You know, Ms. Addison, there's going to have to be some changes once you've testified. No matter what the outcome of the trial, Gilette's people are not going to be happy with you."

Julia leaned her head against the glass. She could see the cars 40 floors below, jostling and weaving for position in the street. How strange it all seemed. She hadn't thought that the Highlands could get beneath her skin so quickly. But she was longing for that moist, cool air of the woodlands and glens near Darach's home.

"Do you understand what I mean, Ms. Addison?" Agent Kennedy's voice pierced her reverie.

"Aye." Julia sighed. "I ken what ye mean. I'll need to go into hidin'."

"You sure picked up the accent in the short time you were in Scotland," Kennedy commented.

"Picked it up?" Julia looked at her. "Hmm. I'd swear it was second nature." She hugged herself, despite the warmth of the room and the sweater she wore. She'd never realized how cold New York could be in the spring.

Agent Williams crossed to the bar of the hotel room and poured himself another cup of coffee. He added skim milk and leaned back against the bar as he stirred. "Do you know anything about the Witness Protection Program, Ms. Addison?"

"Please call me Julia. It's what I'm used to."

"All right. Julia. Are you familiar with the

Witness Protection Program or Witness Relocation Program?"

"I think I saw something about it in a goofy movie once. But that was a long time ago."

"Well, in your case it's going to be mandated by my superiors. Also your friend, Ms. Coburn, she, uh, mandated it as well, as you heard on her tape."

"Am I going to be able to see Martine?"

"You'll see her in court tomorrow."

"That's good. I miss her." Julia had a sudden, frightening thought. "Martine's no' going to be in trouble on my account, is she? Wi' the Gilettes and all?"

"I don't think so. After all, she saw nothing. But she'll have protection as well. We'll see to it." Kennedy nodded reassuringly, but her eyes strayed to her partner. Julia caught the glance of concern that passed between them.

"Ye're thinkin' I'm mad as auld Mad Mac-Phee, are ye no'?" She left the window and went to the sofa again. "I canna say as I blame ye. I don't know what's been happening to me. It's as if one minute I'm here and I'm my old self, and in the next, I'm back in the village, sittin' and talkin' wi' the lairds about the hearth." She looked up from her hands. "But go on. Tell me what you've got planned for me when I've said my piece at the trial."

"We can't tell you much. It's all pretty hush-hush, and for the safety of everyone, no one person has all the information," said Kennedy. "What I can tell you is that you'll be asked to make some changes in your appearance, you may acquire a husband and a family if that's deemed necessary to throw the Gilettes off your trail. You'll be in a new city, a new state perhaps, and you'll be thoroughly briefed as to what to tell people about your background. New ID, new licenses, new names, new family history, everything will be provided."

Julia considered this for several moments. "And if I have another plan?"

"You can certainly ask for anything you think you might need," Williams said. "But we can't guarantee that you'll get what you ask—it's too risky that someone who knows you would be able to guess what you'd do or where you'd go."

"What if I could go someplace where no one else could follow?"

The agents exchanged glances again. "Ms. Addison. Julia." Kennedy came and sat beside her on the couch. "You aren't thinking about taking, well, let's say drastic measures, are you?"

"Ye mean would I tak' my ain life?" Julia shook her head. "Not hardly. I've too much still to do. I want bairns. I want to grow into a troublesome auld crone who can terrorize her grown children wi' one look. No, I'm talking something completely different. But you've got to promise me that what I tell you will never leave this room. FBI scout's honor?"

Williams and Kennedy nodded warily.

"Good. Here's what I need to do."

* * *

Williams and his partner were up late that night after Julia had gone to bed. They sat in silence for a while; then Williams got up to dish up some more of the Chinese takeout they'd had delivered.

"This is the best moo shu pork I've ever had," he said, folding the fragrant mixture up into the delicate pancake. "She may be completely Looney Tunes, but the woman knows her food."

"So you think she's nuts?" Kennedy asked.

"Oh, come on," he said around a mouthful of food. "You were there when she made us take her to Columbia to visit that professor. She wanted a carbon date on that old shirt she brought with her from Scotland. She's delusional about this time travel business."

"The professor didn't think she was nuts."

"That's 'cause the guy's name was Fergusson. And he's nuts over anything to do with Scotland."

"Do you think we should tell the chief about her plan?"

He shrugged. "We might as well. She won't get what she wants. But maybe it'll help him see that she's an eccentric and they'll have to be careful with her in the relocation process."

Kennedy shook her head. "I don't know, Chaz. She seems pretty normal to me. Oh, yeah, she's got this fixation about Scotland, but like you said, so does that professor. You don't see him being booted out of Columbia for upholstering his desk chair in his clan tartan."

"Di. Earth to Diana. Are you serious?"

394

"Yeah, I am. I'm going to tell the chief I think we should do all we can to get her back to Scotland."

"Thank you, Agent Kennedy. I'm that grateful for your faith i' me."

They both whirled to see Julia Addison standing in the doorway to her room. She smiled at them both. "Don't worry. I'm used to being told I'm crazy. It's business as usual for me. But if you'll at least take me seriously enough to grant my wishes in relocating me, I'll be as good as gold." She looked at Williams. "That's what you're worried about, isn't it? That my Scotland fixation, as you call it, will come out at the hearing and my credibility will be shot. And if that happens, Gilette's men get a nice ride home."

Williams rubbed the back of his neck. "Ah, you've got me, Julia. Do you think you can pull this off?"

"I can and I will. You'll see. And then the minute all this is finished, I'm on the first plane home to the Highlands."

"Darach!"

Darach halted in the shelter of a gnarled rowan tree and waited as Alasdair reined in his mount beside him. He had nearly reached the track that led to the gate of the Moreston stronghold.

"Ye mustn't go in," Alasdair said, breathless.

"I have to."

"No, ye don't. At least, no' this way. There's a better spot to catch them unawares."

"What are ye sayin'? Since when do ye have knowledge of Castle Moreston?"

"Since I met . . . someone who lives there."

"What?"

"Darach, as ye love Julia and as ye love your clan, come wi' me now and meet wi' her. She can help us." Alasdair's horse carried him around, then back to face Darach. "But ye must come quickly. There's no time to lose."

Darach hesitated. Julia was in there and God only knew what sort of tortures she was experiencing. He looked at Alasdair. His brother's eyes were pleading. And sincere.

"Let's go."

They raced back over the field to the eaves of the woods. Alasdair caught up a burning branch from Tommy as he rode, and its light showed them the way to the standing stones.

Alasdair swung down off his horse before it had come to a halt. He tied the reins to a low branch and carried the torch into the circle of stones. Darach followed more cautiously.

"Ye can come out," Alasdair called.

A small, cloaked figure stepped out from behind the tallest stone. Darach looked at Alasdair.

"Darach, this is Celandine. Celandine, my brother, Darach MacStruan."

"I'm pleased to meet you," came a sweet, musical voice. "But I know you're impatient. Let us talk." She slipped her hood off her head and Darach stared at the rare beauty who stood before him, beckoning him to the circle.

"I've been living in Castle Moreston for a year and a half," she said, taking a seat on one of the stones. "I'm betrothed to the Moreston."

Darach turned to Alasdair. "Ye fool! What hae ye done?"

"Whisht!" Alasdair shook his head vehemently. "She's no' a Moreston. She wants to help. Let her! This may be our only chance to withstand the Morestons and save yer Julia."

"What hae ye to say to me, woman?" Darach growled.

"Come," she said, beckoning once again. She had a stick in her hand and was rapidly drawing lines in the dirt.

Darach advanced warily.

"See? Here is the way you were trying. You won't survive beyond the blink of an eye if you go that way." She pointed with the stick. "Here. At the back. It's treacherous to climb and there is no absolute promise that you'll come in safely. But if you make the climb, you will come to a small postern door. It's old and needs repair. The walls around it are crumbling. Hardly anyone comes or goes from there."

"Except ye." Darach shot a glance at his brother. He was watching this elfin lass with rapt attention. God in heaven, he thought. Alasdair's in love—with a Moreston!

Celandine nodded, not looking up. "Yes. That is how I got out and came here. I made sure the guard there was supplied with plenty of spirits. He should be drunk ere you arrive at his door."

"And hae you a key to this door? Or do we fly over the parapets?"

She gave him a cool stare from her exotic almond eyes. "I have no key. And I've never learned to fly. But you could get in. You're strong enough. A few tools would permit you to pry out some of the stones in the wall and you could come through that way, if necessary."

"And when I do get in, what will be waitin' for me there?"

"I can't say. But I know where they have your lady." Celandine drew a quick sketch of the tower keep. "She's here. And she'll be well guarded. But you may come in by stealth, especially if you let Craigen believe that you've retreated. It may cause him to lower his guard."

"Are ye the witch of the Morestons?" Darach asked.

"No. I assure you I am not. And even if I were, I'd do anything to help you and insure your safety. I have given my oath on it. To Alasdair."

Darach strode away from the ring. Clouds had been building, extinguishing the light of the stars. Rain would be falling soon, aiding the Morestons in their efforts to quench the fires his men had set. Each moment Julia spent in that tower, he knew, could mean her life. But who was this woman and could he trust her?

"Alasdair," he called softly. Alasdair crossed to stand by him. "Where did ye meet this lass?"

"Here. The night ye were all up at the caves. We've been meetin' here in secret since then. It was she that stood in Julia's place on the parapet. She made a sign to me and I knew that Craigen was playin' us false."

"Is she to be trusted?" Darach put his hands on his brother's shoulders. "Think well before ye answer. My whole life depends upon it."

Alasdair nodded. "I'll stake my ain life on it. She's worthy."

Darach searched his face once more. He could see Alasdair's wholehearted faith written in his eyes. Alasdair might be young and he might be brash at times, but he wasn't a fool. Never had been. Even in the throes of love or lust, he'd always kept his head.

And if this proved to be the exception to that rule, it didn't matter. This woman held out hope for Julia, perhaps their only hope. Darach had to cling to that hope or go mad.

"It is well. Let's hear the details and then be off."

"Darach." Alasdair caught at his sleeve. He waited. "She'll have no place to go after this," Alasdair said. "I want her to come to the village wi' me."

"We'll see."

"You dunna trust her."

"It isna that. It's the Morestons we canna trust. They'll know it was she that helped us. They'll seek her out in the village first off."

"You're right. All right. I'll take her up to the caves."

"That'll do. Now I can no longer tarry here!"

Celandine had embellished her maps. The

two men studied them thoroughly and laid their plans.

As he mounted up to ride to the castle, Darach looked down at the woman who held his hope in her slender hands. "There's one more thing I need to ask o' ye," he said, his face tight and drawn.

"Yes?"

"Is my lady still alive?"

She put her hand on his knee. "I will not lie to you. I do not know if she is alive. Craigen and Edana would not permit me to enter the room where they have her. But I don't know that she is dead either. Take heart, Darach MacStruan," she said softly. "Your faith will be rewarded."

He looked at her, but for his life he could find neither hope nor faith in his heart. Only fear and desperation.

Chapter Twenty-eight

All of Julia's tensions were melting away. The sign on the road told her that Kinloch was only 20 miles away. She was almost home.

She heard a rattle and a squeaking from the backseat and smiled at the thought of all the boxes of supplies she'd brought along. She'd be praying for them to make the journey with her.

A journey. Her journey home, through time. She'd known it all along, one way or another, but while she was in New York she'd sought more proof, just for the sake of her own curiosity. She knew there was no way she was going to convince anyone else. But it was nice to know.

Professor Fergusson had called just before she'd left for the airport, her business with the grand jury at an end, Gilette's men satisfactorily indicted. The professor had dated the small section of fabric she'd left with him, and the cloth was indubitably old, he'd told her. Hundreds of years old. His colleague in the textiles department had been amazed at the piece and had agreed that her examination of the swatch showed it to be, at the least, an outstanding re-creation of old weaving techniques. She wouldn't go so far as to give a date, noting that the cloth was in far too mint a condition to be truly old.

Julia had her answer. The answer she'd known in her heart all along. There was a time and a place where such shirts were the order of the day. And it was there—or then—that she was headed now.

She grinned as she reached for another piece of fruit from the basket on the seat beside her. She was hungry all the time these days.

"Thanks to the MacStruan," she said aloud, patting her abdomen. They'd kindled the common fire, well and truly. She'd taken one of those little tests shortly before she'd left New York and the stick had turned a delightful shade of blue, confirming her hopes and suspicions.

"Aww," she'd crooned to her belly. "A wee ogre for the chief of Clan Ogre."

Said chief had better be ready for her, she thought. Because she was on her way back to him and nothing was going to stand in her way. Nothing.

* * *

"What the devil is he up to?" Craigen Moreston faced Ian Dougal, his second in command.

"He's retreatin'," Ian replied with a grin. "The rain's put out their fires. They know that if they come within reach o' the walls, we'll cut 'em down like weeds in a garden. They're slinkin' away into the night, like good wee MacStruans."

Craigen didn't share his good spirits. "I dunna like it."

"Why not? We knew we'd get the better of them, soon or late. We didna have to lift a hand. They've run away o' their ain accord."

"They left the woman."

Ian's grin faded. "Oh."

"Aye. And it's no' like MacStruan to run off and leave her. Edana says he loves this one."

"So?" Ian's confidence returned. "He left his wee bridie wi' us the last time. He tried to make a parlay wi' us, then refused our offer. He runs off when he kens he's been bested."

Craigen shook his head. "All the same, I dunna like it. I want the watch to stay at their posts until daybreak. And let no one come or go frae this house."

"Ayè, Craigen."

Ian saluted and went off to carry out his orders. Craigen paced the room for a while. He hated being cooped up in this tower. He hated being cooped up in this castle, truth to tell. He wanted out. When he was finished with the MacStruans, he thought, he'd go to Edinburgh again. Maybe to Paris. He'd take Celandine with him, unless she was already too far gone with his seed to travel.

He rubbed his hands. Celandine. What a delicious bit she would be, come the night he'd been waiting for all these weeks. Not like his lovely Caroline, of course, but a worthy substitute as a breeder of heirs. And Edana had practically guaranteed him he'd get a son on the lass the first time he mounted her.

All he had to do was gain the MacStruan lands. And from the look of things this night, he'd have them before the month was out.

Darach's horse moved slowly through the mist. Though he'd taken the precaution of wrapping his steed's hooves in sacking, he wanted no telltale pounding of the ground that would alert his enemies that a horse was galloping toward their walls. Impatience rose within him but he tamped it down. He couldn't afford to lose control now. There was still a long way to go before he achieved his goal.

The hill into which the castle was built rose up suddenly before him. Everything was as he recalled from before. He dismounted and left his horse to graze in the shelter of an oak. Going cautiously in the dark, he traced the landmarks that Celandine had described to him. He found the narrow footpath and began to climb.

The lass had been right. It was indeed a treacherous climb. He had to admit she had courage, if she had indeed taken this path down from the castle to meet Alasdair. At several points, there was no true path at all, merely a jutting of rock no wider than his palm. He inched along, mist and sweat beading on his skin. He lost track of time. It seemed he was on the face of the hill for hours, and that there was nothing else in the world but rock.

At last he clambered over the top. He dropped to the ground for a moment to allow his legs to recover from the strain of climbing and to get his bearings. Through the mists he spied the great bulk of Castle Moreston and knew he had come out in the right spot.

It was no easy matter to get in once he reached the walls. There was no way to enter from the outside; one had to be allowed in by a guard. It took him the better part of an hour to pick away at the crumbling stones that Celandine had described and make a hole large enough for him to squeeze through.

He lowered himself to the floor. A snort brought him up short, his hand on his knife. He peered around into the dim passageway. Another snort went up and he made out the form of a portly guard slumped on the floor, his back to the wall. An ale cask sat next to him.

Thus far, the odd lass Alasdair had found had proven true. But still more dangerous maneuvers lay ahead of him. He set forth to find the tower.

Niall and Tommy were stealing along the edge of the woods, their plaids wrapped over their heads, the glinting of their swords hidden in the folds. Only a few more yards and they would reach their post directly opposite the main gate of Castle Moreston.

All about the outer borders of the castle, the MacStruan lairds were taking their places. Their task was to wait for a signal from Alasdair that Darach was ready to leave the castle with Julia. Then they would set up the distraction that, it was hoped, would draw the Morestons from their posts and permit Darach and Julia to make their escape from the postern door.

"Do ye think this'll work?" Tommy whispered as they crouched under the dripping branches.

Niall shrugged. "We'll not know till we've tried."

"But will it be enough of a surprise to the Morestons?"

"Whisht," Niall growled. "Keep yer doubtin' to ye'self, man. This is no' the time for it."

A sound from the forest behind them brought them both around, swords drawn. They ducked behind some tall bracken as the snapping of twigs told them that several people were heading straight for them.

Niall scowled into the darkness. He drew a sharp breath. "What in the name of—?"

Mairi MacStruan stood before him, cloaked in darkness but unmistakable in her stance and demeanor. He rose and opened his mouth to greet her.

She raised her hand, silencing him. "Niall MacStruan," she said, her voice soft but thoroughly commanding. "What the devil do ye mean, goin' off to war without consultin' wi' the rest o' the clan?"

"Mairi, I—we—" Niall sputtered to a halt as the forms of other women materialized out of the shadows. "Rose isna wi' ye, is she?"

"Nay. She stayed up in the hills wi' the bairns. She's fine. But I brought the rest o' the able ones wi' me."

"Ye must all gang away frae here," Tommy cried, spotting Lara among the group. "It's no' safe!"

"Bosh," said Mairi. "MacStruan women have gone into battle wi' our menfolk before. 'Twas wee Julia herself who brought it to my mind when she was standin' up to my Darach like a lass out o' the auld tales. Now tell me what plans ye have for facin' a force ten times your ain size?"

Niall obeyed. She pursed her lips and frowned. "Ye call that a distraction? A bunch o' trees advancin' on the castle and a couple o' flamin' arrows?" She sniffed. "If it's a distraction ye need, leave it to us. Ye see to my son and his lady."

Tommy and Niall looked at one another. They were outranked and outmaneuvered and they hadn't even entered the fray. They submitted to the inevitable and the indomitable.

Edana felt him near. She was quivering with anticipation. She hadn't expected to see him so soon, not like this, but she knew that destiny had taken a hand. The hour had come to reveal herself to her love.

She sat down on a chair facing the door of the tower room and waited for Darach to come to her.

The path to the tower that Celandine had laid out for him had been treacherous indeed. Darach had fought off several guards, killing four and knocking the others unconscious as he wove through kitchens and hallways. Still, she had warned him it might be so, and he also knew that other, more public ways would be guarded far more heavily.

Now he was at the foot of the tower stairs, waiting in the shadows for a chance to steal up the winding steps. Soldiers were coming and going in the yard near the tower and there was shouting and hooting coming from the walls that faced the woods. More men began pounding past his hiding spot, bent for the walls. He wondered what had attracted their attention. It wasn't time for his men to go into action.

He couldn't think about it. He seized the opportunity and raced for the stairs under cover of the confusion. He gained the top and found the door to the inner chambers unlatched and unguarded.

He drew his sword, sensing a trap. With each step he took toward the door that Celandine had told him led to Julia, he felt the hairs prickle on his arms and the back of his neck. This was too easy. But he had to go on.

He reached for the latch, his stomach roiling with the sense of danger that seemed a part of the very air in this place. He glanced about and eased the door open.

"Come in, Darach," said the beautiful woman who sat before him. "I've waited a long time for this meeting."

"Do ye see 'em?" Gordon demanded of Niall and Tommy.

"Aye," said Niall in a dazed tone, staring toward the castle. "I see it but I dunna believe it."

Out on the meadow, well within sight of the castle walls, a bonfire burned, its flames casting strange lights and antic shadows on the high, sheer stonework. Round the fire several women danced, their hair loose and floating about them, their feet flashing and capering to the music of wild, sensuous piping. They waved their arms and hands, graceful as sylphs.

And each and every one of them was as naked as a newborn babe.

Tommy was all eyes. "She said she'd make a distraction that'd curl the Morestons' hair," he murmured, rubbing the back of his neck with his hand. His Lara was out there, maid though she was, and the sight of her unclothed, swaying seductively in the firelight, had raised his body heat to an uncomfortable peak.

"Well, she's done that," Gordon said. He shook himself free of the sight of his own tall, curvy wife frolicking in the nude like a pagan goddess of old. "It's time to do our part."

The tops of the walls were lined with Morestons leaning over the edges, cheering and howling. Distracted they were, and the women urged their interest to even greater heights with tempting, teasing gestures. The lairds, gathering for their foray, were hard-pressed to keep their minds on their task.

"He should be in the tower by now," Alasdair said. "It's time to make these bastards pay for their entertainment."

They fanned out behind the women, bows and arrows at the ready. They waited, allowing still more men to fill the spaces at the top of the wall. Then, at Alasdair's signal, they raised their bows, took aim, and began to rain arrows on their unwary foe.

Julia hoisted the last of the boxes out of the trunk of the car and carried it to the circle of the standing stones. She was glad she'd rented a sturdy Range Rover with four-wheel drive this time. She'd never have been able to haul all these boxes over the rocks and mud that lay between the road and the stones.

She sat and rested, taking long sips from the bottle of fresh water she'd brought along. It felt so right to be here once more. Even the chill she couldn't shake felt right, familiar. In modern times, fewer trees stood around the old circle, she noted, and overhead a jet droned past, but it was the same. She recalled her first perceptions of the Highlands, how they had seemed to be wild and rough, yet full of life. She felt the same way today, only more so. This place was full of her own life now, as well as the life of her clan and their forefathers, all the way back into the mists of prehistory. How odd and wonderful it was to be a part of something so rich and ancient.

A nagging doubt intruded into her reverie. Was this going to work? During her stay in New York, she'd driven her attending agents crazy ordering books on physics, time, Gaelic and Celtic history and mythology, Druidic rites, even rocks, just in case there was something special about the materials in the standing stones. Was she going to be able to make the journey she had been dreaming of and planning for all these weeks?

Another question nagged at her. When she'd returned to the present, she'd only been gone for about an hour, while weeks had passed while she inhabited the past. Would the same thing happen in reverse? Would she return to the kitchen of Darach's house, an apple in her hand, LC wrapping herself around her ankles?

An apple. She felt an icy finger touch her spine. The apple was the last thing she recalled before she woke in the circle of the standing stones. Had the apple been the key to her return through the centuries? Or was it the stones, as she'd thought all along?

In all honesty, she didn't have a clue about how this mystery of crossing time operated. She knew there was no guidebook, no recipe for what she needed to do. She just knew she would do it if it took the rest of her life. Her soul was waiting for her in another time.

She rose and picked up a shovel. Going to the center of the circle, she sank the blade into the earth and began the task of burying the boxes she'd brought. There was no reason why she should do so, she knew. She was going on instinct and hope. And belief.

When she was finished, she was weary and famished. She got a basket from the Rover and sat down to feed herself and her child, smiling as she dreamed of telling Darach about the babe she carried. She could hardly wait.

The moon was rising as she finished her meal. Full and bright, it was ringed with clouds that glowed from its light. She took it as a good omen.

She wrapped her heavy wool cloak about her shoulders, but let a bit of Darach's shirt, which she wore as a blouse, show white in the moonlight. She emptied her mind of all thoughts but those of Darach, and the clan, and the world of clachan MacStruan.

But something didn't feel right. Instead of flowers, she smelled smoke. Instead of the taste of lemons and oranges, she tasted the bitter tang of burning brush. She searched the landscape around her, expecting to see flames or deep gray billows rising into the night sky. But everything was calm and clear.

She sighed and closed her eyes, trying to concentrate. Voices floated to her on the wind. Screams. Cries of outrage. Jeers and howls.

What was this? She was shaking now, as she opened her eyes and whirled about in a circle. Was what she was hearing real? Was it in the present? Or the past?

Desperation and fear gripped her. She had to get back. She had to find the secret. Something was wrong.

Darach was in danger.

Darach stood in the doorway of the tower chamber, his sword in hand. The woman rose and held out her hands to him.

"Don't you remember me?" she asked, her voice as silken and rippling as springwater.

"Who are ye?" he asked. "Where's Julia?"

The woman shook her head, her red tresses shimmering in the candlelight. "So. It's the same as ever, isn't it? We've met before, Darach. In Edinburgh. At the court."

He frowned. There was no sign of Julia in this place. Had Celandine played him false after all? He peered at the tall, curvaceous woman before him. For his life, he had no idea who she was.

"Ah. Aye," he lied, hoping she would reveal herself. "Edinburgh. That was a while back, but I couldna forget ye, lass." He took a step into the room. "It was Michaelmas, was it no'? A man would ne'er forget your hair by the light o' the candles at court."

She smiled and shook her head. "It was not. And you don't remember me now any better than you did then, though I made every effort to engage your attention."

413

She moved toward him. His eye caught the slight rise of one shoulder and hip. She was lame. Lame. He racked his brain. He knew this was important, but his mind was so concentrated on Julia he couldn't seem to make it work at recollecting this strange woman.

"If I gave offense in those days, lady, it was youthful ignorance and my Scots roughness," he said, taking another step into the room. "I offer my pardon." He made a short bow.

She laughed. The pretty sound was somehow grating and false. "Your Scots roughness has always appealed to me, Darach," she purred. "But I was hurt when you took up with Caroline Farquharson. She didn't appreciate you as I did."

The name jolted him. Caroline! He hadn't thought of her in years. But he remembered her. She'd been Craigen's—saints, what was he onto here?

"Ah, I see you do recall that lady," she said. She picked up a jeweled dagger and fingered the blade. "Perhaps I can prick your memory."

"Edana," he breathed.

"You do remember me!" she cooed. "Oh, I knew you would. In time. Now that we have our introductions out of the way, let us—"

Craigen burst into the room. "Damn ye, witch! Celandine is gone!"

Edana nodded to Darach. Craigen turned and Darach was face-to-face with his old enemy at last.

"MacStruan," he growled, drawing his knife. "Ye're far more stupid than even I believed."

414

"Craigen." Darach raised the point of his sword. "Where's the lass?"

Craigen smiled. "Ye'll never have her, MacStruan. My lady witch here has taken care o' her. As I'll take care o' ye."

"Craigen!" Edana snapped. "You'll do no such thing. He's mine, remember?"

Craigen spoke to her over his shoulder, his eyes still on Darach. "Our bargain is ended, witch. It was broken when Celandine left this tower. She was to be mine."

Darach chuckled mirthlessly. "The twa o' ye make a fine pair. Squabblin' like waistie wanis over what'll never belong to either one o' ye."

Edana waved a hand. "You may laugh at us spoiled and squabbling children, Darach, my love. But neither will you have what you want." She crossed the room and drew aside the tapestry that hung from ceiling to floor.

Darach felt his heart leap up and then freeze. Julia lay on a pallet behind the tapestry, silent and still. Too still. Grief and horror stunned him. The tip of his sword dropped below his waist.

Craigen attacked.

The battle on the meadow was in full pitch. The Morestons, caught off their guard by the women, suffered great losses in the first few minutes of the fight. But when the women fled the scene and the first few flights of arrows found their marks, the Morestons rallied with a vengeance.

"To the woods!" Alasdair bellowed as the portcullis began shrieking upward over the great gate. He turned to the Bruce, who stood beside him, as stout as his oaken staff. "Ready, my liege?"

"We'll lead 'em a chase to rival Julia's *French Connection!*" Bruce cried.

The MacStruans scattered and raced for the trees, abandoning their bows and arrows for their knives and swords. Hordes of Morestons followed their trails, trampling the bracken and hacking at branches with fury.

A high, undulating cry echoed through the woods. A shower of rocks poured down on the attackers, to the accompaniment of unearthly moans and shrieks. The Morestons tried to do battle with their invisible enemies, but their swords only became tangled in the tree branches over their heads. Howling, many retreated toward the meadows, the awful din echoing in their ears. The rest ran on, deeper into the woods.

Mairi called out to her treetop warriors. "Well done, ladies! Now let's be quick. The rest o' these villains are after our men."

MacStruan women dropped from the trees or scrambled down trunks in the darkness. Gordon's tall wife, Annie, lit a torch while the rest hefted cooking pots, cudgels, and battered swords from a pile heaped in the bracken.

"Away the women!" Annie shouted. And they were off, following her torch into the woods, racing toward the fight.

416

The Mirror And The Magic

* * *

Julia felt like a stick caught in a whirlpool as she lay on the grass in the middle of the stone circle. The sky spun over her head, the tip of the great standing stone marking the revolutions. One moment it was raining. The next it was dark, but blazing hot. In another moment there was the moon once again, full and cloud-ringed.

She closed her eyes against the whirling sights. This settled her dizziness and brought her a moment of peace. But she was still so cold, colder than she'd ever been in her life.

Then she heard the voices. So near. Darach's voice! A woman's sweet laughter. Another man's rough cries.

What was happening? She couldn't seem to move.

She tried lifting her arm, wiggling her leg. Nothing. Had she been paralyzed? The voices were growing louder. They were here with her!

"Darach!" she cried. "Darach, I'm here!"

Nausea rolled over her once more. It was a dream, she thought. One of those hideous, terrifying nightmares where she was being chased by something awful and yet she couldn't move, and her mouth wouldn't open to free the screams that strained at her throat.

There was the sound of metal on metal, grunting, and a sharp indrawn breath. It was a fight. Darach was in a fight. She had to get to him.

She managed to open her eyes a crack. A woman's face swam before her eyes. The face in the mirror. She knew it at once. Was she, Julia, in the mirror? She caught glimpses of a stone ceiling above her head, saw the flicker of rushlights such as Darach had in his house.

Was she back?

She tried to call out to Darach, to anybody, but she felt a lump in her throat that cut off all sound. She couldn't draw breath to fill her lungs. Panic filled her and she tried to struggle, to raise her hand to her throat. Her hand stayed at her side, heavy and disobedient to her desperate demands.

She heard a man scream and the thud of a body falling to the floor.

Darach!

"They're settin' fire to the woods!"

Dugan came thundering up to Niall and Gordon, who were resting after they had routed the last of the Morestons who'd managed to follow them. Niall jumped to his feet. "Show me!"

The three men didn't need a torch to light their way. The glow of a not too distant fire showed them what was next in the Morestons' arsenal.

"We canna lose the forest!" Dugan said, panting for breath. "The animals. The huntin'."

Gordon was trotting back and forth amid the trees. "It's no' a circle this time," he reported to his kinsmen. "Not sae far, anyway. Julia told me something that we could try."

"No' a movee tale?" Niall demanded.

"Nay. It's called a firebreak. But we'll need

everyone, women and all, if we're to halt the flames."

Niall put his fingers to his mouth and gave three short, piercing whistles. In a twinkling, the clan was gathering. Alasdair came running, his sword stained, and blood running from a cut on his cheek.

"They're burnin' everythin' from here to the standing stanes," he reported. "We must get back to the clachan before it reaches there."

Niall told him of Gordon's plan. Alasdair listened, dabbing at his wound with his sleeve. The women began to pour into the little clearing, their eyes wide but their spirits undaunted.

"Darach's still in the tower, as far as we know," Bruce told Alasdair. "Ye must be chief in his stead."

Alasdair looked alarmed for a moment, then straightened and sheathed his sword. "Tommy and Ross, ye're the swiftest of us. Run to the clachan and bring back every diggin' tool ye can lay hands to. Mairi, can ye and some o' the others gang to the burn and wet yer cloaks? We'll need somethin' to beat back any flames that get in our way."

Celandine appeared at his side as the clan scattered to their tasks. Alasdair gathered her into his arms and hugged her close.

"Can ye see aught of what's to come?" he whispered.

She shook her head. "All is smoke in my sight, love." She put her hand on his cheek. "But do not despair. You're the chief now. And there's no better man for the position."

He kissed her, hard and swiftly. "Please God ye're right," he said.

A short while later, their weapons mustered, Clan MacStruan set out to do battle with their new enemy.

Chapter Twenty-nine

"Oh, dear." Edana leaned over slightly, eyeing Craigen's body on the floor. "He never was much of a man." She sighed, clucking her tongue. She smiled at Darach. "Good for you, love."

Darach pushed past her. He cast his reddened sword to the floor and stooped to lift Julia from the pallet. Edana tapped him on the shoulder.

"Aren't you forgetting something?" she asked brightly.

He turned without a word and began to carry Julia's body to the door. He felt a sudden pain in his side. He roared and spun to face the witch, clutching his burden to his chest. "What the devil are ye up to?" he said. "It's over. Yer master is dead. I hae no quarrel wi' ye."

Edana waggled the dagger at him. "Now,

now. You know you don't want to leave. You came here because I made you come. Because you wanted to be with me."

He groaned. "Ye're mad, woman." He turned and headed for the door once again.

She was suddenly in front of him, though he hadn't seen her move past him. He halted, sheltering Julia.

"You set me aside once before," she said. A bitter note crept into her musical voice. "You must make up for that."

He eyed her, trying to gauge the extent of her madness. Was it revenge she was seeking? Or an alliance? All he wanted was to get out of this place, to hold his Julia, to wail out his grief. But he had an inkling that this woman was far more dangerous than she appeared.

"I made no promises to ye, Edana," he said. "We scarcely spoke. Besides, ye had Craigen, remember? And he is—or was—richer than I could ever hope to be, and more powerful. He was a far better match than I. Ye deserve more."

"You're trying to flatter me." She smiled, perfect dimples showing in her cheeks.

"I'm speakin' the truth. And now that Craigen's dead, ye'll be the rich one and all, for I've no doubt he's left ye well provided. Ye wouldn't want the likes o' me. I'm naught but an ogre and sae poor my clan's wealth could fit in yer shoe." He lifted Julia higher on his chest and moved to pass Edana.

The door slammed shut, though no hand had touched it. He tensed at the sudden awareness that he was dealing with not only a mad, jealous woman, but a witch besides. He would have to fight.

He turned and crossed back to the pallet. He laid Julia down upon it once more, hating to surrender her. He faced Edana. "Now then, witch. What is it ye want o' me?"

The woman's face broke into a lovely smile. "Why, to love you, of course! Why else would I have gone to all this trouble?" She advanced on him. "We belong together, you and I. And now that Craigen's out of the way, I have made certain that you and I shall lead both the clans."

"And if I say nay?"

She looked amazed. "Why would you?"

"Because ye're the devil's ain true love, no' mine."

"Why, you jealous thing, you!" She giggled. "Oh, pish," she said with a wave of her hand. "Once you have a taste of the power I hold, the power I'll share with you, you won't care about the source." She minced up to him, her smile beguiling. "Once you have a taste of my loving, of this body, you won't care about anything else. I know secrets of lovemaking that will bring you ecstasies such as you've never imagined." She slipped her hands up over his chest. "And don't forget, you owe me. You not only scorned me in Edinburgh, but you stole Craigen's lady love, and now you've killed my benefactor. I know your famed MacStruan honor wouldn't permit you to run away from a debt."

He thrust her hands away. "Ye're too twisted

for words, Edana. 'Twas ye that killed Isobel. Ye that preyed upon my people with sickness and mischief. Ye yoked yourself wi' the Moreston and joined him against me, even as he killed my father and my uncle. Ye took an innocent maid and promised her to that monster Craigen, selling her as a brood mare to please his lustful pride." He stepped away from her. "And ye believe I'll give myself to ye? That I'll love ye? I'd sooner share my bed wi' a she-wolf than take up wi' the likes o' ye."

Edana placed her hands on her hips. "Don't make me cross with you, Darach," she said, pouting. "People don't say no to me."

He shrugged and crossed his arms. "I'm through talkin', witch. Make yer move."

The woman's face suddenly changed from lovely and seductive to wild-eyed and harsh. "You won't get another chance!" she cried. "I've already killed your little black-haired bitch. Would you like me to show you more of what I can do?"

Darach nodded. "Aye. Show me what ye can do when ye're no' creepin' about, working mischief in secret."

Her image began to dissemble before his eyes. She shimmered and sparks flew from her burnished hair. The acrid scent of burning sulfur assaulted his nose. In a twinkling she was transformed from an exquisitely beautiful woman to a flame-haired male warrior, his muscles bulging at his cross-braces, a broadsword in his hands.

"Try me now, Darach, my love," came the obscenely feminine voice from the cruel, masculine mouth. He lunged forward and the battle was pitched.

Darach fought hard, but his opponent was indefatigable. Every blow Darach landed healed up in a matter of moments, while he himself was bleeding profusely from two slashes that caught him unawares. He had to think, to make a plan, for it was plain that sheer strength and skill alone would not win the day.

"Why don't you give up, my darling, and join me?" Edana taunted. "She's dead. Craigen's dead. Your little ragtag clan is already reduced to ashes. Why go on?"

Why go on? The words rang in his ears even as he slashed back at his foe. What was the point, if he had indeed lost everything? His whole adult life had been lived for others. He had no purpose now. Perhaps he was never meant to have any other use in this world.

He was backing toward the door, on the run from his opponent and gasping for breath. He lost his footing on a loose floorboard and stumbled, receiving a nick on the ear for his clumsiness. Why was he still fighting? he wondered.

Don't you ever get tired of trying to make the world go around? Julia's voice was in his mind now.

I am what I am.

Really? Then what you are is a major lunkhead, which is what I thought the first time I laid eyes on you. . . . What you need is a good, swift kick in the kilt. . . .

Julia's words sank into him as he twisted out of the way of the next blow. A lunkhead, was he? Was he really a man who couldn't change, even when he did receive a good, swift kick to the rump?

Ah, hell, he thought. If he couldn't bring himself to fight for others, he'd fight for himself. He'd let go of controlling the destinies of every person he'd ever known or cared about and think of his own survival. Come what may, it would be a fitting tribute to his Julia. He'd change.

He felt a second wind coming on. With a light, dancing step, he spun out of the way of the oncoming blade and wrenched open the door latch. Edana lunged forward, stumbling out into the hall.

Darach pressed her down the hall, their clashing swords echoing off the stone walls and shooting sparks on contact. She was forced into the defensive position now, as Darach cast caution to the winds and fought for the sheer sensation of fighting. If he could get her onto the stairs, he might gain the advantage.

"Darach, what are you doing?" she cried out. "You love me, remember?"

"Aye, witch. I love ye! I plan to love ye straight into hell!" He surged forward, blade raised high.

She thrust out at his unprotected chest. He jumped backward, laughing. "Watch yer footing here, witch!" he called out, kicking at the rough stones. "That lame leg o' yers is near as twisted as yer soul."

She gasped at his words. Suddenly the image of the warrior began to crackle and shimmer. Darach saw the woman behind it begin to form, her hands clutching at the heavy sword. He had the advantage he needed. He rushed her. She stumbled heavily and fell to the floor, just at the top of the stairs. She thrust upward with her sword but she was too late. Darach raised his blade and plunged it straight through her heart.

He stood over the writhing figure, his chest heaving. Her eyes went wide, she stiffened, and died. He left his sword where it was and went back to the chamber.

Julia lay where he'd left her, unchanged. In his most secret heart, he'd hoped that Edana's death might break some spell that she had cast over Julia, returning her to life. But when he held a bit of mirror up to her nose, the glass remained unclouded.

He sank to his knees and howled out his grief.

No one came to challenge him. The Morestons heard the bansheelike cries from the tower and rushed up the stairs. The sight of Craigen's witch, dead on the stairs, impaled on a mighty sword was enough to put them all to rout. With no chief to guide them and no plan for the future, they scattered in all directions throughout the castle. Some looted, some fled the keep. Some tore into the stores of food and drink and made merry long into the next day. None of them saw the tall man stalk away from the tower, the body of a woman held in his arms.

He marched through the forest, edging around the flames with an almost contemptuous grace. Dawn was coming, but the clouds and smoke hung a curtain against the sun's light. He didn't care. He was alive. He'd fought for his life alone, as Julia had urged him. She'd never allowed herself to give up or to give in to self-pity, even when she was a prisoner, locked in a dank cell in his house. She'd entered into his world like a whirlwind, bringing him back to life with her outrageous and beautiful ways. Now he would have to learn how to live that life alone.

He heard shouting and footsteps pounding toward him, but he kept walking toward the clachan. The smoke parted and diminished at the far edge of the woods, and there, before him, were his people, alive and well, and covered with dirt and soot. Their joyous cries died on their lips as they saw the burden he carried.

The lairds formed a ring around Darach, their torches illuminating the limp body in his arms. Some of the women wept openly. Big Dog nudged his way through the circle and came to snuffle at Julia's hand.

"Get back," Darach said, his voice hoarse and strained. "She canna pet ye now." He moved on toward the village and his house, cradling Julia's body to his chest.

He bore her inside and carried her to his chamber, where he placed her upon his bed. He stooped and smoothed the hair away from her face, marveling that it could still feel so warm and full of life. What a mockery! He sank to his knees and buried his face in his hands.

"Darach." Mairi came to stand beside him. He didn't look up. "Darach, she's gone. We must make the burial plans. We canna wait overlang."

"Nay!" he roared. "I'll no' have it!" He drew his knife and it glittered in the torchlight. "I'll no' put my Julia in the ground. And I'll kill the first one who dares to take her frae me."

He leaned over Julia's body, touching her face and hands. "She looks sae beautiful," he whispered. He twisted about to look at the men. "Why is she so beautiful still? Liam, ye're learned—can ye tell me? Alasdair?"

The two men hung their heads. Darach looked back at Julia. "It's as if she were asleep," he murmured. "As if she could waken in a moment."

He tipped back suddenly. "Bruce!" he cried out. "What was that tale she told us one night before the fire? O' the prince who kissed his lady and wakened her from a sleep of a hundred years?"

"Darach, lad, ye must come awa'—"

But Darach didn't hear him. He was pressing his lips to Julia's, holding her head up to caress her cheek.

"Darach!" Mairi's tone was horrified. He ignored her. "Somebody do something!" she commanded.

"Let me through! Dammit, let me through!"

Tommy burst out of the crowd and raced to the bed. Darach looked up at the young man, feeling his hopes draining away even as he held Julia to his chest.

"No, Darach, that's no' the way. Remember?" Tommy was pulling at his hands, forcing him to lay Julia back on the bed. Darach growled at the intruder and raised his hand to shove him away.

"Hit me if ye wish, Darach." Darach heard the authoritative note in Tommy's voice. "Hit me," Tommy continued, "but ye must keep on wi' what ye're doin'. Do ye ken what I'm tellin' ye? Ye must give Julia the kiss o' life. And if ye don't, I will."

A sudden burst of energy exploded in Darach's chest. "The kiss—" He didn't waste time finishing his sentence. He grabbed Julia and pried her mouth open. He heard the gasps of the people around him, but they seemed faint and far away. All that he could see, hear, know, was Julia and what he needed to do.

He inserted his fingers into her mouth. Mairi gasped. Tommy held up his hand for silence. "That's it, Darach. Check the mouth for foreign objects, she said."

Darach's heart contracted violently. Her tongue had swollen to more than twice its usual size. He forced his way around it, probing, as he had seen Tommy do it before. He gave a cry. He thrust his forefinger deeper into her throat and felt something dislodge. He brought the object out. Immediately Julia sucked a breath into her body, her chest bucking upward on the bed.

"What is it?" Tommy asked. Darach handed the lump over to him and began to chafe Julia's wrists and slap her gently on her cheeks. "A bit of apple," the younger man said wonderingly.

"Is she alive?" Mairi's tough demeanor was melting; Darach could hear it in her voice.

"I don't know. I think—"

"The kiss, Darach," Tommy urged. "Ye must breathe for her—"

The room fell silent as a soft, feminine voice came from the bed. "Darach?"

"I'm here, Julia," he said, caressing her hair. "Wake up, love." His throat was so tight he fought to get the words out.

Her eyes fluttered open. "I made it back," she said with a sigh. "I made it back."

"Aye, lass." Darach gathered her in his arms. "Aye, ye made it back."

She rubbed her face weakly against his chest and then drooped. He checked her breathing quickly and smiled in relief. "She's still wi' us," he said to Tommy. "She's only fainted."

"Saints, Darach, don't tell her she fainted," Tommy said, grinning. "She'll be sae angry she'll feed us all Glue Stew for a month."

Darach grinned. "I'm afraid, lad, that what my Julia does is no' in my control."

Conscious or not, furious or purring with pleasure, Darach didn't care, as long as she was alive. He knew it wasn't called for, but just to make sure, he bent down and kissed her, breathing a gentle breath between her parted lips. The kiss of life, he thought. The kiss of life with his Julia.

Chapter Thirty

It was a long time before Julia was allowed out of her sickbed by Dr. Thomas MacStruan, as she now called him. For his firm and forceful bedside manner, she added the honorary title of Ogre to his name. And when she was declared fit enough to leave her bed, Darach carried her straight back into it, loving her with such tenderness that she nearly wept with the sweetness of their reunion.

The fire in the woods had burned out, leaving another blackened scar on the land. But it was a scar that scarcely touched the MacStruan border. Thanks to Gordon's firebreak and the hard work of all the clan, the fire had been turned back before it reached the standing stones. Alasdair and Celandine celebrated that fact, especially.

"She's lovely, Darach," Julia said, watching the pair go about, arms twined about one another's waists, living in their own world. "Who is she? She's a Sassenach, is she no'?"

Darach groaned. "That's no' the half o' it. She says she's one o' the Fair Folk frae over the sea. A Talcott, she calls herself, and says she has the gift o' sight. While our Alasdair has lost his sight for aught save her."

"Oh, I see. One o' those impossible matches between an outlander and a stubborn laird that never work out." Julia grinned at him and they both laughed. "I suppose all we can do is wish them luck," she said, watching the couple with a fond heart.

"Aye," he said, slipping his arm around her waist. "It's all anyone can do."

She looked up at him in surprise. Could this be her Darach? Mr. Duty Calls? Was he actually giving up control over his brother at last? She hugged him and he gave her a grin that curled her toes.

"Besides," he drawled, "the lass is Craigen's sole heir. She'll be bringin' quite a fortune to Clan MacStruan."

"Oh ho! So that's why you're sae acceptin' o' the match." She grinned and shook her head. "Ye're a cold man, Darach MacStruan."

"I'm just lookin' after my ain folk." He smiled down at her, wicked lights dancing in his eyes. "And I'll be happy to show ye just how cold a man I am, if ye wish to gang wi' me back to our bed."

434

She was more than pleased with his demonstration. No question about it, she was warmed through and through. She was home. New York, her old life, was fading like a dream.

When she was strong enough, Julia led the lairds and some of the women to the stone circle once more and showed them where to dig. She was elated. Her boxes were there, and they were still intact.

"Good old Styrofoam," she chortled, hoisting one muddy and squeaking container. "Better livin' through chemistry." She handed it to Tommy, who tore off the lid and rummaged through it, excited as a child at Christmas.

"This one's no' medicines, is it, Julia?" He held up a can with a rich red label.

"Nay," she said, grinning. "That's for the pantry. Artichoke hearts."

"Arty—What?"

"Never mind. Just wait till ye taste them. And there's sun-roasted tomatoes, pizza dough, water chestnuts, and—"

"Ah, be wary, lass." Liam wagged his finger at her. "Surfeits slay more souls than swords."

"Aristotle?" Julia asked, smiling.

He puffed up. "MacStruan."

They toted the treasure home to the village, a triumphant procession of squeaking and thumping. Some wild hens strayed across the path, and Gordon and Liam renewed their ancient argument. Dugan snorted and strode away from them, seeking out his new lady love, a strapping young widow by the name of Tessa.

Having the women back in the clachan made Julia feel even happier.

Julia walked along beside Darach, enjoying her success and her homecoming with a contented grin.

"So," he said, hanging back so that the others were out of earshot. "This looks an awful lot like ye're plannin' to stay."

She sashayed up closer to him. "I am. Wanna make somethin' of it?"

"Aye."

"Oh?" She crossed her arms. "And what might that be?"

"I'm thinkin' it's time to have the priest up here."

She froze. "What?"

"I said it's time we had the priest up to visit. There's somethin' I need him to do, if ye'll be stayin' here."

"Darach! I thought that was all settled! I thought we were all past this witch business. It was Edana, remember, she was the—"

"Whisht, woman! I said I wanted to make something of it. I want to make ye my wife."

She gaped at him for a long, long moment until at last she felt his words truly enter her mind. They took a neat turn and sank, like a golden shaft of sunlight, straight down into her heart. "Ye mean it?" she asked softly. "Ye'd want a fasheous Sassenach for a bride?"

"I'd want ye if ye were Pee-Wee Herman," he said solemnly.

"Oh, God," she said, helpless against the

laughter that bubbled up inside her. "Don't say that."

"Why not?"

"Never mind." She went to his arms, her heart so full she thought she might float off like a balloon. "Just say it again."

"Say what?"

"Say what ye want o' me."

"Julia Addison, I want t' make ye my wife." She sighed rapturously. He shook her gently. "And ye say . . ."

"Oh! Oh, aye. Aye." She laughed and kissed him. "Aye, my ain true love."

Celandine and Alasdair watched the bride and groom as they danced in the center of the crowd. Celandine took his hand and kissed it, then placed it over her abdomen.

"What's this ye're tryin' to tell me, love?" he murmured against her hair.

"It's time, love," she said. "If it's what you want."

He turned her in his arms. "Are ye sure?"

She smiled. "You forget what I am." She pressed his hand to her abdomen once more. "Can you not feel it?"

He closed his eyes. Wonder spread across his face. "Saints. I can! It's like water sparklin' off the loch and stingin' my hand." He opened his eyes and looked deeply into hers. "I'm no' sure I can wait to get ye upstairs to my ain bed."

She laughed, the sweet music of her voice winding about his heart like a living vine.

"You'll have to wait. I've something special in mind."

He sighed. "Love, ye'll be the death o' me. But lead on. I canna say no to ye."

A short while later, he was looking about him in wonder. "Here?"

"Here." Celandine went to the center of the circle of stones and cast her cloak to the ground. Her pale gown shimmered in the starlight as she spun, laughing, her arms outspread. "Here is where it all began," she sang out. "Here is where I want you to love me for the first time. Here is where I want us to conceive our child." She flashed her skirts at him, showing off her slender legs and even a glimpse of thigh.

Alasdair began pulling his sword free of his belt, laughing at her shameless flirting. She held out her arms as he came to her at last.

"So, new chief o' the Morestons, what is your will?"

She smiled. "You know all too well what I will."

"I'm a loyal MacStruan, ye know."

"Yes, I know. But as soon as we're wed, I shall be a MacStruan as well. And your clan shall be my clan, and my clan yours."

"I like the way ye put that."

She stepped back and pointed over their heads. "The moon is full," she said, letting the last of her garments slide to the ground. "I want our son with us come spring."

He shook his head. "Have ye been takin' lessons frae my brothair?" he asked, grinning.

"Ye're awfully bossy a' of a sudden."

She sighed and bent down to retrieve her gown. "Well, if you don't want to, I suppose I can—"

She didn't get to finish her sentence. The full moon glimmered from on high and the stones stood solid, their ancient power blessing and protecting the Faerie child who became, in part, a mortal woman in the arms of her love.

"I'm as happy as anyone has the right to be." Julia sighed.

Darach nuzzled at her neck as he carried her up the stairs to their bedchamber. "I'm glad. But I'd swear ye've put on a bit o' weight, sweet. That or I'm no' the man I used to be."

She smiled and tweaked his ear. "Ye're all the man ye've ever been and more, besides. And I'm more than I was, as well."

"Ye're a MacStruan."

"Aye, that I am. Ye've got me livin' as one, actin' as one, and speakin' as one." She pressed her lips against his ear and whispered, "And ye've got me lovin' as one."

Darach stopped then and there and pressed her back against the wall, kissing her breathless where they stood.

Below them, in the great hall, Liam was engaged in the ages-old tradition of the naming of the ancestors. His audience was well filled with wine and food by this point in the celebration, so few were paying any real attention when he slipped the names Laird Humphrey of Bogart and Queen Ingrid Bergmansdottir into the list. Bess, his birdlike little wife, caught the joke, however, and blew him a kiss from where she sat by the fire, their youngest on her lap, right next to Rose, who was nursing her new infant son, Harrison Ford MacStruan.

Dugan was demonstrating the waltz, as Julia had taught him, to Mairi MacStruan, who had cast aside her staff for the occasion, to almost no one's surprise. Ross, Niall, Gordon, Bruce, and the new priest, Brother Simon, were toasting the happy couple, the clan, the house, the weather, the furniture . . . happily red-faced and cheery. No one had seen Thomas, as everyone now called him, slip out with his Lara.

LC and BD were under the long table, content with the fine scraps they'd managed to cadge from an unwary diner or cajole from a well-oiled laird. LC paused in her munching to lick some tasty chicken grease from BD's muzzle, refining her skills in preparation for imminent motherhood.

Darach pushed through the bedroom door and kicked it shut behind them. He deposited Julia gently on the bed. "More than ye were, eh? I thought it was harder goin' up those stairs."

Julia gave him a catlike smile. "That's because ye've put a babe in your wife's belly."

Darach stared at her, thunderstruck. She laughed. "Don't look so surprised. Did ye imagine after all our sportin' your seed would fail to find its mark?"

"A bairn," he said wonderingly. "How—When—Can we still—"

"We'd better," she said, twining her arms about his neck. "Just wait till ye see the surprises I brought ye from the other world."

His eyes came even more alive with heated interest. "Ye don't mean . . . ?"

She nodded. "I'm no' very far along. I can still fit nicely into some o' those silky briefs and bras ye like sae well. O' course, there might be a wee bit more up top than there was before, but ye won't mind that too much, will ye?"

"I'll struggle wi' it," he said solemnly.

"Good," she said with a soft giggle. She sat back and began to undo the laces at the top of her gown.

"Wait."

She paused, her hand at her throat, her eyes questioning. "Tryin' to control your wife already, Laird Darach?"

He shook his head. "Julia Addison Mac-Struan, I'll say it again and again—ye're like somethin' out o' my dreams." He placed a hand on the soft, slight swell of her abdomen.

"Aye, and so are ye, my husband," she said softly, leaning to kiss him. "And are we no' lucky that dreams come true?"

Author's Note

The Scottish Highlands have always meant magic to me. In creating the world of Clan MacStruan, I learned that magic, omens, and folklore are as much a part of life in the Highlands as heather and pipes. For example, the practice of "smooring" the peat fires in the rugged stone houses was common until quite recently, and there were numerous incantations that could be said to insure a safe, fire-free night and a quick start in the morning. The roots of the ancient Celtic world, with its standing stones and intimate ties to nature, still run deep in the Highlands.

Now as for traveling in time—my physicist husband tells me it's simply a product of my overactive imagination. Just the same, I'm not making up my mind just yet, and I think Stephen Hawking might agree with me. Moreover, scholars agree that there's still a lot we don't know about those ancient standing stones and their purposes. But Julia's journey to find Darach and his people, the one place she could call home, was certainly heavily influenced by the magic of the heart. If anything can carry us across the barriers of time and distance, it's the power of love.

I hope you enjoyed this *sgeula-gaoil*, or love story, of Julia, Darach, and the Seven Lairds. I love to hear from readers! You can write to me at Leisure Books, and my thrifty Scots ancestors would appreciate the addition of a self-addressed envelope, if ye'd like a reply. May the magic of love be with you always.

A Stolen Rose

CORAL SMITH SAXE

Bestselling Author Of *Enchantment*

Feared by all Englishmen and known only as the Blackbird, the infamous highwayman is really the stunning Morgana Bracewell. And though she is an aristocrat who has lost her name and family, nothing has prepared the well-bred thief for her most charming victim. Even as she robs Lord Phillip Greyfriars blind, she knows his roving eye has seen through her rogue's disguise—and into her heart. Now, the wickedly handsome peer will stop at nothing to possess her, and it will take all Morgana's cunning not to surrender to a man who will accept no ransom for her love.

_3843-9 $5.50 US/$7.50 CAN

Seduced

CATHERINE LANIGAN

"Catherine Lanigan is in a class by herself: unequaled and simply fabulous!"
—Affaire de Coeur

Even amid the spectacle and splendor of the carnival in Venice, the masked rogue is brazen, reckless, and dangerously risque. As he steals Valentine St. James away from the costume ball at which her betrothal to a complete stranger is to be announced, the exquisite beauty revels in the illicit thrill of his touch, the tender passion in his kiss. But Valentine learns that illusion rules the festival when, at the stroke of midnight, her mysterious suitor reveals he is Lord Hawkeston, the very man she is to wed. Convinced her intended is an unrepentant scoundrel, Valentine wants to deny her maddening attraction for him, only to keep finding herself in his heated embrace. Yet is she truly losing her heart to the dashing peer—or is she being ruthlessly seduced?

_3942-7 $5.50 US/$7.50 CAN

The ROSELYNDE CHRONICLES
JOANNA

Roberta Gellis

"A superb storyteller of extraordinary talent!"
—John Jakes

Beautiful, iron-willed heiress to power, Joanna secretly burns with an explosive inner passion as wild and radiant as her flaming red hair. But her deepest emotions are tragically frozen by the cold fear of a man's tender love.

Ensnared in the violent lusts and dangerous intrigues of King John's decadent court, the tempestuous noblewoman defies every outward peril—only to come face-to-face with Geoffrey, the knight whose very presence unleashes terror in her heart. Caught between willful pride and consuming desire, Joanna struggles hopelessly to avoid surrendering herself to the irresistible fires raging within her.

_3631-2 $5.99 US/$6.99 CAN